My Fair Frauds

"*My Fair Lady* meets *The Sting* in this fun, fast-paced, Gilded Age tale of Alice, a beautiful and experienced con artist, her young but eager apprentice, Cora, and the colorful cast of grifters who will help Alice wreak revenge upon the greedy and vacuous robber barons who wronged her family so long ago. Rooting for a pack of swindlers has never been quite so fun—or so satisfying! Once again, the writing duo of Kelly and Thorne prove they are the Queens of Capers!"

—Marie Bostwick, *New York Times* and
USA TODAY bestselling author of
The Book Club for Troublesome Women

"*My Fair Frauds* by Lee Kelly and Jennifer Thorne is everything I hoped for—and more. Who knew I'd find myself cheering for a group of con women? But that's exactly what happened. With lost souls who stumble into found family, this cleverly crafted, utterly compulsive story is one I'll root for time and again."

—Jenni L. Walsh, *USA TODAY*
bestselling author of *Sonora*

"*My Fair Frauds* is an absolute triumph—a dazzling tale of intrigue, drama, and female friendship that hooked me from the very first page. Lee Kelly and Jennifer Thorne create a world so cinematic and immersive that I felt transported straight into the glittering, treacherous heart of Gilded Age New York. With complex, un-forgettable characters and deliciously twisty plot turns, this story is as clever as it is compulsively readable. Alice and Cora's unlikely partnership had me cheering, gasping, and eagerly turning pages to see just how far their audacious con would go. Kelly and Thorne are masters of crafting richly drawn settings and dynamic storylines, and *My Fair Frauds* is a sparkling example of their combined brilliance. This book is an absolute delight—readers will not want to miss the swindle of the season!"

—Jennifer Moorman, USA TODAY
bestselling author of The Charmed Library

"What a cheeky blast! Lee Kelly and Jennifer Thorne deliver a clever caper of Gilded Age glamour and smart girl fraudsters in their latest collaboration, and readers will be delighted. This was a delicious escape that entertained me to the last page!"

—Kimberly Brock, bestselling author
of The Lost Book of Eleanor Dare

The Starlets

"Pass the popcorn and settle in for a terrific time with this seamlessly crafted blend of historical fiction and old-school suspense."

—Library Journal, Starred Review

"Kelly and Thorne follow up The Antiquity Affair with a spry and suspenseful crime novel set just after Hollywood's golden age . . . Kelly and Thorne make a clichéd setup entirely their own, wringing surprising depth from Vivienne and Lottie's mutual thawing without skimping on action or sumptuous descriptions of France and Italy. For movie buffs, this will be as welcome as a cool breeze on a hot day."

—Publishers Weekly, Starred Review

"Author duo Kelly and Thorne (The Antiquity Affair, 2023) return with a new historical thriller set in 1950s Hollywood . . . A fun, madcap romp through old Hollywood with an 'enemies to besties' twist, this book will be a hit with fans of Taylor Jenkins Reid's The Seven Husbands of Evelyn Hugo (2019) and Ally Carter's The Blonde Identity (2023)."

—Booklist

"The glamorous 1950s setting, the plot twists, the romp across Europe, the chemistry between Vivienne and Lottie, ambitious, at-odds movie starlets who must join forces to save the picture and their lives—everything about *The Starlets* is a sheer delight! This fast-paced caper from the writing duo of Kelly and Thorne is fresh, fun, and exactly the escape readers need right now."

—Marie Bostwick, *New York Times* bestselling author of *Esme Cahill Fails Spectacularly*

"Kelly and Thorne are a phenomenal duo . . . two brilliant authors with boundless talent and a singularly remarkable voice."

—Elle Cosimano, *New York Times* bestselling author of the Finlay Donovan series

"The glam of Old Hollywood meets the empowerment vibe of *Barbie* in this fast-paced European adventure that turns on-screen rivals into off-screen allies. Energetic, funny, and loads of fun."

—Lori Goldstein, author of *Love, Theodosia: A Novel of Theodosia Burr and Philip Hamilton*

"*The Starlets* captivates from the first sentence. Brimming with Old Hollywood glamour, a twisty plot, and feuding film stars navigating increasingly sticky situations, this atmospheric, engrossing caper is your next must-read!"

—Rachel Linden, bestselling author of *The Enlightenment of Bees* and *The Magic of Lemon Drop Pie*

"Lights! Camera! Action! Once again, Kelly and Thorne have created a heart-pounding story of nonstop adventure and irrepressible fun. In *The Starlets*, cinema icon Vivienne Rhodes and up-and-coming Lottie Lawrence join forces to save the day and steal the show. I enjoyed every moment of this 1950s glamorous adventure that whisked me from Hollywood to Italy, with a delightful stop in Monaco to visit America's favorite Princess Grace, and back to Hollywood again with two leading ladies who know who they are and have the courage to chase what they want. A must-read!"

—Katherine Reay, bestselling author of *The Berlin Letters*

"*The Starlets* is the most fun I've had inside the pages of a book in a long time. The novel flips 'friends to foe' on its head, putting two competing actresses in the spotlight, transforming the starlets from adversaries to allies as they race across Europe to take down a kingpin. Shenanigans, quick thinking, and a cat-and-mouse game ensue. A propulsive, page-turning romp perfect for book clubs."

—Jenni L. Walsh, *USA TODAY* bestselling author

"Well-crafted and deliciously devourable, *The Starlets* tosses you onto a Hollywood movie set filled with everything you'd expect and want—glitz and glamor, love, jealousy, extravagance, jaunts across Europe . . . and murder! Plot twists abound when archrivals unite as real-life heroines who must save the day or all is lost, including their lives! A page-turning, exhilarating wild ride of a story that I devoured in a single weekend!"

—Jennifer Moorman, bestselling author of *The Magic All Around*

"Glamour. Danger. Adventure. Enemies to besties. Yes, please! This book has just the right touches of killer (pun intended) locations that our heroines get to zip around like an exploded champagne cork. Throw in some Hollywood touches, Esther Williams vibes, and this story is served like the perfect cocktail."

—J'nell Ciesielski, author of *The Winged Tiara*

The Antiquity Affair

"Authors Lee Kelly and Jennifer Thorne have written a rollicking tale replete with adventure, romance, mystery, and a sprinkle of the supernatural. *The Antiquity Affair* has been likened to *Indiana Jones*, and it's an apt comparison, as both are rousing adventure stories complete with ancient mysteries, hidden tombs, harrowing mantraps and pitfalls, villains bent on world domination, and fabled relics of power . . . The authors neatly subvert the trope of swashbuckling men and their archeological treasure. A fast-paced and entertaining read that I hope is not the last from Kelly and Thorne."

—Historical Novel Society

"What a thrilling adventure with sisters at the heart of it. When Tess and Lila take the reins—of horse and camel—their stories take off, brimming with cases of mistaken identities, cat-and-mouse chases, booby-trapped catacombs, first loves, encrypted clues, and a long-lost treasure that all want to get their hands on. A rousing, page-turning romp across Egypt!"

—Jenni L. Walsh, *USA TODAY* bestselling author

"A deliciously entertaining, swashbuckling adventure, *The Antiquity Affair* gives readers a mystery to unravel, romances to swoon over, and a sister story to tug at the heart. An absorbing, heart-pounding page-turner."

—Lori Anne Goldstein, author of *Love, Theodosia: A Novel of Theodosia Burr and Philip Hamilton*

MY FAIR
FRAUDS

MY FAIR FRAUDS

A NOVEL

LEE KELLY AND
JENNIFER THORNE

HARPER MUSE

Published by Harper Muse, an imprint of HarperCollins Focus LLC, 501 Nelson Place, Nashville, TN 37214, USA.

This book is a work of fiction. The characters, incidents, and dialogue are drawn from the authors' imagination and are not to be construed as real. Any resemblance to actual events or persons, living or dead, is entirely coincidental.

Any internet addresses (websites, blogs, etc.) in this book are offered as a resource. They are not intended in any way to be or imply an endorsement by HarperCollins Focus LLC, nor does HarperCollins Focus LLC vouch for the content of these sites for the life of this book.

HarperCollins Publishers, Macken House, 39/40 Mayor Street Upper, Dublin 1, D01 C9W8, Ireland (https://www.harpercollins.com)

Library of Congress Cataloging-in-Publication Data

Names: Kelly, Lee author | Thorne, Jennifer, 1980- author
Title: My fair frauds : a novel / Lee Kelly and Jennifer Thorne.
Description: Nashville : Harper Muse, 2025. | Summary: "A high society fraud and a scrappy swindler team up to take down Gilded Age New York in this tale of intrigue, drama, and female friendship"—Provided by publisher.
Identifiers: LCCN 2025024810 (print) | LCCN 2025024811 (ebook) | ISBN 9781400347728 paperback | ISBN 9781400347742 epub | ISBN 9781400347759
Subjects: LCGFT: Fiction | Novels
Classification: LCC PS3611.E4498 M9 2025 (print) | LCC PS3611.E4498 (ebook) | DDC 813/.6—dc23/eng/20250626
LC record available at https://lccn.loc.gov/2025024810
LC ebook record available at https://lccn.loc.gov/2025024811

Art Direction: Halie Cotton
Cover Design: Lila Selle
Interior Design: Chloe Foster

Printed in the United States of America

25 26 27 28 29 LBC 5 4 3 2 1

For Katelyn. We'd never attempt a big job without you.

Principal Shareholders

Manifest Rails
Est. (May 1) 1870

One week after bankruptcy of Midwest Railroads.
This will be the day.

Mr. Harold Peyton

Wife dead in childbirth.
Son, Harold Junior.
No other living relatives.
Angle: Venality

Mr. James Vandemeer

First wife deceased.
Second wife, Olivia.
One daughter, Mimi.
Angle: Vainglory

~~Mr. Sherman Witt~~

Died 1874.
Widow, Iris Witt, retains shares.
Children: Beau and Bonnie.
Angle: Capriciousness

Mr. Robert Ames

Wife, Pearl.
Daughter, Arabella.
Angle: Validation

Mr. Brett Ogden

Wife, Priscilla. No legitimate children.
As per sources, his reputation is unchanged.
Angle: Carnality

PART I

The Pledge

Feed with mystery the human mind,
which dearly loves mystery.

—THE ESTEEMED MAGICIAN HARRY KELLAR

THE NEW YORK HERALD

Friday, November 9, 1883

TENSIONS ESCALATE IN GERMANIC KINGDOM OF WÜRTTEMBERG FOLLOWING RATIFICATION OF "TRIPLE ALLIANCE"

Calvin Archer, New York Office

The historic defensive "Triple Alliance" treaty between the German Empire, Italy, and Austria-Hungary, when initially proposed last year, was met with widespread resistance in the Kingdom of Württemberg, a resource-rich Germanic nation that has suffered both politically and economically since Reich unification. Opponents decried the treaty as overreaching and particularly unfair to Württemberg, and contended that ratification would surely sound the death knell for the southern state's sovereignty.

King Charles I's capitulation to the empire's pressures to ratify subsequently spurred a growing nationalist movement within Württemberg's borders, with key nobility rumored to be setting the stage for a resistance . . .

CHAPTER I

In the Wings

November 9, 1883

Coraline O'Malley—known as "Cora Mack" to her current troupe and company—stands at the ready as assistant stagehand, watching from behind the scenes as her aging boss, Prospero the Great, performs feat after feat of manufactured wonder for tonight's enraptured audience. A parade of ghosts slinking through his labyrinth of onstage mirrors. A kaleidoscope of butterflies spiraling out from the floor and over the crowd. A tree growing in rapid time from a plot of dirt, a sprout unfurling and blooming into an orange plant taller than Prospero himself in a matter of minutes.

But the most confounding magic of the night, at least in Cora's opinion, lies offstage: the wealthiest, most afternoonified audience she has ever encountered, currently seated in Mrs. Iris Witt's two-hundred-guest-capacity private auditorium housed inside her palatial Madison Avenue home.

Incredibly, Prospero's show is only one of the evening's many diversions, a themed "Night of Illusions," which seems intended to herald the arrival of November and another New York social season. The Witts' foyer has been transformed into a circus, complete with fire-eaters. Their ballroom, a ribboned carousel of real live zebras and giraffes. Partygoers decked in costumed gowns riddled with brilliants, skirts swathed in lace, fascinators of gems and exotic feathers. Mrs. Witt's own peacock headpiece is so enormous that it blocks the views of the ill-fated dozens seated behind her.

Cora swallows. The sheer overwhelming excess, the unfairness of *so much* concentrated wealth in one room in one corner of one city—

Just breathe, she tells herself. *Breathe and reset the stage.* Jealousy won't get her back Long Creek Farm, after all—but picking this audience's gilded pockets postshow certainly might.

"Are you sure you can handle her?" Maeve, the show's lead stagehand, sidles breathlessly beside Cora. A hefty magnet—usually Cora's responsibility during performances—is balanced precariously across Maeve's back, further rounding the old woman's stooped shoulders. "Dinah can be a handful, ye know, so if you're having second thoughts—"

"Maeve, I'll never manage a raise if I can't master all the tricks," Cora says.

Maeve's crinkled lips pull into a worried frown. "Told ya, love, Prospero don't give raises."

"And I told you, I'm gonna be the exception." Cora sighs, hiding her frustration with an assuring smile. "I can handle her, honest. You can trust me." *Although, come to think of it, Dinah should certainly be out of the dressing rooms by now.*

"All right, love. Break a leg." Maeve flashes Cora a small smile before glancing at the stage. "That's my cue." Readjusting the large magnet across her shoulders like a donkey pole, Maeve hurries down the backstage stairs and into the trap room.

Onstage, Prospero welcomes his latest volunteer. "Mr. Vanderbilt, would you consider yourself a man of great strength?"

The volunteer flexes his muscles, and the crowd laughs.

Prospero lifts a small box, opening the container for the audience to see. "You all bear witness, evidence that this box is empty."

Cora peers around the backstage area, her concern beginning to mount. Dinah is a handful indeed. She has been Prospero's assistant since the Grant administration and fashions herself a true star—dismissive of Cora and Maeve, generally abrasive, and habitually late. Cora considers dragging her out of the dressing rooms when a high-pitched voice sounds behind her.

"Well, don't just stand there!" Dinah spins around in her glittering stage dress, giving Cora access to the unbuttoned back. "Hitch me up!"

Cora bites back choice words and jumps to, affixing the wooden plank to Dinah's corset, just like Maeve showed her during dress rehearsal. If she can somehow prove to Prospero that she deserves to make as much as Maeve—maybe even work onstage alongside him, split the stage tricks with Dinah—well, she'll be that much closer to getting back her home.

Onstage, meanwhile, Prospero has placed the empty box on a small table before him. "Mr. Vanderbilt, please, if you might lift the box . . . with your unparalleled vigor."

The volunteer pulls on the trick box's handle. It doesn't budge, thanks to Maeve now standing sentinel with the magnet in the trap room below the stage. Mr. Vanderbilt mutters to himself, pulling, yanking, cursing, much to the crowd's delight.

"That box must be made of steel!" he crows, returning to his seat. "I couldn't lift it an inch!"

Onstage, Prospero smiles and bows. "And now, for my final demonstration!"

"Are you finished yet?" Dinah hisses. "Tonight needs to go perfect for this smart set! Why are *you* here anyway? Where on earth is Maeve?"

"She's got the magnet downstairs," Cora huffs, working fast. "Which leaves you to me. Not to worry, you're in good hands, Maeve trusts me—"

"Her first mistake," Dinah scoffs. "This is taking twice as long as it should—"

"Ladies and gentlemen," Prospero cries, "please welcome back my lovely assistant, Miss Dinah!"

Hearing her cue, Dinah attempts to hurry onstage, but Cora yanks her back into the curtains. "I'm not finished!"

Prospero laughs uneasily while the crowd titters. "Come, my darling Dinah, now don't be shy!"

"Just hold still." Hands shaking, Cora finally hooks the mechanical crane's thin metal rod, meant to lift Dinah into the air on Prospero's command, onto the plank's clasp. She fumbles to cover it with Dinah's dress buttons.

"You trying to make me look bad?" Dinah shrills. "Think you're gonna steal my spot?"

"Stop squirming—"

"I know your type, always plotting and scheming. Don't think I don't know about your own act, little thief. If I had my way, we'd have left you in Charleston."

"You're ready, *go*!"

Dinah disentangles herself from Cora, strutting onstage to more applause.

Prospero's finale, his showstopping "levitating woman," brings down the house.

Cora watches the trick with detached, dread-filled certainty.

"Little thief." Forget a raise. She might have just lost her job, and her own home, for good.

🜚　🜚　🜚

"Did you tell her?" Cora demands, cornering Maeve in their makeshift prop room after the show, Prospero and Dinah both having retreated to this evening's dressing quarters, a series of ornate parlors right off the Witts' private theater.

Maeve cocks her head. "Tell who what, love?"

"Dinah!" Cora blinks back tears. "My methods are flawless. There's no possible way she could have caught on, unless you specifically ratted me out."

"I . . . I had no choice!" Maeve's sunken cheeks flush. "Dinah was going through your things one day and—"

"My things?"

"Found a stack of cash and didn't understand how you came into so much money, given what you get paid is . . . well, you know." Maeve clears her throat. "She accused you of far worse vices, Cora. I was only defendin' your honor."

"Hell's bells, Maeve." Cora flops onto a trick box. *Just breathe.* "She's going to tell Prospero. She's going to have me fired."

"No, Cora, no." Maeve hurries toward her. "There's nothing to worry about. I told her I'd handle it, on my honor, set you straight." Maeve takes Cora's hands. "Dinah promised she wouldn't tell the boss—not unless you do it again, anyway. I swear, everything's going to be right as rain."

Cora shakes her head. "Listen, Maeve, you really don't understand . . ." How can Cora possibly explain that at three dollars a week, without her subsidized earnings, her unique style of sleight of hand—pickpocketing, purse-lifting, sneak thievery, all conducted discreetly on select patrons after the show—she might be Maeve's age before she can take back Long Creek Farm? A lifelong dupe, just like her father. Forever a pawn in a smarter player's game.

Maeve keeps staring at her, looking about to cry herself.

"All right." Cora sighs. "Yes, fine. I'll stop the filching, Maeve. Honest."

A cacophony of impatient knocks sounds from the door before Prospero thrusts it open. The magician is now dressed in a clean, crisp white shirt, his face freshly painted, his haughty showman veneer still firmly affixed. "Our hostess desires some parlor tricks. Come. Out we go."

Cora and Maeve follow their boss, Dinah, and the rest of their crew past the temporary dressing rooms. They soon reach the main artery of the stately home: a long marble hall awash with sculptures, decorative armor, and massive oil paintings, where black-clad waiters are busy bussing champagne and canapés through Mrs. Witt's crowd of glamorous party guests, the warm light from her three giant tiered crystal chandeliers coating the entire scene with a dreamlike glitter.

"*The smart set*," Dinah had called them. For once, Cora must agree. The "haves" of this country versus her current company of "have-nots." *By dint of what?* she wonders. Inordinate family wealth hailing back to the *Mayflower*? Else gained through merciless business practices or duping easy marks—like those Ross & Calhoun bank lenders, preying on her father's financial ignorance. What shiny American victors they are, with their fancy balls and private shows and homes large as city blocks.

Cora feels the whole world slipping from her fingers as she trails her troupe into the festive melee. What if she never rises above her current station, playing backstage lackey to a troupe of fools? What is she to do now if she can't pick-pocket on the road? Cora needs *three thousand dollars* more to approach the bank with a credible offer for Long Creek Farm, and that's assuming no one else offers first. Absent thieving, that kind of money will take her twenty years to put together.

Twenty. Years.

"Pardon me, kind friends, please do excuse us."

Cora watches as a bearded, stout gentleman with a cane expertly threads a tall blonde woman through the crowd. The lady on his arm is pretty, dressed to the nines, if a little bit somber in her choice of deep blue velvet. Middle, possibly late twenties, and appearing quite faint.

"Dear Duchess," the man says, "perhaps some air might do you good?"

The blonde woman shakes her head, as if to clear it. "Just a bit taxed from all the excitement, is all," she says in a harsh, thick accent Cora can't quite place.

Mrs. Witt slides between the pair, a superior tilt to her chin. "I cannot imagine the House of Württemberg throwing parties like this, hmm? Allow yourself some respite, Duchess. In my sitting room. Ableton!" Mrs. Witt beckons one of her footmen standing ready in the wings.

The bearded man nods in gratitude, steering his female companion out of the fray as a portly middle-aged woman and a mousy-looking young lady sidle beside their hostess.

"Mrs. Witt, do you really think it proper for the duchess to retire alone with Mr. McAllister?" Frowning, the larger woman glances at her younger intimate—her daughter, Cora assumes. The pair have the same dishwater-brown hair, the same narrow-set eyes. "Arabella and I find it quite concerning that the duchess is without family or friends on these shores looking out for her well-being, and thus we consider it our duty—"

"You have no duties yet, Pearl." Mrs. Witt rolls her eyes. "Now stop angling for the Württemberg crown and let me see to my party." She waves above the crowd, clearly annoyed. "Mr. Prospero? Mr. Prospero, come here!"

Mrs. Witt summons the performer forward, eyeing the man like a new toy she longs to break. "My ball cannot be complete unless you share the methods behind your tricks. I command you to do so at once."

"Ah, but what is magic if not the keeping of guarded secrets." Prospero smiles grandly, deflecting. He drops his voice to a stage whisper. "And if I may say, madame, I do believe you're keeping secrets of your own."

Prospero steps forward, trailing his fingers across Mrs. Witt's monstrous headpiece. A moment later, a dove bursts forth from the bloom of feathers and soars toward the chandeliers.

The surrounding partygoers gasp, erupting into another round of applause.

"I wish the whole dratted thing would fly away." Mrs. Witt adjusts the piece with a groan. "We do what we must for *la mode*, but this headdress is a true cross to bear."

A team of harried-looking footmen rush forward to assist.

From the edges of the gathered crowd, Cora watches as the servants remove Mrs. Witt's dwarfing headpiece—carefully withdrawing, one by one, a series of ornate pins holding it in place. Four pins, to be precise. Each pin a shaped helix of at least two dozen diamonds.

One footman holds out a silver tray while the other lays the pins down in a perfect row.

Cora creeps through the crowd, angling for a better look. The pins are delicate, the bases sparkling silver, and the diamonds are of a significant size—half a carat each, maybe more.

Good God, how much could one possibly fetch for a set like that?

She watches the footmen head down the hall with the headdress and tray, her mind fully racing now. Is this a gift from above, a stroke of incredible luck, right when she needs it? She doesn't have a professional's eye for jewelry, admittedly— her family's treasures were of the cereal and corn variety—but she can appreciate the finer things, always has, and taken as a set, those pins must be worth at least a few thousand. More than enough to walk away from the show forever, cash out, and finally take back her family's land.

All she has to do is follow those footmen, wait for the right time, and swipe the whole lot.

As Prospero pulls a deck of cards from inside his lapel for his next parlor trick, Cora inches farther backward. Ignoring Maeve, who is also standing on the crowd's fringes and currently giving Cora a *very* pointed, bug-eyed stare. Although Cora is just being paranoid—there is no way the older stagehand could possibly sense what she is planning. Besides, Maeve has left her no other choice; without thieving on the road, Cora's future is as empty as Prospero's trick box.

As the crowd shifts, closing in for a better view of Prospero, Cora seizes her moment, slipping away from the commotion, retracing the steps of the footmen. Behind the scenes all night, and dressed in black herself, no one should mistake a young stage-hand for anything but additional hired help for the evening's festivities.

Cora rounds the hall into another narrow corridor.

A wrinkled woman in an apron stops her short.

"Ah, finally. My kingdom for a free hand!" The woman thrusts a heavy box into Cora's chest. *A sewing kit?* "Run this to Adelaide, girl."

Cora pastes on a manic smile. "Right. Adelaide." She nods across the corridor. "Saw her go that way—"

The servant thrusts her chin in the direction from which Cora came. "Thataway! Guest has a tear, yes, yes. It's a parade of fashion emergencies. Out you go—"

"To Mrs. Witt's quarters?"

"Ha, are you mad? They'll be in the guest room upstairs." The woman all but shoves Cora back into the hall.

All right, Cora, reset. Time for a new plan.

She returns to the marble hallway, then stealthily crosses over into the empty theater. Once inside the space, she spies a luxurious velvet shawl discarded on a seat. Perfect. She nabs the piece and heads backstage for Dinah's dressing room.

After closing the door, Cora hastily exchanges her black shirtwaist and skirt for one of the assistant's gaudy, floor-length gowns. As a final embellishment, Cora opens the sewing kit she's been saddled with and, with a few swift stitches, secures one of Prospero's black silk scarves into a waistband that matches the shawl.

Next, she helps herself to Dinah's mess of rouges and pow-ders stacked on an end table, then tugs down her hair and, with a couple of deft moves, retwists it into a piled tousle of curls.

Cora studies herself in the room's opulent mirror.

"Not quite Madison Avenue. But it'll do."

She hurries onto the stage, stopping for a moment to look out at the empty theater, imagining, for just a moment, those elusive spotlights finally shining on *her*.

In another life, perhaps. In this one, Cora is running out of time.

After leaving the theater via the far entrance, she enters the main hall on its opposite end. From there, she walks swiftly into the Witts' grand foyer, holding her head high, as if she owns the place. Disregarding the quizzical tone of a butler asking if she's lost.

"Just taking a break from the festivities," Cora says airily. "These events can be so demanding, do you not agree?"

"Yes, madame, but if I could—"

Ignoring him, she glides headlong past, rounding another hall peppered with marble busts and tapestries. Mrs. Witt's dressing rooms must be somewhere in this expansive maze.

The hall soon dead-ends, and Cora makes the swift decision to turn left, and . . . *Voilà*. She's rewarded with the sight of the two footmen and a lady's maid now holding the feathered headpiece and tray of pins, the lot of them idling and chatting down the other end.

Cora tucks herself into an alcove, waiting, watching as the servants share a quiet joke. The footmen finally disappear into a doorway on the right as the maid takes the bounty, passing two rooms before turning into the third door on the left.

Cora hangs back for one heartbeat, two . . . and then sneaks in behind her.

Mrs. Witt's private quarters.

The room is dark, but Cora can still see enough that pure

envy closes around her, stifling, like a spell box. Such luxury, extravagance. Excess. A canopy bed, damask-patterned walls, a sitting room, a moonlit vanity, and an elevated dressing stage.

She retreats into the shadows, feeling even more determined now.

The lady's maid carefully lifts each diamond pin from the tray and places them one by one inside a jewelry box on the vanity, then crosses the room and lays the feathered headpiece down like a sleepy child into a long velvet box at the foot of the bed.

Finally, the maid returns to the hall, shutting the door with a satisfying *click*.

Showtime.

Cora hurries toward the vanity and opens the box, lifting one of the pins for inspection. The delicate, intricate piece glimmers like a promise under the tall casement window's swath of moonlight. Twenty-four beautiful diamonds.

She swallows a triumphant squeal. No more waking up in one city and falling asleep the following night on the way to the next. No more toiling away in the shadows for her weekly pittance or slinking through the vaudeville crowds, always on the prowl like a famished hyena.

Cora conjures the image of her old clapboard farmhouse, the endless stretch of wheat, the way the sun glints off the winding creek at sunrise. Then, even more satisfying, she pictures the stunned, defeated faces of those avaricious lenders when she walks into their offices and slaps a stack of bills on the table.

Coraline O'Malley, victorious. Nobody's fool.

Invigorated by her fantasies, she affixes the pins inside her skirts.

When she attempts the door, however, she finds it locked. *Good God, nothing is ever easy.*

Slightly panicking, Cora surveys the whole of the room, her gaze soon falling on a second door—this one narrow and latched—on the adjacent wall beyond the sitting room.

Her body wilts in relief. Another way out.

It's hard to tell where the pocket door leads as Cora inches it open, given that the adjoining room is dimly lit. Another sitting room, perhaps? A parlor? Regardless, Cora slides through, emerging in a narrow space between two tall bookshelves. But just as she's about to make her exit . . .

She realizes she is not alone.

"I'd say that was a success, dear Duchess," a male voice quietly crows. "If a brief one."

Cora presses her back against the wall. There are two people here, in fact—the bearded man with the cane and the pretty European noblewoman with ice-blonde hair.

Damn it all. Maybe Cora won't be noticed, wedged between these high shelves. Safer here, in any case, than utterly exposed in the middle of the hostess's bedroom.

She'll simply have to wait them out.

From her shielded vantage, Cora watches the man stride, cane-assisted, across the room. He makes himself right at home with the drinks cabinet, where a decanted bottle of sherry waits to be poured.

"I'm not taking unnecessary risks, Ward," the woman answers in a low, flat American accent—a very different elocution than she had used earlier during the party, Cora notes.

"Time's a'ticking," says the man—Ward? "We don't set this in motion soon and we might forfeit half the season."

He hands his companion a glass of sherry.

The woman swirls it before sipping, scowling a little, as if in deep thought, while Ward sits back down with a contented sigh.

"And we can't risk letting this play into the summer, Alice," Ward says. "Only so long before word gets out about secret mines."

Cora's heart ticks like a metronome. *Forfeit the season? Secret mines?*

How . . . fascinating.

Also . . . none of her concern!

She's hiding on her person a collection of stolen, hopefully exorbitantly expensive diamond pins. Whoever these people are, if they catch her, they'll no doubt rat her out to Mrs. Witt. She'll not only lose the score, but she'll also lose the farm and likely her job, low-paying as it is. Perhaps she could even wind up in jail.

Cora focuses her entire being on willing their departure. *Leave, you wretched interlopers!*

"An excellent point," says the duchess—or Alice, as this Ward fellow just called her. "And four of the five families are now at play, thanks to this social outing, so you were right about that as well."

"As to the fifth . . ." Ward strokes his impressively pointed beard. "Are you dead set on Peyton? We could—"

"Peyton is nonnegotiable." The tall woman's voice has gone stiff. "He's the worst of them."

"As well as the most intractable," Ward mutters. "I laid the groundwork with his business manager, but no dice. Silas posed the proposition, told him about the mines. Peyton shut him right down: 'Not interested.' I fear he'll need a more subtle form of persuasion, but I'm unsure as to how to achieve that without an actual tête-à-tête. And like I said, Alice, the man's a veritable hermit. No one other than Silas—and I mean *no* one—has seen him for years."

"We'll simply have to find a way to draw him out." Alice sits up straighter, eyes sharpening. "Perhaps we could approach him at his ch—"

"Church? What *church*?" Ward laughs. "The man's the devil himself, as you said. What use has he got for God? He hardly lets his own son see the light of day anymore."

"His son. *There*—that's an angle. The son has got to be, what? Twenty-three by now?" Alice paces the room, thinking.

Cora feels her own heart pounding.

"Twenty-two, I believe," Ward answers quickly. "Now, what are you pondering, Alice? That the younger Peyton might be lured into—"

"Forget it. It won't work." The woman sighs. "He's too young."

"You are very beautiful." On the bearded man's lips, it feels more like a clinical observation than a flirtation. "And twenty-eight is hardly elderly."

"How kind," Alice says with a sardonic glint in her eye. "But I'm afraid you have more faith in my charms than I do. Twenty-eight may not be elderly, but it is decidedly spinsterish, not exactly the prime attraction for a young man. Even if it were, playing him off Ogden would risk losing them both." The woman waves her hand, exasperated. "It's not worth muddling over tonight. I'll find a way to drag Peyton out of his house and into our trap. Within months, he'll be left without a rag to wipe his forehead."

Cora flattens herself against the shelves. A magic trick

would really prove opportune right now. She's learned quite a bit about deception from watching Prospero's acts, but an escape stunt remains far outside her current capabilities. Her mind free-falls through increasingly outlandish possibilities: Could she fold herself in half, stuff herself between the books?

"And we'll be filthy too," Ward chuckles. "Filthy rich!"

"Precisely." Alice nods in a way that suggests punctuating the end of the conversation. "The plan is in place. The through line of it, at least. All that's left are mere details."

Cora closes her eyes, shifts her legs, which are starting to turn numb from remaining in place so long. Praying for reprieve, until finally, *finally*, those prayers are answered.

She hears the door to the main sitting room open and close. *They've left.*

Cora bursts toward the door.

And collides straight into the waiting duchess.

CHAPTER 2

Leave Them Wanting More

I sn't this an interesting magic trick?" Alice says in a decidedly German intonation, gripping the younger woman's elbow. "Levitating into our hostess's private quarters. I don't suppose you've received a personal invitation."

"Whereas you got yourself a plum one," the girl answers, a smart tilt to her chin and a smirk playing on her Gibson Girl lips. "You can drop the accent, by the way. You may have others fooled, but I just heard plenty to suggest where you're really from. And it sure as heck isn't Europe. Unless Upstate New York got annexed sometime in the past few years and I didn't know about it?"

Alice's grip loosens ever so slightly. *Upstate New York.* This girl has a good ear. Too good.

"Aren't you the clever one," Alice retorts dryly, dropping the accent as requested. The girl rocks back onto her heels like a precocious child who's just won a spelling bee. "You're not the one I took you for, are you? The magician's assistant, up there on the stage. But surely you're not an invited guest. And in any case, I can't let you waltz out of here with that."

She nods to the side of the girl's long skirt that she's clearly gripping with the fingers of one hand. The girl feigns bewilderment, but that hand doesn't budge.

"Don't know what you mean," the girl says. "I was just relieving myself, if you must know, in cleaner facilities than that dank little cupboard in the servants' wing. There. You got me. Haul me off to toilet jail!"

She tries to saunter off, but Alice blocks the way, arms crossed, unimpressed. "Go on. Let's see it."

The girl's eyes flit here and there, as if to assess whether a physical scrap might get her out of this one. Alice is tall, over five feet nine inches, and of a slim but formidable build. Even so, she knows it's her expression of absolute intractable marble that manages to dislodge the younger woman's confidence.

The girl sighs in capitulation. Immodestly she digs into the skirts of her gaudy dress, her hand emerging with four slim diamond pins. Iris Witt was wearing them earlier, wasn't she, to affix that horrendous headdress? It's a score so obvious that Alice nearly laughs aloud at the foolishness of Iris making such a show of removing them from her head.

If this girl successfully absconds with the jewels, she'd create a ruckus that would, as a best-case scenario, merely distract from the impact of Alice's own introduction into society; at worst, she'd put these grandees on their guard for the rest of the season. Unacceptable.

The easiest way to stop this little thief currently rests in a discreetly sewn pocket in Alice's gown—the derringer pistol she never leaves the house without. But perhaps there's a more delicate way to approach this.

"They're fakes," Alice says with a pitying cock of her chin.

The girl's eyes widen with surprise, but only for a blink. She's suspicious now, as well she might be. "How can you—"

"Watch." Alice leans close to the piled pins, enjoying the sight of the girl flinching, then breathes hot air into her hand. "See all this fog? The stones caught and held the humidity. Diamonds don't do that. This is crystal."

The girl shuffles back with a scowl, having a look on her own. "I don't see any fog."

"It takes a practiced eye, especially in this light." Alice raises her eyebrows. "It occurs to me that instead of giving you trade secrets, I ought rather to turn you over to the police. This sneak-and-grab routine appears to be a well-honed trick."

"You? Turn *me* over?" The girl laughs. "I'll be out that window and gone before you can even shout 'thief.'"

As if to test that theory, she edges closer to the far wall.

Good, Alice thinks, *the conversation has moved on from the gemstones.*

"An escape artist, are you?" Alice blinks. "I must have missed that part of the act. I'll have to ask the magician for your name."

"He doesn't know my real name," the girl volleys back, chin lifting again—more with pride than defiance, Alice thinks. "But I know your fake one. And if all goes south for me and I wind up in custody, I'm sure the boys in blue would love to hear what I have to say about the upstanding member of European aristocracy who blew the whistle on me. Makes for *quite* an interesting story."

They watch each other for another moment in tense silence.

Alice shrugs, motioning to Mrs. Witt's bedroom door. "Put those fakes back where you found them and no harm done.

If you heard as much as you claim to, then you'll understand why I can't have any kind of scandal arising while I'm here."

"Yes, that's all *crystal* clear," the girl says, spinning the pin with a smirk. "Go on, then. I'll put them back. Deal's a deal."

Alice shakes her head. "I think I'd prefer the evidence of my own eyes."

"Touchy, touchy."

Alice watches the girl sulkily glide back through the pocket door and into Mrs. Witt's dressing chambers, placing the pins back inside the lacquered jewelry box, shutting its compartment up tight with visible reluctance.

She's got a restless mind, Alice observes. *For her, it's as much about winning as the winnings themselves.*

She can certainly relate to that.

"We square?" the girl whispers as she slides the pocket door shut behind her.

"Indeed," Alice answers, with her German cadence back in place. "I wish you better luck in the future than what you've found tonight. And here's something more for your trouble."

She hands the thief a shiny coin.

"A fiver?" The girl squints. "I'd think my silence was worth something more like—"

"Don't press your luck."

The thief sinks like a tethered balloon, the bare regret in her expression making Alice wonder if she was right in her assessment of the girl—perhaps she really does need the money. But then, with a blink, the girl slides smartly away, turning the coin over in her hand with a neat spin to make it disappear. A well-practiced act. She's underutilized in that troupe of hers.

With perfected wariness, Alice watches the girl sidle out of the sitting room and back down the hall.

She lingers for a minute before rejoining the party, where Ward waits inside the game room with a group of male chums, all laughing at some quip she suspects she should be glad she hasn't heard. Ward straightens smartly and hastens from the room at the sight of her.

"Shall we away, Your Grace?" he offers. "I'm sure this has all been taxing."

"And I have some correspondence to reply to," Alice says quietly.

"To your brother, no doubt," Mrs. Witt loudly whispers, faux-conspiratorial as she takes Alice's arm in the corridor. "Tell me, is it really true that Prince Wilhelm's been corresponding with Arabella Ames, that little mouse? If he's looking for an American debutante, surely he can do better. Not that I'm offering up my Bonnie. She's got more suitors than she can juggle at the moment."

Alice affects a disarmed laugh at this crude performance. She must make Iris Witt believe that her particular brand of boastful vulgarity is a balm to the duchess's troubled mind.

"I'm afraid I'm writing back on more somber matters," Alice answers. "There have been raids by our supposed allies at our nation's southern border . . . But I really must say no more. I'm sure all your fine guests are beyond reproach, but I cannot risk any wisp of information reaching the ears of our Austrian oppressors."

Her eyes dip low before rising through the game room's doorway to meet the gathered men's curious and appreciative glances—in particular, Brett Ogden's arrogant gaze. He cuts the handsomest figure at this party, even in middle age, but he wears his beauty like a threat. Alice takes pains to fight off a shudder at his curling smile, especially while her sharp-eyed hostess is also watching.

"The truth is, I always reply promptly to my brother so that he will not worry about me." Alice laughs softly. "It is ironic, is it not, given the state of affairs in Württemberg and my safety here, but oh, he does fret, thinking of me alone on foreign shores. Thanks to your aid, dear Mrs. Witt, I'll have much needed artillery funds to convey to the resistance along with my letter. And your continued prayers for Württemberg's freedom will help us greatly."

"And now let us allow the duchess some rest." Ward turns to Mrs. Witt with a gallant bow and a wink. "A triumph, as always, dear Iris. I'll be sure to say as much to *Mrs. Astor*."

At that promise, Mrs. Witt draws a deep, exultant breath. No one in this sphere, not even one so apparently disaffected as their hostess, is immune to the power the name "Mrs. Astor" carries.

With that adieu duly delivered, Ward and Alice turn together to sweep down the grand corridor and out of the party, knowing all eyes will remain fixed upon them until they step out of the front doorway, into their carriage, and away.

Inside the lacquered car, Alice's shoulders drop. Her breath steadies. A postmortem drink at Ward's and then back to her own home, and sleep. Nearly done tonight.

It's a relatively brief ride south to the McAllisters' townhome on Thirty-First Street, offering just enough time for Alice's mind to wander, to adjust as needed, to plan further, but as Ward keeps up a monologue of wry observations for most of the ride, mainly recounting the series of events that led to Mrs. Witt's falling-out with Mrs. Astor a month prior, Alice's musings haven't slipped dangerously into the realm of needless anxieties.

Ward's right. This evening went well. She achieved what she needed to, stepping alluringly onto the public stage and then away again, letting the gossip that will inevitably ensue in her absence do much of the work for her.

The only glitch came at the end. That girl, the magician's assistant, or so Alice assumes.

But that was resolved neatly enough. Didn't even have to use her gun. Five dollars is far less than those pins were worth, even if they had been crystal, but as far as a trouble-free bounty goes for someone of that chit's station, it's nothing to sneeze at.

Neither, for that matter, is the five-hundred-dollar banknote Mr. Ogden passed her earlier in the evening while whispering a declaration of admiration into her ear.

"For your own troubles," he'd breathed. "You mustn't neglect yourself, Duchess. You are *far* too beautiful to bury yourself in worry."

She'd had to fight the urge to scrub the humidity of his breath from her ear, along with the memory of a dinner party long ago, that same ever-so-handsome Mr. Ogden sliding his hand over her mother's wrist, murmuring into her ear. Her own mother, fighting to hide her horror, for the sake of propriety.

Brett Ogden may well prove the easiest of the five marks.

Alice mentally recites their names in a loop as she steps from the carriage onto the night-damp street and up the stoop into Ward's home.

"Allow me a moment to loosen my tie," Ward drawls, motioning Alice toward the sitting room while he trots upstairs, tugging a bell string as he passes, to rouse some poor house-maid or other.

Ward's wife is also abed, but Alice doubts he'll wake her. She may not have even realized he'd been out to a ball to-night. All social invitations include Sarah, but she always declines, due to her ill health and borderline agoraphobia. Alice herself has only met the wan woman once in these past few months of her business acquaintance with Ward McAllister, and came away with the impression of an ac-tress who had been assigned the role of "Wife" but not been given any lines to memorize. They have three grown children, Alice recalls, spotting their childhood portraits in oil hanging upon a wall in triptych. Clearly they had some degree of rapport before Sarah's convalescence, but even so, Mrs. McAllister feels akin to so many other aspects of Ward's life—his Southern grandiosity, his "working farm" in Newport, his highly placed social intimates—all a matter of well-thought-out conspicuousness and clever misdirection. Distractions from his bevy of male companions and, perhaps more importantly, his perpetually strained finances.

As predicted, a maid appears in the sitting room doorway, hastily dressed, her hair still rumpled from bed beneath her white cap. Alice is too exhausted to sympathize with her at the moment.

"A glass of claret before you see to the fire," she says, retain-ing her royal hauteur and Germanic accent.

The servants have more power than most people realize. And goodness, do they talk.

"Very good, miss," the maid replies, swallowing down a yawn.

Alice resettles her gaze on the tired woman. "Just leave us

the bottle when you're finished. I shouldn't expect we'll need anything else."

After the maid gratefully retreats, Alice sips her heady wine, basking in solitude on the settee, listening to the fire crackling back to life, along with her own habitual recitation:

Ogden. Vandemeer. Ames. Witt. Peyton.

Ogden, that cut-rate Don Juan. Vandemeer, that overgrown child, who must always be fastest, first, best. Ames, who hates that he's new money. Witt, the merry widow with her vicious, ever-changing whims. And Harold Peyton Sr., the ringleader, the mastermind, the one who put it all in motion, and therefore the true worst of them.

All five of them complicit. Those fine families. Their upstanding reputations built on rotten foundations.

And her own family, their greatest victim.

Alice sips her claret, taking in Ward's modest sitting room with its charmingly chintzy furniture. Still larger than any room in Alice's current home, though her apartments a few blocks uptown are certainly respectable enough for the exiled duchess she purports to be. Lolling her head against the back of the settee, she recalls the first bolt-hole she landed upon returning to the city, a small hostelry run by a woman of exquisite confidence, who didn't bat a single eye to see Alice step out day after day in the very same elegant gown (indeed, the only one she owned). When she'd given her landlady her final rent payment and announced she'd be moving on, she was greeted with a knowing wink and a "well done, my dear" that made an unaccustomed smile rise to Alice's own lips.

She thinks now also of the places she lived before that. The indistinguishable stream of lodgings in out-of-the-way corners of Montreal, one to the next, so she'd never get waylaid or caught. Before that, the years upon years squandered in that ancient, claptrap, falling-down mansion-turned-boardinghouse in Poughkeepsie. The single room she shared with her mother and, for a time, before he made his escape, her little brother. And the baby, of course. So very briefly.

She remembers the shuddering sobs of her mother from the other side of the tin bed, shaking the thin mattress night after night. The swarms of flies in the summer and the chill of winter seeping in through the cracks in the ill-fitted window frames. And all around them, the sounds of other boarders, wracked with coughs, or barreling drunken laughter, or singing softly to children who were born hale and healthy, unlike her own little sister, who barely was.

And though she's not in the habit of training her mind back that far, now Alice remembers her sitting room on Madison Avenue. Her nanny holding her by the hand as she greeted the grown-ups in their glittering gowns and smoking jackets, the sweet smell of pipe smoke filling the room. Her mother rosy-cheeked then, eyes bright and innocent. Her father with his straight smile and white teeth and bristled mustache.

Alice stands, inhaling deeply. Her pulse roars in her temples as she grips the stem of her glass.

"Your Grace?"

Alice stifles a flinch as she turns to see the housemaid standing in the doorway, looking bewildered. "I believe you may have a visitor."

CHAPTER 3

Loose Ends

Compared to the grandeur of the Witt home on Madison Avenue, Ward McAllister's residence is modest, a narrow, three-floor townhome on Thirty-First Street, although Cora supposes there is a certain unmistakable care and pride in its keeping, the set of rosebushes encased inside the wrought iron fence, the potted plants lining the stoop.

She steels herself with a fortifying breath, watching the home from a ways down the block. She can see movement through its front window. A maid, perhaps, or butler. Given that she followed Alice and Ward here by carriage—having spent the bulk of Alice's measly five-dollar payoff on this trip—she knows they're inside too. Scheming, no doubt.

Cora understood why the fake duchess shooed her away a few hours ago, concluding "no harm done," or however she'd put it. Meaning no harm done to *her*. There was loads of harm done on Cora's end. Her score was foiled, and now with Dinah on her scent, her days are numbered with the show—unless Cora keeps her word to Maeve and stops her side hustle, but that means Long Creek Farm is as good as gone. There's also the undeniable fact that Cora will never again meet a fake duchess, or rather, a woman so astute at playing a fake duchess that she had a party of hundreds fooled.

This woman might prove a bigger score than thousands of sneak-and-grab jobs, as she called them. And Cora cannot let her slip away.

Before losing her nerve, Cora approaches the house, passing a well-dressed couple stepping out from another carriage on the corner, laughing, cheeks flushing in the cold November night, Manhattan showing no signs of slowing down, although it must be nearly five a.m. by now, the sun threatening to rise over the distant glimmering East River. There is something intriguing about city life, Cora will admit. The frenetic pace, bustling hustle, high society and all their elaborate social rituals. And yet she's made an oath to herself, signed her name in blood: Long Creek Farm will be hers again. It fully consumes her, nearly all she can think about, since Ross & Calhoun swept in like a storm cloud on the Great Plains, blotting out the sun.

She'd—*they'd*—lost the farm almost eighteen months ago, to be exact, though the money troubles started long before that. Long Creek Farm was getting pinched on all sides by overproduction and skyrocketing distribution prices, thanks to the railroad tycoons. The boll weevil plagues of '81 only added insult to injury. And it was just her and her father, besides the temporary hands he'd bring on during the season—her mother, dying of a fever when she was just a baby, and her wayward older brother, not suited for farm life, long since scramming for the West and the promise of striking it rich.

A couple of neighbors looking to round out funding for a new grain elevator started pressuring her father, telling him he had to "mechanize production" on the farm or risk falling behind. "Industry is the future of this country," she'd hear them argue at night in their kitchen, hard-pressing him over round after round of whiskey.

Then came the meetings with the men from Topeka in their dark suits with their sham smiles, offering loans at obscenely high interest rates. Cora could smell a noxious scheme afoot, strong as manure, but Da kept shrugging her off, telling her he knew what he was doing—he'd taken care of her all his life, after all; he wasn't about to start kowtowing to her hang-ups now. With the loans from Ross & Calhoun, Da purchased three John Doe plows, reapers, and that share in the grain elevator, all with his own farmland pledged as collateral.

In a matter of months, it all went up in smoke, Cora watching like a patron at a magic show—shocked, disbelieving, powerless to do anything to stop the spectacle. Despite the new machinery, they couldn't keep up with the larger Topeka competitors and fell behind on payments. Da defaulted on the first, then the second and third loans, until Ross & Calhoun Loans swept in and seized their home straight out from under them.

Out of money, no land, Da became a tenant farmer, bringing Cora along to help with grunt work in the stables and kitchens. She watched him grow smaller and smaller all winter, ground down by labor and despair, until he eventually succumbed to whooping cough that following spring.

"Can't trust no one anymore." Da's dying words. *"Whole country's full of cheats."*

From Cora's vantage, though, that wasn't wholly true. There were confidence men and their marks, weren't there? Schemers and dupes, the whole country polarized right down the middle. There were people like Da, the over-trustful, hapless fools with targets on their backs, and then there were people out on the hunt to make theirs: bankmen, railroad magnates, folks like those crooked politicians in Tammany Hall. The fancy set, too, like Mrs. Witt at the party, wealth wielded as a weapon, determined to take down whoever, pay whatever, in order to preserve their reign.

It had seemed like fate when Prospero rolled into town last June, one of the many traveling vaudeville acts at the local Shawnee Circus & Fair. Cora had watched the magician's show of fire, lights, and illusions, rapt. Prospero was a professional grifter of the highest order. A man who could stand onstage and fool scores of patrons every show. Cora had already started thieving alone on the streets of Topeka, a purse here, a pocket watch there, hoping to cobble together enough to buy back her land—come out on top after all—but she had so much to learn and so far to go. Here was someone who could help her. She approached Maeve and the backstage crew after the performance, gushing with compliments, and they introduced her to Prospero. Cora left with the troupe for Lincoln, Nebraska, the very next morning.

But Prospero, the show, the road, it's all a dead end now, what with Cora stuck backstage making three crummy dollars a week and Dinah threatening to have her sacked if she tries crooking more.

This fake duchess, however, could very well be Cora's solution. Her ticket to greener pastures, in more ways than one.

With new resolve, Cora taps the bronze knocker against Mr. McAllister's door. She knows it's far past the appropriate time to call, but Cora can't afford to wait. It's right now or joining the troupe on their way to Providence, Rhode Island— first stop on a lifetime journey to Nowhere Fast.

She knocks again.

A bone-weary-looking housekeeper finally answers. "Yes, miss?"

"I'm here to see the duchess . . ." Cora blanks, trying to recall if she actually heard the sham name of the woman in the library, landing on "Duchess Lady Alice."

An arched eyebrow tells Cora she guessed wrong. "Is the duchess expecting you?"

Cora smiles. "In her own way, most likely."

The housekeeper gives a curt nod and retreats into the house, not inviting her in. Cora resists the urge to bite her nails, resting her gaze on the McAllisters' small but lovely fenced garden beside the stoop.

"Grand Duchess Marie Charlotte Gabriella of Württemberg will be with you in a moment," the housekeeper announces behind her with a barely contained sigh.

She leads Cora into a modest parlor with a striped settee, matching armchairs, and a crackling fireplace. "Please. Make yourself comfortable."

Comfortable. What a tall order. Cora settles for perching on the edge of a chair.

"What on earth are you doing here?"

Cora leaps to her feet at that voice, then internally curses herself for her jumpiness.

She spins to take her first long look in the light at her mark, who must have been lurking in here all along. The Grand Duchess Marie or Alice or whoever she truly is has perhaps ten years on her. She really is a beautiful woman, although hard-looking, with a long, straight nose and that severe, pale hair—although, who knows, her entire face might soften when she smiles. Cora has yet to see a smile and cannot quite imagine one, but she can see how the woman can get away with claiming nobility. There's a timelessness to her appearance, a weariness too, as if she carries the weight of many generations.

"I'm here to talk to you," Cora says. "I didn't feel we were quite done with our earlier discussion."

"We most certainly were," Alice says.

Cora spies the home's owner, Mr. Ward McAllister, lingering in the hall, now dressed rather informally in a maroon smoking jacket and slippers. "Your, ah, Grace? If I may—"

"You may not," the fake duchess says. "I'll handle this myself, Mr. McAllister."

The man gives a ceremonious bow, then brightens as he spots the decanted wine.

"In that case, I shall take my nightcap in the study."

He plods languidly between them, swirls the rust-red wine inside the crystal decanter, then with one more smirk, glides out of sight.

"Nice place he's got here," Cora says wistfully once his slippered footsteps have retreated.

"Yes. But again, why are you in it?"

"I remember what you said." Cora sweeps forward. "And I understand that we *could* let sleeping dogs lie or whatever."

"It seems you *don't* remember what I—"

"The thing is," Cora charges onward, "I believe we can help each other."

Her Fake Grace lets out a thunderclap of a laugh.

Cora persists. "I think I could learn quite a bit from you. You see, a turn of unfortunate circumstances led me to Prospero's employ in the first place, and try as I might to flourish under his tutelage, I feel stymied, stuck rather, and I don't necessarily see a way out . . . which is why I had found myself in Mrs. Witt's chambers in the first place. But then when I fell upon you, I just . . . I truly feel like fate had a reason for bringing us together."

The duchess's face remains blank, carved of stone.

Cora feels dizzy but refuses to relent. "I only mean to say that I have plans to . . . well, I suppose I have lofty goals, but there's a divide between what I know and what I need to know in order to make them happen, which is why I could really stand to benefit from a mentor. A real one. Prospero the Great hardly qualified, and I think—"

"*I* think it's past time for you to go."

But Cora isn't stopping now, not after practicing her speech at least ten times on the carriage ride here. Obviously she was prepared for friction. She knew this woman was not just going to throw open her arms and say, *Yes, of course, I've always desired a mangy mutt as a protégé.*

Cora has to go all in or else it's all for naught.

She takes a step closer, drops her voice. "See, the thing is, I believe I can do far more damage with the information I gleaned tonight than you can with the hypothetical crime you claim you saw committed. And anyway, I'm a puff of smoke, a nonentity. Prospero doesn't even know my real name. Besides, no one cares about a sly act from the likes of some nobody like me. Not a princess or duchess or . . . whatever you're pretending to be. And I have a feeling whatever prize is at the end of this, it's a big one. One you're not about to jeopardize."

Only Alice's brow betrays her. One crinkle between the eyes.

"Prospero's troupe leaves for Providence soon. Another

private show, of which I'm sure he'll pocket all the proceeds, but this time I very much hope I won't be part of the act." Cora hands the woman the calling card she's prepared by hand. "I go by Cora Mack. I'm staying with the troupe at the Hopper House, near the river. We're scheduled to depart at five o'clock sharp this evening. You can send a servant or a messenger or come yourself, however you like. But if I don't hear from you by the time I'm expected to load up and out, I'll assume I need to resort to my contingency plan."

The duchess arches an eyebrow. "And what is that?"

"I'll be forced to alert Mrs. Witt that she was not hosting royalty but rather an outright fraud."

The woman laughs again. "Who in their right mind would believe a magician's stagehand over Ward McAllister?"

"I'm not sure Iris Witt *is* entirely in her right mind," Cora notes.

A glimmer of a smile sparks in Alice's eyes. Enough to give Cora hope that this might possibly work and keep going.

"From what I've experienced of your world, its access feels quite . . . tenuous. All it might take is a shadow of doubt. A wrinkle ruins an entire dress, as they say. Just think about it." Cora smooths her own skirt, partly to avoid the reaction on Alice's face, then nods curtly. "I can see myself out."

It's only when she's stepped out into the rising sun, emerging to pierce the brisk New York morning, that she gasps, residual fear seeping out of her as she hurries down the McAllisters' steps, a rogue tear running down her cheek.

Oh yes, she could learn loads from that woman. An entire trade. Enough to get her farm back and maybe a brand-new life to boot.

Here's hoping she gets the chance.

CHAPTER 4

A Widening Circle

Ward sits in his study with a pipe and a fresh glass of madeira. He tips his glass curiously at Alice.

She lingers in the doorway, taking in the morning light filtering through the bay windows with a troubled squint.

"Picked up a new friend at the party?" He nods vaguely in the direction of Thirty-First Street.

"She'd like to think so," Alice groans, stepping inside. "Not just a stagehand, this one. I caught her trying to pilfer Mrs. Witt's diamond hairpins. I think she'd have gotten away with it if we hadn't been positioned to intercept her. Alas, she was even better positioned to eavesdrop on our conversation."

Ward's brow furrows. "How did you stop her? Heaven forbid it got physical."

"I can assure you, I avoided a scrap." Alice smiles wryly. "I told her they were fakes."

Ward lets out a boom of a laugh, hands resting on his belly. "And she believed you? After walking through that party? Real zebras in the ballroom but fakes on the hostess's head? She can't be very bright."

"Oh no, she's a sharp one. Merely young." Alice lounges against the arm of a leather sofa. "And eager. Followed us here, didn't waste a minute. She's an admirer of mine, she says. Wants to learn from me."

"Now that is smart."

"But again, young," Alice counters. "Naive. First rule of what we do is to keep the circle small."

"I'm not sure I agree with you there." Ward polishes off his wine. "Look at my Mystic Rose. Look at Alva Vanderbilt. Hell, look at all these captains of industry around us. They thrive on ever-widening circles, and make no mistake, they're every bit the con artists we are."

"I can't argue that," Alice says.

"And there is a certain danger in being seen to be isolated," Ward goes on. "It begins to look like an illness that the members of society would be keen to avoid contracting. I fielded quite a few sentiments of concern for your well-being tonight, my dear duchess. People thought it was not quite right that you should be sent all the way out here on your lonesome. It wasn't enough to make people question your story, but even so . . . something to consider."

"What are you suggesting? I hire a theater troupe to pose as my royal retinue?" Alice gazes sidelong at Ward.

"Heavens, no. Actors are entirely too untrustworthy to make good criminals," he quips. "But to build out our case a little further, just a touch of extra pathos—the brave resistance, the noble nationalists of Württemberg, giving their all for freedom from Austrian mistreatment and exploitation . . . I'm merely spitballin' here, my dear. Feel free to shut me up."

"I welcome your spitballs," Alice says. "But you do understand there is an end goal to all this storytelling. And it is entirely personal for me."

"I wish sometimes it weren't." Ward shakes his head, his

smirk dropping off. "It's so much easier to achieve your goals when you don't care one way or the other about the people involved."

But Alice's gaze has drifted out the window, her mind reciting those names again. *Ogden. Vandemeer. Ames. Witt. Peyton.*

"Now that I consider it," Ward says, "there is another wrinkle that girl might be able to iron out for us."

Alice turns to him, surprised. "Which? She's skilled at sleight of hand; I noticed that."

"Oh, that's not exactly what I'm referring to." Ward chuckles. "Along with being extremely young, she's downright pretty, but not in the way of someone whose face will remain in your memory like a tintype. And you say she's eager to learn?"

"Frothing at the bit."

"So teach her," Ward suggests, turning back to the house. "And then turn her on Mr. Peyton. The younger, I mean, not the old recluse. Just the thing we need to draw out the father."

"Interesting," Alice says, carefully noncommittal.

Ward sets down his pipe and rises from his chair. "The more the merrier is my conclusion. But now I'll bid you good night, or rather, good morning. Sarah will be awake soon, and I must fall asleep before she catches me up or she'll force me to describe the party to her in exhaustive detail over breakfast, a fate I'd much rather postpone. I'll ring for my coach to see you home."

As Alice rides the few blocks north to her apartments, she ponders Ward's marriage dynamic with more befuddlement than ever. But then, she finds most relationships perplexing. There has been precious little intimacy in her life since leaving Manhattan under a cloud of tumult. Only wariness and trials.

The moment she decided not to let anyone divert her from

her course was the moment that course finally took a steadier bearing. Six years ago, during those months after Mama died, Alice continued her employment with an upright, moneyed local family, assisting in the education of their daughter, a dull but obedient girl who stared out the window through most of her lessons, especially when Alice would read aloud to her in French from novels like *Le Comte de Monte Cristo*. Alice was never sure how much this listless girl only a few years younger than her was actually absorbing, but oh, what an education it afforded the teacher. When the girl made her debut, Alice was released with the gift of a cast-off day dress and a ten-dollar bonus.

It was enough. Enough for train fare to Montreal under an assumed name, wearing that secondhand dress, and the first of many nights in modest lodgings. Enough to make her look respectable, a necessity for pulling off her first and simplest deception—a tearful and shocked accusation of theft in a crowded area, in which kind souls were inclined to provide charity. Over the next several years, the sophistication grew. A bump into a gentleman, resulting in a broken vase— the very one she was supposed to sell for her employer. With the loss of the income to come out of her wages and Alice to be tossed out on her ear! "Oh, but how much were you expecting to receive for it? Here, I'll give you the money and no harm done."

From there, a dipping of Alice's toes into the plan she'd forged back in Poughkeepsie during her teaching days. Just to see how far she could carry it in Canada where, if there were repercussions, they wouldn't be felt beyond the border. A duchess from a European country who dared to defy the whims of the kaiser. The financial hardships facing the people of her homeland. "Oh, but that's terrible. How can we help?" A donation to the national cause would not go amiss.

Alice made certain of that, stockpiling them fastidiously in preparation for her larger game. The move to New York this past year. All careful, methodical, nothing rash.

Until that day in Union Square when she met Ward Mc-Allister. She ran the vase trick. He'd seen it pulled by others before. But rather than turning her over to the authorities, he offered her a partnership. He'd been running a bit of a scam himself, it turned out, practically his whole life. Playing the role of a family man of sustained and considerable means. Styling himself as the sole arbiter of taste and good breeding, along with his patroness, Mrs. Caroline Astor. Pretending he didn't completely loathe all the society denizens who surrounded him day in and day out.

When he learned her plan, he was all in, for a fifty-fifty split, with the understanding that anyone else Alice brought along—like that French-Canadian pickpocket, say, or that brute of a Hun woman from the Battery—would draw their cut from her portion.

Alice doesn't trust Ward McAllister. She knows better than that. It is an arrangement of mutual usefulness. Isn't that what all friendships are in the end?

But by that logic, why *not* offer the same to this Cora girl? Perhaps Ward's right and all it will take is a pretty face and an eager ally to gain access to the last, most important target, the as-yet elusive Peytons.

She slips inside her home without waking her own servants— if she can even truly call them that—slides into her small bed, and sleeps on it. Briefly, as ever.

She wakes just after noon with the next stratagem, and ten

to follow that one, clear in her mind. And by the time she's finished her lunch, she's got it all lined up—the adjustments, the improvements, the new lures and tightening hooks and locked door traps, bespoke to each family—all the way from this very moment, today, November the tenth, until the first of May.

The final stage of a revenge fourteen years in the making.

CHAPTER 5

The Vanishing Ladies

Upon first seeing her, Cora assumes she is a mirage, a trick of the light, just like Pepper's ghost. Or else an angel, with her white-blonde hair, smart fur-lined coat, and matching wide-brimmed hat, descended from on high to the hellish bustle of West Forty-Ninth Street. But no, the fake duchess is real, and *here*, right at 5 p.m. as requested, standing outside the front doors of the Hopper House.

Cora bursts out of the dingy lobby and into the cold, late afternoon air like a child rushing toward a Christmas tree.

"You came for me." Cora longs to wrap her arms around the woman but doesn't dare.

"Whether I leave with you remains to be seen." Alice archly looks over her shoulder. A few paces down the road, two of Prospero's burly crewmen guard the show's caravan of props, while another hefts Dinah's many pieces of luggage toward the back. "Not the safest place to talk."

"Perhaps the lobby?" As soon as Cora suggests it, though, she winces. "Although my fellow stagehand, Maeve, will be down at any moment."

Alice nods down the road, toward the river in the distance,

sparkling blue between the rows of dilapidated tenements. "Walk with me."

Cora folds her coat tighter around her waist and sets out with the regal woman. Past the line of desperate street vendors shouting into the crowded streets from their wooden carts, the sagging front stoops, the elevated Ninth Avenue line rumbling over it all like a gloomy thunderstorm.

"Charming place," Alice muses.

A gust of frigid wind blows off the water as they turn the corner. Cora tries not to react. This conversation may well be her audition, after all, and instinct tells her that this cunning, ruthless woman beside her might consider shivering a weakness.

"Believe it or not, this is quite nice compared to where we stayed in Philadelphia," Cora says. "Although I believe one of the buildings down the road from the Hopper is called Hell's Kitchen. And there was some sort of squabble between street gangs transpiring when I arrived in the wee hours this morning, but they hardly noticed m—"

"Now that we have some privacy, I think it's best to discuss next steps," Alice interrupts. She has dropped the accent, at least, but still cuts an intimidating figure, looming over Cora with her perfect posture.

"Yes. Right. Next steps." Cora nods. "I'm ready. And have some suggestions. Some ideas, rather, given what I overheard between you and Mr. McAllister. I've been running plays on my own, you know, for a while, and—"

"A while?" A faint smile lifts Alice's lips. "How old are you?"

"Twenty-two." Cora tries to ignore Alice's eye roll. "I'm not claiming to have pulled any big jobs, but I'm a quick study, and I've long thought about—"

"I'm not interested in your thoughts." Alice purses her lips as they sidestep two young men quarreling in the street. She takes Cora's elbow swiftly and pulls her along. "I have a very discreet, specific need and believe that you might be able to fulfill it. I expect you to do exactly as I ask, without hesitation, objection, or embellishment. If you are so willing, we can continue this conversation. If not, it looks as though your troupe is minutes from embarking on yet another magical adventure. So which is it to be?"

Again, Cora resists the urge to bristle, this time from Alice's chilly tone. So she is expected to play a lackey once more, a mindless minion to a greater star. Not exactly the type of angle or experience she was hoping for when she solicited this woman as a mentor.

Then again, given the circles this confidence woman moves within, Cora suspects she'll get everything she wants in the end—the money, her farm, a real future. Besides, who's to say Cora can't work to earn the woman's trust, just as she once hoped to do with Prospero? After all, there is always room for upward mobility, for growth.

Cora nods. "I am so willing."

"Good." Alice turns her attention forward, setting a new pace, as determined and brisk as a military general. Cora has to scramble to keep up with her. "The game I've begun, and that you have now entered, is already fully laid out. The rules. The players. The strategy. So it's best that you simply listen from here on out. Mr. McAllister and I have recently concluded the first stage, establishing credibility—"

"With whom, exactly?" Cora interjects, genuinely curious.

Alice glares her way. "I will get to that."

Cora mimes locking her mouth up tight, resisting her impatience. "Right. Sorry. Simply listening now."

"Do you recall the name I went by at the party, when you found Mr. McAllister and me conversing in Mrs. Witt's sitting room?"

Cora stares at her blankly. "Oh, understood—now it's time to speak. Yes, the duchess, Grand Duchess Marie of . . . Wertingpark?"

"Goodness, no. That sounds like the title of a half-rate dime novel. *Württemberg*," she corrects, with caustic emphasis. "A small Germanic principality, still sovereign, with its own nobility and crown, which has tragically found itself in economic and political turmoil since joining the German Empire." Alice adjusts her elegant hat, protecting her face against the cold as they turn another corner. "Our nation of Württemberg . . ."

Cora marks that "our" with a surprised blink but keeps her mouth shut.

". . . is extremely rich in a *very* valuable natural resource. Emerald mines, to be exact, which are scattered across Württemberg's topography—and which were unfairly and secretly pledged as an incentive in the brokering of Germany's recent treaty with Austria-Hungary and Italy. Our king, Charles I, wildly unpopular with the people, failed to protect our great nation by not only capitulating to this treaty but also by allowing our mines and other assets to be ruthlessly pillaged by these new supposed allies."

Alice waits a moment to continue as they edge around a bustling fruit cart.

"Understandably, this has led to a growing national resistance, helmed by my brother, Wilhelm Karl Paul Heinrich Friedrich, the grand prince and current heir to the throne. I believe, in my very soul, that with a little financial help from our American friends, we will gain Württemberg's independence—but all of this has made us reconsider the future, you see, including the management of our most valuable resource. Perhaps it is time to join the modern age. Allow a select number of *trusted* foreign investors to join the efforts of our sovereign-backed mining company—"

"Quick question. Only one at present, promise." Cora winces. "This Württemberg . . . is it real? I've never heard of it."

Alice stares at Cora as if she's grown a second head.

"Yes," she says evenly.

Cora feels her cheeks warm, even in the cold. "I just wasn't sure where the truth ends and the con starts."

"Please tell me you are following this. The nation, the treaty, King Charles, even the recently widowed Prince Wilhelm, all real. We have created a *fictional* sister, played by yours truly, who is helping the prince's *fictional* national resistance to protect Württemberg's *entirely fictional* emerald mines, which we are going to posit as a discreet, early investment opportunity to select New York families in order to rob them blind. Yes?"

Cora swallows hard. "Ah yes. Got it. Crystal clear—I mean, right as rain." She ignores her jumping pulse. She is game for this kind of subterfuge, is she not? A detailed, mindful game, with high stakes and great rewards. She simply needs to get up to speed. "If we could just go over the bit about the sovereign-backed mining company—"

"There's no need for that at present." Alice closes her eyes. "You will be playing the role of my cousin—my sweet, *simple* cousin, I'm thinking now, who knows very little about economics or the inner workings of Württemberg mining. All you'll need to do is look and act the part while Mr. McAllister and I work our targets and secure their pledges to invest."

"The part," Cora repeats, "the part of—"

"A Württembergian emerald heiress."

Cora shakes her head. Coraline O'Malley, an *emerald heiress*.

Hardly a backstage gig, as suspected. No, it sounds as though Cora will be on the front lines of this endeavor. This could be quite satisfying. In truth, she cannot think of a more rewarding game, infiltrating the smart set by proving them foolish, waltzing right into their showy parties and fleecing them. Things are coming together indeed.

"The trouble is," Alice goes on, "this sort of scheme is finite. These marks, as insulated as they are in their Manhattan, upper-crust world, are also quite resourceful and well connected. Mr. McAllister and I estimate we have the span of one spring social season to lock in our targets and realize our aims. Our endgame—their investments—*must* be attained by the conclusion of the social calendar, with the first of May as our closing date. And I am not leaving New York without achieving what I've come for."

"And where exactly did you come *from*?" Cora ventures. "Was I right about Upstate New York?"

Alice's eyes narrow, as if to physically lock her mind up tight.

Cora opts for a shrug over a smile. "I figure I should know a little bit about the person I'm working for. Beyond all the lies, that is."

She watches Alice consider. Then: "Poughkeepsie."

Cora nods. Presses her luck further. "Some grand mansion in town, I assume."

"A boardinghouse. Can we get back to the matter at hand?"

"Right, of course." Cora nods smartly. "Who are our targets?"

"Five families, some members of which you may have already been exposed to, but we will cover them in detail, and in due course," Alice says, stepping carefully around a large pile of horse manure steaming on the walk. "All you need to know right now is that they are part of high society, including the *nouveau riche*, the type who hold tightest to their newfound wealth and power and thus who need to be approached extremely carefully."

The nouveau riche. Robber barons, she's heard them called. Steel and railroads. Banks. Not Ross & Calhoun, those devils, but exactly the same ilk.

"You will be staying with me, your elder cousin," Alice continues, "and after your long sea journey, you are quite eager to join the season's festivities here in New York. You've been studying abroad, perhaps in England. I'll teach you a Württemberg accent; the British influence will explain why it differs slightly from mine. You have a good ear. Hopefully you'll prove as skillful a mimic."

Cora opens her mouth to enthusiastically agree, perhaps even to attempt a posh British lilt, but is spared the effort by Alice plodding onward.

"Following the tragic death of your father, the king's exchequer, who secretly supported the resistance—"

"My fath . . . Um. All right. I—"

"Your mother has decided to send you to me, safe from potential repercussions here in America, where perhaps you may also meet a suitable husband. Since unfortunate circumstances have forced me to these shores as well, we are in great sympathy with each other, you see. There could be no better mentor for you."

Cora is more inclined to agree than ever. She nods.

Alice leans forward. "I'll introduce you to society. The dinners, the balls. At these events you'll help us gain access to one particularly elusive mark and draw him into the emerald scheme."

"And then what?"

"And then we're golden until the first of May, at which point all our preparations will coalesce into one glorious confidence game. Then we'll go our separate ways as far wealthier individuals. Where you go and why is entirely up to you."

Cora nods again, exhaling, as they round the block once more, the Hopper House's stodgy entrance now coming back into view. Long Creek Farm has never felt so attainable, so inevitable.

"Oh, and Cora?" Alice takes her arm, pulling her back slightly. "I hope it goes without saying that if you breathe a word about this to anyone . . ." She smiles, although the expression is neither warm nor charming, as Cora had assumed it might be. It's curling, wicked, with far too much tooth. "I'll ensure you truly disappear."

Cora deflects that clearly genuine threat by glancing at the doors. "Well then. I suppose I should get my belongings. Am I to assume we are to start right away?"

"Right away, as in immediately." Alice gently guides her in the opposite direction, gesturing toward a hansom cab parked under the elevator line across the road.

"Wait, I need to . . ." Cora sighs. "I have some money. It's in a safe place, stowed in my luggage. It isn't much, but it's a start, to buy my farm, you see, and I—"

"One hundred fifty? Maybe two?"

The correct number is one hundred eighty-nine dollars, but Cora has to assume Alice's question was rhetorical.

"It's imperative to cut ties immediately, as goodbyes will only prompt explanations as to where you're going and what we're about to do." Alice lifts her chin. "I assure you, you'll have five thousand times that amount when this is through."

Five thousand times. Meaning her cut is . . . *one million dollars?* Cora laughs incredulously. "And I'm just meant to take your word for that?"

"I'm not going to draw up a legal contract, if that's what you're asking," Alice says crisply. "You requested that I teach you. That is going to require a leap of faith. Are you prepared to jump?"

She supposes Alice makes a point. Cora nods.

As consolation, when they set off, she keeps her eyes trained on that flat expanse of water tucked between the long rows of shanties in the distance—beyond all the filth and squalor, the promise of something far bigger and brighter than even this city can contain.

Alice remains silent as they ride across town, which is just as well—more time for Cora to gape at the homes and mansions growing in increasing proportion as they inch toward Fifth Avenue. The iconic street itself feels like another world from the one she left, all tall, majestic buildings and shining horse-drawn carriages, frilly ladies and well-dressed gentlemen strolling on either side of the road, as if they have nowhere to be but part of a perpetual parade, fashionably whiling away the early evening. This is her new show, Cora supposes, her chance to perform front and center on a real stage, although she can still hardly believe it.

She finds her mind drifting back to her prior days on the road, her old gig, the troupe, Prospero, Dinah, and Maeve. Well, mainly Maeve. She pictures the kindly older woman now, stammering possible explanations to Prospero about where Cora could have gone. Pleading with Dinah to convince the boss to wait for her, just a while longer. Maeve is likely worried sick about her, fearing the worst, as she tends to do.

Cora shifts in her seat, trying to get comfortable with this unfortunate ramification. If Cora ever wants to set foot on Long Creek Farm again, she is going to need to be as merciless, and single-minded, as the men were who stole it in the first place. She will make it right with Maeve one day. Find her, somehow, when this whole Württemberg scheme is through.

The carriage stops in front of a well-kept townhome on the corner of Third Avenue and Thirty-Eighth Street. It's quite nice, actually. High-end.

"You live here?"

Alice arches an eyebrow. "New York is its own illusion."

She exits the carriage without further explanation.

Frugal with her words, Cora supposes. *Let's hope that frugality doesn't extend to anything else.*

As Cora climbs down after her, she gets a better look at the place, realizing it isn't one home but several—a manse divided into different units, different flats. Though a step up from a boardinghouse in . . . Poughkeepsie, Alice had said? Perhaps she and her new mentor really aren't so different—at least, not in all respects.

Cora stops when her gaze falls upon a young man lingering on the front stoop, dressed in a crisp, multipiece suit and a derby hat. Smoking a cigarette, as if he owns the place. He's tall, Cora notes, with even features, striking blue eyes . . . Quite handsome, actually. Almost distractingly so. His smile rises when he sees Alice accompanied by Cora, one eyebrow quirking.

Alice spins around, cursing under her breath, dragging Cora backward a few steps.

"Who is that?" Cora whispers.

"That is no one," Alice mutters. "A nuisance."

Cora steps forward. "Well, can't I—"

"You cannot *do* anything. You're not ready. He's a newspaper man—and a particularly dogged one, if you must know." Alice glances over her shoulder, then sighs. "Wait here by the carriage and do not say a word."

Cora does as she's told. Still, she attempts to glean whatever terse words are exchanged between them. The man trots off with only a smirk and a tip of his hat before she can parse much of anything.

Interesting. She makes a mental note to ask again about him later. A woman posing as a fictional grand duchess would hardly welcome the attention of the press. Then again, much of Alice's con seems based in truth (if Cora was rightly following any of it).

She hurries forward, trailing Alice up two flights of stairs, and into a meticulously furnished apartment: mahogany bookshelves in the entryway, a homey sitting room with a lovely view of the tree-lined street below. And then all the way down a central corridor and into a tiny back bedroom, one containing no more than a bare cot, a small washbasin, and a decidedly less lovely view of a manure-speckled alley.

"This will be yours while we prepare. Luckily, we had it ready. It's sat empty these past months, surplus to our needs."

Cora nods, trying not to show her disappointment. Though what did she really expect at this juncture, a Württembergian castle with an emerald keep?

Alice watches her closely, eyes narrowing. "The others have taken the servants' quarters, but I'm sure they'd be happy to trade for a room with a window if you'd rather lodge near the kitchen with them."

So much for hiding her reaction.

"This is perfect," Cora says. Then: "The others? Who—"

"My cook, Dagmar, and my housemaid, Béatrice." Alice pronounces the latter in the French way. "And in case you're wondering, yes, they know all about our plans and have their own parts to play. Though not as showy a part as yours."

That gets Cora's heart racing again.

"The season is already in full swing, I take it, considering last night's affair?" she says. "I'll need some fine dresses, not that that's a priority, obviously. Just building out our checklist. Emeralds too, I suppose?" Cora swallows, attempting to recall the deluge of details Alice rattled off on their walk. "And if I could just get a *little* bit more detail on my backstory—"

"Plenty of time for that," Alice says. "The parties won't begin in regular fashion again until late January, starting with the Patriarch's Ball."

"January?" Cora says, appalled. "But that's months away. What am I meant to do in the mean—"

"You are to stay with me. Here. Hidden until you're ready."

"But . . . I am ready." She spreads her arms impatiently. "Ta-da!"

Alice lets out a startled laugh. It's a surprisingly infectious sound.

"We 'ave a guest, Your Grace?"

Cora turns to see a petite woman in the doorway, attired simply but immaculately in the dress of a housemaid. Her dark hair is piled atop her head, and it strikes Cora that she might be quite pretty if not for the jagged scar that mars the length of one cheek.

"Ah, Béatrice." Alice's entire body seems to soften at the sight of her. "You can dispense with the formalities. This is Cora. She's one of us now."

Cora feels an unfamiliar warmth spread through her at the sound of those words. *One of us.* She never had a true family, not really. Her brother left when she was just a girl, and the relationship between her and Da always felt more obligatory than fond.

She shakes her head. *Come now, Cora, don't be a fool.* This is a job, same as the troupe was. It is silly, even dangerous, to think of this arrangement as anything else.

That shrewd thought is only further underscored by the sight of Alice's second servant.

Dagmar is easily six feet tall, too wide to fit through the doorframe, and as solid and serious as a railway car. She eyes Cora with open dubiousness.

"One more for dinner, Dagmar," Alice says, breezing past them all into the hallway. "She'll be with us until our project concludes."

"Will thees affect our cut?" Dagmar asks. Her voice is as deep and Germanic as Cora expected. Dagmar's eyes dart sharply to Cora's, as if daring her to smirk.

"Our new friend's contribution in firmly securing our fifth investor will ensure even larger cuts for all of us," Alice says, prompting a grunt of approval from Dagmar. "If, that is, she proves amenable to instruction."

"But that's just it," Cora sputters. "Instruction in what?"

"Everything," Alice says, helpful as ever.

Béatrice smiles warmly, which sets Cora more at ease. "We shall need to turn you into a lady."

"By January. A matter of months. There are infinitesimal

ironclad rules governing this world, and any violation of them will mark you as a fraud, and by extension, the rest of us." Alice straightens, prim as a schoolmarm. "An early dinner and then to bed. Our lessons will begin promptly at eight o'clock tomorrow morning."

The three women size Cora up and down in a detached, circumspect way that makes Cora feel very much like chattel. Is there something wrong? Does she have something on her face? She absently wipes her cheek.

Alice sighs. She turns to go, murmuring to Béatrice in a voice just loud enough for Cora to hear, "You should rest too. I'm afraid they're going to prove very long days."

CHAPTER 6

Metamorphosis

LESSON ONE: COMPORTMENT ~ NOVEMBER 11

We shall begin with the very fundamentals," Alice says, pacing the sitting room as Béatrice watches from the doorway. "Rise to greet me."
Cora stands from the settee with a smile.

"No." Alice's voice sounds like a hatchet falling.

Cora gawks at her. "What did I get wrong?"

"Nearly everything. Stand where I am now and I will demonstrate." Alice takes Cora's place on the settee. Her eyes alight on Cora's and brighten very slightly. She rises like a marionette pulled by strings. "You see? Upward without lurching, a faint smile, no teeth, mainly in the eyes. Extend a hand."

Alice bends downward like a willow bough as she presses her gloved hand into Cora's.

"What a pleasure to see you," Alice says quietly. Her smile sloughs off. "Your turn. Try again."

Cora sits. Stands. Glides elegantly to the doorway to take Alice's hand. "What a pleasure to see you."

"That," Alice says, closing her eyes, "was deafening. Quiet decorum. *Quiet.* You must learn to modulate your voice."

"But . . ." Cora stops, adjusting her volume. "What of the rest of it? The movement. Better?"

Alice and Béatrice exchange a glance. Béatrice laughs, then muffles it with her hand.

"Again," Alice orders. "This time a little less like a puppy bounding from a basket, more like, I don't know . . . a self-possessed young woman?"

LESSON FIVE: TABLE MANNERS ~ NOVEMBER 14

"Wrong. Try again."

Cora squints so deeply at the intricately laid table that Alice worries the girl will start to form wrinkles on top of all her other now-apparent deficits. "This one?"

Cora holds up the salad fork.

"You guessed that last time." Alice closes her eyes, breathes slowly through her nose. "The *oyster* fork, Cora."

"Why don't you just point to it?"

"We learn best through struggle."

By the time Alice has opened her eyes, Cora is at long last holding the correct, small, three-tined utensil from among the fourteen other bits of silver.

"Good," Alice says. Cora slumps with relief. "Identify the rest for me, and *then* you may eat."

LESSON TWELVE: FRENCH ~ NOVEMBER 17

"Il fait beau, n'est non?"

"N'est-ce pas."

Béatrice's corrections are a far sight gentler than Dagmar's German tutorials. It's almost enough to make Cora actually look forward to these French sessions. Nevertheless, after correctly repeating the pleasantry, she cannot help but grumble, "Am I really expected to be fluent in two other languages? German, yes, that makes sense, but French as well?"

Béatrice offers a kindly wince. She opens her mouth to answer, but Alice's voice cuts through the sitting room.

"Any well-bred young lady of New York society, let *alone* European, will have learned French from a very young age."

"What about you, then?" Cora asks. "You taught yourself perfect French back in that Poughkeepsie boardinghouse? I find that hard to swa—"

"You need only be conversational," Alice says. "Memorize key phrases you can drop here and there, as the occasion warrants."

Dagmar pokes her ruddy face into the salon and says something in her native language that Cora can't even begin to sort out.

As Alice follows the cook out of the room, her German reply makes Dagmar boom with laughter.

"Say, Béa, what expletives can you teach me?" Cora asks sweetly. "I do believe the occasion warrants it."

LESSON TWENTY-TWO: WHIST ~ NOVEMBER 22

Alice, Cora, Béatrice, and Dagmar sit about the card table.

Alice has her eyes shut. "And what have we learned?"

Cora shrugs in desperation. "Never play against Dagmar?"

"Correct." Alice sighs.

Dagmar gathers the loose coins and bills from the table. With a single swipe of her large arms, the cook strides away, whistling.

LESSON THIRTY: THE HISTORY AND POLITICS OF CENTRAL EUROPE ~ NOVEMBER 27

"It's actually rather fascinating," Cora says as she paces the perimeter of the living room rug, practicing a gliding gait as requested. "The rapid progression in the past twenty years from North German unification to the Treaty of Frankfurt in 1871, then the—"

"You cannot appear too intelligent," Alice interrupts, once again. "*And* you're beginning to slump."

Cora straightens with a tight, sardonic smile. "I hadn't realized you wanted the other Cora's views. In that case . . ."

She rearranges her features into a gauzily dim expression—an imitation of a sheep she was fond of back on the farm, not that Alice need know that—and recommences her gliding along the rug's fringed edge.

"Ach, you see, eet is not unlike zees United States, excepting zat our states are ruled by kings and princes. Now imagine eef your Presseedent Arthur made an arrangement wiss Mexico, saying, yass, go ahead, you may take all the cows from Texas, thees ees fine. Zee people of Texas vould not be happy, I think?"

Alice has her fingers pressed to her mouth—whether to keep from laughing or crying, Cora can't tell.

"Pull that accent way back, if you please, to match my own," she finally says, her eyes sparkling. "But better. *Much* better."

LESSON THIRTY-SIX: TABLE MANNERS (AGAIN) ~ NOVEMBER 29

"Asparagus tastes like roasted dirt," Cora grumbles. "Must I actually eat it?"

"Some of it, yes." Alice drops her a sidelong glare.

Cora reaches for a fork.

Alice swats it away. "With your *fingers*."

"You're joking."

"That's what the finger bowl is for." Alice nods to the crystal dish with lemon water beside Cora.

"I thought it was for drinking," Cora deadpans.

"Feel free." Alice shrugs. "But I prefer this."

She hoists a bottle of Roper Frères Brut. Dagmar, seated across the table, rises, impatient with Alice's efforts to uncork it. With a triumphant *pop*, it fizzes loose from the bottle. Béa hastens to dab the mess with a napkin and pours for them.

Cora's eyes widen as she reaches for her own sparkling drink. "I've never had real champagne before."

"Oh, another rule," Alice adds, offhand. "Never fully empty your glass."

Cora blinks. "Even if it's champagne?"

"Especially if it's champagne." Alice nods for Béatrice to pour herself a glass too. "But as this is Thanksgiving, I think we can bend the rules a bit."

They all raise their glasses to clink above the turkey crown.

LESSON THIRTY-EIGHT: GENERAL
COMPORTMENT ~ NOVEMBER 30

Cora sits pinioned between Béatrice and Dagmar on the settee, half of which is consumed by Dagmar's derriere.

Cora continues smiling blandly at Béatrice. "The opera is rather diverting, isn't it? Which is your favorite composer? I'm partial—"

"You've not given her time to answer before proffering your own opinion," Alice drones from the doorway. "Which would be seen as inordinately boorish. Never mind the fact that you've publicly slighted poor Miss Dagmar by not directing that question to her as well. When in the company of two people, whether at a table, a drawing room, or an opera box, one must always divide one's time equally."

Cora huffs, exasperated. "Any other critiques?"

Alice smirks. "Since you've asked, you might practice modulating your volume. A low murmur forces one's companion to lean in closer in order to hear, and we want young Harold Peyton to draw very close to you. Remember, a lady always projects quiet decorum."

It takes immense quiet decorum to keep Cora from bursting into expletives—German ones, learned by eavesdropping on Dagmar when something's gone wrong in the kitchen.

LESSON FORTY-TWO: DANCING ~ DECEMBER 2

Cora partners with Dagmar, Alice with Béatrice, the parlor furniture pushed to the far walls to afford them more room for their waltzes and quadrilles. Béatrice sings various popular tunes for them to keep time to in a sweetly lilting alto.

This is the easiest lesson for Cora by far. She could do these dances in her sleep, though Alice doesn't seem to notice, or give any credit (perish the thought). She's barely even looked Cora's way since they swapped to the polka.

If Cora didn't know any better, she could swear Alice is too busy actually enjoying herself.

"You are very graceful," Dagmar grunts grudgingly down at Cora.

"This is nothing," Cora crows, twirling herself away, the stress of the past three weeks of relentless instruction finally coming to a head, the desire to let loose, just for a moment, proving too much to bear. She hoists her skirt and launches into a lilt jig, feet flying with expert precision, movements she hasn't made in years coming on like a fever dream.

Béatrice claps, but Alice wearily shakes her head. "Never show—"

"Your ankles, I know. It's impossibly vulgar, far too Irish, but also ever so fun," Cora breathlessly argues. "You should give it a try sometime!"

Dagmar, to Cora's shock, does just that, pulling up her own thick skirts and having a go.

And Alice lets out the most wonderful laugh.

It's enough to shock Cora into stillness once again.

LESSON FORTY-FIVE: WARDROBE ~ DECEMBER 9

This lesson, held in Cora's chamber, concerns a set of newly purchased garments laid out upon her bed. Outside the narrow windows, it has begun to snow.

Nearly Christmas, Alice thinks absently, *which means nearly*

January, nearly the ball, and the girl is not ready—and yet she can't help but be charmed by the image of Cora standing reverently beside the mattress, considering the garments as one might regard priceless artifacts.

Alice is careful to keep her voice mechanical, businesslike.

"Two chemises, skirts, dresses, demi-toilette for daytime. Two dresses that will suit for balls and dinners. And one"—Alice carefully lifts the last, a pale pink chiffon embroidered with silver rosettes, and Cora lets out a blissful sigh—"for the opera."

"Thank you, Alice," Cora breathes. "I hardly know what to say."

The moment feels strangely intimate. Rather too affecting. Like sisters might feel, like a normal family, warm with trust.

Perhaps it would have been like this with her own little sister. Had she lived.

A stab of tears threatens Alice's eyes. She turns quickly away. "No need to thank me, as this is not a gift. We'll sell each ball gown after use in order to purchase another. My entire budget for the season is forty thousand, not a penny more, so it is imperative we keep costs low. We're not actually aristocrats, after all."

"Of course not," Cora murmurs.

Still, a second after Alice shuts the door, she hears Cora's quiet squeal of delight.

And Alice allows herself a small smile of her own.

LESSON FIFTY-ONE: FRENCH AND GERMAN (AGAIN) ~ DECEMBER 12

"Es ist schönes Wetter, nicht wahr?" Cora remarks. Her voice has quieted to a demure purr.

"And in French?" Béa prompts.

"*Qu'il fait beau aujourd'hui,*" Cora supplies, just as sweetly.

Alice, watching from the doorway, catches Béatrice's questioning glance.

Alice offers a nod. She smiles minutely, disappearing before Cora can spot any sign of approval.

The girl must not grow complacent. Nothing can slip or this house of cards will tumble.

LESSON FIFTY-FOUR: STREET COMPORTMENT ~ DECEMBER 19

Cora stands ready in her spring demi-toilette, day jacket buttoned up, hat pinned just so, and parasol in hand.

"The streets in the city are filthy," Alice starts.

Cora snorts. "I've noticed. My room overlooks the alley where they shovel the horse manure."

"Better it go there than on your skirts," Alice says. "You'll need to hold your hem out of range of spray from the carriages, but not high enough to showcase even a hint of ankle. Like this."

She demonstrates. And Cora repeats the movement.

Nothing above her boot shows, nothing drags, and she does not display any discomfiture whatsoever.

"Good," Alice says.

Cora squints. "That's it? No corrections?"

"I'm not asking you to perform an aria, merely a skirt hike," Alice shoots back.

But she's pleased. The gesture looked effortless. Elegance has crept into every aspect of Cora's bearing. Gentility has become second nature to this scrap of a thing, who mere weeks ago moved like a hayseed queued up to audition for a chorus girl slot.

But the best thing Cora's learned, for Alice's purposes anyway, is to keep her face neutral. That mind of hers is constantly whirring—Alice never would have brought her in otherwise—but she doesn't show it anymore. That will be crucial.

"I shan't be surprised if you suddenly insist I appear on stage at the Metropolitan," Cora quips as her face remains perfectly, prettily dim.

"You may want to work on some scales just in case," Alice says dryly.

Cora winks—and in that split second looks like her old self again. "Be careful what you wish for."

LESSON SIXTY-SIX: STREET COMPORTMENT (AGAIN) ~ DECEMBER 23

The snowstorm begins with a few flurries, and then day after day of solid, silent precipitation, quieting the grind of the city, replacing it with the hush of a world wrapped in cotton wool and the occasional peals of laughter from delighted children on the street below. The plows come now in the morning, pulled by great bay horses, their tread rendered entirely invisible within an hour.

When Alice notices Cora's initial delight souring to sullen restiveness as she gazes out the window day after day, she sends Dagmar on an errand, passing the cook a few dollars extra from the ever-dwindling kitty. The expense proves worthwhile if only to see the joy on Cora's face when Dagmar returns hours later with thick woolen cloaks and fur-lined boots, perfect for tromping in the snow.

"Shall we attempt a lesson outdoors?" Alice offers.

The walk to Central Park that would have taken a mere thirty minutes under other conditions becomes an epic march northward under continuous swirls of flurries.

Alice bears it stoically. Cora is downright exultant.

"It's like we're on an Arctic expedition," she marvels, throwing her arms as wide as her tight cloak will allow. "Perhaps we'll find poor Greely and his men."

Alice muses over that reference before remembering that Cora has recently taken to poring over each morning's edition of *The New York Herald*, reading first all mentions of European politics, as Alice had instructed, then every other article of note she can lay her eyes upon.

I shall have to remind her yet again not to sound too informed when we go out into society, Alice notes peevishly. *That mind and mouth of hers will raise alarm bells if I'm not careful.*

When they reach the park, a fringe of snow thickly caking the hems of their skirts and cloaks, they find a line of enterprising fellows who have set up sleigh ride rentals. Alice finds the smallest, a little trap that will fit the two of them, pulled by a single draft horse, and helps Cora to mount beside her.

"Hoods up," she says. She's already noted several society faces in the surrounding parklands, some with children building snowmen, others in their own sleighs, waving to those of their acquaintance. She turns to Cora, adjusting the fur-lined hood of her cloak back a little. She secures it in place with a pin drawn from her glove so that it displays just enough of Cora's face that she'll be remarked upon, with an air of demure mystery remaining.

It does the trick. As they *clip-clop* through the smoothed snowy paths of the park, curious heads turn. Men's white-dusted caps are tipped. Women in broad woolen hats whisper to one another.

Alice knows that Ward has been making the pre-Christmas social rounds all month, speaking warmly of his friend the duchess and the debutante cousin who's come to join her from abroad. This enticing little peek at the two Württembergian ladies will add one breath of air to the spark of society's interest, feeding the flame without blowing it out entirely.

"Thank you so much for that, Alice," Cora murmurs, in her American voice, as they tromp back around the corner to their brownstone building.

"Consider it your Christmas present," Alice says quickly, Württembergian accent in place, hoping to quell any further displays of sentimentality.

NO LESSONS ~ CHRISTMAS DAY

There is, in fact, a parcel waiting for Cora beneath their modest, nearly bare Douglas fir. One for Dagmar too, and Béatrice.

Alice's heart beats strangely quickly, her mouth growing dry, as she waits for them to unwrap their gifts. Perhaps it was foolish for her to buy them. Perhaps they'll hate them, lose respect for her. Perhaps—

Cora claps in delight, taking in her new hat with its feathered brim.

"For you to keep," Alice blurts, her voice awkward to her own ears. "We won't sell it on."

The other parcels are rapturously opened.

Dancing shoes for Dagmar, in just the right hard-to-find (enormous) size. She wastes no time in trying them on—then trying a few dance moves that shake the floor beneath them.

Béa cradles her glass bottle, filled with hand lotion scented in lavender. A memory of where she grew up.

"You did not need to," Béatrice says, her eyes downcast, lips pulling into a smile.

"Of course I didn't," Alice says. "If I did, it would be payment, while this is a gift."

Her eyes sting a little when they meet Béa's. She likes it. She's putting it on her hands already.

Relief akin to joy floods warm through Alice's body.

But she still startles when a parcel falls onto her own lap.

Alice looks up to see Cora standing like a triumphant child, hands on hips.

"Merry Christmas, Duchess. Go on, open it."

It is a book, leather bound. But when Alice opens the cover, she finds only blank pages inside.

"You're always keeping so many plans and ideas in your head," Cora says. "I thought maybe you'd like a place to write them down."

The last thing Alice would ever do is keep a record of her plans, providing concrete evidence of wrongdoing to anyone who happens to lay eyes upon it. She has jotted notes but immediately burned them in her study's stove.

Any other day she might have admonished as much, provided another key lesson to this upstart fraud in her charge.

But something about the hope in Cora's blue eyes makes her press the book to her heart instead.

"This is ever so thoughtful, Cora. Thank you."

She'll find some use for it. Perhaps as a ledger.

LESSON NINETY-NINE: STREET COMPORTMENT (YET AGAIN)... AND KEY INFORMATION ~ JANUARY 19

Cora perches beside the frost-fogged window in the dining room, reading *The New York Herald*, an activity that has started to feel illicit, given Alice's glare every time she catches her.

When footsteps approach briskly, Cora is prepared to fold away the news headlines she was reading—political trouble in Egypt, an alderman convicted of embezzlement, the dispute over ownership of a new coal mine, a forgery plot foiled, murders galore right here in this very city.

Perhaps she's afraid all this reality will send me running for the hills, Cora thinks, but then Alice appears in the corridor, dressed for an outing.

"Béa's laid out clothes for you and will set your hair," Alice announces, perfunctory as ever. "We're going for a stroll."

Cora is thrilled—but leashed like a puppy, she realizes, as once out in the brisk city air, Alice dictates a strict path of no more than a two-block radius for their little outing.

"So we're not overheard," Alice says lightly. "I want to go over the marks again. And every time someone notes us as we pass, with a nod or a tip of the hat, we will switch to German, or close enough. Understood?"

"*Verstanden*," Cora answers, not a little smug.

"Have you ever been fishing?"

That question confuses the smirk right off Cora's face. "I . . . Yes."

"Good. Then you'll understand this analogy. My overall strategy is to hook all five families in tandem, but to then reel them in one by one. Carefully. And in a bespoke fashion."

As Alice outlines the backgrounds and foibles of all the marks, she keeps her voice light and sweet as a tea biscuit. A few times, when passing men tap their canes to their bowler hats, they switch quickly to Germanic nonsense, with an accented "good morning," and then continue their conversation where it's left off.

It feels like no time at all has passed when they draw up outside Alice's steps once again.

The moment they step into the blessedly toasty interior, Alice removing her gloves and coat, she fixes her eyes stonily upon Cora and says, "Let's see what you've retained. Ames."

"Robert and Pearl. First-generation wealth, which has kept them excluded from places like the Academy of Music. Their daughter, Arabella, believes herself to be in correspondence with your brother, the prince."

"Your angle?"

"They want a royal title in the family. A pedigree. Make Arabella believe an engagement is possible."

"Vandemeer," Alice goes on.

"Old money. James and wife, Olivia. Daughter . . ." This takes her a moment. "Marion, known as Mimi. My angle is to flatter, while dropping subtle hints that others may offer competition."

"Witt."

"Iris." Cora smiles, recalling the widow's ridiculous headdress at her Night of Illusions ball. "Son, Beau; daughter, Bonnie. With them, I must offer entertainment. Render myself ridiculous."

If she's half hoping Alice will correct her on that last point, she's quickly disappointed.

"Ogden." Alice's face tightens at this one.

"Brett. Wife, Priscilla. Endear myself to the wife. Steer entirely clear of the other."

"And Peyton."

Cora glances back to see Béatrice laying out tea for them in the sitting room.

Alice snaps her fingers. "Focus. Peyton."

"Harold Senior, a recluse," Cora answers hastily, longing for nothing more than that hot tea. "Harold Junior, also rarely seen these past few years. I am to . . . entice him."

"You are to make him fall headlong in love with you. Let's not dance around it," Alice snaps. Her voice softens, however, when she adds, "I'll be doing the same with Ogden, so you needn't feel martyred. It's the oldest con there is, and perhaps the easiest to pull off."

"How do you know so much about these people?" Cora asks once they're situated for tea. "From Mr. McAllister?"

"Only partly." Alice raises her eyebrows. "Although I'm sure he'd gladly claim full credit. No, certain details I remember from my childhood, the gossip I used to hear around the sitting room and in the downstairs quarters. The servants have always been the ones who actually hold the city's secrets."

From the kitchen, Dagmar grunts in agreement.

"But . . ." Cora shakes her head. "What kind of society gossip could you have heard growing up in Poughkeepsie?"

"Ah." Alice's eyes twinkle like a cat that's cornered a mouse. "I told you I *arrived* here from a boardinghouse in Poughkeepsie. Not that I grew up there. I suppose your last lesson is this: Pay as much mind to what people don't say as what they do."

It takes Cora a moment to read between the lines of even this statement. Then hope crests upon her in a swell.

"Did I hear you right? Did you say *last* lesson?"

"Last formal one. And not a moment too soon." Alice rises from the table—a move that Cora knows by now is designed to keep her from seeing any sign of approval or, God forbid, warmth. "The first event of the season is approaching quickly."

"The Patriarch's Ball," Cora dutifully recites, catching up.

"And Ward's been true to his word. As founder of the Patriarchs, he's secured us both invitations." Alice fixes Cora with a discerning squint. "I do believe you're ready. Please don't prove me wrong."

Cora struggles to conjure the appropriate response—a promise or a thank-you or a smart reply?—before landing on an obtuse nod, and a silent prayer for good measure.

This is it. The show begins.

All she can do now is hope to God that Alice is right.

PART 2

The Turn

Magic is the only honest profession. A magician promises to deceive you, and he does.

—THE GREAT MAGICIAN KARL GERMAIN

THE NEW YORK HERALD

Friday, January 25, 1884

WÜRTTEMBERG'S GRAND PRINCE WILHELM BECOMES A BEACON IN NATION'S DARK TIMES

Calvin Archer, New York Office

The once-prosperous, resource-rich Germanic nation of Württemberg has fallen on hard times in recent years, with consensus assigning King Charles's timorous leadership and deference to larger neighboring powers with much of the blame. Hope for a more prosperous future, however, has taken the form of Grand Prince Wilhelm Karl Paul Heinrich Friedrich, a widowed Württembergian noble who has pledged to protect his nation's greatness from outside influence and further exploitation.

Prince Wilhelm, described as a thoughtful, courageous, quiet man, is no stranger to overcoming misfortune himself, having lost his wife and stillborn daughter in childbirth in 1882, as well as his infant son, his only male heir, just two years prior . . .

CHAPTER 7

Welcome to the Season

The Patriarch's Ball
January 29, 1884

AMES

Angle: Validation

The hair . . . the hair still isn't *setting*." Pearl Ames paces behind her daughter, who remains statue-still before her dressing room's cheval mirror while her lady's maid and three additional temporary hires for the evening flit about, attempting to forge Arabella's determinedly straight hair into piles of curls.

Her daughter bites the corner of her lip, her eyes starting to well.

"It keeps! Going! Limp!" Pearl squeaks, picking up a lank, uncurling lock. "And rouge, we need *rouge*. She looks more like a mouse than a future queen."

They cannot turn up to the first great social event of 1884 looking chintzy. There will be snickers no matter what they do—"*Ah, that family has arrived. Can't recall their name. Is it the Parvenus?*" "*I can smell the steel factory on them from here!*"—and Pearl knows there's no culling those backhanded jibes entirely.

Not without something to wave in their smug, old-guard faces. Like a *royal title.*

"I think we're getting a bit ahead of ourselves, Mama," Arabella whispers in a tone that makes Pearl wonder whether her choice of insult was a little rash, in the way of a self-fulfilling prophecy. The girl's always been self-conscious about her diminutive height, her round ears, and timidity only renders her more mouselike. "We've only exchanged a few letters."

Arabella's gaze darts to her bedroom door, toward the little desk where she keeps the letters she receives from Prince Wilhelm of Württemberg—in which he recounts his love for his country, his courage in the face of oppression, his grief over his late wife and longing for new companionship, and his gratitude for these warm correspondences with his new American friend. Pearl knows all this because she's read every letter. What responsible parent wouldn't? And how else would Arabella have known to enclose just the right sketch of herself to send along with her last reply?

"Arabella, keep your head still." Pearl huffs a breath, attempting to collect herself. Too much emotion, fretting, and she's going to begin to sweat and ruin the three coats of powder she applied earlier. She nods to the servants. "Twirl and pin a few pieces like so, I suppose, and then we must just accept failure here and move on, or risk missing the event entirely."

Pearl will *not* be compensating the extra help for this "acceptable failure," but that can be addressed by her housekeeper after they've left for the ball.

"The duchess will be there tonight, won't she?" Arabella adds. "I must admit, I get a bit nervous in her presence."

"As well you should, child. Your entire future rests on her opinion of you," Pearl says. "If all goes according to plan, she will become your sister-in-law—oh, and that reminds me. You must immediately take her young cousin under your wing. We wouldn't want the duchess to consider you entirely self-interested."

"I'm not self-interested," Arabella weakly protests. "I can't think of a single thing I want for myself."

"Well, that's not exactly a useful attitude either, is it?" Pearl huffs a breath, praying for patience. "Listen closely, Arabella, since you are new to all of this and I am not. Tonight is the Patriarch's Ball. You, along with every other debutante in attendance, have been invited for a reason, and that reason is to be presented to a bevy of bachelors, all proven eminently suitable by the fact that they were invited in the first place. But they are mere *distractions*, as our sights are set far beyond 'suitable.' Across the Atlantic, mind you. International royalty. Do you understand?"

At that, Arabella seems to brighten a little, her eyes drifting away from her own reflection in thought.

"The cousin will make ripples, no doubt," Pearl muses. "Even if she's ugly. We must create the illusion of having been introduced to her previously, so that all of society sees our place in the affections of the Württemberg royal family. And above all, we must reassure the duchess that we are her greatest friends on these shores."

Pearl's heart begins to hammer against her corset's boning.

She has successfully cornered the market on the duchess's affections, has she not? Though it has struck her that the duchess has only accepted her invitations for tea, never dinner. Does that mean something? It's only a matter of time before other families begin angling for her attention, as well as that of the eligible heiress in her charge. And through them, a connection to the prince for their own unmarried daughters.

Real competition for his affections could start as early as tonight.

Pearl must move their relationship forward in some manner, immediately. Perhaps a shared personal detail, told in confidence, in order to knit them together as bosom friends . . .

She realizes Arabella is staring at her.

"Mamma, have you thought about *which* bachelors might be in attendance tonight? Other friends and acquaintances with whom we might be afforded a reunion?"

"Are you sleepwalking, child? I just said they do not matter!" Pearl scoffs. "Except to introduce the cousin to, I suppose."

Arabella steals a breath. "I did hear a rumor that Harry Peyton would be invited."

Pearl startles at the name but waves to the maids. "This will do, thank you, time's up. Now, the headpiece."

After the maids secure two matching diamond wings into Arabella's hair, they gather their things and go.

As soon as they are alone, Arabella continues, "I haven't seen him in years. Do you remember how close we once were? During those days of the railroad merger, when Father and Mr. Peyton were working together? It's been ever so long, and I know the Peytons do rather keep to themselves these days, but I had wondered whether Harry might step out tonight, given that he's only a bit older than me and hasn't gone off to university or anything like that, if the rumors are to be believed.

Which surprises me, as he always was so intellectually inclined during our lessons and in his letters . . ."

Through this insipid speech, Pearl steals a centering breath. Why her otherwise malleable child decides to be obstinate only at wholly inconvenient times, she'll never know.

Truth be told, Pearl does now remember how well Arabella and Harry got on when they were small. They shared the same governess, ever together chasing butterflies in Central Park or making up games in the parlor as their fathers conducted business in the library, and their mothers . . . Well, Harry didn't have a mother. Dead in childbirth. As for Pearl, she was busy. Securing her daughter's future through society connections.

That was all before the Manifest and Midwest mess, obviously. Before the unpleasantness. Before Harold Senior collected his substantial winnings and disappeared into retirement, eventually walling himself and that son of his in that Upper East Side palace like Fortunato and Montresor.

She forces a dismissive laugh, severing Arabella's monologue like a snip. "Why on earth are you thinking about little Harry Peyton when the latest letter from the *Grand Prince of Württemberg* is sitting on your bedside table? Unopened!"

Arabella blushes. "I'll admit there's something in me that's afraid to see what he's written. To respond to it, to feel anything at all—"

"Yes, yes, yes. Well, all of this is just to say, best not to concern yourself with the likes of Harold Peyton Jr. For goodness' sake!"

In a rare display of affection, Pearl pinches Arabella's cheek. Her daughter flinches.

Robert pauses mid-stroll down the hall, examining his

pocket watch. Even in his beautifully fitted tuxedo, the wallpaper seems to absorb him entirely, as if his body is disappearing as quickly as his thinning hair.

"Doesn't she look lovely, darling?" Pearl calls out to her husband.

He looks up, utterly incurious, and continues away without a word. Absolutely typical.

"We have far grander aspirations tonight than the son of a railroad man," Pearl whispers peevishly to her daughter. "Come now. It's twenty minutes to ten. We don't want to be late!"

CHAPTER 8

The Line and the Lure

nother ten minutes, I think," Alice calls over her shoulder. "We won't want to be early."

She gazes into the mirror. She looks rather drawn, pallid, but it suits the character she's playing. The gown is secondhand but doesn't seem it, procured discreetly from a shop in Philadelphia. It took Béatrice twenty hours to go there and back, but the expense of her rail ticket was offset by the money they've saved not having a dress made to order. This is a Worth gown, Parisian, cast off by a Pennsylvania debutante only last season. It suits Alice's complexion well.

Béatrice has an eye for these things. She really is remarkable.

Here she is now, behind Alice in the mirror, frowning so charmingly as she tries to add a little life to that French twist, but Alice waves her off. "See to Cora one more time, final details. She must be the object of all eyes tonight."

"That will be difficult standing next to you," Béatrice says quietly.

Alice smiles just as faintly. Only Béa would believe that.

"We won't be locked at the hip tonight as we've been these past weeks," Alice notes with a sigh. "I hope she's ready."

"She is. It is all lining up exactly as it should."

Béatrice presses a hand to Alice's shoulder before she goes. Alice feels her touch lingering there even after she's left the room.

She draws a few deep breaths, soothed somehow by the confines of her corset, a reassurance that she is here, she is real, even if all else is illusion. That she is held in, not over-spilling. Calm and prepared.

"My bustle barely fits through any of the doors!" Cora's giggles erupt from the sitting room. "This dress is divine, though. Even you have to admit it, Dag. *Gefällt dir mein Kleid?*"

Alice hears Dagmar's amused grunt of acquiescence as she rises to make her own careful way down the hall. When Alice reaches the sitting room, her shoulders drop in relief. Cora is exactly as she'd envisioned—warm where she herself is cool. Her champagne silk dress dazzles in contrast to Alice's deep plum fabric. Cora's strawberry-blonde locks set in playful curls, one ringlet dropping loose, where Alice's pale hair is pulled back tightly in a more austere and old-fashioned style. The younger woman will draw eyes while Alice works in shadowed corners. Just as she has planned it.

Béatrice stands watching for Alice's verdict on her handi-work.

Alice nods, appreciation lifting the corners of her mouth.

Color returns to Béa's cheeks at that and Cora outright beams, twirling about in her shining gown.

"It's a good thing we're selling this one or I'd be tempted to wear it every single day."

Alice notes the wistful pleasure in Béa's expression and wonders if she looked like this back in Montreal, in the years before her first arrest—a young teen working at a dressmaker's shop, learning the trade, only close enough to the gowns to stitch them up, never to wear them herself.

I'll buy her dresses to wear when this is done, Alice thinks. *All the gowns and slippers and gloves she wants.*

The front doorbell rings and Béa turns to see to it, jarring Alice out of her foolish thoughts.

Béatrice will be able to buy *herself* dresses when all this is done. They all will.

"Mr. McAllister's carriage is ready," Béa returns to announce. Every inch the well-trained housemaid. One would never guess she was ever anything else.

Béatrice holds the door for Alice and Cora to step out onto the street. Alice can feel more than hear her warmly murmur, "Good luck," as Alice sweeps past her into the waiting night.

Ward peeks out from his carriage door, held ajar by a footman, with a saucy grin. "My goodness, you do clean up well, Your Grace. And I am so very pleased to at last make the acquaintance of . . . is it *Lady* Cora?"

"We are going with 'Miss,'" Alice murmurs, Württembergian accent back in place as she settles beside Ward inside the carriage, Cora filling the spot opposite.

"I may have told a few people 'lady,'" Ward frets. "Never mind that. This is going to be a night to remember."

"In a good way, I hope, Mr. McAllister," Cora says demurely.

Ward goggles at Alice. "That accent. She's nailed it!"

Alice can't help but smile as she shushes McAllister. He takes the hint, changing the subject.

"You know, there was a young fellow loiterin' outside your house when I arrived," Ward announces. "Didn't much like the look of him. He told me he was a reporter and I liked him even less."

"Probably angling for a quote on the situation in Württemberg," Alice says, looking away.

"You're givin' quotes to reporters on a fictional resistance movement?" Ward gawks. "Do you think that's entirely wise?"

"How did P.T. Barnum put it?" Alice shrugs. "There is no such thing as bad publicity?"

"I couldn't disagree with him more," Ward drawls. "Lawd knows there's plenty about myself I don't plan on publicizin' anytime soon. But I have nothing but faith in your own judgment, my dear duchess."

Cora, Alice notes, has followed this turn in the conversation with barely concealed alertness. Even so, she asks no questions and remains uncommonly silent for the rest of the short drive down to the Financial District.

Nerves, Alice thinks. Or perhaps Ward drawing attention to her Württembergian accent has made her self-conscious about it.

Alice herself is more relieved than anxious when they arrive at last outside Delmonico's flagship building alongside scores of other carriages bearing guests to the brightly lit doorway.

At the entrance to the restaurant, McAllister hands all three of their invitations to the doorman with a wink, then parts from them as the two women are ushered by a waiting maid into a dressing area that's already awash with women. The sudden chatter and flash of color that assaults them as they walk in is such a contrast to the cozy insularity of the past several months in the flat on Thirty-Eighth and Third Avenue that Alice has to bite back a gasp as they step inside. The overall effect is one of an aviary full of tropical songbirds.

For her part, Cora looks, if anything, more at ease. Perhaps it reminds her of dressing rooms before performances.

"Your *Grace*," comes a saccharine voice from across the room—Mrs. Pearl Ames, her many-layered gown of yellow charmeuse giving her the look of a mangled canary.

Alice straightens elegantly as she greets Mrs. Ames, knowing all eyes in the room have now turned away from their mirrors and firmly onto her.

Her own performance has now begun.

She meets Mrs. Ames halfway across the room, Cora and Arabella trailing behind the two elder women like dinghies pulled by yachts.

"So the rumors are true," Mrs. Ames coos. Her smile is bright, tinged with desperation. "Your Grace's cousin, is it?"

"Mrs. Ames, may I present Miss Cora Ritter, daughter of my late uncle Reginald."

Cora, as rehearsed, dips her head in grief, even as she extends her gloved hand to Mrs. Ames.

"Oh, he's . . . he's dead, then?" Mrs. Ames sputters, her hand flying to her broad bosom. Then she leans in to whisper, "It wasn't the Austrians, was it?"

"In a way, it may have been," Cora murmurs. "He pledged his heart to Württemberg and his king, *mein* papa. In the end, it could not withstand the strain of all that we have lost."

There is a somber silence before Mrs. Ames chirps, "My daughter, Arabella. You two will be quick friends, I'm sure of it. Arabella, don't be rude. Take Lady Cora to meet your other young acquaintances. She doesn't know a soul on these shores, do you, poor thing?"

"I'm afraid I do not," Cora answers, turning to Arabella with a shy smile.

"Come with me, then," Arabella answers eagerly, the pink of her cheeks flushing to match her rose gown. "I should love to ask you about Württemberg, if you don't mind. Mamma tells me you fled here for your safety? That must have been terrifying for you . . ."

As little Arabella and Cora break away toward a clutch of gathered debutantes, the two arm in arm already like childhood friends, Alice notices not for the first time that there's a genuine sweetness to the younger Ames woman's expression that does not appear to have sprung from either of her parents.

She swallows away the stab of compunction that accompanies that observation. There is no leeway for mercy in this plan of hers—not even for Cora, who shoots Alice an alarmed look over one champagne puff of a shoulder. Sometimes you have to push the baby bird from the nest in order to get them to fly.

"Dare I ask about the resistance?" Mrs. Ames asks, her face a rictus of feigned worry. "Your brother, safe, I hope?"

Before Alice can draw breath to answer, Mrs. Ames glances in apparent panic over Alice's shoulder. Alice follows her gaze to see Mrs. Witt flinging her fur warmer and winter cloak at an attendant maid and rapidly crossing the room to intercept the conversation.

Mrs. Ames leans in and frantically whispers, "*My* brother nearly died in an ice-skating accident when he was seven and I've had a terror of ponds ever since. Isn't that silly? Don't tell anyone; it'll be our secret."

She laughs shrilly as Mrs. Witt reaches them. Thank goodness Alice has the other woman's cheek kisses to use as an excuse not to bother conjuring up a reaction to whatever bizarre display of intimacy Mrs. Ames was clearly attempting.

If they are all birds, then Mrs. Witt, in her feathered lime-green gown, is an Amazonian parrot. An exceedingly gangly one.

"My darling friend," she drawls, acting for all the world as if they've been intimates since childhood. "You're looking ever so well, considering. Did you see I dressed in your honor tonight? Emeralds! I've got tiny ones sewn into the bodice, you see—not Württembergian ones, alas, but I did try. Now, where's your poor orphaned niece? I'm sure she's as pretty as they say, but it amuses me to picture her as some haggard waif out of Dickens. It'll be a shame to spoil the illusion, but either way, my son will want to meet her."

"My cousin," Alice corrects gently, "who does still have a mother living, I'm pleased to say, is making new friends, thanks to Miss Ames."

She nods to where Cora seems to be engaged in pleasant enough conversation with a decidedly unpleasant coterie of pretty young women.

"Ah, there she is! Pretty, alas, how dull. Eyeing up the competition, is she?" Mrs. Witt swipes a restless hand over the white streak in her hair. "Including my own little debutante doll. Strange to feel envy for one's own daughter, but I do miss those days sometimes. Leaving blood on the dance floor after every ball. Proverbially, of course."

"I can imagine it," Alice says, feigning admiration. "And I'm very glad to have met you as a friend rather than a rival."

As Mrs. Ames grows pallid at the word *friend* used for anyone but her, Mrs. Witt laughs so loudly that she silences all surrounding conversation. "You are such a tonic, Your Graci . . . ness."

Now Alice is quite sure Mrs. Witt's had a pre-party tipple.

She grasps Alice's arm and wobbles with her toward the now-opening ballroom doors, leaving Mrs. Ames abandoned behind them.

"You've no idea how boring it is, season after season, the same dull faces, the same excruciating conversations. You're the only thing that gets me out the door and into society these days, I swear— Oh, Sarah!" She waves past Alice as they walk down the hall. "I must say a swift hello and goodbye to Sarah Newbold or she'll corner me later with anecdotes about her newborn, nothing in the world more agonizing. Back in a flash."

She won't be back. Alice smiles to herself. *I was right about her weakness. A desperation for novelty. Anything shiny and new.*

Two smart footmen stand at attention beside a wide set of white-painted doors, leading to the brilliantly lit ballroom beyond. Romantic, baroque-style lanterns pepper the large room's perimeter, lushly draped balconies looming over like the loges of gods, the teeming space awash with frothy ball gowns and elegant tailcoats. Darting back and forth through the crowd are servers distributing pebble ice trays of oysters and caviar, rounds upon rounds of sherry and Green Swizzles. The air itself is thick and scented with perfume and powder. It's all one big champagne coupe come to life.

The only thing marring the view is dour little Mrs. Ogden, who has afforded herself few favors in her choice of a bronze gown that gives her complexion a greenish tint. Priscilla Ogden's expression is even more sour than usual as she turns to eye Alice with a hostility that is almost shocking in its baldness.

What affects Mrs. Ogden most is being bypassed in favor of others—and so Alice does just that, gliding straight past her as if she were a servant standing ready with an unappetizing hors d'oeuvre. She catches the eager eye of Mr. Ogden instead. He stands waiting beside a flower arrangement in rather careful three-quarter profile, all the better to highlight his Byronic silhouette, complete with a lock of dark hair falling upon his brow.

Alice slows her step ever so slightly to allow him to dart in front of her and bow in greeting, the very picture of ardent but respectful regard. She alone is positioned close enough to note the lascivious gleam in the aging lech's eye.

"A vision," he breathes. "Your Grace, as upon our last occasion to meet, I feel I've conjured you from a dream."

The band starts up, a violin sonata—a Corelli *sonata de camera*, if she's not mistaken.

Mr. Ogden cocks his chin, listening, highlighting a sweep of muscle in his neck. Alice wonders if he's practiced that expression in the mirror.

"I don't suppose you'll favor me with a dance?" He leans close enough to fog up her cheek with his breath.

She affects a tragic stare. "I would love nothing more. But I have vowed not to dance until my country is free."

He closes his eyes as if moved. "Naturally. You *angel*." And pivots neatly away to take his livid wife's arm and lead her into the dance instead.

Ogden likes the game. The chase as much as the act itself. I must make him believe there is only one possible path to my bedroom.

Alice steps back, momentarily alone as the dance begins. She spies Cora across the room. Notes the appreciative, if perhaps a bit intimidated, glances of the men who approach to ask others to dance but not Cora.

How odd. They may have made her a little too beautiful.

Either way, it makes no difference if her intended audience fails to turn up.

Perhaps he's already here. Unless he closely resembles his father, he'll blend right in with the rest of these bright young knickerbockers and slightly slicker, richer parvenus.

Ward, appearing from nowhere, presses a glass into her hand. Champagne. She lifts it to him in thanks before sipping.

"I'm glad you're so tall," Ward drawls. "You can hide me."

She laughs quietly. "From whom?"

"Vandemeer. Beelined for me as soon as I walked into the men's lounge. Has a bone to pick, somethin' about not introducing you to him before the Ameses, but I've managed to evade him so far."

"Don't stay too evasive." Alice smiles. "I'll need to speak with them before the night is out."

"Never you worry, my dear duchess." At her sidelong expression, he raises his bushy eyebrows. "Before you ask, no, the Patriarchs did not receive an answer one way or the other from young Mr. Peyton, but I can assure you, the invitation was hand-couriered to the lad while he was out observing a surgical procedure at the New York Academy of Medicine—a particular hobby of his."

"One might even call it a peculiar hobby," Alice mutters, a slight wrinkle forming between her brows.

"Beneficial to us, however. I knew better than to send an invitation to his place of residence, where his father no doubt has a standing order to the servants to discard any social correspondence before his son can catch whiff of it."

"The New York Academy of Medicine?" Alice frowns. "I don't suppose there's a ladies gallery there. If he doesn't come tonight—"

"Put aside your contingencies for one night, my dear," Ward says, voice light with jollity as he takes his leave to greet other guests. Then, with a droll wink, adds, more loudly, "Enjoy the ball, Your Grace. I can assure you, no bombs are going to drop here tonight."

CHAPTER 9

Quiet Decorum

C oraline O'Malley feels like a bomb about to detonate right here inside this ballroom. Months of planning, training, sitting straight, talking softly, laughing in just the right key, whispering in French as she nibbles on asparagus—everything, all of it, comes down to tonight's introduction to society, and somehow, mere hours into the evening, she has been rendered a *debutante non grata*.

Not *one* suitor has approached her on his own accord since Cora stepped foot inside this grand wedding cake of a building, with its dwarfing chandeliers and glittering ball-room floor. Could her Württembergian accent be too harsh, off-putting? No, that's ridiculous; she has barely had the chance to speak to anyone. And it's absolutely not about her appearance—Béa's cosmetics skills tonight have sharpened Cora's features to the point where they could cut glass—nor her gown, as this champagne silk rental is especially stunning.

Cora peers around the party from where she's currently marooned, near the refreshments table, beside a trio of vapid young ladies—Arabella Ames, the Vandemeer girl, and Mrs. Witt's boresome daughter, the pug-faced brunette Bonnie

Witt. Cora spots Alice across the ballroom, currently pre-occupied, she and Ward both being paraded from one fine family to another by Mrs. Ames, like pets on a leash. No, Cora will need to figure this out on her own, and fast. If she cannot ensnare the attentions of some of these gentlemen before Mr. Peyton arrives—assuming he *will* indeed arrive—she's going to appear to her mark like unwanted, damaged goods.

"If Robert Davenport doesn't approach me in the next ten minutes, I am going to throw a fit," mutters the curvy blonde beside Cora.

"Marion Vandemeer, known as Mimi." Alice's tutorials flood Cora's mind like a spring. *"The spoiled rotten daughter of old money James and his second wife, Olivia, a glamorous laudanum addict—or so the rumors go."*

"I'm sure he'll come around, Mimi," Arabella whispers. She smiles gently at her scowling friend. "He probably assumes your dance card is already full."

"What a conniving little attempt to point out my short-comings." Mimi's eyes narrow. "The card is *half* full, Arabella, which means half *empty*. And I've already made far too many compromises. Boys with immigrant parents, paltry inheritances, overbites—"

Cora seizes the opening. "At our balls in Württemberg, young women are encouraged to approach the men."

She flinches. Her accent came out much too harsh and her proposal far too desperate.

The trio all turn to stare.

Cora swallows. "It is seen as deferential and, ah, honorable, in our country. Perhaps we might all—"

"No suitor is going to want to speak to *you*." Mimi laughs.

Bonnie barks out a chuckle. "Besides my nutter brother, but who wants him?"

Cora's face must show her confusion plainly as Mimi adds, "I mentioned to Edward Livingston that you practice the occult with your little green gems." She smiles sweetly. "Perhaps he spread it around?"

Cora grits her teeth. *Why, you vicious little twit!* Alice's voice, though, sounds through her mind, drowning out her own thoughts: *"A lady always projects quiet decorum."*

Through sheer will, Cora resists the urge to throttle her.

"Forgive me." Cora forces a smile. "I do not understand why you would say this."

"Because you're pretty," Bonnie drones, "and a beautiful emerald heiress is compet—"

She cuts off when Mimi elbows her in the waist.

"Ladies," Arabella puts in softly, glancing at Cora. "We would do best to *welcome* new friends to our shores—"

"Oh, lighten up, Arabella, it's harmless fun." Mimi's eyes sparkle. "A *welcome* joke between Lady Cora and me. To break the ice."

"It's Miss Ritter."

At Mimi's arched, challenging eyebrow, Cora amends, in a softer, more Württembergian accent, "I am not titled. But call me Cora, if you please."

Arabella gently cups her elbow, gracefully diverting her attention. "Cora, then. I, for one, would love to hear more about your nation, the landscape, the culture, the emeralds. About everything concerning your homeland, really. I confess, I've come to greatly enjoy the posts from your cousin. The grand prince spoke so hopefully about the fate of Württemberg in his last message."

"You cannot know what a service you've offered him," Cora says, attempting to reclaim her footing. "In your words, he sees the hope of true support from abroad."

Arabella smiles. "The pleasure is mine. It has been a long while since I've engaged in such frequent correspondence."

"Ah yes, since sad little Harry Peyton," Mimi says flatly as she inspects her nails.

Cora's pulse jumps at his mention, while Arabella blushes.

"I hear his father keeps him chained in the basement now," Mimi muses. "Only time he's allowed to leave the house is to watch quacks hack up dead bodies."

Arabella blurts, "So he has an interest in anatomy. As do many of the greatest minds of our time."

"Speak of the devil," Bonnie drones, nodding toward the restaurant's large doors, and Arabella's voice gulps into abrupt silence.

Cora follows her gaze toward the restaurant entrance.

"So he's finally decided to show his face again," Mimi says. "And my, *my*, how he has grown."

Arabella shakes her head, still reeling. "Oh . . . He's . . . You're right."

"Harry Peyton just arrived," Bonnie announces to Cora in a bored monotone. "The one we were just discussing."

Cora feels upended. Dizzy. As if she's levitating herself.

Harry Peyton. Son of Harold Peyton the senior, Alice's white whale, the supposed "worst of them."

Cora's ultimate mark has finally walked through the door.

"The years have treated him kindly, I see," Mimi adds. "Although that attire. How . . . misguided."

Through the crowd, Cora spots the young man Mimi's speaking about—and a wave of relief crests over her shoulders.

Sometimes in the past weeks, at night, when cold rain pelted the windows or when the fire would pinch out and Alice's apartment turned frigid, Cora's mind turned chilly too, imagining the very worst that lay ahead—far worse than mastering dances and place settings. Harry Peyton could have proved a true ogre, after all, one she must spend months fawning over and charming for the sake of her payout.

Thankfully, the young man working the crowd—shaking hands now with Mr. Vandemeer—looks more like a hapless prince than a gruesome ogre. Tall, slim physique, a big smile. Animated, bewildered eyes as he takes in the ballroom. Cora can't tell what color they are from here, but she wouldn't mind finding out.

Mimi mutters, "Harry should save that getup for your mother's costume ball, Bella."

"Hush, Mimi," Arabella says, unusually sharp.

Mimi does make a point this time. Good heavens, no wonder Cora thought of a prince. What *is* Harry wearing, and why? A blue satin coat that doesn't quite fit, scuffed shoes, a clearly borrowed and worse-for-wear *powdered wig*?

No matter. Cora's mind clicks into performance mode, nerves singing now that her target has taken on tangible form. Now that the plan is no longer theoretical but here, curtains opening, the act about to start. And a wrong first step could foil the entire show.

She considers her move as Harry turns to approach Mrs. Ames.

"Lady Cora, allow me to introduce myself."

Cora startles, turning to find a pale, spindly young man hovering on her heels.

The man's dull gray eyes narrow, his rounded spine hunched like a question mark as he bows. "Beau Witt the Third, heir to my father's empire. Once my mother passes and gets out of the way, obviously."

Bonnie's "nutter brother." *Oh no, not now.*

Beau straightens somewhat, smiling to reveal a set of crooked gray teeth.

"Ah yes, charmed, Mr. Witt."

"My sister has been monopolizing your time," Beau coos. "I take it you have an interest in the occult? I myself . . ."

His voice sinks into the party's swells as Cora tracks Harry out of the corner of her eye—still with Mrs. Ames, though Arabella has wisely used Beau's interruption as an excuse to cross the room and join them.

". . . and so I was hoping the two of us might have a word," Beau concludes, to his own apparent satisfaction.

Cora blinks. "I believe we just had several."

Beau laughs like a hyena, so loud that even his sister grimaces and shrinks away. Mimi, too, slinks off to a nearby table, eyebrow crooked again.

Wonderful. Now just the two of them.

"I should think you would be excited for some conversation, a chance to practice your English. Cora—I *can* call you Cora, can't I?" Beau waggles his haywire eyebrows. "I notice that no other gentleman has been bold enough to approach. I assure you, we Witts are confident stock, not easily intimidated by matters of the heart, mind, or even the supernatural. It is not every day one meets an international, powerful princess—"

"I am not a princess, Mr. Witt."

"And all this talk of mystic gems—"

"Emeralds." She glances away, searching for rescue.

"Not to mention how truly enchanting you look tonight." Beau winks, his smile stretching wide. It's like a cemetery in there, she thinks, a mouth of ancient headstones on a gloomy eve.

Cora's pulse begins jumping faster than the orchestra's rag. From her vantage, she can see that Arabella and Harry are speaking now, both of them smiling. Beaming, really. Friends from childhood, it sounds like, correspondents, although it looks like more. There's obvious chemistry between them. Not a spark necessarily, but . . . something. A simmering.

A simmering she supposes she'll need to quickly cool, which is hardly possible when one is trapped by a young Grim Reaper.

"Did you hear me?" Mr. Witt presses petulantly, fiddling with something in his pocket. A pencil. What the dickens, is he about to ask her to dance? "I said *enchanting*."

"Yes, a play on . . . the occult, is it? Very clever." Cora smiles brightly. "But I'm afraid the thing I feel most at this moment is overheated. If you'll excuse me—"

"Join me for punch, then."

"Oh, Mr. Witt, that won't be necessary—"

"I insist." He leads her toward the refreshments table.

Cora swallows a groan, although at least they're headed in Harry Peyton's vague direction. As Cora approaches, she can see Mrs. Ames's expression more clearly now. She's also watching her daughter and Harry's little reunion, and looks none too pleased herself.

A plan formulates in Cora's mind—a slight pivot from *quiet decorum*, though Alice will have to forgive the hasty improvisation—and hasty it will have to be.

Beau twists the ladle like a sword before sloshing the red

punch into a glass. "After this moment of respite, I do hope you will honor me with a— Say!"

Because she's already started swaying, one hand to her forehead, the other held out as if bracing for a fall.

Beau fumbles to place down the drinks and help, but Mrs. Ames has already caught sight of Cora's impending tumble and is mercifully quicker.

"Miss Ritter, Cora dear, are you ill?" Mrs. Ames bustles to her side, Arabella and Harry on her heels.

"I'm . . . not sure," Cora whispers, stumbling a step. Two, for good measure. "I—"

As Beau approaches, Cora spins dramatically—and in one fluid motion, discreetly lifts the small pencil tucked inside his pocket—then wobbles, falling backward toward an approaching Harry Peyton, uttering a silent prayer that he'll catch her.

She lands softly into his wide, outstretched arms. *Good boy.*

Harry hovers over her, blue eyes widening.

"My goodness, miss." He gently places her on the floor, pressing his fingers to her neck. Not exactly what she'd expected, but she can work with it. "Your systolic pressure has plummeted. At these levels, I worry about your heart—"

"My heart," she whispers, gazing deeply into his eyes. "It does feel rather transfixed at the moment."

A hint of red flashes on Harry's skin.

Cora bites her lip to stop her smile from growing any farther. Up close, Harry looks even more charmingly guileless. High cheekbones, dark hair peeking out from that ill-fitting wig, literal wide eyes. His thick eyebrows stitched, still studying her with concern.

She begins to rise, and he hastens to offer a hand.

"Thank you for your exquisite timing, but I promise I am

more than all right," Cora says in her Württembergian lilt, smoothening her skirts. "Although also quite . . . mortified."

"Then you should consider yourself in good company," Harry says, still holding her arm for balance, gesturing down at his outfit with a frown. "I thought tonight was a costumed event. I had it in my head that all balls were costumed balls. Obviously that was an ill-informed presupposition."

"We all make mistakes," Cora supplies kindly. "At least this is a charming one. Fortunately, I do feel a bit better now."

"You should always carry smelling salts on your person," Harry says gravely. "And drink plentiful liquids to keep yourself hydrated."

"I told her she needed punch," Beau mumbles behind them.

Cora ignores him. She peers down at Harry's hand, still touching her, then away, as if shy. "Truly keen advice."

"It *is* hotter than Dante's inferno in here," Mrs. Ames coos in sympathy, offering her a second arm. "Please, do take your time, Miss Ritter."

Harry adds, "Fresh air can also help with syncope."

"Syncope?" Cora asks, gazing up at him.

He looks beyond flattered to be asked. "The scientific term for swooning. Caused by a decrease in blood to the brain."

"We'd both be happy to escort you outside, Cora," Arabella cuts in, too quickly.

Beau clears his throat, stepping forward.

"That won't be necessary. Harold, good to see you out and about." As they shake hands, Beau adds, "Allow me to take it from here. Lady Cora and I were just in the middle of discussing the possibility of a dan . . ." He stops, searching his pocket.

"Oh. How?" Beau glances up. "Ah, excuse me, but . . ." He

pats his pockets again. "Can't find the dang pencil. Keep your card ready, Lady Cora. I'll only be a minute."

Mrs. Ames rolls her eyes, sweeping forward, her wide frame blocking Beau out entirely as he hurries away.

"Mr. Peyton, this is *Miss* Cora Ritter." She looks inordinately proud to have gotten the honorific right. "Cousin to the Grand Duchess Marie Charlotte Gabriella of Württemberg."

Harry's forehead wrinkles. "Württemberg . . ."

"A nation within the German Empire," Mrs. Ames chirps.

"Ah. How fascinating." Sincerity rings in Harry's voice. He bows. "I'm delighted to make your acquaintance, Miss Ritter."

"The grand duchess was kind enough to bring Miss Ritter along to New York for the social season," Mrs. Ames explains. "A welcome respite for them both. Our family has pledged to do everything we can to make their time in our city as comfortable and memorable as possible, haven't we, Arabella?"

"Ah yes," Arabella mumbles, but only after her mother has nudged her.

Harry smiles. It's a nice one, Cora notes, just a shade flummoxed, with dimples and those doe-like blue eyes, his gaze never wavering. It's the perfect opening moment, really . . . if not for the anxious-looking Arabella beside him.

"I wonder, do you find yourself homesick at all, Miss Ritter?" Harry asks. "In the somatic or figurative sense?"

"Heavens no, Mr. Peyton," Mrs. Ames answers for her, "it is a gift they have reached our shores. Don't you know Miss Ritter's country is on the brink of a civil war? The governing king has wronged his people, and a national resistance, led by *her cousin*, seeks to restore order and prosperity for all."

Harry's eyes dart back to Cora's—wide with interest or concern, Cora can't be sure.

Mrs. Ames drops her voice an octave, murmuring to Arabella, "Speaking of, dear daughter, I do believe we should ask the grand duchess if she's heard from the prince. I overheard Mrs. Vandemeer inviting her to an intimate dinner. It might be prudent to remind the duchess of the particular bond between our two families, wouldn't you agree?"

"But—"

Mrs. Ames turns toward Harry. "We shall leave you two to become better acquainted."

Before Arabella can further object, her mother whisks her across the ballroom.

Cora lets out a low, steady breath. *And now the stage is mine.*

Harry inches closer. "Tell me, Miss Ritter, how are you acclimating to our city? I am always captivated by the effects of new environmental factors on the body."

Goodness, the boy really does have a fascination with anatomy—Harry is most certainly a far sight quirkier than Alice had intimated. Still, Cora manages a doting laugh. She studies the dancers surrounding them, the kaleidoscope of silk, lace, color.

"I suppose I find it quite beautiful. Busy. *Lonely.*" She glances back, offering him a sad smile. "I am . . . still finding my way."

"Manhattan is not a hard city to master once you're accustomed to it. I never get lost during my weekly jaunts to the Academy." Then Harry adds, more hesitantly, "But I understand how it might feel lonely. I've often wondered how other cities might compare."

Cora swallows her surprise. A young man of Harry's station . . . She would have thought he'd grown up summering in Newport, vacationed for months on end across Europe, same as the rest of this privileged set they're rubbing shoulders with.

"Surely you've been to other cities besides New York?"

"I'm afraid my natural habitat has shrunk to the size of twenty blocks and two avenues." His smile turns wistful. "I am fulfilled, mind you, having thrown myself into my studies, the Academy, the pursuit of a greater calling. Still . . ." Harry trails off. There's a new glimmer of yearning in his eyes.

"They've become recluses these past few years," Alice explained during training. *"The father has cut them both off from the world."*

But it sounds as though Harry has been shuttered on this island for much longer . . . and Cora can definitely tap into that yearning.

"Well, I have done enough travel for the both of us," she says kindly. "I can be your field guide to other places, if you like. And perhaps one day, with some luck, your horizons might extend far beyond Fifth Avenue."

"With some luck." Harry's eyes dim. "I'm lucky in some senses. Not so fortunate in others."

"One's fortune can always change, Mr. Peyton."

As if on cue, a new song begins. Talk about luck.

"Well," Harry says, a hedging, cautious tone, "if your nervous system is now fully regulated, might you . . . be interested in joining me for a waltz, Miss Ritter?"

Would she be interested? Alice had Cora waltzing, quadrilling, practicing the four-step across her living room with Dagmar for evenings on end. Though Cora has some natural skill, it took a full week to master the intricacies of all the variations of ballroom dance. She's excited to show off her skills, put all of Alice's meticulous training to the test.

"I should love nothing more."

The crowd parts, scores of eyes watching them with curiosity, as they step onto the floor.

Cora resists the urge to look around, else risk seeming less than fully taken with her partner. But as they begin to glide across the parquet, she would wager her cut, maybe even bet the farm itself, that Alice is watching her.

She hopes her mentor is delighted. Proud of her even, perish the thought. She and Harry Peyton, sailing across the ballroom, just as she'd hoped. The night had its obstacles, most certainly, but Cora has triumphed. Sheltered, unusual fellow this Peyton is, and still, ensnaring the lad was far easier than she anticipated. Painless, really, as a stroll around the park.

As they spin about the floor, Cora catches Arabella's watchful, worried eye.

Just a pity there will be some unforeseen casualties.

CHAPTER 10

Pepper's Ghost

February 3, 1884

Directly after breakfast, Alice calls to Béatrice, "Ready the velvet, once you have a moment, the one we've been saving. It'll go nicely with your new hat, Cora."

Cora blinks blearily up from the needlepoint square she's been struggling with. "Where are we going?"

"It's Sunday." Alice pauses in the doorway, wondering if the girl's gotten quite enough sleep. "We're going to church."

"I . . . But . . . we haven't been to church before." Cora looks almost terrified. "*I've* hardly been to church before. Our congregation was tiny back home, and Lutheran, not . . ."

"Episcopalian," Alice supplies wryly. "If you're concerned that God's wrath will descend upon you the instant you step into Grace Church, I can assure you, you're perfectly safe. Plenty of far worse sinners have filled those pews long before you or me, and stepped out just as hale and healthy as before. Not to mention more securely sewn into the social fabric of New York City, which is what our aim is in attending, now that you've been properly introduced to fashionable high society."

"Fashionable by whose account?" Cora asks sardonically.

"Ward's account, mainly." Alice leans against the doorjamb with a smirk of her own. "As informed by his friend, the great Mrs. Caroline Astor."

"And when am I going to be meeting the great Mrs. Caroline Astor?" Cora looks more hopeful about that prospect than the one facing them this Sunday morning.

Alice's smile drops away. "If I can help it? Never."

She turns and sweeps into her bedroom before Cora can pry any further.

Béatrice dresses them hastily, then readies herself in practical woolens and a thick winter cloak.

As she holds the door for them to step out of the brownstone, Alice glances sharply back at her. "Are you sure—"

Béa shakes her head, waving away her concern. "I will be fine. This is a task best accomplished alone."

Alice nods, continuing down the icy steps with Cora, leaving her housemaid to attend to her even more crucial errand. In terms of capability, she trusts Béa almost as much as herself.

She can't think further than capability. It's too dangerous to think of trust in more sentimental terms. As much as she might hope for more . . .

Everyone leaves, Alice reminds herself, closing her eyes against the bright winter morning as Ward McAllister's carriage crunches up the road. *Don't be the fool who thinks otherwise.*

"Why, a very happy Sunday to all! Your Grace, Miss Ritter," Ward crows. "And is that a new hat I spy?"

"It was a Christmas gift," Cora replies. "From my cousin."

She nods to Alice. Ward's eyebrows rise, wrinkling his brow.

"And nothing for me? I'd claim to be wounded, but then again, I didn't get you ladies any gifts either, now did I?"

There's a glint in the older man's eye that makes Alice suspect he is, in truth, offended at the oversight. She'll have to watch to make sure that bit of irritation doesn't grow into something bigger.

Once the carriage door is shut and they're on their way downtown, Ward drops the small talk, lowering his voice into an octave meant for business.

"Mrs. Astor will be in attendance today. Easy enough for me to make an introduction. Rather harder to avoid it, don't you know."

"And yet I'll find a way," Alice demurs firmly. "I'd really rather not cross her path."

"I've snuck you both onto the guest list for her ball," he notes.

"And we've declined."

Cora lets out a surprised squawk. Her eyes have been following the two of them like she's in the crowd at a summer tennis match.

Alice ignores her. Again. "The next engagement must be the Vandemeers' dinner party. You know how James is—if he's not first in line, he's not interested. In order to draw them in more deeply, they must be seen to be our preferred hosts, our preferred everything."

"Seen by *all* to be preferred. Including Mrs. Caroline Astor? Society will see your declining her invitation as a purposeful snub. Perhaps even a scandalous one."

"You never should have included us in the first place," Alice puts in, more sharply. "Then we wouldn't be in a position to cause scandal."

Ward's face reddens. "I'd thought it a strategic move. Clearly you disagree. But I assure you, I would not have taken the risk of offending my Mystic Rose by intervening for anyone else."

The risk. Of course. The reason he's entered into this arrangement with the likes of Alice in the first place. To secure a safety net beneath his ever-precarious social position. When one relies on the generosity of richer patrons, the kind who savor nicknames like "Mystic Rose," for goodness' sake, one is forever at the mercy of their whims. But all of that is set to change in only a few months' time.

"I know how much you esteem her," Alice offers.

"*Respect* is a better word," Ward says wryly. "In the way that an explorer respects the grizzly bear he encounters in the wild."

"You see?" Alice cocks her head. "You've put it better than I could. Mrs. Astor is no mere chorus member in this production of ours. How could she be, when everything in this world turns upon a word from her? Better just to leave her out of it. She needn't know we were even invited."

"Oh, she knows already." Ward sighs. "At least she will as soon as she receives your regrets."

Alice softens. Presses her hand into his, her form of an apology.

He squeezes, accepting it.

"I'll send a further letter of explanation," she says. "Cora's brother died yesterday. Shot by Hungarians as he attempted to stop them from entering the mines. We are both in mourning for the next several weeks."

"How shocking." Ward tips his hat to Cora. "My sincerest condolences."

Cora smirks, but her face drops as the carriage slows behind the train of others arriving at Grace Church's Gothic Broadway entrance. "Oh hell, I'll need to look tragic, then."

"Indeed," Alice says dryly. "And you may consider watching your language while inside a public place of worship. It might be different for Lutherans, but this is—"

"Episcopalian," Cora grumbles. "Let's get this over with."

As they parade inside the building, leaving Ward behind at the doorway to attend Mrs. Astor's arrival, Alice recalls past services here as if from the other side of a dream.

She was much smaller then. The pew backs much taller, the windows and ceiling endlessly high. Filing in along the stiff-faced clerics, exchanging dry, wordless greetings with everyone already seated in their carefully negotiated pews. Squirming in her scratchy lace-collared dress, her governess pinching her to make her sit still, her mother's sweet voice rising as they began the hymns. Her father heartily shaking hands with well-wishers and business associates.

With Robert Ames. With Witt and Vandemeer and Ogden and—

"Are you all right?" Cora whispers in her correct accent as they take a seat in a pew toward the middle of the church.

"Yes, obviously," Alice mutters back, in case anyone is listening. "Only praying for your dear brother's soul."

Taking the cue, Cora lowers her head, eyes closed in silent prayer of her own. A murmur rises among the more cheerful parishioners, signaling a new and notable arrival.

Alice averts her eyes, only glancingly seeing Ward glide

past, his arm on loan to a stately older woman dressed in deep cranberry.

"There she is," Cora whispers breathlessly. "*The* Mrs. Astor."

Her sister-in-law might take issue with that declaration, Alice thinks, but she can't quite get the quip out, even to whisper it. Her breath is growing tight.

As the service begins, Alice feels her heart pounding forcefully within her. She can barely hear the words of the reverend leading them in prayer, through the readings.

It takes her a moment to realize everyone is standing for the first hymn. Cora's voice rises with "The Son of God Goes Forth to War." It is a triumphant, restoring sound.

Alice could swear it is her mother who is now restored, standing beside her, peering down at her daughter with a smile. Mother always loved the singing best, but Alice finds she cannot bear it, the sound of these hymns, let alone force a tune through her own dry throat.

Her eyes spill over in a flash too quick for her to possibly quell.

With a gasp, she lurches for the end of the pew.

From above, Christ and all his saints watch her flee for the exit, the safety of the sidewalk—and they're not the only ones. All of New York society watches her run from her mother's ghost out of Grace Church, tears streaming down her foolish cheeks.

Cora finds her out in the cold a moment later, shivering, holding both of their cloaks. "What happened back there? What's the matter?"

"This was a mistake," Alice sputters in a whisper, barely clinging to her accent. She snatches her cloak from Cora, then starts quickly away, up north. They won't wait for Ward; they'll walk.

Cora struggles to keep up. "But it was your idea! I don't understand."

"I thought it would help secure our respectability, to become a regular part of the congregation. I didn't calculate . . ." She shakes her head, willing her breath to steady again.

To her credit, Cora has learned not to press, only walks quietly beside her for a good half mile, a silent sentinel, both of them listening to the cacophony of sounds filtering out of the buildings around them, families spending the day of rest in their own ways from city block to city block.

"That was your church, wasn't it?" Cora finally ventures. "When you were a child."

Alice stops and fixes her with a sharp glare.

It doesn't dissuade the girl from placing a light hand on her shoulder before they continue walking.

A headache has set in by the time they reach their own corner, but Alice has mulled a solution to this small debacle along the way. She'll write to Mrs. Ames, apologize that their hasty departure prevented a proper hello, explain that they were still overwhelmed by the news of her cousin's death. It was all too fresh for the both of them. There. Done and settled. Now she can go inside and regain her equilibrium.

Alice stops walking. And stares.

Cora presses a hand to her arm. "The reporter. The nuisance."

Nuisance, indeed. Cora doesn't know the half of it.

The young reporter, now dressed in thick tweed and a derby hat, lounges against the banister of their stoop like he's waiting for a trolley. His smile rises when he sees Alice accompanied by Cora, one eyebrow rising inquisitively.

"The very same," Alice mutters. "You go on inside while I speak to him."

He tips his hat to the two of them as they approach. "Happy Sunday."

"And to you," Alice says with stiff formality, her accent thickly, almost forbiddingly Germanic. "Miss Ritter, my dear—"

"Miss Ritter, is it?" He steps forward, eyes sharpening on the younger woman's face. He pockets the pencil to extend a hand. "Cal Archer. *New York Herald*."

"*The Herald*!" Cora exclaims. "We read that every day."

"Do you really?" A slow grin creeps across Cal's face as his eyes slide to Alice's.

"I do believe I've seen your byline," she goes on, continuing to ignore Alice's express orders. Small consolation, but at least she's maintaining her false accent. "Why, yes, I enjoyed your story about France's military ventures in Tonkin."

A loud cough from Alice at least manages to rattle the rapt look from Cora's face.

Cora laughs breathily. "Though I have no idea where Tonkin even is!"

Too little too late, Alice thinks, closing her eyes to keep from rolling them.

"I'd be happy to show you on a map anytime, Miss Ritter," the reporter goes on, leaning lazily against the stone stoop.

"Call me Cora, if you please, Mr. Archer," Cora murmurs smoothly. She presses her fingers lightly, briefly into his, flushing slightly before dipping into a curtsy.

Oh, for heaven's sake, thinks Alice. *Of all times to master quiet decorum.* "Cora, go inside straightaway now and warm from the cold. I will not be but a moment."

With obvious reluctance but markedly improved grace, Cora inches her skirt upward, mounts the steps, and disappears inside. Alice raises her eyes to find Dagmar glowering down at the scene from an upstairs window like a particularly fearsome guard dog.

Alice keeps the requested conversation short, seeing young Cal Archer quickly on his way, and when she rejoins Cora upstairs, she is prepared for a peppering of questions.

"He seems to come by often," Cora starts in. "How are we to handle him?"

"We can start with not appealing to his inflated sense of self-regard by naming other articles of his we've enjoyed."

Cora reddens. "What do you do? He's here to ask for updates on his Württemberg stories, clearly. What do you tell him?"

"The truth, to start with," Alice lies. "That I cannot give him any information for fear of endangering my loved ones. He can read into that however he likes—or more to the point, however *I* like—and run his story on a resistance movement so secret that it's barely even spoken about from the safety of American shores."

"But why would he turn up now?" Cora's forehead wrinkles. "You don't think he heard about the scene at the church, do you?"

That theory startles a laugh out of Alice. "Even I can recognize that my little outburst hardly constitutes front-page news."

And yet, it was odd, wasn't it? All those memories, that surge of emotion. It's as if she'd summoned him.

"Never mind *The New York Herald*, anyway," Alice announces. "It took us twice as long to get home on foot than if we'd waited outside to take a carriage back. If we delay our Sunday dinner any longer, Dagmar will toss the lot of it away in protest of our rudeness."

From the doorway, Dagmar grunts her agreement.

Béatrice must have returned mere minutes before their little confabulation with the press. Alice finds the maid warming her hands before the iron stove, her cheeks still pinkened from the cold.

"Did you get it?" Alice asks.

Béa looks confused, which stops Alice's heart for a beat. "Of course I did."

Alice lets out an enormous breath, warmth returning to her own body for the first time since she fled Grace Church. Or perhaps, long before that.

As Béa passes her the parcel, Alice lets her hand linger against Béa's, her eyes downcast as she whispers, "I hope you know how invaluable you are."

Béatrice lets out a shy breath of a laugh, but she doesn't pull away until they hear the clank of platters against the dining table—Dagmar's version of a dinner bell.

After Dagmar lays out the Sunday meal, the most formal one they tend to share over the course of a week—under this roof, anyway—they all four sit together. The sweet German Riesling flows as freely as the conversation, even Béa and Dagmar uncharacteristically matching Cora for chattiness. Alice, finally content, sits back and listens to them, her strange provisional family.

Her mind wanders again to the sidewalk, to the reporter, but she blinks the thought of him away. Tonight is no time for worry or discontent. Not when everything is lining up exactly as it should.

As Dagmar serves up dessert, Alice excuses herself from the table and retrieves the parcel Béatrice passed her earlier.

The spoils of Béa's discreet and well-timed journey downtown to Maiden Lane's Diamond District fit neatly into a small muslin cloth. Purveyor Albert Lorsch of Albert Lorsch & Co. may have been at church this Sunday morning, but other, more key members of his "and Co." were more than willing to accept a covert exchange on a day they don't consider the Sabbath.

"Do you remember when I asked you if you could fish?" Alice asks, returning to the table.

Cora laughs around the bite of pie she's just taken. "Mm-hmm."

"Well, the best thing to lure a big fish . . . is something shiny."

Alice lays the parcel on the table still wrapped in its muslin, then peels the fabric back to reveal it, just as she'll do for the others. The marks.

"Goodness," Cora breathes. "That is shiny."

And shiny is the least of it. A thirteen-carat stone dangling upon a slim, twenty-inch gold chain, its solitaire setting adorned with finely carved roses and vines, creating the illusion that this astonishing gem has simply sprung up from the ground.

The more apt word, to Alice, is *perfect*.

"And so big," Cora says, her fingers hovering over the necklace without daring to touch. "Is it a real emerald?"

A fair question, Alice must admit. They've spent easily half of their forty-thousand-dollar budget on this piece of jewelry alone.

"Not only is it real and practically flawless"—Alice turns it so that the light catches on the green and reflects it onto the wall—"this is a *Württembergian* emerald."

Setting it down, she leans back in her chair, her hands folded upon her lap.

"Friends, it's time I laid out to you the next and final stage of our plan, from today through the first of May." Alice smiles with deep and bitter satisfaction. "The day we take them for all they're worth."

CHAPTER II

Unexpected Battlefields

February 8, 1884

The carriage *clip-clops* down ice-lined Fifth Avenue, past a parade of gleaming white mansions and stately townhomes, the snow-dusted promise of Central Park growing ever closer from the distance. New York in February is a good sight more frigid than winter in Kansas, though this afternoon's jaunt has warmed Cora indeed. Béa recently secured the truly marvelous necklace as a lure to intrigue their marks (which admittedly does make Cora wonder about the limits of Alice's budget), Cora has captured Harry Peyton's unique attentions, and Alice is thankfully beginning to trust her.

Case in point: While Alice has run off for some mysterious errand involving real estate, Cora was sent back alone from the dressmaker's early to ready herself for tonight's dinner at the Vandemeers'. The first time she's traveling singly as "Miss Ritter" in the three months she has been living in this city.

She settles herself against the bench, bracing for the inevitable turn onto Thirty-Eighth Street, for the now-familiar front stoop of Alice's home. This is what it must feel like to be part of a family—a *team*, rather, a crew. She never felt valued by Prospero and the troupe, always relegated to behind the stage, hardly embraced as one of their own, even after so many months on the road together. No one besides dear old Maeve even bothered to show her the ropes or teach her the tricks. And yet with Alice, Béa, Ward, even Dagmar, she finally feels she's where she belongs. On the front lines and, hopefully, on the march toward victory—preparing to take down the city and get exactly what she wants.

They turn off Madison. The driver of the hansom cab helps her down.

"Miss . . . Ritter, is it? Or can I still call you Cora?"

Cora stops at the bottom of Alice's front steps with a frown.

She turns to find that increasingly omnipresent reporter from *The Herald* leaning against a lamppost a few yards away. Cal Archer. Goodness, Alice is right. The man is relentless. Cora is beginning to wonder if he is really seeking out more information about Württemberg or if he's onto them. And if it is the latter, how long Alice will be able to fend him off.

Cal's well-fitted brown suit shows off his tall, lean physique. He's smiling at her, his derby hat set jauntily askew today, a notepad in one hand, a pencil in his other.

Seeing no polite way out, she smiles too. "Cora, yes. It's lovely to see you again, Mr. Archer."

He cocks his head, wry. "Is it?"

The question is apt. He's truly the last person Cora wants to be detained by at the moment, especially without Alice here as chaperone and buffer.

"A joke," he adds quickly, as if apologetic, but humor lingers in his eyes. "I know how people of my profession are often perceived, even by fans of our work."

Cora's cheeks grow hot. Alice was right to glare at her in that last encounter. What had she been on about, declaring her "love" of his writing?

Cal hoists his notepad, seizing on her moment of discomfort. "I was only hoping for a few minutes of your time and then I'll let you get on with your day."

"Right now isn't ideal, I'm afraid," she says. "I have a dinner engagement tonight and I'm already late."

Cal glances at his pocket watch. "It's three in the afternoon."

She laughs, flustered. "Late to get *ready*. Obviously."

He nods, eyes sparkling. "It seems you've ingratiated yourself quite quickly into New York society."

"Simply lucky to find a host of generous, welcoming friends."

"Impressive for someone so new to these shores."

"Though surely *un*impressive to arrive late to a kind invitation." She resists the urge to grit her teeth. "Another time, perhaps, Mr. Archer?"

With a curt nod, she begins to ascend the stairs.

Cal calls out, "You seem different from the last time I saw you."

Cora stops, neck prickling. Is he referring to her accent? No, it's impeccable and she knows it. Her demeanor, then? Some other element of her carefully constructed persona that isn't rendering consistent?

Cora slowly turns around again, smile stitched tight as a corset.

"More . . . settled," he finishes with a smile. But there's an uptick to his tone again.

"The last morning we spoke, I had just received word of my brother's death, at the hands of the Hungarians." Cora lifts her chin archly. "I was not, as you say, myself that day."

"Ah. Right. My condolences. The Hungarians, you say?" Mr. Archer flips his book to a page full of dark ink. "Speaking of, I haven't been able to connect with the grand duchess lately. She's quite hard to pin down. I've been trying to get her for days, but even when I manage to find a window, she's as opaque as a front door."

Cora can't help but smile at that. Another apt comment from Mr. Archer. She feels the same way about Alice. Often, in fact.

Sensing her resistance crumbling, Cal pounces, "Truly, Miss Ritter, just a few questions on Württemberg, the nation's state of affairs—"

She sighs. "Why, may I ask?"

"The paper wants to cover the situation in full." He surveys his notes, murmuring, "I don't think anybody fully knows what in Sam Hill's going on over there and the place is suddenly the talk of the town. My editor wants a longer feature piece, but there are a few loose ends I'll need to tie up first."

Longer feature piece. Meaning the front page of *The Herald.* Real, legitimate news. A piece like this could actually help Alice, now that she thinks about it—those horrible railroad men seeing their story confirmed in black and white while they sip on their early morning tea. A perfect next step in the plan.

With all Alice is managing, perhaps Cora should take more initiative. Alice could be in over her head, despite what she says to the contrary, overwhelmed with all she needs to achieve in a few months' time, as she desperately seemed last Sunday. Cora has proven she is a trustworthy member of the team, has she not? What did Alice tell her about dealing with the press? *"Start with the truth."* Surely

there is a way to spin the truth just so to this man, in order
to sell their lies?

"Loose ends," she repeats. "What type of loose ends?"

"Well." Cal considers her carefully. "I suppose I'm perplexed as to how Württemberg has kept its apparent bounty
of natural resources out of all the history records."

His stare becomes penetrating.

"I'm not sure I understand your question, Mr. Archer."
Somehow Cora manages to keep her tone both accented and
cool.

Tucking his pencil behind his ear, Cal takes a step closer.

"These lavish emerald mines that have the entire town in
a tizzy," he says softly, one perfectly arched eyebrow rising.
"Why is it that this spring is the first time I've . . . well, I've
ever even *heard* of them?"

A dull buzz mounts between her ears, building to a voice-
less scream.

How, again, did Cora think she could "spin the truth" to
cover a gaping hole of a fabricated investment opportunity?

"Ah . . . yes. I do appreciate your confusion there."

Just breathe, Cora. Breathe and reset the stage.

The stage. One thing she learned from countless hours
watching Prospero . . . if a performer expects the audience
to *believe*, to ignore the lies and suspend their doubts, the
performer must lead them. Must evoke certainty incarnate, a
confidence so unflappable that the audience has no choice but
to pledge their poetic faith.

Lead him there.

Confidence.

Think.

Cora's thoughts slip-slide through all of Béa's lessons, Alice's training, those arcane history books and papers on the German Empire, which she's studied for hours on end.

She knows Alice warned her not to appear too informed or intelligent, but it may be time for yet another pivot.

"Well, to fully understand, you simply need to consider our nation's history."

Cal slowly tilts his head. "Go on."

Cora steadies her hummingbird pulse. *Unflappable.*

"Württemberg has always been a nation of secrets," she explains. "One need only look to the decisive battles of recent times."

Cal retrieves his pencil from his ear. "The decisive battles, you say . . ."

"The Battle of Tauberbischofsheim, as one prime example."

The reporter's eyes almost evacuate his skull, which gives Cora a rush of satisfaction.

"The Battle of—" Cal coughs, clearing his throat. "Sorry, can you spell that?"

Cora proudly obliges.

"The Battle of Tauberbischofsheim was a crucial conflict in the Austro-Prussian War, where Württemberg, along with the rest of the Eighth Army, faced the mighty Prussian forces."

She is careful to keep her tone somber and disguise her delight, now that Cal is writing copious scribbles in his notebook.

"It is well known that Württemberg was comprehensively defeated. What is less well known, *secret* even, was the forced indemnity payment and clandestine treaty between Württemberg and her conqueror."

Cal's brow furrows. "I . . . see."

"And then? Only a mere decade later, Württemberg is again pillaged for the sake of peace, the terms of its entrance into the German Empire wholly unfair, and *not* widely known." Cora steals a breath. "Consider the current devastated state of our once-great nation, Mr. Archer. After all this theft and exploitation. I do hope you appreciate why we Württembergians are unwilling to proclaim what is left of our riches to the world."

She pauses, understanding how crucial it is to choose her next words carefully—to keep the mines themselves out of the papers and yet still sell the story.

"And I do hope you will honor that . . . reluctance, Mr. Archer," she says. "When and if you choose to write your piece."

Cal studies his notes and then nods, looking up at her.

"I believe we understand one another, Miss Ritter." He snaps his book closed decisively. "You certainly know your history. This has been very enlightening—"

"I'm sure my cousin would be most pleased to give you more details," Cora hastens to add. "At some point, anyhow. But I really must be going now."

"Of course. Thank you for your precious time."

Cal smiles. It's quite a nice one, actually. Cheeky and lop-sided. With a tempered sort of cockiness that she might find appealing in other circumstances.

He waves his notebook by way of goodbye.

As soon as he's gone, Cora wilts with relief. Along with elation. What she just concocted for Mr. Archer might keep him at bay for the duration of their scheme. Who would have believed it possible? Miss Cora Ritter, capable of conjuring news stories straight out of thin air!

She stifles a laugh on the stoop, excited to tell Alice.

"I expect you to do exactly as I ask, without hesitation, objection, or embellishment."

Though she realizes there is a *slight* possibility that Alice may be less than thrilled by this latest improvisation.

In any event, Cora will need to banish that concern for another time because there is a more pressing matter at hand.

Dinner. Tonight.

Their first mark. The Vandemeers.

CHAPTER 12

Fine Gems

February 8, 1884

VANDEMEER

Angle: Vainglory

Olivia Vandemeer feels another headache coming on. If they expect her to host graciously, beautifully, impeccably—and they do, for everything in her husband and daughter's life seems to rest heavily upon her own slim shoulders—then perhaps they could take care in the moments before a dinner party to maintain some level of quiet.

"I don't see why I can't take dinner in my room." Mimi trails her mother relentlessly through the house, barking like a Pomeranian. "It's not as if there's any purpose in my being there, given that you've not invited any young men who might possibly show any interest in *me*."

Olivia glides past the parlor, hoping James might intercept

their daughter in conversation, appeal to her himself, so she can see to the last-minute arrangements with the servants.

No such luck.

"I hope to hell you haven't put McAllister near the head of the table," James Vandemeer shouts into his brandy glass. He steadies himself against the marble fireplace. "He likely expects it. Don't know why we had to invite him in the first place. We're the ones honoring the duchess and that niece of hers."

"Cousin," Olivia puts in quietly.

"We deserve every bit of the credit." He slams the crystal lowball glass against the mantel.

Olivia closes her eyes. "It will be through Mr. McAllister that we receive credit for being the first to host a dinner party in their honor. No one is a bigger gossip, I assure you."

That assuages him a little. The level of red in her husband's old Dutch face has at least receded a shade. "And you're quite sure we are the first? This late in the season?"

"Apart from Mr. McAllister, only the Ames family have enjoyed the company of the grand duchess in any intimate capacity. Tea, I believe, if Mrs. Witt is to be trusted."

"Mrs. Witt? Trusted? That blasted woman is the very last person . . ." James launches straight into a vitriolic rant, and Olivia curses herself for even mentioning the name.

"That's another thing!" Mimi stomps her foot, rattling the beading in her gown—and the teeth inside her mother's head. "I'd thought surely the Witts would be invited tonight. Not that I'd ever entertain Beau's affections, but at least there would be the appearance of someone courting me. Mother? Mother! You don't seem to take any of this to heart."

Mimi's voice raises to the pitch of a buzzard cry.

"Three seasons stand between me and spinsterhood and . . ."

As she continues her tirade, Olivia studies her daughter afresh. Pretty enough, certainly, but the sourness emanating from the girl's every pore is a powerful repellent. She'll never be as beautiful as her mother and she knows it, siphoning attention instead through sheer force of noxious personality.

"All will be well," Olivia announces, as much to herself as to her family. "You will attend dinner, Mimi. I'll make it worth your while, I promise. And James, you'll be at the head of the table, as you always are, and by noon tomorrow, every family on Madison Avenue will know that we are the favored first to host a duchess at our table."

Then she slides down the hall, away from their droning voices.

Whether it's the spate of strategizing she's just undertaken or the predictability of her daughter's and husband's responses, she feels abruptly and utterly drained. James has always been like this. *Everything* is a competition, a race to the top. She suspects it ultimately has to do with him being hungry to prove himself better than his forebears with their Knickerbocker pedigrees. She may be a second wife, but fast upon their wedding—the *first* of that season—James insisted upon becoming the *first* new family to build a manse along Fifth, just as he longed to be the *first* to garner a central box at both the Academy and the Met, the *first* of the old families to invest heavily in railroad, and the *first* to break ground with a vacation cottage in Newport. She suspects these feelings of inferiority also drove him into that messy Manifest Rails debacle, now that she thinks on it, which she tries not to do unless absolutely necessary. Thinking about matters of money, apart from spending it, aggravates her nerves almost as much as her husband.

Olivia cannot wait to be rid of the man. Him and Mimi *both*. But one step at a time. Marry off the girl, encourage James's insatiable appetite for brandy in the hopes it brings about an expedited death, and then . . . freedom.

Freedom and exorbitant wealth. Thirty-five isn't so old to begin a new chapter, after all. She'll just have to drift along in the meantime.

And to that end . . .

She finds she's drifted into her own, blessedly dark bedroom, a small glass bottle of laudanum now in her hand. Final preparations, indeed.

"What would I do without you, my darling?" Olivia coos to the bottle, uncorks it, and drinks.

🍸 🍸 🍸

Alice and Cora are already dressed, powdered, and coiffed when the messenger boy arrives with a note written in Mr. McAllister's hand. The message inside precipitates a few adjustments.

"We'll need rouge after all," Alice calls over Cora's shoulder to Béatrice. "Perhaps a bit on the lips. And bosom."

"I thought I was meant to look wan, to allow the emerald to stand out," Cora protests. She nods down at her gown's low neckline, the solitaire emerald necklace shining against her pale skin.

"We shall have to compromise." Alice holds up the note so Cora can read it:

Mr. Peyton the Younger has accepted the invitation.

"We'll have two gems in play tonight," Alice says briskly. "Both it and you."

"I'll take that as a compliment," Cora says, closing her eyes as Béa sees to her face.

Alice nods in approval, and they set out. The Vandemeers have sent one of their own carriages to escort them to the dinner. It arrived half an hour ago and has been waiting ever since. They'll be thirty minutes late for the party, by careful design. As she patiently explained to an irritatingly confused Cora, "On time is embarrassing. Fifteen minutes late is polite, twenty-five pushing the bounds of rudeness. Thirty will maximize our entrance. We're not after decorum tonight so much as impact."

Sure enough, when the carriage arrives at the Fifty-Seventh Street and Fifth Avenue beaux arts mansion belonging to the Vandemeers—the first in its style to be built in New York City, James will have you know—Alice and Cora are introduced by an English butler into a parlor already full of guests sipping champagne and nibbling canapés.

Relief breaks through the ever-present haze in Mrs. Vandemeer's eyes when she turns from her conversation with Mrs. Ames to greet the new guests.

Ward shoots Alice a surreptitious wink as she passes. He's played his part well, then. Sowing doubt as to whether they'd turn up.

"I must apologize wholeheartedly for our delay," Alice says. "I received a telegram from my brother, you see, and it was such news that we felt we had to reply tonight, which delayed our departure. I hope you don't find us too terribly rude."

"Of course not," Mrs. Vandemeer murmurs distantly. "Not

me, anyhow. Pearl thought it might be a European custom to arrive late."

Over Mrs. Vandemeer's elegant shoulder, Alice sees Mrs. Ames begin to sputter. "Not that I've ever observed *you* to be late, merely that I believe I read somewhere about the differing habits between our continents, perhaps—"

"In Württemberg, we are very prompt," Alice cuts in. "Though I myself have set a poor example tonight."

"Shall we to dinner, then?" Mrs. Vandemeer announces abruptly, drawing a look of reproach from her husband, who appeared to be on the brink of offering the new arrivals aperitifs, as would be customary.

Her over-hastiness rather suggests an eagerness to get tonight over with, Alice notes, along with her hostess's trembling hand.

"Wonderful," Alice agrees.

"Thank heavens you came at last," Alice hears Arabella whisper to Cora as they progress down the checkered marble hall to the dining room. "I thought I was going to be trapped alone with Mimi all night."

Alice passes Cora a look of warning—don't engage in petty gossip—but no need. Cora has simply flashed a brief, indulgent grin, then gathered her composure once more. Just in time for Harry Peyton to step forward and offer her an arm, to Arabella's thinly masked discomfort.

It's Mr. Vandemeer himself who escorts Alice into the dining room by arm, prompting a glower from Mr. Ogden worthy of Heathcliff stalking the moors.

Alice is seated between Vandemeer and Ogden, the couples split up according to custom. As she sits, she takes in the gathering around the candlelit table, noting their arrangement as if they are cutouts in a shooting gallery: immaculate Mr. Vandemeer at the head of the table to her left, then plump Mrs. Ames, Ward McAllister in a jaunty cravat, beautiful and glassy-eyed Mrs. Vandemeer, the thus-far entirely taciturn Mr. Ames, Cora seated beside Harry Peyton—Alice can only assume this was Ward's influence—then sulky Mrs. Ogden, almost-as-sulky Mimi Vandemeer, little Arabella Ames, and Mr. Ogden to her right, already laying the smolder on thick.

"I'd thought the Witts might be joining us," Ward notes lightly, reading the question in Alice's expression.

Mrs. Vandemeer closes her eyes. "You *had* to mention the name."

Too late. Mr. Vandemeer's face has already gone red above his neatly trimmed beard. "That dreadful woman! That harridan! I don't know who she thinks she is, won't listen to a word—"

"She retains her husband's shares in Manifest Rails and refuses to sell," Mr. Ogden breathes into Alice's ear. She smiles as if interested, while successfully fighting off a shudder. "I think Mrs. Witt enjoys turning up to shareholder meetings just to watch the rest of us squirm. She'll be back in Vandemeer's good graces within weeks, though. We all fall out, again and again, like clockwork automatons, but it never lasts. Too small a society to hold on to grievances. That's why it's so refreshing to have you and Miss Ritter brightening our drawing rooms."

His finger plays on her bare forearm, his eyes dancing up to hers teasingly.

Alice is unsure how she is going to stomach this meal. All twelve courses of it.

The menu is written in French. Alice wonders how much of it Cora can now read. She's caught her in conversation with Béatrice from time to time, in their apartment, working on her fluency beyond the limits of her earlier tutelage. A hungry mind.

And a hungry stomach too, by the looks of it. Cora nearly inhales her first course of oysters, but she slows down for the consommé printanier, careful not to slosh any drops onto that dress of hers. They'll need to sell it on in good condition, after all.

By the time the blue trout and lobster rissoles arrive and Cora reaches for the correct fork and knife for each, Alice realizes she can safely turn her attention away from her protégée and onto the rest of the table . . .

Like Harry Peyton, hanging off Cora's every soft-spoken word, his own lips parted as if in expectation of a kiss. Mrs. Ogden glaring in Cora's direction between bites, clearly affronted by her tablemate's preference for the younger, prettier conversationalist. Mrs. Vandemeer also staring across the table at Cora—though not at her face, exactly. She appears to be hypnotically transfixed by the gem hanging about Cora's neck. Perhaps it looks all the more sparkly through Mrs. Vandemeer's chemically altered gaze.

Alice smiles. Cuts another bite of her terrapin steak. Ogden, thank goodness, has taken enough of an interest in his meal to stop attempting to murmur into her ear, so she dares glance past him at Arabella, who of all the assemblage looks outright miserable. She turns her narrow-set eyes from a downcast position fixed on her plate up to Ogden from time to time, either hoping or fearing that he'll engage her in conversation, then, rather more desperately, across the table to where Harry sits leaning ever closer to Cora.

Her mother has taken note of it as well, Alice can see.

Mrs. Ames clears her throat loudly enough to cut through

the clatter of silver and chitchat, then turns to Alice with an overbright smile.

"I must say, we're all desperate to hear what news you've received of home, Duchess. Although I confess . . ." She dabs her lips with her napkins as if playfully locking a secret inside. "From what your brother has written, it seems Württemberg will see political changes within the year . . . Your brother on the throne, God willing . . . and perhaps a royal wedding to follow?"

"Mother!" Arabella's shout silences the table. She looks a little startled herself when all eyes turn to her. A miniature lobster has tumbled from her plate with the force of her jolt. "You're reading my letters? They're personal."

She stares down at her lap, her face bright pink. Across the table, Harry's brow furrows with concern.

"A mother needs to know," Mrs. Ames soldiers on. "I promise your secrets will be entirely your own once you're in charge of your own home. Or castle, as the case may be."

She sips her claret, smug as a cat, eyes darting around the table for everyone's reactions. If she's expecting envy, it's cut off quickly by Mr. Ames's sudden sniff.

"What *is* the situation in Württemberg?" he pipes up. Alice starts with a slight jolt, realizing this may very well be the first time she's ever heard the man speak. His voice is surprisingly high, even for a man of his diminutive size. "I need to know I'm not sending my daughter into an impending war zone. No child of mine is going to go traveling around the world begging for guest rooms as some princess in exile."

A gasp goes around the table on Alice's behalf. Ogden puts a hand to her wrist and starts to rise, as if preparing to engage in fisticuffs in her honor right here at the table, but Alice preempts him with a sad smile.

"You are a kind father, and a thoughtful one," she says to the rattish Mr. Ames. "It is a lonely life, being uprooted from one's home. But thankfully, what Mrs. Ames said is correct. My brother, the grand prince, has told me the tide is turning for the nationalists. The last harvest has been disastrous, and King Charles spends most of his time on holiday in Nice rather than with his people. An envoy has been dispatched to discuss the terms of his giving up the crown."

"Abdication," Mr. Ames says, as if informing her of the word.

She nods. "Indeed."

"Well, that right there is news to be celebrated," Ward crows, standing up himself, wine lifted high. "To the people of Württemberg and their freedom to come!"

"Hear, hear!" resounds around the table.

Ogden awkwardly sits. "Once the resistance has proven successful, you can finally turn your mind to yourself. No need to be a saint any longer."

He keeps his voice dry and neutral, but the expression in his dark eyes, barely visible through his thick, falling dark hair, broadcasts his meaning plainly enough.

For goodness' sake, the man is shameless.

"I'm afraid Württemberg will have more need of me than ever before," Alice says.

"How so, Your Grace?" Ward strokes his pointed beard.

"In the service of commerce," Alice says, and she swears that all the men at the table lean forward slightly at the word. Apart from Harry, anyway. "One thing these past years have highlighted is how passive we have been, allowing Berlin to make decisions for our people in Württemberg. We see what those decisions led to—Austrians and Hungarians marching in and plundering our emeralds, harassing our peasants, trampling our fields, as if our proud land is but a clearinghouse for the spoils of their treaty. With my brother as king, it will be a different matter. We can set the terms of trade once again, including, of course, our principal export."

She nods to Cora. Everyone turns to look.

Cora blinks. Utterly blank. Alice glares downward at her bosom.

"Oh! Yes!" Cora startles, then fiddles rather inelegantly with the gemstone. "Silly me, yes, this is our, ah, principal export. Württembergian emeralds. I have so many at home, you see, dozens and dozens, that I didn't . . . know to what you were referring."

"You're wearing one tonight?" Harry asks, courteously avoiding looking down at it. "An emerald from—"

"From home, yes." Cora sips her wine, dipping her chin as if shy and not entirely caught off guard, but Alice knows better.

"And you say you have . . . dozens and dozens of similar jewels back home?" Mr. Vandemeer asks, a keen light sparking in his eye.

"There is a folk saying among our people," Alice chimes in, her eyes dancing. "'When the well runs dry, dig another and look for green.' It is not so common as all that, but 'tis true that there are real accounts of peasants finding a very pleasant surprise as they've turned over their gardens. The vast majority of our emeralds are in the royal mines, the property of my family and Cora's."

"Must be nice," Mimi says with a sniff. "Being an emerald

heiress instead of dirty old railroads. Can't wear a train car around my neck, now can I?"

Mr. Vandemeer's eyes go electric. "I'll buy it."

Alice's head whips to him in surprise.

"The necklace," he barrels on. "I'll bet my boot that's the first genuine Württembergian emerald in New York City. Name your price. I'll get it for you, Mimi darling."

Harry's mouth has opened as if ready to protest, as Mimi's own eyes sharpen viciously on Cora.

"Sounds like a good plan to me, Daddy," she says. "Seeing as you have dozens and *dozens* back at home, Miss Ritter."

Alice turns to Olivia Vandemeer for her reaction—an objection, surely—but the woman sits as placidly still as an oil painting, either entirely uncaring or simply oblivious.

There may have been a moment when Alice thought her the more likable party within her family, trapped within these walls with these poisonous people through no fault of her own. That may well be the case, but her medicinally aided apathy is a poison all its own.

If Alice felt any qualms about ruining her along with the rest of them, they evaporate here and now.

"You cannot buy it," Alice answers.

Mr. Vandemeer's chest puffs up. "Now see here—"

"Because it will be our gift," Alice continues. The table goes quiet. "You have been so kind to us, welcoming us tonight into the warmth of your friendship. It is more of a comfort than you could possibly know."

"The bonds of friendship are powerful indeed," Mrs. Ames pipes up. "Almost as powerful as the bonds of family."

Dessert is served. Not a moment too soon.

It's over coffee that Mr. Ogden turns his forceful attentions back to Alice. "You wear no jewels, I see."

"It is different for the young, like dear Cora." Alice sighs. "They need hope, while I am cursed to fret."

"Not forever, surely," Ogden breathes. "You deserve to be draped in emeralds and diamonds and silks and anything else you choose. I can imagine it. The pleasure it would bring you."

Across the table, Alice sees a muscle in Mrs. Ogden's jaw twitching, fury and humiliation swirling in her seething glare.

Alice forces herself to look away and meet Ogden's eyes instead over the brim of her steaming coffee cup. "Perhaps one day you will see that, my friend. Now that change is on the horizon."

He leans back, satisfied.

Alice glances about the table, sure now that she'll see some sort of reaction from the others at this flagrant escalation of Ogden's flirtation, but the Ameses and Vandemeers alike have turned their attention to their wine, continuing to chat with their neighbors as if nothing is amiss.

Almost like they've seen this exact scenario play out several times before and have grown entirely bored of the sight.

"Gentlemen," Mr. Vandemeer crows at last. "Shall we retire to the study? I've just had a delivery of brand-new Cohibas, the first of their brand in the city, best out of Cuba. You've never tasted the like."

Harry looks reluctant to leave Cora's side. He bows to her before turning to take leave of the ladies, who are all now standing to follow Mrs. Vandemeer into the parlor.

Out in the hall, Alice feels a hand grip her wrist roughly, pulling her back from the gathering.

Cora glances back from beside Arabella. Alice shakes her head slightly: *Go ahead.*

She turns to see Mrs. Ogden still gripping her arm.

"I know what you're doing," the woman hisses, her shoulders drawing in like a witch in a fairy story. "You think you'll get your claws into him, don't you?"

"Into whom?" Alice widens her eyes in bewilderment.

"My husband. You . . . you . . ." Her mouth forms a circle. Daring herself to say the word: "Whore."

Alice dips at the knees, looking Mrs. Ogden in the eye.

"Shh," she whispers. "You're humiliating yourself. For no reason. None at all."

"I'm not the one making a show of mys—"

"You *are*," Alice says, glancing at the quickly filling parlor. "My darling friend, you are. I've suffered great hardship of late, and I think I see the same in you. It hasn't been easy, your life, has it, Priscilla?"

Mrs. Ogden looks stunned by her sympathy. "I . . . N-no. It hasn't. None of them. No one understands. I don't have children to parade around. I don't—"

"Neither do I," Alice murmurs. "I understand. I would like to be your friend, if you'll let me."

Mrs. Ogden pauses as if paralyzed. Then she nods.

But as they progress into the parlor again, she grabs Alice once more, this time to whisper, "I was very beautiful once, you know. More beautiful than you."

Alice smiles warmly. "And you still are."

As Mrs. Ogden glides to chat with Mrs. Ames, mollified, Alice sits, hiding the shaking in her hands by tucking them beneath her skirts.

It feels an eternity before the party officially breaks up, everyone taking their leave in staggered clusters in the grand foyer.

Ward pats a few of the men on the back, grinning as he approaches Alice.

"Did he ask?" she whispers.

"Before the door was even shut, don't you know," Ward murmurs back. "Wanted to know all about those emerald mines. I told him they were privately held, and that no matter how much I try to convince you to open the family company up to foreign investors, you've remained firm. He reckons he can change your mind."

As Mrs. Vandemeer approaches, heavy-lidded as she bids good night to a somewhat queasy-looking Harry—unaccustomed to Cuban cigars, no doubt—Alice turns to Cora. "Ah! I nearly forgot."

She reaches around Cora's swan neck to unclasp the necklace. She lets it pool in her hands before passing it to a vacant-looking Mrs. Vandemeer, Mimi standing by with a smirk triumphant enough for the both of them.

"Good night, and as always, my sincerest thanks," Alice says. She catches the look on Harry's face as she turns away. Positively stricken.

On the steps, he jogs to catch up to Cora and whisper in her ear before helping both her and Alice into their coach and bidding them good night with a tip of his hat.

"What did he say?" Alice asks once the carriage sets off.

"That Miss Vandemeer requires the, ah, *ornament*, whereas I do not." Cora looks uncommonly pensive. "He asked to call on me. I suggested a walk in the park."

"Good," Alice says.

"The necklace," Cora asks hesitantly. "Was giving it to them part of the plan?"

"No," Alice admits after a leaden pause. "I'd meant to offer it as a sample to be evaluated and then returned to us, but after your boast of having so many jewels lying about, I was forced to improvise. We cannot let it show that this is the only stone we can afford. The one creates the illusion of many. Trouble is, we do not, in actuality, have the funds to purchase 'the many.'"

"So what are we going to do now?" A moment of silence passes, then Cora huffs. "I can hear the wheels turning in your brain. You don't have to do this in silence, you know. I might be able to contribute to the strategy if you'd only allow me a glimpse of it."

Alice still doesn't answer. Weariness has settled over her like an illness.

Funny. Improvisations aside, she'd expected to feel exhilaration at a moment like this. A pond full of fish, all of them readily taking the bait. But she feels nibbled away every moment she spends in their company. These parasites. These frauds.

Only a matter of months now, she reminds herself as she makes her way out of the carriage ahead of a still clearly frustrated Cora, past a quietly inquisitive Béa waiting at the door, and straight up to the blessed solitude of her own bed. *Weeks, really. And once it's all done . . .*

Alice finds she can't quite finish the thought.

For all her planning, all she can envision is a massive void.

THE NEW YORK HERALD

Tuesday, February 12, 1884

WÜRTTEMBERG'S FRAUGHT HISTORY FUELS NATION'S CURRENT TURMOIL

Calvin Archer, New York Office

In order to understand the escalating homeland conflict within the Germanic nation of Württemberg, one need only consider the polity's complicated past, say sources close to the crown. Württemberg's history of exploitation by its more powerful neighbors has created a culture of wariness concerning future military or economic alliances, as well as ignited the current growing nationalist movement to protect Württemberg's resources.

Consider the polity's historic relations with Prussia, the decisive Battle of Tauberbischofsheim . . .

CHAPTER 13

A Stroll Down Memory Lane

Cora tightens the collar of her borrowed coat, a beautiful yellow wool with wide, fur-lined sleeves and a matching stole. The wind has kicked up to an almost comical degree, an audible *whoosh* sending dead leaves whipping across her high-heeled boots.

"Still keen to press onward?" Harry says, teeth chattering. "A fascinating reflex, shivering, is it not? Tiny contractions meant to manufacture the sensation of warmth."

Cora resists the urge to roll her eyes, along with the urge to mention that she, too, is hard at work manufacturing an altogether different sensation, one of a mutually satisfying, blossoming relationship.

Somehow she defers to her better angels.

"I do appreciate the fresh air," she assures him, using the excuse of the cold to nestle tighter into his side. "Let's keep on. I am very grateful for your tour of Central Park."

It's probably the truest thing she's said all day. Central Park still feels like a well-kept secret, a marvelous green oasis that astounds her every time she happens upon its grounds, even after all these months. Sprawling green meadows. Lakes and woodlands and babbling brooks. It's as if God dropped Kansas right in the middle of Manhattan, unfurling plains tucked into the heart of the bustling city.

It makes it hard not to pine for Long Creek Farm, the old rolling pastures, the endless sea of wheat . . . and yet her goal has never felt so possible, so close. If Alice's plans continue falling into place, absent the latest wrinkle—with four of the families intrigued and soon to be hooked, and Harry's adoration building, hopefully, to the point where he simply must convince his father to finance along with them—Cora could be signing a purchase agreement for the farm come May. Dreams attained. Coraline O'Malley, victorious.

She swallows around the tiny lump in her throat, watching as Harry marvels at a group of squirrels parading around a nearby tree, all the while absently narrating the unlikely adaptive mechanisms of the city park vermin. He really is so absorbed, so sheltered, all the money in the world not enough to buy him any worldly shrewdness.

Then again, does any mark like Harry honestly stand a chance against the likes of a cunning woman such as Alice? Or against Cora and the rest of her team, for that matter? Not to mention months of careful orchestration, meticulous planning, schemes . . .

She hasn't thought about her father in quite some time, but now Cora finds herself pulling out old memories, considering them from different angles, like prisms in the light. She always blamed Da for his foolishness—his credulity was the sole reason Cora lost everything; she was so sure of it. But there were so many people working and conning him, from all sides, weren't there? Neighbors pressuring him to join the grain elevator. Friends warning he was falling behind. Those slick lenders from Ross & Calhoun, flipping lightning fast through their thick pages of legal jargon, promising him the world, and goading him to sign.

Maybe the story she's been telling herself is a bit too simple.

"You seem far away, Miss Ritter," Harry says now. "Thinking about home, perhaps?"

She startles, turning.

"Your pupils have expanded," he explains excitedly, "a telltale sign of daydreaming."

Harry, she reminds herself, is referring to dreaming of her fictional homeland.

"Indeed," Cora recovers. "It's been so long since I've graced Württemberg's shores."

Hell's bells, focus, Cora—Württemberg is landlocked.

"That is an expression in my country," she ad-libs quickly. "Württemberg's magnificence seems to expand beyond its borders to the mountains, the seas, and the shores."

Harry nods thoughtfully at that hogwash, as he tends to do, never too eager to press or venture too far out of the confines of his own little world. One minor blessing, as Cora has taken to wandering off script frequently these days, often out of necessity. Of late, Alice is off with Mr. McAllister more than she's home, always claiming some emergency meeting about the new embassy or now, this latest complication about the emerald that they must address.

"Württemberg does seem a fascinating place," Harry says. "Arabella relayed the contents of an article she happened upon the other day, discussing your nation's history. I do support your cousin's efforts, by the by. The national resistance. You ask me, a country should have autonomy over its own resources."

Cora nods, straining for solemnity, but finds she has to bite back a smile. That story she cooked up for Cal Archer ended up gracing the front page of the latest World News section of *The Herald*. And true to the reporter's word, there was no mention in the slightest about emerald mines.

Mr. Cal Archer may well prove an unforeseen asset, in addition to a nuisance.

"Let us hope, Mr. Peyton. Let us pray that our homeland's future is as warm and bright as the sun."

"I would enjoy hearing more about this magnificent Württemberg." Harry smiles his trademark befuddled grin. "You can play field guide again for me, if you like."

She nestles another inch closer. "I assure you, it is one of the most beautiful places on earth. As well as one of the most blessed. Rolling hills, sparkling emeralds, as far as the eye can see—"

"Arabella, too, is always keen to mention the minerals." He bites his lip. "This is, perhaps, humorous . . . When we were children, she and I had once envisioned a made-up land of sparkling jewels, one you could only find using a very detailed and specific code of coordinates. We would travel there all the time, on these ill-advised adventures—from our chosen spot in the park and straight into a land of our own creation." He shakes his head at the memory. "How silly we were."

"How silly, indeed."

The "simmering" Cora had detected at Delmonico's between the Ames girl and Harry most certainly would have built into something more serious given time. Bit of a pity, as the two odd ducks might have made quite the flock in another life—given, say, the absence of a fictional emerald heiress.

Speaking of, maybe it's time to change tack. Move things forward with a time-tested appeal to other, more *biological* instincts to seal the deal . . .

"Mr. Peyton," Cora murmurs demurely, spinning to look at him. "I do hope this is the correct phrasing in English . . . You'll have to forgive me, I wish to impart the right sentiment. I appreciate your past . . . adventures, but I have many, *many* thrilling exploits to offer you myself."

Harry swallows, his Adam's apple jumping. "Thrilling, ah, exploits?"

"Mm." She leans closer, smiling, batting her eyes—quite a difficult feat in the midst of a windstorm. But she must be achieving the desired effect, because a distinct red is now creeping up his narrow throat.

She drops her voice another octave, spoon-feeding the sensual overtones so there is no confusion: "And please know that I would always be delighted to play your field guide, Mr. Peyton."

Harry has turned red as a tomato.

"Why . . . I believe I should like that." He swallows. "I should like that very, very—"

"My, what a coincidence, Miss Ritter!"

Cora freezes. That distinctly brazen tone.

Cal Archer steps toward them in long strides, that cocksure, determined gait ever so strangely familiar. He's sporting a top hat and a thick, black overcoat in this weather, but the bulk does nothing to hide his athletic physique. He appears taller than the last time she saw him, which is obviously impossible. He's not taller, is he? He sidles up beside them, towering over Harry.

Cora straightens. "I am beginning to get the sense you're following me, Mr. Archer."

His blue eyes glimmer, his words visible puffs against the cold. "I do cover other beats, Miss Ritter. Believe it or not."

"Ah," she says primly, surprised to find herself game, even

excited, to volley with him once more. "Tell me then, what is today's top story? Park pigeons, perhaps? The perils of winter picnics?"

He smirks. "Don't believe we've met." Cal turns to Harry, extending his hand. "Cal Archer."

"Very good to meet you, sir. I'm Harold Peyton."

"The Peytons, ah," Cal says. "Of course. I'm familiar with your father's work."

"Is that right?" Harry waits for Cal to elaborate. He doesn't.

Cora starts, "Mr. Archer—"

"Now that we're all acquainted, I'm hoping I might take advantage of this serendipitous encounter." Cal pulls his notebook from his pocket. "Your sob story went over well with my editor, Miss Ritter, so he's hoping for a follow-up. A humanitarian story this time, perhaps," he muses, flipping pages. "Something on the everyman of Württemberg. How the plight of your country is affecting the homestead. Make people really sympathize. You don't mind, do you, Harold?"

"Only insomuch as Miss Ritter minds."

Cora opens her mouth, priming to share a litany of facts about Württemberg's people, before she promptly closes it. She has yet to garner Alice's reaction to her first published improvisation, after all. Until she does, perhaps it's best not to pull the same trick twice.

"Mr. Archer, I believe this conversation is best suited for another time. Or another person altogether," Cora says. "Perhaps the Württembergian Embassy can help you."

Cal's eyes brighten. "Embassy? Where's that, now?"

She bites her lip. Goodness, she lacks focus today. Does the embassy even exist? She tries to recollect what Alice last told her. Comes up blank.

In fact, maybe it's best to stop talking altogether.

"They are obviously ever so busy," Cora amends quickly. "But I can speak to them on your behalf. Or accompany you. Eventually. When the time is right. Which is not right now."

"I should quite like to accompany as well," Harry marvels.

They both turn.

Harry clears his throat. "Should you need your own field guide, Miss Ritter."

"That won't be necessary," Cal says as Cora coos, "How chivalrous of you, Mr. Peyton."

Cal frowns, which, to her surprise, sends a trill of delight up her spine. Is it really possible he tracked her down in the middle of Central Park only to see her again?

No, that's ridiculous, and far too self-indulgent.

"Sounds like it's settled, Mr. Archer," Cora adds breezily. "I'll send word for when we might all visit together. Now, do you mind if we continue on with our stroll without further imposition?"

"Of course." Cal tips his hat and steps aside.

"Though I dare hope you don't consider the free and independent press an imposition," he calls after her.

She smiles and turns.

"If you ask me," he says, "my paper's playing quite an important role in your whole affair."

That strangely loaded term, *affair*, might alone be enough to send her off-balance, but the scoundrel also has the cheek to wink at her.

That said, this off-kilter feeling is not an entirely unpleasant sensation.

"Good day, Mr. Archer," she says.

"Good day, indeed."

"Are you all right, Miss Ritter?" Harry ventures, once Cal's gone. "You seem very flustered."

"Oh, I'm perfectly fine, Mr. Peyton."

"The blood vessels around your cheeks have dilated and your eyes appear glassy—"

"Simply because I'm with you."

She winces, having meant for the words to come out as a flirtatious purr instead of a growl. Thankfully, her retort still does the trick: Harry's stopped walking and is now blushing himself.

"If that man was bothering you," Harry says, puffing out his chest, "I am more than happy to have a word with his employers."

As if this wide-eyed lad could even find his way to *The Herald* office alone.

"Oh, ah—no, no, Mr. Peyton, that won't be necessary." She flashes him her brightest smile. "Please. Let us enjoy our afternoon. Now, what were you saying earlier, about your favorite spot in Central Park?"

CHAPTER 14

A Precision of Mind

PEYTON

Angle: Venality

Harry Peyton watches Cora Ritter slowly spin around, a delighted smile on her lips as she takes in the old-world resplendence of Belvedere Castle. She looks right at home. Obviously she does, Harry chastises himself; she is a princess. Or rather, a duchess twice removed. Royalty, in any event. Harry was always more interested in the sciences than in history, was never very adept at keeping names and titles straight during his governess's lessons or in school. A fact that he should probably attempt to remedy, he supposes, if he intends to parade through society with Miss Ritter on his arm.

The notion makes him equal parts eager and queasy. He is mightily aware that he needs to change his current circumstances: Harry has become his aging, temperamental father's preferred caregiver (a role that has increasingly resembled servant, and then, as the years have dragged on, *victim*), tasked with fulfilling the old man's every obscure, demeaning, and occasionally vindictive "need." And yet Harry is also far from comfortable rubbing shoulders with Württemberg nobility as a matter of course.

Perhaps he can frame this courtship of Miss Ritter as an experiment of sorts. One he can prepare for, research, and control through various elements, same as he does with all his examinations. He'll need to eventually secure his father's blessing . . . and yet Harry's father finally agreed to his weekly visits to the surgical theater at the New York Academy of Medicine for further training, did he not? And didn't, or couldn't, stop Harry when he had hurried out the door for the Patriarch's Ball? A mere few months ago, such respite from their Sixtieth Street home would have felt like a dream. And look at Harry now, attending real live parties, walking about the park with a beautiful, charming, *interested* woman. Perhaps Cora was right, that one's fortune can always change. Yes, it's simply a matter of time before he can secure aid for his father and flee for good—and if he manages to escape halfway around the world, so much the better.

Harry shivers against the cold as he observes Miss Ritter. There's a sad sort of irony to this young woman standing in precisely the same place where he and Arabella used to frolic in their imaginary world those many years ago, before the Manifest Rails deal swelled the family's wealth exponentially, before his father grew more and more ruthless in his business practices and more insatiable in his quest to bring up the perfect heir. Then, ever more and more furious, as his body deteriorated and he became wheelchair bound, eventually shutting out the world entirely for them both. Through all of Harry's frustration and heartache, he'd had one constant beacon of hope: his childhood friend, Arabella Ames. She had been his playmate, then his confidante, and then his correspondent—until his father put an end to their letters too.

Ahead, in the wide cobblestone square, Cora claps her hands, her perfectly proportioned silhouette angled upward as light snowflakes begin to fall.

She laughs, eyes glittering with delight—another anatomical wonder, he notes absently, how a person's eyes can appear to shine when they are joyous. "As if this place could be any more enchanting."

Harry forces a smile. "I'm so glad you like it too."

He summons his courage and goes to her. Takes her hand.

"Look at us," Cora whispers, her eyes so wide, her features so stunningly symmetrical. "Already having a new adventure."

Harry can't help but redden again, recalling the lady's earlier, unintentionally evocative declaration about "thrilling exploits."

For the first time, he allows himself to truly imagine a future with her.

He thinks about walking with Miss Ritter in a garden half-way around the world, the sound of native birds chirping as they stroll along together.

He imagines tending his own garden, planting various specimens from the foreign countryscape, watching them grow, taking notes (perhaps writing his own Württembergian equivalent of *Origin of the Species*).

He might even pursue his particular interest in anatomy, institute a royal surgical club (one can dream).

Dining with international kings and queens (he will become far better with diversified small talk as the years go on).

Emerald prospecting on an idle day (if that is indeed a Württembergian pastime—he shall research).

Harry swallows. It really is high time to gently escort Arabella to the recesses of his mind. It is the only way to truly be free, by marrying international royalty, settling overseas. Besides, it's not as if Arabella isn't moving on. Mrs. Ames has made it beyond clear that she's two letters away from a formal engagement with the Württembergian fellow, anyhow.

If they both marry Württembergian nobility, at least they'll travel in the same circles, remain friends forevermore.

There is also the simple, primeval consolation of knowing that Miss Cora Ritter of Württemberg is undoubtedly the most beautiful young woman Harry has ever seen.

He smiles, an authentic one this time, new snow melting on his cheeks. "I wonder, Miss Ritter, if I might have the honor of escorting you to the Ameses' ball this Friday?"

She beams up at him. "If it pleases you."

"It would please me very much."

Harry wonders what it might feel like to kiss her—but that would be too untoward, much too fast, especially without any promises made between them.

That, however, is a variable that *is* in his control.

He can change that. Soon.

CHAPTER 15

A Bit of Misdirection

I'd expected Mrs. Vandemeer to join us." Alice smiles vaguely, affecting the bewildered dignity that has served her so well in the past several months.

"She's . . . indisposed today, I'm afraid," Mr. Vandemeer says, rather awkwardly motioning her into the study. "Besides, she finds matters of business dull. Doesn't have a mind like yours, Duchess. Please, sit."

She thinks for a moment that Mr. Vandemeer is going to take the seat behind his desk in his study, as if directing a message to subordinates in his railroad business. He pauses, however, perhaps noting the expression on Ward McAllister's face, and appears to rethink it, doubling back to claim a studded leather armchair, which he drags closer to the chairs he's just offered his guests.

It makes a grating sound against the floorboards, dragging the Persian rug along with it, no doubt damaging both. The man doesn't care, Alice realizes. He'll simply replace them.

"What sort of business did you want to discuss, Mr. Vandemeer?" Alice asks, accepting the coffee the footman brings her with a cool nod. "I can certainly make introductions, if it's a trade agreement you have in mind."

"Of a sort," he says. "Listen, I won't waste your time beating around the bush. That necklace you gave my Mimi? I had it evaluated."

She raises her eyebrows as if amused. "Did you?"

"He's a fellow who dots his i's and crosses his t's, don't you know." Ward chuckles.

Mr. Vandemeer leans on his knees. "My man called that emerald 'eye-clean,' one of the clearest, highest-quality emeralds he'd ever inspected. He was very interested to hear about these mines in Württemberg. Said that stone was as green as a Colombian emerald."

Given that it really did come from Colombia, by way of the Financial District, Alice is far from surprised, which adds to the effect as she shrugs politely.

Vandemeer's eyes widen. He sits back. "Fellow wanted to invest in those mines himself."

"Oh dear." Alice laughs. "I'm not sure what Mr. McAllister has told you, but I'm afraid the Württemberg mines are far from an investment opportunity. They've been in my family for ten generations, perhaps more. We will happily export them again once our political unrest has ended, but as to—"

"I've heard as much from Ward, yes," Vandermeer says, lowering his voice conspiratorially. "But we both know the real money's in ownership."

"It is not merely a matter of money, Mr. Vandemeer." Alice shuffles in her chair.

She turns to Ward, as if for help.

He winces, hands spread wide. "As you say, Your Grace, but may I gently argue that it's also a matter of . . . friendship?"

She goes still, ceding the floor to McAllister.

"You've come to our shores in search of allies," he says, his voice taking on the cadence of a politician giving a stump speech. "And you've found them. A group of friends so moved by the plight of your fine people that they've opened up their pocketbooks and granted you their help. With nothing asked in exchange, mind you."

Alice frowns. "For which I am very grateful."

"What I'm sayin' is that now is the time to strengthen those alliances, so nothing like this ever happens again to your proud nation," Ward declares.

"You're suggesting I open up what has been a privately held mining company from time immemorial to anyone who wants to invest?" Alice sputters. "I-I couldn't—"

"Not to anyone," Vandemeer cuts in. "That's the last thing we're suggesting. Don't want the hoi polloi getting their dirty hands into this, no, far from it. An extremely select few. Even just me, if you like. And, ah, Mr. McAllister here, I suppose."

McAllister nods in thanks, valiantly ignoring the poorly disguised look of dislike on Vandemeer's face. "You'd be one of the primary foreign investors, Vandemeer. Perhaps the very first. If I myself can scrape together enough for a share, it would be paltry, a mere token of my affection for the people of Württemberg."

Alice stands up, affronted. "Gentlemen, you are letting this idea run loose. As I have said, our mines have been in the family for—"

"I'll give you a million," Vandemeer blurts. "Write you a check today. Ward here knows I'm good for it."

A million.

Alice's awed reaction is a real one. That's a sizable chunk of the man's net worth to throw out in afternoon conversation.

But it's too soon. And only a small fraction of what she's after.

"Mr. Vandemeer, Mr. McAllister," she says quietly. "You have given me much to ponder. But if you want an answer today, then I am afraid my answer is no. I'll bid you good day now."

As she leaves in a feigned huff, seen out to the foyer by the maid, she passes Mimi, who's positioned herself in a carefully conspicuous spot in the conservatory. In the little chit's hands is the emerald necklace, which she dangles this way and that, casting refractions of green upon her hands.

"Lovely little plaything," Mimi drawls lazily. "Thanks again, Your Grace."

It takes all of Alice's composure not to snatch the necklace out of Mimi's hands. The maid brings her coat just in time. She smiles at Mimi and carries on outside.

Ward trots out, close on her heels, buttoning himself hastily into his own winter garb. "You played that one rather severely. Thought for a moment you'd decided to call the whole thing off."

"Far from it," Alice says, accepting his hand up into his waiting carriage. "People like Vandemeer need to hear the word *no* in order to insist upon a *yes*. It must feel like his idea. Better yet, his secret."

"It's everybody's secret," Ward chuffs. "I've heard from Ames and Ogden. Even Iris Witt's gotten a whiff of it now."

"Good," Alice says. "I'll have to arrange a cornered moment for her to ask me about it at the ball."

"What costume have you chosen, by the by?"

"A hoopoe," Alice says. "A bird native to our country."

"Ever the patriot." Ward chuckles. "Thought you'd dress in emerald green, but perhaps that's a little too on the nose.

Would be like Mrs. Astor dressing as a Mystic Rose just because I gave her the nickname. Speakin' of which . . ."

Alice had wondered how long it would take for the conversation to whip back around to Mrs. Astor.

"Caroline's not too miffed that you missed her own ball, to my great relief," he says. "Didn't seem to mind one way or t'other. She's got me designing her costume today. Demeter, goddess of the harvest, don't you know. She needs me on hand to keep the seamstresses from going overboard with the sewn-on fruits."

"You're invaluable to her," Alice notes.

"It's what keeps me in fine suits." Ward sighs.

"For now." Alice pats his hand. He looks startled by the fond gesture. "You'll be a man of independent means to rival the best of them here in a matter of months."

"If I deign to stay here," Ward says, a mischievous light dancing in his eye.

Alice might be tempted to succumb to curiosity and pry into his plans, but they've already arrived outside her house.

After stepping out with the aid of the driver, she turns back. "I keep neglecting to inquire after Sarah."

Alice has met her only twice, and briefly, but it seems polite to ask.

Ward looks genuinely perplexed.

She raises her eyebrows. "Your wife?"

"Oh! Her. Yes, she's fine. Usual aches and pains and general malaise. Nothing life-threatening. Yet. Well, I'm off to the Union Club. Might run into some of our mutual friends there, and will certainly keep you apprised of any developments."

He tips his hat with a wry smile as the carriage pulls away. Of all of that, what Alice is left remembering is that "yet." An odd phrasing, sinister in the casual way he tossed it off.

She shakes her head to rid herself of unease as she mounts the steps to her front door. As slippery as she knows Ward to be, he has in word and action become a true ally to her. A rare thing, she knows too well.

Her mother had friends but not allies. Close companions. From childhood up until her husband's death, at which point all but one of them shut her out in the cold, shunning her completely. Mrs. Vandemeer was a new addition to their circle, a young thing having only recently married into New York society, but that excuses her but little. She followed the flock in turning her back. Alice doubts very much she ever spared a thought for her "dear friend" Mary from that moment on.

No. In her own addled way, Mrs. Vandemeer is every bit as bad as the rest of them.

As Béatrice takes her coat, Alice peers into her eyes. "They cannot keep the necklace. When this is done, they must be left with nothing of worth. Nothing *at all*."

Béa looks alarmed and then saddened, but she nods. "You'll figure it out. You always do."

CHAPTER 16

In Decent Proposal

March 1, 1884

WITT

Angle: Capriciousness

T he bonnet is falling off your goose, Mamma."

"Then pin it back!" Iris Witt smacks her daughter's arm. "Don't just sit there like a rag doll."

Bonnie lets out a leaden sigh as she leans the slight distance across the carriage to reaffix the bonnet onto Iris's goose headdress. "You couldn't have chosen something simpler?"

"Like a fairy queen, such as you?" Iris snorts derisively. "There will be ten Titanias there tonight, not that you two care if you're absorbed by the crowd."

Beau's too busy picking at his gums with a toothpick to bother looking affronted.

"Bad enough to endure yet another costume ball." Iris sighs. "I don't suppose we can expect the likes of the Parvenu Family to innovate."

"The Ameses?" Bonnie corrects.

"That's what I said." Iris sneers. "The *Parvenus*."

The carriage stops before a stately manse on Sixtieth Street.

"Still don't understand why we're collecting Peyton," Beau moans. "To protect his maidenly virtue?"

Bonnie slaps her brother with her clutched fan, but she's smirking right along.

"We're bringing him with us for the fun of it," Iris declares.

"Here she goes," Bonnie mutters.

"The monotony of this social sphere, the endless cycle of one predictable setting after another; it's enough to drive one to an early grave. The same people, the same conversation, with nothing novel to break it up. You're both too young and frankly too boring to know the agony I'm in," Iris cries. "Comfort, wealth, it is a pernicious trap. At least the poor have work to pour themselves into, and surely the fight against starvation affords a certain level of novelty to each day."

"Go on, Mamma, try out poverty, see if you like it," Beau snickers.

Iris lifts her chin. "Perhaps I will. Perhaps—"

She gasps. Clutches at Bonnie, who recoils as far as the carriage will allow.

"Oh yes, we'll throw a poverty party. That will be quite a distraction. Haven't been to one of those in ages—now, smiles in place, children, here comes the young shut-in himself. Harry! My goodness, what a costume, and . . . what's that you're holding? Now, now. This will be an interesting evening after all!"

❦ ❦ ❦

"So the others will want an emerald valuation as well?" Cora stands in the middle of the parlor, adjusting her Egyptian headdress. "Do we have the funds for another emerald, even a smaller one?"

No one pays her any mind, a sensation she is growing alarmingly accustomed to. She might as well be here as a *tableau vivant*—meant to be looked at, certainly not listened to.

Cora truly doesn't understand: Has she not done whatever Alice has asked of her since coming aboard—day after day playing the demure heiress, doing her part to conquer Harry and, through him, ruin his father? Has she not proven herself through tedious training, study, countless social engagements, keeping reporters in the dark, literally spinning the news in their favor? And still, Alice refuses to see her as an equal . . . or even as someone capable of adding value. Someone who deserves respect.

Alice continues pacing, running rivulets into her parlor floorboards, while Ward sits at the window, frowning down at the bustling avenue below, his hand absently screwing his cane into the rug. He's supposed to be Henry VIII for tonight's costume ball but looks rather more like a sad clown in his chosen attire—cockeyed velvet cap, a slightly too-snug burgundy doublet, puffy brocade breeches.

"We need to find a solution before Thursday," he murmurs. "We're set to dine with the Ogdens and—"

"Thursday?" Alice spits out the word like venom. "Far too soon. Even assuming this forgery idea would work—a *big* assumption, mind you—we'll absolutely need to delay."

Ward grimaces. "Time is of the essence in general, is it not, my dear?"

"A forged emerald, you mean?" Cora cuts in, now desperate

with confusion. "For me to, what? Wear to dinner with the Ogdens? Surely you aren't going to risk someone wanting to buy a bracelet off me too—"

"*Surely* nothing. This isn't a two-bit production, Cora. Your advice is neither relevant nor helpful." Alice turns on her, blue eyes frosty. "These people are serious players with deep pockets and aren't going to just accept green glass and say thank you. As to your earlier question, yes, each of them may want the stones evaluated, which would be more than understandable. Now, pray be silent and let the adults talk."

Cora reels back as if she's been slapped.

"Don't cry, *ma puce*," Béatrice murmurs kindly, hovering near the entry. "Think of the makeup."

Alice sighs, turning toward the window, dismissing Cora with a wave of her hand. Somehow the feathers of her hoopoe-themed gown lend extra hauteur to the gesture.

"Cinderella's carriage has just arrived, anyway," she mutters. "Go be useful. Ward, do buy me more time if you can. Even a week would . . ."

White-capped rage—or is it hurt?—crests between Cora's temples, drowning out the sound of Alice and Ward's further plotting. She hurries past them all, blinking back hot tears. Past Dagmar too, who has chosen to remain in the kitchen, polishing pots, agnostically silent on the subject as always.

Cora hurtles down the narrow steps.

"Enjoy the party, Cora," Béatrice calls gently after her.

Cora ducks into the corner of the narrow, stuffy stairwell, attempting to catch her breath, calm her juddering pulse. Alice could not have possibly meant those cutting gibes. No, she is overwhelmed, obviously, ever more anxious as they hurtle toward this grand production's final act on May 1.

Just breathe, Cora tells herself. *Breathe, reset the stage.*

She carefully wipes her eyes, attempting to preserve Béa's handiwork. This is hardly the time for self-pity. And this is what she wanted, after all: to be part of a winning team, to star in a lucrative performance, with instruction from a master (however cold or ruthless that master might be). Alice will fill in Cora, eventually, of course she will, when the time is right. Alice needs her, after all.

Cora only wishes Alice were better at showing it.

She takes a few fortifying breaths and steps into the respite of the night, taking in the picturesque New York winter evening in all its splendor. The warmly lit lanterns, the horse-drawn carriages clopping down the road, the frigid air laced with perfume and expectation. As for her escort, the carriage is already parked at the curb.

Alice was right, per usual: The Witts' cab is indeed lifted straight from a fairy tale, ornate white wood, gilded frame, and hitched to four majestic gray steeds. A reedy, well-dressed driver stands ready to assist.

Get into character now, Cora. Calm, regal, earnest, doting.

She lifts the beaded skirts of her Egyptian princess costume, her heaviest and most exquisite gown yet this season—though calling it "hers" is a stretch, as it will be sold on, same as all the rest of them, soon after the party. She blinks the less-than-glamorous reality away and glides down from the front stoop just as Harry steps out from the carriage.

Harry bows, offering his hand. Thankfully, his attire tonight is loads better than the hasty, misconceived getup he threw together for the Patriarch's Ball. He's dressed as a Scottish Highlander, with a sharp cap, full cape, and gentleman's kilt. Will wonders never cease; he must have finally hired a tailor.

"Miss Ritter," Harry says. "You're as exquisite as a *Nymphaea caerulea*."

Cora cocks her head.

"An Egyptian lotus," Harry hastens to explain. "You know, given the, ah, costume."

He gestures manically toward her Cleopatra dress.

Goodness, he seems more off than usual.

She affords him an indulgent smile.

"Thank you, Mr. Peyton," she says with perfect Württembergian inflection. "You look very dashing yourself."

They settle into the crowded carriage, onto one of the car's long velvet benches. Seated across are the Witt twins, Bonnie and Beau, dressed as a fairy and a silken-clad jester, respectively, with their dreadful mother, Mrs. Witt, sandwiched between and overlapping them. The older woman is puffed up like merengue in frills and lace, with some kind of taxidermied bird both posing as a hat and wearing a hat of its own.

"Mother Goose," Mrs. Witt explains proudly, as she likely will all night.

Cora smiles. "How clever, Mrs. Witt."

As Alice explained earlier this week, it would be untoward for Cora and Harry to attend the ball on their own. Given Alice and Mr. McAllister considered it more strategic to ride with the Ogdens tonight—one thread of their exclusive debates that she *was* able to parse—Cora has been tasked with suffering the Witts.

"My, my, how beautiful you look, Miss Ritter." Mrs. Witt smirks. "The detail in that gown is astonishing. Everyone will wonder how many emeralds you had to sell to pay for such a costume. I'm surprised your cousin is allowing any expense to be allocated anywhere but back home to the resistance effort."

Mrs. Witt's shrewd eyes flash dangerously. Was that a knowing cut? Was this costume a misstep? Does she see through their resistance ruse, or is she just being vicious?

Here and now, Cora decides that out of all the marks, she dislikes Mrs. Witt the most.

With an airy laugh, Mrs. Witt leans across the cab and pats Cora's knee. "Quite right to bring your best tonight. *Of all nights.*"

She flashes Harry a little smirk.

Harry starts nervously laughing, which quickly devolves into a choking cough.

"Goodness, Harry, are you all right?" Cora places her hand on his shoulder.

"Quite," he heaves, flashing her a demented smile. "I'm in a fit about this ball. I'm sure it will be one for the ages!"

"It'll be flashy, no doubt," Beau muses dryly. "Too bad money can't buy class."

Beau adjusts his jester hat, peering out the window with a sneer that at least manages to cover his gray teeth.

Mrs. Witt laughs along. "Pearl Ames will always try. I suppose she thinks a royal title for her little mousy daughter might help. What do you think, Miss Ritter? Would marrying your prince of a cousin do the trick?" Mrs. Witt hardly waits for a reply, her smile curling into a simper. "Although, why bother talking of the Ames girl when there are far more exciting developments afoot?"

She winks at Harry, adding in a faux-conspiratorial whisper, "I bid you all the luck in the world tonight, dear boy."

Harry descends into another fit of nervous coughs.

Before Cora can figure out what the devil is going on, their carriage jostles and turns onto Thirty-Fifth Street, all talk falling away as they join the long procession snaking up to the Ameses' front walk, the mounting ballyhoo on the street and surrounding sidewalks ensnaring everyone's attention.

"Goodness, how many did they invite?" Mrs. Witt says. "What a circus this is!"

"The press is even here," Beau mutters. "How delightfully vulgar."

Cora looks out. There are hundreds upon hundreds of guests filtering toward the Ameses' stately brick residence. Several Marie Antoinettes in pink silk; a few Catherine the Greats in brocade mantles; a collection of ancient kings, Renaissance knights, and medieval princes blurring together in velvet and lace-lined tunics. And Beau was right about one thing: Buzzing about the glimmering set, Cora can make out reporters, distinguishable by their comparatively drab brown suits and muted toppers.

Cora's pulse stutter-steps as she spots a rather tall man on the fray, currently stooped to catch a quote from a fellow dressed ostensibly as Richard III, complete with a pillow stuffed into his jacket as a hump. Good grief, what beat *doesn't* Mr. Archer cover?

She watches the reporter with an odd mix of wariness and suspense. Mr. Archer will no doubt have at the ready at least five questions for her. *What angle could he be after this time?* she wonders. More inquiries about the people of Württemberg? Perhaps the noble lineage? She finds she is oddly anticipating the next round in their ongoing volley—as well as another chance to prove, even if just to herself, that she is more than merely a prop in this affair.

Cora smiles. She might also be eager to see how the handsome reporter will react to her appearance tonight. All made up, eyes lined in kohl, lips berry-reddened. This dress. Like true, non-Württembergian royalty.

The reporter laughs, scribbles something in his notepad, and turns—

It isn't Cal Archer. Looks nothing like him, Cora realizes.

"Miss Ritter? Are you all right?" Harry stands outside the carriage now, hand extended, waiting. Apparently they have edged to the front of the line and started to disembark.

She pastes on another smile. "Just struck by the scene. Yes. Off we go."

Off they go indeed, moving along with the throng up the front walk and through the grand entrance.

The Ameses' interior has been transfigured floor to ceiling into an enchanted garden—Mrs. Ames's garbled theme, A Midwinter Night Costume Ball, on full, mystifying display. Garland draped across every mantel and along every entry, chandeliers bursting with hydrangeas and white lilies. Cedar pines and potted cypress lining the marble halls, the trees themselves adorned with white, beaded costume masks, as if some of the guests themselves have transformed into topiary.

The entry gives way to the largest residential ballroom Cora has ever seen, larger than the Witts', one that rivals even Delmonico's, where revelers costumed in every age and era have already taken to the dance floor, the wide, gleaming room bordered by numerous tables, all adorned with gold leaf and sparkling candles.

As Cora accompanies Harry deeper into the party, she spots Mrs. Ames and Arabella ahead, greeting their guests. The matron of the hour stands beaming and rosy with pride, while Arabella looks as though she's contemplating hiding under a nearby table.

In some ways, Cora supposes, this ball is being thrown for Arabella's benefit, however misguided that honor might be. A grand affair to demonstrate to the Grand Duchess of Württemberg that the Ameses are worthy allies in the quest for world dominance or self-importance—or whatever other base motive is spurring the Ameses to marry their daughter off to a man they've never seen (and who, of course, doesn't know she exists).

Cora nearly feels bad for the girl . . .

Nearly.

They cut through the bustling crowd, Harry awkwardly summoning her forward, clearly eager to introduce her to a cadre of young men on the opposite side of the dance floor. Extended family—second cousins once removed—if she heard him right over the growing party din.

"Harold!" A man of about twenty-five or so steps forward, slapping Harry on the back. "How long has it been, old chap? Feels as though you've been locked away forever."

Harry goes quiet, considering. "Six-hundred and ninety-five days," he says numbly. "Minus around forty hours for a handful of excursions to the Academy."

Good Lord, just how cruel is his father?

"Ha!" The man lets out a befuddled laugh. "As precise as ever, Harold!"

Harry steps aside. "Please allow me to introduce Miss Cora Ritter of Württemberg. Miss Ritter, please meet my cousin, Mr. Ernest Denning."

As Cora steps forward with a small curtsy, Ernest nods approvingly, murmuring, "Clearly congratulations are in order."

Congratulations? Cora blinks. *For what?*

There's hardly time to ask given the subsequent flurry

of introductions, all going more or less the same, with Harry growing noticeably more emboldened—or is it distressed?—by the reactions his presentations of her are eliciting. He seems particularly perturbed tonight; Cora doesn't know what to make of it. They are far too late in the season for her to lose his attention now, not when the emerald plans are already in motion, not when Alice is already preparing the fictional embassy for their showdown on the first of May.

"I wonder, Mr. Peyton, if we could steal away for some air, just the two of us?"

"I love a good quadrille, don't you?" Harry blurts awkwardly, once the music changes.

He doesn't wait for a response, simply pulls her toward the dance floor.

They fall in line with three other paired partners, any hope of conversation dashed for now. One dance leads to three. And then four.

When a waltz starts up, Cora seizes her chance. "I must admit, you seem awfully distracted tonight, Mr. Peyton." Then, more softly, "Harry."

He's too busy scanning the room to note her dulcet tone, tightening his grip around her hand as he spins her away. His hand is clammy, she notices, as he pulls her inward. His forehead damp too.

"Oh, thank goodness," Harry mutters, eyes widening. "I can hardly wait any longer."

Cora follows his gaze as they spin again.

Oh. No, no, no.

Her frame feels like an hourglass, her insides disintegrating into sand.

Harry is blatantly staring at Arabella, who stands huddled together with her mother and Alice in her bird costume. He is flagrantly pining for his childhood sweetheart. So Cora has lost Harry's interest after all. Ruined everything. Good God, how many times has Alice insisted that without the Peytons, there *is* no con? Forget Alice letting her in; she'll never forgive her. Maybe Cora will be Alice's next revenge target. She can picture it perfectly. A lifetime of running away from the cold-blooded wolfhound.

Oddly, though, buried under all these mounting vexations, there is the strangest, slightest tinge of . . .

Relief.

"Cora, now that your cousin has arrived, I . . ." Harry swallows. "Well, I cannot keep this up any longer."

He leads her off the dance floor and toward the refreshments table.

"Perhaps some punch first?" Cora suggests, hand shaking as she grabs the ladle.

"Cora." He grabs her wrist. "I have something I must ask."

She turns queasily. Her own nerves are out of control now, a careening carriage with loose wheels. And is it her imagination, or is the crowd closing in? Beau Witt has appeared in the fray, staring at them with that gloomy sneer. A few young men Cora met earlier have stopped their own conversations and are now staring at Harry. But a couple paces away, Mimi Vandemeer and Bonnie Witt, too, have both turned, smiling at Cora in sick fascination.

"I do believe it's time," Bonnie intones ominously.

Time for what?

Mimi smirks. "From recluse to bumbling showman in a matter of weeks. It's a turnout for the ages."

Cora has the distinct sensation of the entire parquet floor being pulled out from under her.

Showman?

"I was at a loss for how to do this, but they have assured me this is the correct method." Before her, Harry lowers himself onto one knee and brandishes a small box from his pocket. He opens it carefully, revealing a large opal-cut diamond flanked, quite thoughtfully, by two emeralds.

The room goes quiet.

He takes her hand. "I know that you and I will be compatible."

Cora's mind free-falls. She's floating, divorced from time and space. She hears feet shuffling behind her, whispers, gasps of contented delight.

On instinct, she looks around for Alice, but Her Fake Grace's eyes are locked on Harry kneeling on the ground, her expression demure as ever. Utterly opaque.

Beside Alice is Mrs. Ames, cheeks rosy, hands clasped with glee.

On Alice's other side stands a demolished Arabella.

"So, Miss Cora Ritter," Harry continues, his blue eyes wide and expectant, his brow now gleaming with sweat. "Would you do me the honor of marrying me? Of joining me as my field guide to life?"

Cora closes her eyes, heart hammering like orchestra drums. She should feel victorious. A sense of accomplishment. She knows this. This is the most important piece of the puzzle clicking into place.

But of all things, her traitorous mind has conjured Harry months from now, alone the day after she and Alice run off with his inheritance.

Will this hapless lad remember this very moment? Will he remember the moment he decided to stumble off the ledge and ruin himself?

She forces herself to smile.

"Of course I will."

The crowd breaks into cheers.

"There is no time more enticing than as soon as possible," Harry says into her ear as the crowd descends upon them, the waiters hastening off to fetch glasses of champagne. "I shall have to speak to my father about wedding details, but I am thinking next weekend? Or the weekend after that—"

Cora bites her lip. "Oh, Harry, weddings take time to plan."

Harry shakes his head, more energized than she's ever seen him.

"I don't want to wait one day longer than necessary to start our lives." His eyes alight. "The weekend of Easter, then. That Saturday. It will be a perfect time to celebrate."

Cora pales. "I don't believe I heard you over the noise? Easter Saturday? But that's—"

Weeks before their ultimate fleece.

"To the future Mr. and Mrs. Peyton!" someone cries.

It's like a starting bell, the crowd swallowing them whole, gnawing them apart with aggressive cheers before Cora can speak another word on the matter. Pats on Harry's back, hands offered in congratulations, younger girls fawning over Cora as Mrs. Ames laughs in obvious relief. "What a grand surprise!"

Easter weekend. A mere six weeks from now.

How on earth is she to become Mrs. Harry Peyton in April and rob him blind in May?

And where the hell is Alice, given the grand mess Harry has just made of her carefully constructed plans?

Cora tries to magically summon her, to conjure the elusive woman to appear from thin air, right here beside her in the dining room.

But Alice is the true magician. She's disappeared.

Nowhere to be found when needed most.

CHAPTER 17

Shuffle the Deck

As inconspicuously as she can walk in a songbird costume, Alice cuts her way through the gathered crowd, following the encouraging chill of a draft of night air. Passing the grand dining room, she sees that final preparations to the table have been made, the servants standing ready. Perhaps Harry's proposal delayed the schedule somewhat, but they'll call for the meal within minutes, leaving Alice only the space of a few breaths to herself to gather her thoughts and form a new game plan, now that the hand they've been dealt has been altered.

Out in the garden, the air is thick and cold, threatening more snow rather than delivering. It's enough to make for a lonely setting, which is just as Alice wants it. She walks the boundary of the courtyard past wintering plants and silent statues.

Leaving aside the newest development—that marriage proposal was not on her list of possible events tonight—Alice has been anxiously preoccupied with what she and Ward were discussing all the way up to the Ameses' front door tonight.

Thanks to her gesture of amity at the Vandemeer dinner

party, Mrs. Ogden has felt compelled to issue an invitation of her own to her new bosom friend via Ward McAllister, who had popped by to talk emeralds with her husband. To move forward with an investment in the mining company, Ogden will want one of two things. One: an emerald to have valued. Or two: something Alice is not going to give him.

Before their next meeting, Alice will have to supply him that Colombian gemstone for valuation. As she cannot afford to purchase another, she had determined there was only one option. She will have to replace that necklace with a credible fake so she can remove the stone from its setting and present it to the potential investors as another example of Württembergian riches.

She'd hoped to do it tonight, but it will be another week at a minimum before the commissioned replica is ready to be collected. Even had she been prepared, it wouldn't have mattered, as it happens. Mimi, dressed as a Florida flamingo, declared the gem too much a mismatch with her fuchsia gown tonight, Mrs. Vandemeer told Alice, almost but not quite apologetic.

"She'll wear it to the opera on the seventeenth," Mrs. Vandemeer dreamily announced. "It's *Carmen*, so nothing is too showy."

To which her husband hastily added, "Say . . . now that abdication looks all but inevitable, perhaps you might finally afford yourself a night out. We'd be very happy to host you in our box."

Alice had graciously accepted. She does the math in her head now. Two weeks remain for her to take possession of the false necklace she's commissioned. She'll have to set the date to meet Ogden for the week following, which puts her into late March, leaving April for emerald valuations, last-minute financial machinations, and formal hush-hush invitations being doled out for the event itself.

No sense in agonizing over every step between today and the first of May, however, only the very next one: How to retrieve the actual emerald without anyone the wiser?

Sleight of hand has never been a strength of hers. It is, however, a particular skill of Cora's. One that Alice did not until now anticipate requiring.

She'll have to speak to the girl. Not at present, though, not with everyone filing in to dinner, the happy couple veritably swarmed with well-wishers.

Not at dinner either. They're stationed at separate tables— a blessing, given the desperate look Cora fixes Alice with as she passes her on the way to be seated.

Not as they leave the ball either. Alice rides away with Ward just as Cora and Harry emerge from the Ameses' mansion to claim their own carriage.

She plans to use the ride to lay out her plan to Ward, but he's imbibed too much madeira and brandy to make any truly cogent suggestions. By the time she's reached her home, her mind may be more muddled in its fevered thoughts than his.

Inside, she goes straight to her study and shuts the door.

The journal Cora gifted her sits on the desk, tempting her to fall prey to the cardinal sin of committing her machinations to paper.

She's not such a fool as to succumb but remains too anxious to take herself off to bed, so she runs sums instead, using the book as a ledger, as she'd originally planned.

She enters a figure for the newest projected expense, a

counterfeit necklace. Offset against the group's likely earnings of twelve million, as best estimated, it's nothing. A drop in the bucket.

And Mr. Vandemeer willing to write a check for a cold million right there on the spot.

Alice hears the front door open. Footsteps stomping steadily toward her. She turns her attention back to the ledger and braces for the inevitable.

CHAPTER 18

Queen Rook Pawn

Cora bursts into Alice's private study without knocking, momentum and fury twin stallions hurtling her into the center of the room.

Alice pushes back from her desk, all sure mannerisms, carefully calculated gestures. "By all means. Enter."

"No, I will *not* be made to feel like a fool by you! Every time I attempt to speak with you, there's something more important, and surely there can be nothing more important than *this*."

Cora brandishes her new engagement ring as if she's gesturing with a very different finger. Closing the door behind her, she begins pacing alongside Alice's settee on the far wall. "Not that this is news to you. You obviously saw what happened at the ball."

"Of course. Congratulations."

Alice coolly resumes writing—in the notebook Cora gave her for Christmas. Is she using it as a *ledger*?

"Need I remind you that is *good* news—"

"Harry wants to get married right away. *Right away*, at his father's estate. He mentioned a wedding Easter weekend, which obviously changes everything."

This finally stops Alice's hand.

She looks up again, her face controlled, but Cora can see the glimmer of a frown. "You're certain that's what he said?"

"I'm certain I didn't hallucinate, if that's what you're implying."

Alice places her pencil down, sighs thoughtfully, and stands, positioning herself at the window. Outside, the huge elms lining Madison are still blanketed in snow, the streetlamps turning the winter wonderland luminous, all of Manhattan coated in a gilded shimmer. "I don't consider that a problem."

Cora shakes her head. "Whatever do you—"

"Marry him," Alice says, turning. "There, fixed. Actually, now that I think about it, this is better. Harry will feel duty bound to invest, and he'll have no reason to suspect your influence if you're already his wife. We can proceed as planned without worrying about any last-minute jitters on his part. Right on the heels of your celebration, in fact."

Cora feels a mounting pressure between her temples, a building urge to roar. "You do realize this will make me a married woman, Alice. Essentially ruining all prospects of me ever having a normal life. Of being able to marry again, not to mention ever showing my face in New York—"

Alice quirks an eyebrow. "Please tell me you weren't expecting to do that after we scam most of the railroad industry. And marrying again? I didn't take you for a sentimentalist."

"It isn't . . . sentiment, it's *life!*" Cora blurts, voice shaking. The temper flaring in her belly now too, building like a low roll, threatening to boil. "Real life!"

Alice shrugs one shoulder. Infuriating, emotionless woman. She'll have to meet her where she lives. Encased in steel.

"This isn't acceptable." Cora crosses her arms. "I won't do it. *No.*"

Cora sees the flash of surprise in Alice's eyes at the word, and feels a tiny thrill of satisfaction.

Alice takes a swift step forward. Cora resists the urge to flinch.

"Need I remind you, Miss *O'Malley*, that when we made this deal, you agreed to do whatever I asked, *whenever* I asked. And in exchange, you would be handsomely compensated. Do you not remember that?"

"*Yes*, I remember that, but this is going too far, Alice. I am a member of this team and I deserve a say. The stakes have changed!"

"And yet the game hasn't," Alice says icily. "We will do whatever is necessary to make May the first happen. And since Easter falls before May, you *will* walk down the aisle with that man and you *will* say 'I do,' and before you ask, yes, you *will* consummate the marriage. Or . . ." Her expression defrosts a degree. "Figure out some plausible reason not to. I'll leave that to your own discretion."

Cora's head goes swimmy. Perhaps she is actually hallucinating. "Alice—"

"My God, Cora, *enough*. This matter is settled."

"I honestly can't believe you'd do this to me," Cora says hollowly. "After everything."

"I don't care what you believe." Alice snaps a laugh. "You wanted me to teach you? This is me teaching you. From the very first day, I was completely transparent: I am in charge, and you simply listen. You may go."

"And *you* may go to—"

Cora has at least the presence of mind to bite back the rest of those choice words. She jumps up from the settee instead, flying toward the door, where she nearly barrels into Béatrice and Dagmar, who stand there like mismatched gargoyles, horrified by what they've plainly overheard.

Cora elbows past, barreling toward her room, where she slams the door and crumples onto the bed, finally succumbing to the tears that have been building.

She knew Alice was capable of anything. It was part of Alice's allure, the very reason Cora appealed to the woman in the first place. A confidence player who knows no limits. Has no scruples. A canny mentor who could take Cora under her wing and actually make things happen for her. A huge score, a better life, a fresh chance of getting back her home.

But she cannot deny the truth any longer. Alice isn't her *mentor*, just as she herself doesn't amount to a player or accomplice or anything but a pawn in her hardened boss's game.

Cora has learned *nothing* since that fateful day when the men from Ross & Calhoun gleefully waltzed in and upended her life. She's no better than her father.

Just a fool under the thumb of a sham, heartless duchess.

CHAPTER 19

Genuine Fraud

Alice glances up as Béatrice slides into the study, closing the door behind her almost as silently. Alice hides the hitch in her breath as best she can.

Béa stands staring at Alice for a long beat before she says, "This is too much."

Alice raises her eyebrows, prepared to debate the point, but the disappointment in Béa's eyes as she draws nearer silences her.

"Alice, you cannot force the girl to get *married*. To take vows, to change the course of her life like this. It's too much, it is ridiculous, and you know it is."

"What's ridiculous is how much you're both blowing this out of proportion." Alice rolls her eyes. "What is the difference, really, between a marriage and a long engagement, if at the end of each, you run off, never to be seen again?"

"A legal remarriage, for one," Béa suggests softly.

Alice exhales a *pah*, muttering, "Not you too."

A knowing glint lights up Béa's eye as she draws closer. "It's different for Cora than for you. You would never marry a man, so you cannot conceive of anyone else legitimately wishing to do so."

Alice reels with the plain truth of that. She's never understood the appeal of marriage. And yet . . .

She peers up into Béa's warm hazel eyes, taking in her high cheekbones, her sweet smile, the scar that cuts through it all. A wave of tenderness washes over her.

She blinks hard and looks away, pointlessly straightening the assorted objects on her desk. "I admire your attempt to instill empathy in me, Béa, but it's a question of practicality, not emotion. A new element has been introduced into our plan, and we must adapt to it. It's that simple."

"Adapt in a different way, then."

"How?" Alice's voice takes on a hard tone. She hates the way Béa flinches at the sound of it, but she cannot help herself. "If you're so clever, you tell me."

"You're the planner and we all know it." Béatrice drifts like a feather into the nearest chair, her energy for this argument plainly flagging. "Dagmar has her hundreds of Bowery connections, and I have my assorted skills. And Cora . . . is the beauty."

The quick-fingered beauty, Alice thinks, remembering what else she needed to talk to the girl about—but this is clearly not the time to bring that up.

"But that's not the only reason you brought us in, Alice," Béa goes on, her eyes piercing in their raw affection. "I remember the day we met. Two years ago, in April. Montreal's Bonsecours Market. You saw me pocket that cruller, saw that the vendor saw it too, called out to me by the wrong name and bought it for me on the spot rather than see me get thrown in prison yet again, this time for desperate hunger. Brought me to a tearoom, heard my story, pathetic as it was, and took me in, then and there. I still don't know why you were down in the city's old town that day, but *grâce à Dieu*, you were."

I was there to find accomplices to bring with me to New York, Alice remembers dully. And Béa's story was far from pathetic. She'd been a seamstress's assistant, yes, but she'd also worked for years as a forger and fence before being caught and imprisoned up in Montreal, then released into a world that would never employ an ex-convict, no matter how capable. Alice didn't care about her record. She simply wanted someone useful on the payroll who could also pose as a housemaid to sell the lie of nobility.

She'd taken Béa in because she could use her.

It was only later that she'd become more. Her home. Her person. Even if she couldn't say it out loud.

"You have a good heart," Béatrice says. "I see it. It's real. Not counterfeit."

She smiles, her mouth quirking shyly upward in the way that always stops Alice's heart for a beat.

"Speaking of counterfeits," Alice says, clearing her throat. "It's imperative that I have the replica of the Württemberg solitaire in hand as soon as possible."

A frown line forms between Béa's delicate brows. "Yes. They've said—"

"I'll need you to go down first thing tomorrow and check on their progress. I fear some people need to be overseen closely in order to perform their work to a satisfactory degree."

Béa looks stricken by the change in tone. She swallows hard. "I'll leave before dawn so as not to be seen."

"Good," Alice says, standing briskly. "I'm off to bed. You'd best get some sleep as well, as you'll be off so early."

She breezes past her maid—the woman who cannot, must

not be anything more, not while all of this is swirling in her mind, not while they are so damned close to the first of May.

"You know . . ." Béa's voice rises quietly behind her. "Sometimes I wonder if the person you're bent on punishing the most is yourself."

Alice's eyes burn. She closes the study door behind her as she goes with a bit more force than necessary.

CHAPTER 20

Bottoms Up

Cora digs her head into her pillow, past the point of letting the coarse feathers muffle her sobs that came in the first flush of her outrage last night. She hadn't let herself go like that since Da's funeral, eyes aching, nose wet, a dull headache that consumes her whole face.

She's stayed like this all day, since returning from the ball. As the sun rose soon after, she took to her room. At the soft rap on her door, Béatrice offering lunch, then tea, all ignored. As a pair of pigeons decided to have a noisy squabble just outside her window, Cora remained buried under her blanket and slept.

Now, as she finally digs herself out from her stupor, her stomach rumbling in irate protest, she finds Dagmar standing in her doorway, the cook's bulk filling the entire space.

"I'm fine." Cora sits up, wiping her eyes. "Just tired."

Dagmar grunts, skeptical. For some reason, the German woman's disgusted expression is even more insulting than Alice's cold castoff.

"Trust me," Cora mutters. "I've been through worse."

"Then you know nuttink goot iz going to come lying dere crying your eyes out," Dagmar huffs.

Cora looks up. This is the longest sentence she's ever heard the cook put together. In English, anyway.

"Get dressed," Dagmar adds gruffly, "and nothing too fancy." Her red nose wrinkles on the word. "You are not going to be recogneezed where we are going, but I will take no chances."

Cora jumps up to sift through her wardrobe, just like a good soldier. Highly skilled now in doing as she's told. How on earth did she ever convince herself she was an accomplice, an equal?

In minutes, she has changed into a plain shirtwaist, modest hat, and patterned skirt, with a sensibly sturdy but decidedly unstylish jacket to complete the understated look. Reemerging in the hall, Cora finds no signs of Alice or Béatrice. Dagmar, meanwhile, stands waiting at the door, her hair neatly combed, the lines of her reddened face softened with powder. She takes one of the two parasols she's holding and hands it to Cora, then pulls a thick-knit toque onto her head.

"Come on then," she grunts. "Ale will not drink itself."

They move briskly together down the stairwell, outside into the early evening, and onto the avenue, where Dagmar hails a hansom cab. Cora has no idea where they're going and doesn't ask.

Dagmar is a woman of very few words, which usually is off-putting to Cora, but today there's an odd comfort, allegiance even, in her silence.

It's almost like they're in mourning together.

When the carriage turns off Fifth Avenue and into the mess of the Bowery, though, curiosity finally gets the better of her.

"Where are we going?" Cora asks.

Dagmar lifts a lazy finger to the window, though offers nothing more.

"And why, pray tell, are we here?"

"If you cannot get rid of sorrows for goot?" Dagmar shrugs. "Drown zem for a while."

Cora considers this, hardly game to argue with that airtight logic.

They pull onto a narrow road, past tanneries, shoddy storefronts, tenements with windows scrubbed opaque with dirt. The streets are crowded down here, businessmen heading home after a long day, horses and carriages hitched on both sides, little urchins peddling papers on the corners, wild hogs scampering across the roads. The carriage groans to a halt in front of a nondescript saloon, a flapping wooden sign that simply reads Beer.

"We will have to go in zee back," Dagmar explains.

Cora swallows, reconsidering the sign. "We're going in here?"

"In zee back," Dagmar says again, impatiently. "Women's entrance."

Cora's suddenly feeling . . . nervous? Unprepared? The most she's ever had by way of spirits is the odd glass of wine or champagne here and there, and always in moderation (as per Alice's instructions). Brandy too, once, that Maeve slipped her while they were on the road.

"I've never had beer," she admits.

Dagmar's already halfway out of the carriage, her hat pulled low, parasol extended. "First time for everyzing. Now, come on. Beers are only a cent 'til six."

Cora follows the cook into a dingy alley, around to a door marked Ladies Entrance. The tight, dusty corridor eventually gives way to a cramped saloon, dimly lit, well kept, and packed, with a long oak bar along the opposite wall. Most of the nearby tables are filled with female patrons clustered together chatting or huddled around a card game, half-drunk pints of golden liquid by their sides. The front of the saloon is all men. Workmen in uniforms, soot-stained hands clutching their glasses alongside businessmen in suits and loosened neckties.

Cora feels a wave of shame. An imposter, that's what she is, among all these honest folks putting in their time to eke out a weekly paycheck. People like her old cast members, Dinah and Maeve. Her father too. Meanwhile, here she is, crying about getting married to a millionaire?

Dagmar claims two seats at a table and plunks Cora down into one of the empty chairs.

"Give us four pints, love," she orders, once a waitress appears. "We need to catch up with zee others."

The server returns shortly with four glasses overflowing with foam.

Dagmar slides two Cora's way. "Bottoms up."

Cora nearly chokes on the first sip—the foam isn't sweet, as she assumed, but tart and bitter, the liquid underneath reminiscent of the way the farm smelled in the morning— dewy wheat, sunshine, cut grass. It goes down easy, fills her belly with warmth.

When it's all gone, Cora surprises herself by reaching for the second one.

"Thing is, there are far worse men than Harry," she says, pausing to quietly burp. "He's smart, in his own way. Observant. And without a doubt one of a kind."

"Doez not sound so bad," Dagmar grunts.

Cora takes another long pull from the glass. "Though, fine,

if you insist on the full story, he is . . . also a fair sight peculiar. Truly obsessed . . . with science, particularly the human body. Also coddled, despite his father's ruthless reputation. Bit of a fool, really, when it comes to the way of the world."

"Ze kind of person one might like to dupe," Dagmar amends with a shrug.

Cora sighs. "I'm beginning to worry we're alike in that way."

Dagmar finishes her glass.

"I simply don't understand how Alice could do this to me."

"Alice ez not your friend, *mädchen*." Dagmar holds her gaze steady. "Alice does not have any friends. Only . . . what iz the word in English? *Associates*."

"That's the thing." Cora's stomach twists. "She'd never pull a stunt like this on you or Béa."

"*Ja, freilich*, she would. Besides, you are different. You are face of . . . operation. *Her* operation. One-way street. Ze sooner you get that through your head, ze better it will be." Dagmar's face changes as she scans the room. "Speaking of, I need to conduct some buzness of my own." She nods to Cora's glass. "Put zem on my tab, zey know I am *gut* here."

The cook crosses the room, exchanging hellos with two young women who've just entered—housekeepers, maybe, or ladies' maids. In moments, Dagmar's face positively ignites with pleasure at the sight of a round-faced, burly bartender newly back on break.

The barman throws a rag over his shoulder, ducking under the counter, before spying Dagmar. A bashful, boyish grin curls underneath his thick mustache.

Cora's confused. Could he be part of the Württemberg scheme, a player she doesn't know about?

Dagmar coyly slides over to the bar, the beguiling smile

she's wearing so incongruent with her menacing features that Cora has to stifle a laugh.

Is Dagmar keeping a sweetheart in the Bowery?

Does Alice know?

A laugh bursts out of Cora. She is about to join them, or at least eavesdrop; she's beyond curious . . . but then promptly stops herself. Dagmar is here off the clock. She has her own circle, a real life, an existence outside of Alice's machinations. Whereas Cora has become a puppet, Alice pulling the strings behind her every move.

What has happened to the girl who longed for the spot-light, who had her sights set on besting the world?

Who is she now anyway, besides Phony Miss Cora Ritter from the Kingdom of Balderdash?

Cora chugs the remains of her glass, stands decidedly—if surprisingly unsteadily—and heads toward the bar. Alice would obviously not condone a third pint of ale in the course of twenty minutes, especially not on an empty stomach, which makes securing another glass a *grand* idea.

She edges beside a group of businessmen, thrilling in the impropriety of being a woman alone among men. "Pardon, excuse me, on a very important mission. Barkeep! May I have another?"

Dagmar's sweetheart, who is still busy exchanging sweet nothings with the cook, stands and grunts a reluctant ac-knowledgment. He pours Cora another round and slides the foamy pint across the counter.

"Bottoms up, Alice," Cora declares and downs half the ale.

"Who's Alice?"

She turns. For a second, Cora worries she's imagining things. Again.

But no. Cal Archer, newspaper man, dogged journalist for *The Herald*, is standing in front of her with a half-full glass and a very satisfied smirk.

"What a delightful surprise to find you here, Miss Ritter."

Cora's thoughts ricochet, a game of whiff-whaff. As she was carrying on with Dagmar, taunting her boss halfway across town, was it in her Württembergian lilt? Did Cal spy her earlier and listen in? And how on earth is she going to explain why an emerald heiress is drinking with their cook down in the Bowery?

"I . . ." Cora's mind keeps free-falling. "Württemberg is a country very known for its ale!"

Goodness, is she slurring? A hot, sudden awareness overtakes her. She is not only slurring but swaying. When did that happen?

Cal's blue eyes glimmer from under the bar's lantern light. "Is that so?"

"Yes, er. Indeed, it is. I ask my servants to accompany me down to this area of the city when I'm feeling particularly lonely," she over-enunciates. "It helps with *home*sickness."

Cora scans the room for Dagmar—although, would she make this situation better or worse?

She thrusts her glass forward as evidence, sending half of it sloshing to the floor. "This, here, is the finest in town. In my opinion."

Cal's eyebrow quirks. "If it's so fine, you might want to do better at preserving it."

She places the glass on the bar top, nearly trips.

"Fancy sitting down, Miss Ritter?"

She scoffs. "And where would I sit?"

Cal Archer gestures downward. That smirk again.

There is indeed a stool sandwiched between them.

Her cheeks redden. "If you insist."

She steals another look at the reporter, noticing that he's doing a fairly pitiful job of hiding a laugh. He's looking particularly handsome at this moment, she must admit. Tie loosened, suit jacket off, shirtsleeves rolled just so. A slim vest, no hat.

"I always assumed you had brown hair," she blurts. She managed to hold on to her accent at least.

"Thinking of me when I'm not around?" Mr. Archer smiles. "How thoughtful you are."

"Do you want to buy me another?" She nods to the taps.

"Is that a good idea?" His eyes, still twinkling. Blue eyes, tousled blond hair.

Cora squints. Really, was he always this attractive?

She knows the answer, though—feels it flush across her skin.

"Then again, who am I to pass up the chance to converse with the esteemed Cora Ritter of Württemberg?"

He flags down the barkeep, then turns, refocusing on her.

"Want to tell me why you're really here?" he asks.

"Oh, please. Anything I say, you'll print in . . ." She waves her hands, momentarily and mortifyingly forgetting the name. ". . . that paper."

"I'll have you know I'm more than just 'that paper.'" He slides a drink her way with a wink. "Anything you say tonight is off the record. You have my word."

"Off the record?" Cora takes a sip, picturing Alice in her study, dismissing Cora's entire future with a simple wave of her hand. "Just been a bad day, I suppose. Got some bad news . . . about Würtemberg. My future plans. It seems my cousin . . ."

Cora stops. She's probably breaking at least five different rules of propriety, being here in this bar with a man she's neither engaged nor married to, pretending to be someone she isn't, talking about someone she shouldn't. But now that she's started, she desperately wants to unload to someone—and who better than this charming (no, no, not charming, *worldly*) reporter? The only person in this city who's ever seemed to care about what she has to say? Who is so interested in what she might contribute that he's pursued her around Manhattan? Who's currently looking at her as if he's desperate for her to let him in?

She simply needs to spin the lies this time, in order to confess the truth.

"I am to be married this spring," she begins.

"Ah." Cal's smile hardens. "When?"

"Easter weekend."

"That's soon."

"Yes, it is."

"Tell me, is he an upstanding man? A gentleman?"

"You've met him." She takes another sip. "The young man in Central Park. When we ran into each other several weeks ago."

"Ah yes. Mr. Peyton." Cal turns abruptly, calling, "Barkeep? I'm gonna need a whiskey."

He sighs, stiff smile still fastened on tight. "I suppose congratulations are in order."

"I suppose."

Cal's gaze roams across her features. "If you aren't yet in

a blushing bride state of mind, maybe . . . there is time to reconsider? Postpone for a while? Can't imagine you're in the right headspace to make such a decision, with everything that's going on. In Württemberg."

"No, unfortunately, this needs to happen," she counters. "Immediately. My cousin . . . well, she is a very demanding person."

"The grand duchess?" Cal supplies. "Demanding?"

"You have no idea."

"Enlighten me." Cal leans against the bar. "Here I thought you two were peas in a pod."

Cora lets out a bitter laugh, studying the swirling gold liquid in her glass. Good God, she cannot cry in front of this man.

She blinks the swell back. "She considers it my duty . . . *to Württemberg* . . . to do whatever she asks, whenever she asks, including going forth with this wedding. Thing is . . ."

Cora hastily raises the pint to her lips, the ale a strange sort of temerity fuel.

"I wanted to come to America, you understand, to assist my family. To be on the front lines of . . . soliciting help for our great nation. But I worry that I'm . . ."

Cora pauses, recalibrating. "My late father, you see, the current king's exchequer, was an overly trusting man. He understood that Württemberg has suffered greatly for years, that King Charles has stood by idly for far too long as outside forces took advantage and pillaged our homeland. My father had *agreed* with Prince Wilhelm and the other nationalists calling for change." She pauses. "And yet he still fiercely believed that his king would do the honorable thing. My father blindly deferred to him, trusting him, doing his bidding, until his dying day, just like a fool."

Cora stares once more into her frothy, fast dwindling glass. "I suppose I worry that I'm more like him than I ever realized."

If Cora's ad hoc, thinly veiled soul-baring is giving Cal any pause, he doesn't let on. The man appears wholly engaged, even empathetic, those blue eyes considering her, nonjudgmental. "Is that so?"

"Maybe I am no more than my cousin's pawn. My personal interests, welfare, barely considered, if at all. Maybe the grand duchess values her mission more than anything else, *anyone* else, and in serving her so unquestioningly, I'm only ruining my life in the process." She looks away, cheeks burning. "Please understand, I do admire my cousin greatly. Really hoped I could learn from her—*be* like her, rather. Emulate her. You understand what I mean. She's so regal, elegant—"

He murmurs, "You are more like her than you both realize, I'm afraid."

Cora finds the compliment vaguely disappointing, which emboldens her. "Are you trying to call me pretty, Mr. Archer?"

"As a reporter, that's a hard fact to deny. But no, I wasn't calling you pretty," he repeats with disdain. He downs his whiskey, eyes never leaving hers. "*Resilient* was perhaps the word I was looking for. Resourceful, and ever so refreshing." His eyes lose their playful sparkle, turn serious. "Possibly even exceptional."

As she struggles to recall how and when Cal Archer would have ever spoken at length to the "grand duchess" in order to glean their similarities, he leans closer.

And all thoughts scatter from her mind.

"Your cousin would be a fool herself not to be proud of you," he murmurs. "Though I must come clean. The only reason I'm admitting all this"—he gently taps her head—"is that I don't think you're writing anything down in there either."

The rest of the night is dark and murky, most of the evening's details opaque . . . although fragments flash across her mind like summer lightning:

Dagmar dragging her out of the beer saloon.

The sick-inducing cab ride home.

Singing up the stairwell together.

Béatrice scolding them both as she shuttled them off to sleep.

Cora sits up fast in bed, morning light searing through the curtains.

Another flash, of Cal Archer smiling, leaning over her in that Bowery bar. A sharp throbbing blooms in her head, descends into her chest, and laces all the way down, deep past her abdomen.

She bites her lip.

Good God.

Does she have *feelings* for this man? And far more importantly . . .

What in the Sam Hill did she confess to him last night?

CHAPTER 21

Nobody, a Nuisance

C oraline O'Malley is acting decidedly odd. Alice watches her warily from across the breakfast table as she stirs milk into her coffee.

For one thing, her skin's gone gray. Alice had assumed Cora had taken to her bed all of yesterday out of pique at what Alice has demanded of her, but now she wonders whether an actual stomach ailment is to blame. When Béa laid out the platter of sausages and poached eggs, Cora pushed back a bit from the table as if with revulsion. Now she sits nibbling the edges of a piece of dry toast, furtively, like a mouse, her wide—now bleary—eyes darting to the front entryway every minute or so.

Alice clears her throat. "Expecting a visitor?"

Cora outright startles. "No. At least I hope . . . no, just. The morning papers."

"They've arrived already." Alice frowns, nodding toward the parlor, where she'd left them for later perusal.

Cora jumps from her chair, rattling the table. "Sorry. I . . . Just a moment."

As the girl runs from the room, ostensibly desperate for the latest news headlines, Alice smiles in bewilderment. She attempts to share a look with Béatrice, but Béa has studiously avoided eye contact for days.

Which is all for the better, probably. Best to keep things strictly professional, cut and dry, uncomplicated—

Cora rushes back into the room, her cheeks freshly flushed. As she reclaims her seat at the table, blinking hard as if against a wave of nausea, Alice peers aghast at her fingers, all of them smudged with newsprint ink. She'd admonish the girl to wash her hands before eating, if she was planning to eat anything this morning.

"Anything interesting in the paper?" Alice asks casually.

The color leaves Cora's cheeks again. "No. I . . . was, ah, looking for something. But it wasn't in there. Perhaps tomorrow . . ."

That last bit said more to herself, with a look of swirling dread in her expression.

At the now-obvious scrutiny in Alice's eyes, Cora blinks hard. "I thought they might have posted a society mention about what went on at the Ameses' ball. Or a formal engagement notice. Harry had mentioned he wanted to announce it as soon as possible."

"Ah." Alice sips. "And that concerns you because . . ."

"It doesn't concern me." There is a manic edge to Cora's smile. "I'm excited, is all. To see my name in print. Even if it's, you know . . . not my real name."

Curiouser and curiouser. The last time she and Cora spoke on this subject, Cora was as far from excited about an engagement announcement as a young woman could possibly be.

Alice chooses not to press the point. She cuts her sausage with a smirk. "If your real name winds up in the papers, something has gone terribly wrong."

Cora lets out a shrill laugh, startling the knife out of Alice's hand.

Alice draws a deep breath. "What has gotten into you today? Are you really that jittery over all this? Of all potential liabilities, I did not predict in you a nervous disposition—"

"Nor should you." Cora leans back in awkward imitation of a lady at ease, but Alice can see her gray skin breaking into a sweat. "I've had some time to think, and it's a fine plan, as you said. All of this is going brilliantly. It's all going to work out. It has to."

Alice's frown deepens into an incredulous grimace when the bell rings in the front entry, sending her rising from her seat.

"We're not expecting Ward," she murmurs to Béatrice, who turns to meet her eye at long last.

"Perhaps a message boy," Béa says.

But when Béa opens the door, the person waiting there cuts rather a larger figure.

Cal Archer at least has the courtesy to remove his derby hat before barging inside.

Alice lets out a cry of outrage as the young man breezes past her into the parlor—as if he pays rent here.

"What are you doing?" she cries, trailing him closely.

"Warming up," he says, rubbing his hands together by the lit stove. "Warming up to what I have to say to *you*, that is."

Alice can feel her face purpling with anger. She lowers her voice to a fervent whisper, her eyes darting to the hall, assuring herself no one is approaching. "How many times must I tell you not to come here? Anyone could have seen you come inside!"

Cal turns to face her, his own expression thunderous. "Oh, I was careful. Which is more than I can say for you."

"You're being thoughtless," Alice hisses. "And keep your voice down."

Cal doesn't bother to whisper. "And you're being heartless. How could you possibly sanction this? An actual marriage? Against her will, against common decency—"

"How do *you* know it's against her will?" Alice snaps. "How is this any business of yours?"

He waggles a finger at her. "Oh, don't you play the 'stay in your lane, I'll stay in mine' line with me. That might work on some downtown fence or forger. Hell, it might even work with old McAllister, but not me. I know you far too well for that."

Alice scoffs. "You say you know me? That is a bold claim."

Cal points. "There. That's it. This isn't about clean lanes, not completely. You are punishing me."

"Don't be ridiculous." Alice turns away, waving her hand in exasperation.

"Maybe I deserve it. Hell, I know I do. But if you would only let me atone, Alice—let me in at all. Let *anyone* in!"

"I . . ." A hollow voice echoes from the hall. "You . . ." Cora stands on wobbling legs, staring between the two of them from the doorway as if waking from a dream. "I think this time I'm actually going to . . ."

Cal rushes past Alice to Cora's side, just as Béa steps into the room, ready to drag an armchair near. Between the two of them, they ease Cora into a seat before a legitimate swoon can overtake her.

"Hiya, Béatrice." Cal offers the maid a rueful smile. "Sorry to barge in without a proper hello."

"A proper hello to you too." Béatrice laughs. "Cup of tea?"

"I'd kill for one. You're a *saint*," he drawls, the idiot, then has the gall to call after her, "And I don't suppose Dagmar's made any of those spice cookies lately?"

Alice turns away, pressing a finger against her temple to stave off the stress headache she can already feel building.

"He called you Alice," Cora murmurs. "And your accent . . . You're not . . . doing the accent."

She shakes her head as if trying to clear it of dust.

Alice glares at Cal. He shrugs.

Alice rolls her eyes. "Fine. As you're already apparently better acquainted than I had either expected or planned, I suppose a formal introduction is in order. Cora, this is Calvin Archer. My brother."

"Your *bruh*," seems to be all Cora can say.

"Let's lay it all out for efficiency's sake," Alice says.

Cal snorts. "Quite. Why waste time softening any blow?"

It's lucky she's so practiced at ignoring him. "He's been a part of the plan from the beginning, as he was already well placed as a feature writer at *The Herald*."

Of all things, Cora is starting to look relieved. "So . . . you know?"

"There's no Württemberg resistance movement, there are no emerald mines, there's no duchess or prince—well, actually, the prince is real," Cal recites, fixing Cora with a gentle—one might even call it affectionate?—smile.

Alice leans forward, suspicious.

"I write it all up in the paper as fact," he adds, "jeopardizing the core principles of my very livelihood, knowing full well it's a load of hooey. That, as of today, the only authentic elements of this plan of ours are a single Colombian emerald and a marriage proposal."

Cal whirls on Alice again, livid. She stalks away to stare out the window.

"One that you, apparently, intend to see through?" he goes on. "Ah, bless you."

Alice glances back to see Béa's brought him both tea and those spice cookies he asked for, the traitor.

"I don't understand," Cora says. "Why didn't you tell me?"

Cal keeps his eyes fixed on his sister. "Because Alice asked me not to. She likes to keep things separate, you see. Clean. You're not the only pawn on the board, Cora. God forbid any of us get the full story. Only she can hold it all in her mind, like Athena toying with us mere mortals."

His voice has taken on a poetic tone. It's too much. Alice picks up an embroidered pillow and chucks it at his head.

He swats it away. "Oh! Very mature!"

"But why did you talk to me?" Cora's voice is so soft, Alice can hardly make it out. She's never once seen the girl look so vulnerable. "Wouldn't it have been easier just to stay away?"

"I suppose it would have." Cal frowns, considering the question seriously. Then he grins. "But not half as fun. It gets pretty lonely out there, you know." He nods to the street view. "Staying in my lane. I suppose I thought if my sister wouldn't speak to me, at least I could get little glimmers of how things were going for her through you."

"So you used me." Cora's voice is flat, unreadable.

"I mean, perhaps, at first, but . . . then, no, no, that's not what it was at all. I liked you. Still do. Quite a lot."

Cal and Cora stare at each other in silence.

"You know what's at stake here, Calvin," Alice puts in quietly.

He turns back to her, his cocky smile wiped clean. "I do."

He slumps, apparently chastened. Alice thinks for one blessed moment that he's succumbed to the overriding logic of her strategy.

Then he stands. "But there's got to be a better way, one that doesn't involve throwing a lamb to the wolves."

Alice snorts. "Harry Peyton is hardly a wolf."

"I think . . . he'd be the lamb in this analogy," Cora reluctantly admits.

"Listen, you've said your piece." Alice sighs. "But we are running a risk having you in here for this long. Take your . . . your spice cookies—"

"They are called *pfeffernusse!*" Dagmar shouts from all the way in the kitchen. Lord, the woman really does have ears like a bloodhound. "Not spice cookie."

"Do what you're best at, dear brother." Alice wraps the *pfeffernusse* in a cloth napkin. "Pick a moment no one is watching and go."

"Ouch." Cal accepts the bundle with an unblinking glare, submits to Béatrice's apologetic fetching of his hat and coat.

He bows to a still bewildered Cora, then draws a breath as if to speechify once again.

"Heaven's sake, surely you can speed this up!" Alice snaps.

Cal whirls around. "That's it. That's what we'll do."

Utterly exhausted now, Alice flops onto the settee so ungracefully that even Cora's eyes widen at the sight of it.

Cal hands Béatrice his coat and hat again, then strides to the fire to stoke it—an ominous sign of his intention to settle in once more. "We'll speed it up. All of it. What was it you told me, Allie-girl?"

"Allie-girl?" Cora mutters incredulously.

"It's all coming together more quickly than you'd anticipated?" Cal's eyes have lit up.

Alice blinks in protest. "By which I meant the marks. Getting them all in the same room and—"

"And now they're all lining up to invest in the mining
company. Isn't that so, Cora?"

Cora sits up. "Well, yes, I think so. All but the Witts."

"The Witts are interested," Alice reluctantly admits. "Ward
dropped a surreptitious mention over tea. Iris chased him out
the door, demanding to know more. The only one missing so
far"—she stares meaningfully at Cora—"is Harold Peyton."

"I don't know Cora all that well yet," Cal starts. Alice notes
that *yet* in judgmental silence. "But something tells me she
could wrangle an investment out of that Peyton kid by six
o'clock on a Sunday morning."

"He did propose rather quickly," Cora says, her expression
brightening with hope. "I don't think a pledge will be much of
a leap for him at this point."

"Interesting," Alice says. Also interesting is that her brother
is gripping his teacup so tightly it looks like he might shatter
it. "So what are you suggesting?"

"We move it up," Cal says, eagerly grasping onto the slight
subject change. "The gem evaluations, the sting, all of it."

Alice's heart starts to race. "You mean before—"

"Before Easter, yes," Cal says, glancing at Cora. "So our
dear friend here doesn't have to tie any knots." He smirks.
"With *him*, anyway."

"You do understand that carves our remaining timeline
in half, putting investment day, what? Little more than a
month from now?" Alice rises, walking the length of the

room, processing it all. "And there's still the matter of the embassy—"

"I may have an answer there too," Cal says. "Chum of mine in the international beat says Finland can't afford the rent on Embassy Row anymore. I can put in a deposit—today, even. Not in my own name, naturally."

"Naturally," Alice repeats dryly. "You really are hell-bent on this, aren't you?"

Cal meets Cora's eyes. Something passes between them that Alice can't decipher.

He turns back to Alice with a shrug. "Sooner we all get paid and get gone, the better, right?"

At long last, he takes that as a cue to exit.

Alice follows him to the door.

As he adjusts his hat, Alice reaches for his hand. Warmth fills her at his reaction to the gesture—so open-faced and earnest, just as he was as a boy.

"You need to stay away from her now," she says.

He winces. "I—"

"I don't care what there may be between you. She has a job to do. And she can't do it with you filling her head with nonsense."

A muscle works in his jaw. After a moment he nods, buttons his coat, and goes.

And as Alice watches him leave, unnoticed by any onlookers on the sidewalk, she feels the loss of him as freshly as the day he packed his bag and set out from Poughkeepsie with nary a look back.

But there's no use in sentiment. Not unless you can leverage it to a greater cause.

"Cora," she calls sharply, summoning the girl from the kitchen, where she's apparently launched into an impromptu celebration over her potentially canceled nuptials, she and Béa both sitting atop the counter, emptying glasses of liqueur from a bottle Dagmar is still holding high. "I've noticed you've got a particular skill with *legerdemain*."

"Béatrice?" Cora looks to the maid. "Care to translate?"

"I believe that in this context," Béa says, "it means robbing someone. Without getting caught."

"I'd like your guidance here, Cora," Alice says lightly.

"Ah." Cora's face, already growing rosy with fresh hope, brightens a few watts more. "Right. Happy to oblige."

"Let's say you were at the Metropolitan Opera House and you needed to replace the necklace Mimi Vandemeer was wearing with a fake. What would be your strategy?"

"Oh. Well, first, I suppose, we'd need to arrange to bump into her. Naturally, of course. Stage some kind of accident. We should choose somewhere either completely solitary or chaotically crowded." Cora's eyes dart to Alice's. "I do assume we can drop the hypothetical now?"

Alice shrugs, caught. "A fair assumption."

Cora grins. She straightens, hands clasped to her heart, sighing, "I'll finally get to wear the opera gown!"

Alice has to turn quickly away to keep in a far-too-fond laugh.

CHAPTER 22

High-Wire Act

March 17, 1884

W hat a wonderfully appropriate performance to-night, wouldn't you agree, Mr. Peyton?" Mrs. Ames winks like a doting aunt at Cora and Harry before taking her seat beside Arabella and her husband of few words in the first row of their private opera box. "A story of love, romance, *amore!*"

From what Cora's heard about *Carmen*, it's actually about the power of one selfish woman to destroy the life of the man who falls in love with her. But given that Harry, her own intended object of seduction, is sitting rigidly beside her, it feels best to keep that observation to herself.

Harry glances briefly at Arabella before taking Cora's hand and giving it a perfunctory kiss. "Indeed, Mrs. Ames. Maybe the Met knew we would be coming."

The performance already began before they could take their seats. A cigar factory scene, female choristers singing. Apparently it would be beyond the pale to arrive on time for the opera, she learned recently. That's when all the more inexpensive seats below are filled. On this level, arrivals are far more leisurely.

Cora must admit, she'd have liked to hear the overture.

A woman enters the scene, draped in beads and gossamer scarves, exotic even for this Spain-set scene. All eyes onstage and off turn to her, just in time for her to begin to sing, deeply, soulfully, and yes—seductively.

Cora flashes Harry a suggestive smile before she, too, considers Arabella. Her smile turns hollow. It's impossible to ignore how positively peaked the poor girl looks tonight. She appears to be wearing powder, as if to cover splotchy skin, but it's her puffy eyes that bear the marks of recent crying.

As if to consciously block Cora's view of her daughter, Mrs. Ames whips her fan open and puts it to immediate use. Cora herself feels no need of her fan, clasped daintily in her lap. The air up here is rarified in more ways than one, nice and cool against Cora's skin—of which, in this particularly low-cut gown, much has been bared, as per usual these days. Up here in the Diamond Horseshoe, as they call these prized box seats, she feels laid open to society. On display. Exposed.

Or perhaps that's her mounting jitters over just how much she's meant to achieve tonight, and the height of this upper-level private box is not helping quell the vertiginous sensation of being about to fall off a cliff.

The Metropolitan Opera House, Cora's learned, has been open only since October, which may explain why this magnificent space still smells of fresh paint. Despite how new she is to this world, she can clearly see why the house has asserted itself as *the* fashionable place to convene on Monday evenings in the span of one season. A true feat of design, ingenuity, and the power of persuasion. Huge, sparkling chandeliers float atop a pasture-sized audience, the curved walls lined, floor to ceiling, with spacious gilded boxes, like lace on the bustle of a massive dress. Downtown's Academy of Music hardly stands a chance of survival when faced with this competition. One triumph among many for the "new money" millionaires who helped fund the place, including the company Cora is currently keeping.

The Ameses' box is situated close to the center of the upper ring, though still not as central as Mrs. Ames would have liked (she's mentioned something to that effect at least five times tonight), and most certainly not as primely positioned as the Vandemeers' box, which Cora has been watching surreptitiously since the moment they took their seats.

The pretty, perpetually scowling Mimi Vandemeer, dressed all in white, is hard to miss. She's somehow positioned herself so that the lantern light reflects against the emerald solitaire, making it shine like a green beacon even from this distance. The woman seated beside Mimi is far more subdued in a gown of deep blue, in keeping with her perpetual state of somber fretting over the fate of Württemberg.

No amount of staring will amend the situation, but Cora can't help but inwardly gripe over Alice's placement—right beside the damned necklace! If only *Alice* had the deft hands. For once, she could be the one carrying out someone else's strategy. And if only Cora's own invitation into the Vandemeers' box hadn't been preempted by Harry Peyton's insistence that they attend the opera together, as a newly betrothed couple, in the box of his dear friends, the Ameses.

Alice, as usual, was unperturbed.

"I'm sure you'll figure out a pretext for visiting us," she'd said and left it at that. What a time to finally have trust placed in her.

And now here Cora is. In position and out of ideas.

Down onstage, a sweet-voiced soprano sings to the tenor hero. Thanks to Béa's lessons, Cora can make out a few of the words in the French libretto. Something about a letter, an engagement?

Cora presses her hand to Harry's and nods to the stage. "Who is she?"

"Michaëla," Arabella supplies. "His childhood sweetheart. Still in love with him, the fool."

The box grows quiet. A discomfited Harry begins pulling at his collar.

"Apologies." Arabella's pale cheeks turn rosy. "You were asking Mr. Peyton, not me."

She buries her face in her program.

"And yet, very useful," Cora chirps. "Thank you, Arabella. Have you seen *Carmen* before?"

Arabella stays quiet.

"You'll have to forgive my gloomy daughter." Mrs. Ames leans conspiratorially toward Cora and Harry. "She's pining for your cousin, the prince. Perhaps this opera is a bit heavy for her current spirits, but I thought this a perfect introduction to the opera for our Württembergian friends." She flashes Cora a cloying smile. Then her eyes dart resentfully across the theater to the Vandemeers' box. "Pity the duchess was unable to accept our invitation."

"It was only that the Vandemeers asked her first." Cora dares a little wink. "You know how they do so love to be first."

"Indeed!" Mrs. Ames covers her snicker with her fan. "Very

aptly observed, my dear. I dare say, one visit to New York and you're as canny as a native . . . and may I also say, we so hope to enjoy the closest possible relations with your dear family for many years to come."

Cora valiantly resists the urge to roll her eyes. Had the devil himself arrived in New York and offered the Ames family a royal title, Mrs. Ames would have had her daughter penning letters to hell for the past three months. *Who has been keeping up the other side of this princely correspondence?* she wonders now. *Béatrice? Mr. McAllister? Alice herself?*

Cora lets out a giggle at the very thought. Mrs. Ames blinks, affronted.

"Forgive my wandering mind," Cora says carefully. "I was caught in imaginings of all of these good times. Our new beginning here in this grand city."

As Mrs. Ames nods, apparently mollified by that, Cora moves on, gazing across the open space, scanning the boxes surrounding them. There's Ward in ridiculous white tails beside the stout, regal Mrs. Astor. The Witt and the Ogden booths side by side—Mrs. Witt ignoring the opera entirely while whispering something into the ear of her guest. Mr. Ogden staring rather obviously at Alice in the next box.

And Alice staring daggers at Cora.

Cora sits back, face flushing. Perhaps it's time to use her own damned fan.

"There will be many visits to Württemberg on the horizon as well, no doubt," Mrs. Ames says, drawing Cora's attention once again.

Cora blinks, perplexed.

"Once the conflict has been resolved." Mrs. Ames leans closer to speak over the swelling orchestrations filling the opera house. "We'd thought perhaps to divide our time between there and here once Arabella is wed."

Harry leans across Cora. "After the weddings, I expect our families will grow closer than ever," he says emphatically. "Like we used to be. For all the years to come."

Arabella turns to peer at him with those waiflike eyes of hers, not exactly looking as if she's happy with that forecast.

Harry looks away, suddenly flushed.

Cora chases away the guilt, teasing her throat like the start of a cold. She has a job to do tonight, no room for doubt. Alice may never think of her as an equal, or value her to the extent she might Mr. McAllister or Béa, but she is uniquely relying on Cora tonight.

And it's time to deliver.

The theater erupts into applause as the curtain closes and houselights rise throughout the vast space.

"Intermission," Mr. Ames grunts, walking out of the box more quickly than Cora's ever before seen the man move. Not a fan of the opera, apparently. "Let's go find a drink."

"Oh, darling!" Mrs. Ames laughs awkwardly. "He does have a knack for putting into five words what it would take me seventy to say. A drink. Yes, let's."

Across the expanse of the Met, Mimi Vandemeer rises from her seat and turns to speak to someone. Alice stands more slowly, staring at the exposed clasp on the back of Mimi's neck. Then back at Cora.

Not the most subtle reminder, Alice. Cora nods back: *Message received.* Get the necklace. Swap it with another. Don't get caught. Simple, yes? It's only a matter of where and when.

She turns to Harry, ready to suggest a visit to the Vandemeers' box, citing a burning desire to visit with her dear friend

Mimi—given how Harry's been sequestered from society, Cora can't imagine he realizes that no one considers the gossiping Mimi an actual friend—but the view across the theater scuppers that plan before she can even attempt it.

Apart from Mrs. Vandemeer, who has settled in next to Alice with two fresh coupes of champagne, the box across the way has emptied out. For whatever reason, Mimi is on the move.

"Shall we stretch our legs?" Cora suggests.

"Let's join the Ameses in the saloon." Harry offers his arm. He turns back to the still-seated Arabella. "Will you come too, Arabella?"

The girl shakes her head with a tentative smile. "I'm all right here."

Most certainly for the best. Last thing Cora needs right now is Harry's own "Michaëla" tagging along all night. She ignores the fresh stab of compunction at the toll this is taking on Arabella . . . which, she realizes, is truly nothing compared to the fate due to befall her entire family, and her old friend Harry, in a matter of weeks.

Harry smiles blithely as they pass among the crowds in the gilded outer halls. "Would you care for champagne? Believe I could use a glass myself."

"That would be lovely," Cora agrees, throat still tight.

Inside the central saloon, there is a sprawling ornate bar, with several barkeeps behind it pouring drinks for the well-heeled men approaching, while waiters in long tails circulate the room with trays bearing champagne glasses. The room is a swirl of color and flash, even finer gowns and jewels on display than at the Patriarch's Ball. But the one jewel Cora's looking for, she cannot seem to locate.

Wherever Mimi Vandemeer has wandered off to, it isn't this saloon.

First of three intermissions, Cora reminds herself. *There is still time.*

But not much, goodness knows. Given that their timeline for the embassy coup has now advanced, getting those emeralds back is crucial; the gems *must* be in Alice's possession when she meets with the Ogdens for their own valuation tomorrow. Mimi Vandemeer needs to walk out onto Broadway tonight with green glass around her neck or—

"Are you enjoying the show?" Harry asks, dutifully taking her hand as they make their way through the milling crowd. "I wonder, does your homeland have an opera house?"

"We do indeed, Mr. Peyton. The grand Württemberg Opera House, in Stuttgart. I am sure you will love it as much as I do."

"I do hope Arabella will love it too—ah, rather, will feel at home. There. In your country." Harry swallows, his grip tightening around Cora's hand. "She seems so out of sorts tonight, does she not?"

"I think she's preoccupied with the play." *Enough of this.* Cora loops her arm through his, pulling him closer. "You are a very good friend, Mr. Peyton, worrying about her well-being," she purrs. "A very upstanding man."

This finally draws a real smile out of him, his face igniting with relief.

By all appearances, they do make for a handsome couple tonight—Harry in his new navy ditto suit, his dark hair slicked and parted. Cora's truly exquisite gown, her favorite yet, the pale pink chiffon embroidered with stunning silver rosettes. Does Harry suspect it's all a performance, a trick, even on some subconscious level?

Cora steals another look at him, but he's now preoccupied, flagging a waiter, who approaches promptly to offer them both champagne.

As she's halfway through her glass, however, the bell announcing the end of the first intermission sounds. The flow of traffic shifts back to the hallway, pulling her and Harry along in its wake, all the way back to the Ameses' box for the opera's second act.

And that's the first chance gone.

Nerves singing now, Cora dares a glance at the Vandemeer booth as the houselights dim once again. Mimi's back beside Alice. And Alice looks absolutely livid.

Cora turns her attention pointedly to the stage, roiling herself.

What does she expect me to do? Sprint away from present company all the way to the other box and tackle Mimi Vandemeer in plain view of the entire theater?

Actually, that may be exactly what Alice expects.

As the sunken orchestra jumps playfully into a jaunty tune, Carmen and her female friends process around the stage, dancing flirtatiously with the men seated around what looks to be an inn. Then there begins a sort of ballet in the style of bullfighters—the men showing off their youthful vigor to the women—before Carmen begins to sing her sultry song.

Cora's cheeks grow hot in the dark, thoughts turning, of all things, to that night downtown with Dagmar. And . . . Cal Archer. She still cannot wrap her mind around the reality that he is Alice's brother, who has been duping her all the while she thought she was duping him. She also cannot wrap her tangled mind around her feelings for him. Cal has no doubt been an unforeseen and welcome diversion to this whole undertaking—but he is also a liar.

Although, she supposes, that does make two of them.

In quieter moments, she's taken to replaying every single interaction between them, searching for signs, moments she could consider a different way, like a gem that takes on new dimensions under the light.

Like, say, an *emerald*.

Cora swallows hard. Time is ticking, options dwindling.

Across the theater, Mimi idly strokes her necklace, unknowingly taunting her.

Carmen's second act is quite stirring. Cora is pleased to find that even with her limited French, she can follow the plot just fine. Without really intending to, she sinks into the story. The curtain close at the end of act 2 subsequently comes as a jarring surprise.

Second intermission. The lights turning on, the crowd below rising into animated conversation.

Cora looks again to the Vandemeers' box, readying herself to begin tracking them, trailing them. But this time Mimi stays in her seat, stretching her arms with an extravagant yawn.

"I should like to stretch my legs, beat the crowd this time," Harry says, standing. "You stay here."

"Oh!" Cora shakes her head. "But—"

"I insist." And he's gone, right on the heels of Mr. and Mrs. Ames, off to visit with the Ogdens, if Cora's heard correctly.

Cora stands staring at the Vandemeer booth, rendered immobile by newly learned social mores. She'll drink her champagne when Harry returns and then she'll go; she'll run if she has to.

"Do you think I'm a fool?"

Cora startles and turns. She nearly forgot Arabella was still here.

The girl looks ghostlike in the corner, ivory dress making her milky skin appear bone white.

"Of course not," Cora says, careful as porcelain. "Whyever would I?"

Arabella sighs. "Pinning all my hopes on someone I've never met. Rather than . . . well, it doesn't matter, does it?"

Cora's heart settles down to a more manageable pace. "You mean my cousin? I can assure you, he's a man of honor. You couldn't choose anyone more solid to, ah, pin your hopes on."

"He sounds like Harry," Arabella says, rather wistfully. She brightens, with effort, extending a hand to Cora. "You've made such a good choice, Miss Ritter. I've known Harry my entire life. He is such a find. Brilliant, in his way. A truly thoughtful, curious person, who sees the good in everyone."

"Yes," Cora agrees, perhaps too hastily, taking Arabella's hand. "I could see that about him from the start."

"I only hope I shall find a happiness equal to what you two have found." Arabella sounds the furthest thing from happy right now.

"The barkeep convinced me to purchase a bottle," Harry says sheepishly as he enters the booth again, cradling three empty coupes in one arm. With hope, he looks to Arabella. "I'd love to *uncork* one smile out of you tonight, Bella."

Arabella's eyes glisten, but she musters a grin.

As Harry begins happily pouring, Cora seizes on the momentary distraction.

"Oh heavens," she blurts. "Mimi will be so put out if I don't at least say hello—"

And then she's out the door like a cannon blast . . . only to be waylaid by Ward McAllister, who appears to be standing in wait for Cora, his hand outstretched like a horse tamer, a look of sharp amusement in his eye. "Not so fast, my dear, not nearly so fast."

A sour taste rises in Cora's mouth at the sight of him. She cannot say why, but she's most certainly grown to dislike the man. Perhaps only because she's jealous. He's clearly a true associate of Alice's, or however Dagmar put it during their visit to the saloon. And by that logic, Ward knows the whole game far better than she does.

Cora supposes she'd be wise to listen to him.

"We're halfway through intermission," she whispers, drawing nearer.

"Which leaves me just enough time to stop you from making a colossal mistake," he drawls, that "cat who stole the cream" expression plastered thick on his bearded face. He takes Cora's arm and strolls with her farther down the hall from the saloon crowd. "If you undertake this swap of yours in the booth, as you are no doubt planning, you'll have all of New York high society as witness to it. That emerald's already drawn their eye. The Vandemeers' box is practically a second opera stage tonight. I know you're a consummate performer, but surely this is a magic trick you'd prefer not be talked about all over town for days to come."

There's a whole lot of sense in what he's saying, loath as Cora is to admit it.

"What are you suggesting?" she whispers back.

"Something a bit more intimate?" He shrugs, nodding at the ringing bell signaling the end of the second intermission. "And I urge you to make it snappy."

He pivots away with his walking stick before she can grab it and slap the man with it.

Back in the Ameses' box, Cora takes her seat beside Harry with a manic smile.

Intimate. Not in the box itself. Someplace private.

Farther along the box seat arc, she sees that Mr. McAllister has returned to Mrs. Astor's box with refreshments, looking irritatingly undaunted as he takes his seat.

"Do sit down, Arabella; you're blocking the way." Mrs. Ames settles into her seat, nudging her daughter back into the corner.

As the houselights sink, so do Cora's spirits, her head pounding with the realization that she may well have minutes before it's too late and their entire plan—all the ground they've laid this season—is destroyed, and all because of her shortcomings. But what is there to do? She cannot fly across the opera house and force Mimi Vandemeer to use the water closet.

"Good grief, I've overfilled this," Harry says, handing her the glass. "Sorry, dear."

She looks down at her wine.

Yes. Wine. That's it!

Cora perches on the edge of her seat and stares at the Vandemeers' box. For once, Alice isn't watching her. Of all the luck!

Cora takes her own turn boring holes into Alice, wishing she could channel Prospero and will the woman to look up and see her. Seconds pass. A full minute, a quiet romantic scene below, and then finally, *finally* Alice takes a sip of her wine as she glares accusingly across the theater.

She catches Cora's pointedly wide eyes, her own expression faltering.

Cora furtively downs her glass of champagne. She discreetly mimes dumping the glass beside her, careful not to draw any unwanted attention.

Alice raises her eyebrows. Cora knows this expression. It is Alice's signature "have you gone entirely mad?" look.

Cora puts her glass down, clandestinely rattles her hand back and forth, before miming dumping the invisible contents of this invisible glass onto Harry's lap.

"Everything all right?" Harry murmurs, wide-eyed, beside her.

"Quite," Cora says. "This scene is just so romantic. I feel rather fevered."

"Your temperature is rising?"

"Only in the figurative sense," Cora hisses, eyes on Alice, who now glances at Mimi. *Perhaps she understands?*

Alice shifts in her seat, eyeing Mimi's lap.

Do it, Cora pleads silently, an incantation. *Now, now, now—*

But rather than spill her own glass, Alice adjusts her body suddenly so that it's Mimi's glass that's jostled, dumping its contents straight onto her lily-white gown.

Mimi leaps up, shaking her dress—fully splattered, not with champagne but cabernet!

Alice, clever thing that she is, backs away in apparent horror, signaling to the box steward to bring fresh napkins.

Cora rises, clutching her fan tightly.

"On second thought, Mr. Peyton, I do think I need to excuse myself. In the corporeal sense. Be right back."

Cora whisks out of her box just as Mrs. Vandemeer and Mimi exit theirs.

She picks up her skirts, racing down the lush, red-carpeted hall and around the nearby circular set of stairs. She needs to beat the Vandemeers to the parlor water closet or this is all for naught.

"Do be careful, madame," an opera officiant tells her as she rounds another corner.

"This *is* me careful," she mutters, flying past.

Cora hears muffled voices—complaints?—emanating from the opposite side of the hall. She ducks into the parlor's water closet, shuts the door. She attempts to calm her breath, arranges herself right at the entrance, braces for impact.

The door to the water closet hits her squarely as Mimi and Mrs. Vandemeer barrel inside.

Cora stumbles forward, knocking shoulders with Mrs. Vandermeer exactly as her hand finds the back of Mimi's neck as if scrabbling for purchase and—

Mimi's necklace clasp comes undone, the emerald solitaire sliding to the floor with a *clink*.

"Goodness," Cora mutters dazedly, staggering one step forward so that her long gown overhangs the necklace on the floor.

"Why, Miss Ritter." Mrs. Vandemeer sounds more irked than concerned. "Oh, what a night this has been."

She waves vaguely at her daughter's ruined dress, appearing just as dazed as Cora herself is feigning to be. But then, Cora is getting the distinct sense that "dazed" is very much Mrs. Vandemeer's modus operandi.

"More drama offstage than on," Mimi mutters, swatting furiously at the stain. "And not even the fun kind."

"Are you all right?" Mrs. Vandemeer asks Cora, inspecting her rather reluctantly.

Cora feigns wooziness, clutching the washbasin.

"Yes, I . . ." She blinks rapidly, reeling back, as if confused. "Oh dear, your necklace, Mimi."

She stoops down to pick up the glass counterfeit she's

slipped from between the folds of her fan and hands it to Mrs. Vandermeer with a frown.

"Perhaps the clasp broke?" she says, carefully handing her the fake. "Let's hope it's a simple fix."

"I didn't feel it fall off," Mimi squawks.

Mrs. Vandemeer swats at her idly with the edge of her fur stole. "And yet *another* moment of carelessness. You simply do not value a thing we buy you."

"And your lovely dress . . ." Cora frowns in sympathy as she considers Alice's handiwork. She isn't entirely unskilled in dexterity—Alice succeeded with a direct hit, a large bloom of red from beaded waistline near to the hem.

"It wasn't my fault, Mother. It was that *German* woman." Mimi spits the word out.

Mrs. Vandemeer's pretty face goes pale in the mirror. "Enough histrionics. My nerves simply cannot take it. Oh la. At least there will be few people milling the halls to watch us go."

"Go?" Mimi whines. "Now? But I wanted to see Carmen get stabbed."

Mrs. Vandemeer closes her eyes and inhales. "Mimi, darling, you're the one who looks like she's been stabbed. I do believe I'd like to call this night what it is—a disaster. Let us cut our losses and go."

Cut our losses. They have no idea.

"I'm sorry to hear that." Cora sighs in commiseration. "Would you like me to accompany you out?"

"That is hardly necessary." Mrs. Vandemeer stares down lovingly at the green glass pendant cupped in her hand, none the wiser. "If you don't mind letting my husband know . . . and better invite your cousin into the Ameses' box. Oh, what a muddle. Give the duchess my thanks, I suppose. This emerald had the entire mezzanine in a tizzy."

Mrs. Vandemeer shares a laconic, superior smile with her daughter.

"They do like to gawk." Mimi smirks. "The peasants."

Any sympathy Cora might have felt for either of them evaporates once again.

Still, Cora laughs along with them. "Part of the price of admission, I am sure."

Then she bids adieu to her unsuspecting marks, only allowing herself a hearty exhalation once she's out the door, the real Colombian emerald safely tucked into the cutout compartment in her fan.

A showstopper of a trick, if she does say so herself.

PART 3

The Prestige

Fiat justitia, pereat coelum.
(Let justice be done, though heaven fall.)
—JOHN QUINCY ADAMS

CHAPTER 23

Water Tank

OGDEN

Angle: Carnality

Priscilla Ogden's lady's maid rubs chamomile-scented lotion into Priscilla's forearms before presenting her with the long gloves she'll wear until dinner is served. Her husband finds her raised veins unsightly. He tries to hide his reaction—his good heart will not allow him to hurt his wife's feelings—but Priscilla has noted it nonetheless and covers her legs, ankles, and arms as much as she possibly can. Thick, layered necklaces draped tight around her neck disguise the increasing crepe effect of her skin. Cosmetics do the rest. And prayer.

She was so beautiful once. Long and languid, like a painting of the pre-Raphaelite school. Artists once begged her to pose for them. Young men jostled across a crowded ball to secure dances with her, and she received no fewer than four proposals that first social season. There was no question whom she would choose. Brett Ogden was like a knight on a steed, just as beautiful and well mannered and wealthy, and he loved her ardently. He truly did. He still does and Priscilla knows it, even if he doesn't visit her bedroom at night anymore. That's to do with his grief over their lack of children, not her. He's said as much.

No, Brett is the soul of faithfulness and honor. It is only that womankind is so treacherous! There are so many traps set throughout the city every day, women whose eyes turn to her husband, who intend to draw him away, to lure him into their bed and into ruin. Cruel creatures, these females.

Priscilla has even begun to wonder about her lady's maid. She'd selected her precisely because she was the plainest of all the options her housekeeper presented to her, but there's a certain blush to her cheeks now. A confident swing to her slim hips that was not once apparent. She'll have to send her packing. But that's a problem for tomorrow.

"That will be all," Priscilla says coolly, as her (temporary) maid affixes a pearl comb into her piled graying hair.

She has one ally, at least, among the fairer and fouler sex. The duchess truly has no designs upon her husband. Priscilla can see that now. Her new friend's mind is dispassionately and reassuringly affixed upon the fate of her nation.

Priscilla rises from her dressing table with a smile that sours quickly as she remembers the other guest tonight. She shall have to watch the young heiress closely.

"Fefu! Fritz!" She calls for her dogs and they rush to follow at her heels.

What a comfort they are. At least they still come when she beckons them.

※　※　※

"Spectacular," Mr. Ogden breathes.

For once, he's not looking at Alice.

The emerald, now loose from its setting, lays before them on a simple square of silk.

Mr. Ogden reaches for the stone, then pulls his hand back with visible effort. "May I?"

"Of course," Alice replies softly. She glances past Ward, sipping his post-dinner madeira in the corner of the parlor, where Cora makes a fuss over Mrs. Ogden's two terriers, to Priscilla's grudging approval. If Cora isn't in fact an animal lover, she's putting on one hell of a performance. Even Mr. Ogden's eyes dart over to her from time to time.

"I hope you don't find this too forward," he murmurs now, subtly adjusting his body so his shoulder grazes Alice's. "But I should like to have this stone appraised."

Alice affects a practiced bewilderment. "For what purpose?"

"Why, for yours alone," he says, his voice an intense rumble as he holds the stone up to the lantern light, as if he has a keen enough eye to check for inclusions himself. "So that you know your worth at last."

There are ways to feign a blush, Alice has learned. Not the color itself, but a tipped chin, averted eyes, lips lifting at the corners as if compelled to do so by a flood of unexpected emotion.

"McAllister here tells me there's been interest in your family's mining company," Brett Ogden goes on. Ward raises his glass in acknowledgment. "I would not be a true friend to you if I didn't do everything in my power to make sure your interests are fully looked after. In fact . . ."

He shoots her a rueful smile. No doubt, in his youth—perhaps even now—that plaintive expression coupled with his roguishly handsome features would make some women weak at the knees.

He presses his hand to hers, his pinkie finger playing against the fabric on her knee. "If you were to get into bed with any New York businessman, I would hope it would be me. If you'll forgive the expression."

There's a momentary silence in the parlor, Mrs. Ogden's attention caught afresh on their conversation, then Cora squeals. "And look how he can fetch! What a darling."

One of the terriers—is this one Fritz?—darts past Alice's legs and back. She adjusts her skirts to keep them from being trampled yet again. When she looks up, she finds Ogden's attention has wandered across the room.

"Your niece is very charming," Ogden says. "How old is she?"

"Cousin," Alice corrects. "Miss Ritter is twenty-two."

"Ah. In the first bloom of womanhood."

Across the parlor table, Ward's eyes meet Alice's, flashing consternation. He sets down his wineglass. "Now, I might be talkin' out of turn here, but I don't think the duchess is completely averse to the idea of you investing in this company of hers."

"It is a matter of trust," Alice puts in, returning to the script. "Nothing is pure business in Württemberg, unlike here, you see. Friendship is a commodity of its own and—"

Ogden stands, newly distracted. "What do you say to a little music? Miss Ritter, an accomplished young lady like yourself must possess some musical gifts, no?"

Cora glances between Alice and Ward, eyes wide.

Mrs. Ogden attempts a wavering smile as she strokes the dog on her lap. "I myself was quite skilled at the pianoforte at your age. Some said I could have pursued a career in music, before love came along and scuppered those plans."

She gazes adoringly up at her husband, but when he strides across the parlor, it's Cora to whom he offers a hand.

Taking it, she stands. "I . . . suppose I do have a fair singing voice."

She does, Alice recalls. The girl has a habit of drifting around the Third Avenue house singing to herself like the heroine of a two-bit operetta. It's a sweet tone. Rather *too* enchanting for tonight's audience.

Alice waits for Cora to look at her so she can offer a slight head shake, a flash of her eyes, any subtle signal she can muster that this is not a man whose attentions the girl will want fixed upon her.

But Cora does not look over.

"Excellent!" Mr. Ogden claps, invigorated. "Priscilla, darling, perhaps you'll serve as her accompanist."

He points his wife toward the piano.

Before she can assume the bench, Alice jolts upright.

"Cora, dear, will you be so kind as to sing one of our Württembergian folk songs? They are among the great gems of our culture"—she is careful to insert that word back into the conversation—"and we would so love to spread our songs beyond our borders."

Priscilla Ogden frowns deeply. "I wouldn't know how to begin to play along with that."

"No need!" Alice smiles. "Our songs are traditionally un-accompanied by instruments."

She lifts her nearly empty glass and Ogden moves to fill it, though his eyes remain raptly fixed on Cora. They erred in dressing the girl quite so fetchingly tonight. Alice hadn't predicted this wrinkle, but she ought to have. She could kick herself now.

"That's right." Cora smiles in apparent relief. "They are extemporaneous expressions of—"

"Yodeling," Alice cuts in sharply, praying the girl understands the assignment. "You may know the style best as yodeling."

Cora swallows around her smile. "Yes."

"Yodeling," Mrs. Ogden repeats.

"Well, I for one would very much like to hear this," Ward crows, turning his chair around to face Cora.

"I'm not sure I'm in very good voice tonight," Cora demurs. "Bit of a tickle in my throat."

"Oh pishposh." Alice laughs. "Why, I heard you singing '*Unt Demelische in Pleinden*' just this morning. Your sudden variations in tonality were thrilling. Go on, why don't you give that song a go? I'll note for our audience that this song is sung in an old dialect of Württemberg, rarely spoken these days apart from some of our elderly rural citizens."

Now Cora's stormy eyes meet hers, relaying fresh alarm. Alice tries to remain placid, with all eyes upon her, but feels her forehead begin to crease.

Do it, please, she silently signals. *It's for your own good.*

Cora's eyes clear. She understands.

"Very well." Cora clasps her hands formally in front of her bosom. "'*Unt . . . Demelisk . . . in Pleinum.*'"

As Alice sits, she motions for Mr. Ogden to retake his seat beside her.

Cora draws a deep breath and begins.

"*In de pelleper gons phillipa, den shutten goss ver plitti-plat—*"

"She is describing our brooks and rivers," Alice murmurs low into Ogden's ear, her own voice like velvet. She feels his attention returning to her, bit by bit.

"*Unt fa bellingen sha pilsner . . . ,*" Cora goes on, her voice rising rather too prettily.

"And here is where the warbling really kicks in!" Alice announces, clapping.

Cora grits her teeth for a beat, before going on, "*In Pl-EI-ei-EI-ei-EI-num.*"

"Heavens," Mrs. Ogden breathes.

"And again!" Alice chirps.

Cora's yodel is even more impressive in the recapitulation: "*In Plei-EI-ei-EI-ei-EI-ei-nuuuuuuuuuum.*"

If this song reminds Alice of anything, it's the howling of stray cats in heat in the alley below their house. The poor girl is perfectly—and she does mean *perfectly*—wretched.

She grants Cora a standing ovation, putting her out of her misery rather than torturing her—indeed, them all—with a second verse. Ward and Ogden clap along, Ward with a hearty whistle, while Mrs. Ogden glances bemusedly around at the rest of them before applauding and murmuring, "That's how it's meant to sound. My goodness."

"Here in America, you have the expression 'voice of an angel,'" Alice says. "In Württemberg, we say, '*Stimme einer Schleiereule,*' which means 'voice of a barn owl.' Much more highly prized. Well done, Miss Ritter, *Stimme einer Schleiereule,* indeed."

"Thank you, cousin," Cora says sweetly, sitting beside Mrs. Ogden once more. "Where are the dogs? Oh, they've fled, haven't they."

Ogden now watches Cora with a mix of amusement and disgust. Objective achieved.

"Returning to our earlier discussion," Ward begins.

"Yes." Ogden pivots back to Alice with renewed enthusiasm. "The mines. My dear friend . . . I hope I may be informal in calling you by your own given names, Marie . . . Charlotte . . . Gabriella . . ."

He draws each name out like a caress. Ridiculous man.

Alice slowly lifts her eyes to peer at him through her thick lashes. "My intimates call me Marietta. And so may you."

With a swift glance to check that his wife is occupied—she is, as the dogs have deemed the room safe to return to—Ogden takes Alice's hand and presses a kiss to it, murmuring against it, "Darling Marietta."

"As to the *mines*," Ward cuts in, thankfully breaking the moment in two. "I think it's fair to say there is nobody on our fair shores Her Grace would rather be financially entangled with than you, Mr. Ogden. Not even yours truly, though goodness knows I've tried."

"We may yet come to an arrangement." Alice laughs dotingly. She widens her eyes as she turns to Mr. Ogden. "And if my brother, the grand prince, does see the value as I've expressed it of forming stronger alliances abroad, opening up our company to a very select group of American investors, you would be my very first and most essential . . . partner."

A look of almost sensual rapture overtakes Mr. Ogden's marble statue of a face.

Before he can act on it further, Alice stands.

"Oh, Cora, you're looking very fatigued since your performance. Perhaps you are growing ill. Come, let us take our leave." She hurries across the room to Mrs. Ogden, kissing her fervently once on each cheek. "You have honored us beyond words with this invitation. It was a night we will not soon forget."

"Nor will I," Mrs. Ogden says, her eyes bugging a little as they dart to Cora, no doubt in reminiscence of that "stirring" performance.

Their hostess sees them to the door, her fingers picking idly at the seam on Alice's sleeve.

She stops Alice as the others take their leave. "I wanted to apologize again for my earlier accusations."

"Heavens." Alice laughs. "There is no need, dear Priscilla. For we are friends now, are we not?"

"We are, but you see . . ." Mrs. Ogden glances behind her, as if wary of her husband's hearing. "There was another friend, years ago. I'd thought she was a lady of good virtue like the rest of us, but she turned out to be no better than the basest of whores. The temptations she dangled before my husband." Her lips press together in a white line. "Well, it was a miracle he never succumbed. And in the end, she got what was coming to her. I'll spare you the gory details, Your Grace, and I'm afraid they are rather gory."

She titters.

A chill runs up Alice's spine at the sound.

"What happened to her?" Alice asks, as if amused.

"She was run out of town with her disgusting spawn, penniless, friendless," Mrs. Ogden says with thick satisfaction. "We never heard from her again, good riddance. God's justice, I say. Although why the Lord would grant a strumpet like her children and leave me barren, I'll never know."

"Well," Alice cannot resist getting in, squeezing Mrs. Ogden's gloved hand, "at least you have your dogs."

And in the moment of the loathsome woman's momentary shock, Alice smiles and takes her leave.

Out on the sidewalk of Fifty-First, Alice seizes a moment to gather herself, breathing in the fresh night air, while Ward holds the door for Cora to step inside his carriage.

Another lure set and bitten. But she knows what restraint, what absolute control it will take to reel them all in at last.

Alice wanted to slap that woman, right then and there, for saying such vile things about her mother. But she didn't. She wanted to flee from Ogden's touch. And yet she didn't; she held firm and even managed to reel his attentions safely away from Cora and back to her.

That yodeling! Alice can't help it. She breaks into a smile at the memory. She wishes Dagmar and Béatrice had been there to hear it. Once the girl gets over her obvious resentment of the trick Alice played and understands the reasoning behind it, she might even be convinced to give an encore performance back at home.

"McAllister!" Ogden's baritone voice rises from the marble stairway behind her. "You go on with Miss Ritter. Her Grace and I will follow."

Ward looks to Alice in momentary perturbation as Ogden approaches from behind her, clasping one of her hands in his and whispering, "You are among trusted friends. You need not worry for your reputation. No one will breathe a word."

"Cousin?" Cora calls tightly from the carriage, her face peeking out from the window. But before she can voice any argument to this plan, Ward taps his hat with his cane, enters the carriage, and shuts the door behind him.

"I saw you lingering," Ogden says, spinning Alice around to face him as her ride home rolls away without her. "Unwilling to let the night end."

"I was taking the air," Alice says, careful not to directly contradict him. "Needed to catch my breath."

"As do I, my *dearest* Marietta, as do I."

"I am rather fatigued."

"Fear not, I've sent for my brougham." He lifts a hand as the two-seat, single-horse carriage is brought out from the stables. Then he slides his hand around Alice's waist and whispers, "Fewer windows."

Apprehension begins to creep up Alice's spine, growing ever-lengthening tendrils. This is a wrinkle she cannot think how to iron. Not this quickly, not while he opens the door for her and offers her a hand to step inside.

It is a short drive back to her home on Thirty-Eighth Street, she reminds herself. Surely he can't think to make a move that quickly.

In fact, he can. And does.

The wheels of the carriage have barely begun moving before he falls to his knees in front of her. "I've longed for this moment since the first time I saw you. That Night of Illusions, the lamplight shining on your golden hair, the sadness in your eyes that I longed to erase with my touch—"

"Mr. Ogden, we c-cannot," Alice sputters. "You are a married man."

"And you unmarried at twenty-eight, the crime of the century—"

She startles at the expression, then at the feel of his hands, steadily hunting for her legs beneath her skirts.

"You are royalty, my love, living independently, like no

other woman in the world," Ogden practically moans. "You set your own rules, your own mores, and inside here, we are merely two humans desperate with want. Why should we not have what we desire?"

Those last set of lines sound practiced. Decades practiced. Alice wonders whether he tried them on her own mother.

She slides down the bench, almost, but not quite out of reach. A light sparks in his eyes like a flint match. A predator enjoying the chase. But ready for the kill.

He pounces. Not genteel, not seductive, nothing now but brutal impatience.

Before she can block him with her arms, his hands have found her underskirts and lifted them high, his mouth shoved hot against her neck as he growls, "You want this as much as I do."

"Mr. Ogden," she protests, terror a vise around her neck. "Brett!"

His left hand flies from her skirts to cover her mouth as he scrabbles with the other to shove her drawers aside. Alice feels the fabric begin to rip.

And something within her shifts. Her fear rises into white-hot rage. And then . . . nothing. Emptiness.

She's like a magician in a water tank, the trick gone wrong, the lock holding fast, only one option left for escape.

She kisses the hand that's pinning closed her mouth. He glances up at her in delighted shock, then dives in again, kissing her neck, suckling her ear, all the while desperately positioning himself between her bunched skirts.

Alice feels nothing at all except her unpinned hand as it reaches smoothly into her inner jacket pocket, its fingers wrapping around the grip of her derringer pistol. She closes her eyes, her lips curling into a snarl, and cocks back the hammer.

The carriage stops with a jolt that sends Ogden flying off her, glassy-eyed and wild.

Breath held, Alice keeps her hand and weapon concealed, hearing the sound of approaching footsteps.

A rap rattles the door before it opens.

Alice manages to shove her skirts down, but the look on her face—the bald rage on Ogden's—must say it all. McAllister's face goes sheet white for a stunned moment. Then he recovers himself.

"I'm afraid my carriage has thrown a wheel. Lucky you were following after. Bit of a squeeze, but might Miss Ritter ride with you while I see to repairs?"

Ogden blinks hard, his jaw working angrily. "There's hardly room. I—"

Cora runs over, breathless, her dinner party dress flouncing. "What a misadventure!"

To Ogden, no doubt, Cora appears perfectly oblivious, but Alice can see through the girl's acting by now, the tightness with which she clutches her skirts.

"As I say, rather too much of a squeeze for me." Ogden abruptly rises to exit the carriage. He slides past Cora, then offers her a hand inside. "I'll bid you both good night. A walk in the cold air will do me good."

Alice stares at him, still incapable of speech, her teeth clamped tight to keep them from chattering.

Before he shuts the door, he seizes at her hand and leans into whisper, "We shall have another chance. *Soon.*"

She's unsure whether in his mind it's the promise of a sworn lover or the threat of someone who knows himself to be a monster.

The door shuts and then the carriage starts away again with a crunch and rumble.

Cora's facade crumples into concern. "We suspected this wasn't on the up-and-up. Ward ordered his carriage to be stopped. Please tell me we weren't too late. What hap—"

"I nearly killed him." Alice's voice feels muffled to her own ears. Very distant. She draws out the gun. "I was going to shoot him in the head. Just like this." She lifts the weapon, demonstrating. "It would have ended it all, right here and now. All our plans, everything I've worked so hard for."

"You were . . . you were defending yourself." Cora inches away from the gun barrel. "You—"

"I *wanted* to," Alice says, fixing her eyes intently on Cora's. "I wanted to see him bleed, watch as life left him. I wanted so badly to murder the man. I think I always have."

The carriage stops. Alice and Cora sit in sickly silence, listening to the movements of the driver as he hops from his seat and opens the door for them.

Alice erupts from the carriage and starts quickly up the stairs. The moment the house door closes safely behind them, she begins to shake.

"Alice? Alice!" Cora jogs to catch her, resting a tentative hand on her shoulder. "Wait, please! Talk to me. What happened to you?"

Alice flinches away. "I'll not speak of it."

"I don't mean tonight," Cora persists, a desperate hitch to her tone as she continues down the corridor. "I mean earlier, before, before . . . all of this."

Alice turns to face the girl, eyes aflame. "I will *not* speak of it! Least of all to you!"

Cora flinches in turn. It's as Alice intended, but she still feels the insult as if she's launched it at herself.

She runs to her room and locks the door for good measure, protecting herself against any kind of intrusion against her person. Her mind, her body—what's the difference?

Outside the door, she hears Cora's rustling skirts. Pacing footsteps. And finally, silence.

Alice places the derringer on the floor between her bed and the door and stares at it, unmoving.

She begins to cry but forces herself to be quiet. She can hear that Cora has returned and is now speaking in a low voice to Béatrice outside. She waits, knowing the gentle knock will come, and when it does, it hurts more than anything else she's experienced tonight.

"Alice?" Béa's sweet voice seeps through the door. "Are you all right?"

She doesn't answer. Half of her wishes Béa would knock again, perhaps try a bit harder, but she doesn't. Alice can feel her standing there, however, keeping silent vigil, as Alice balls up in her undergarments, not bothering to change further, and falls into a shaky dreamless sleep.

☙ ☙ ☙

She rises early. Before the others. She is dressed, ready. She can rely on Dagmar not to say a word beyond, "Coffee?" which feels to her the most beautiful word in the world at the moment.

She is seated upright and alert by the time Cora rouses

herself enough to poke her head into the study. Alice doesn't look up from the letter she's penning.

"Good morning," Cora ventures.

Alice lets her squirm for a minute before acknowledging her. She's not even sure why. "Can I help you with something?"

Cora's smile drops off completely. "No. Just letting you know I'm stepping out for a bit."

"Bring Béa with you," Alice blurts, her foolish heart pumping wildly all of a sudden.

Cora shakes her head. "She's at the dressmaker's. Picking up—"

"Dagmar then."

Cora's face softens with understanding. "Alice, you don't need to worry for my safety—"

"For appearance's sake," Alice snaps. "Can't have rumors spreading about Miss Ritter's lack of propriety. Not now, when we are so very close."

Cora nods, the image of practiced possession, despite the new shine to her eyes. "I understand. You can rely on me. Entirely, Alice."

She turns away and shuts the door quietly behind her before Alice can gather her defenses once again.

Not now, Alice repeats to herself, spreading her fingers wide to keep them from shaking as she returns to her letter. *Not now, Alice. So very close.*

CHAPTER 24

Chasing Headlines

Cora shifts awkwardly as Dagmar lets out a loud, late morning yawn, stretching her thick legs across the hansom cab.

"Comfortable?" Cora asks.

Dagmar, always a lady of loquacity, simply shrugs.

Cora gathers her jade velvet skirts, edging closer to the window, covering her mounting, soul-consuming vexation with a practiced smile. To say something is going on with Alice would be a colossal understatement, and even still, Alice expects Cora to merely nod and smile demurely and obsequiously obey her every command.

Well, that ship has long sailed away. Cora has grown to deeply care about the woman—as a mentor, as a friend—and moreover, she suspects the fondness might even be mutual. If Alice will not let her in, she simply needs to find another door, another window. She *will* get access, insight, today, unforeseen complications be damned—all it will take is a very slight detour to shed her culinary keeper.

The carriage careens around Washington Square Park, bustling now with promenading ladies, a rainbow of fashionable dresses and parasols, businessmen striding purposefully across the gravel walks ribboned through the green oasis. The palette turns rather sharply into monochrome as they venture into the Lower East Side, the soot-stained tenements and tight alleys grayed by shadows and overcast gloom, as if even the sky is leached of joy south of First Street.

As they pull around a narrow corner and to their supposed destination, Cora grows reminiscently queasy but attempts to buck up. *I'm not going in, after all. Don't even have to smell the ale.*

Below the saloon's Beer signage, in the folds of the alley, she spies a burly, mustached man smoking a cigarette.

Ah, that's right. Cora places his face now. Dagmar's sweetheart, who was tending bar the last time they were here, the reason Cora was crawsick for the entire next day.

Dagmar's face alights at the very sight of him. "Konrad," she murmurs, voice now soft as cotton down. "Come on, zen," she tells Cora. "We go."

But before the cook can kick open the carriage door, Cora grabs her wrist.

"Oh, Dagmar, I am a goof." She winces. "I only just remembered I've got an errand first."

As evidence, she holds up the bracelet she tinkered with for this very occasion, a gold wristlet with three counterfeit emeralds and a now-broken clasp. "I don't want to delay you from your, um, *fellow*, so go on without me. I'll just be a quick trip to the jeweler and back."

Dagmar glances hungrily at Konrad and then again at Cora, narrowing her beady eyes. "You zaid you needed to drown sorrows wis a morning maroon—"

"I did. *Do!* But you know Alice. She'll shoot me with that pocket pistol of hers if I don't get this fixed before Mrs. Witt's ball." The Witt gala has been crassly billed as a "poverty ball," hardly the place for jewelry, but Dagmar doesn't need to know that detail. "I won't be but an hour, and then we can get to the real matter at hand."

Dagmar studies her, finally offering a grunt. "Not a word of zis to Alice."

"Naturally."

"Soot yourself." Dagmar saunters out of the cab, whistling.

In ten minutes' time, Cora has fixed the bracelet herself, slipped it back on, and arrived at the corner of Park Row and Spruce known as "Printing House Square," home to the many various presses that uncover and distribute—and these days, even apparently fabricate—New York's front-page news. Tall, looming facades border the sprawling gravel forum, pockmarked in hidden corners with dingy clumps of lingering, soiled snow. The buildings, all more than ten stories tall, are still dwarfed by the engineering marvel of the Brooklyn Bridge shining in the distance, a true feat of architecture, a sprawl of monumental towers and great sweeping wires. Cora heard Alice and Béa speaking of the design only a few nights past, sharing rumors that a *woman* oversaw the design, her credit stolen by the prominent men around her.

Cora allows this rumor to rouse and embolden her now. If those stories are true, surely she is capable of merely crossing this square, one boot in front of the other, and confronting the less-than-prominent man who owes her some honest answers.

She strides into the marble foyer of the lobby of *The Herald* building, greeting a bellman who directs her to take an elevator, of all things, to the eighth floor. Within a spacious freight platform lined with wood paneling, its uniformed attendant stands ready at the pulley with a vacant smile.

"Eighth floor, sir," Cora says, her voice wavering. "Please."

They lurch upward, and Cora has to stifle an alarmed cry—but the ride itself is nothing compared to the frenetic madness that's revealed when the elevator stops and the door clanks open.

Cora looks around, aghast. Is this a regular day for Cal Archer? Dozens, if not hundreds, of frantic-looking young men donning sweat-stained shirts and waving notepads like little white flags run back and forth through a labyrinth of desks. Bells ringing—telephones?—warring conversations, desperate shouts about Wall Street and President Arthur overtake her in a cacophonous symphony, gray-haired gentle-men opening and slamming wooden doors along the open floor's perimeter as added percussion.

Maybe this was a mistake, she wonders hastily. Chasing Cal down for her own scoop. What was she thinking?

Abashed, she turns to leave.

"Miss Ritter?"

She turns to find Cal Archer standing in the center of two long rows of desks, his face hitched in confusion as his eyes meet hers.

She hasn't seen him since he waltzed into Alice's living room, demanding her delivery from a loveless marriage with a side of spice cookies. Or *pfeffernusse*, rather (sorry, Dagmar). Was his intervention motivated solely by pity? she wonders now. And yet she remembers, exquisitely, the way he looked at her that night in the Bowery (one of the very few things she actually remembers).

Does he think of her as often as she thinks of him?

"Hello," she says, suddenly feeling foolish.

Cal steps closer with a strangled laugh. "What are you doing here?"

Cora lifts her chin, careful to inflect, in a perfect Württembergian lilt, "I have some questions of my own, Mr. Archer. Some concerns. And I hope you might enlighten me."

He glances around at the frenzied scene, almost sheepish. "All right. But how 'bout somewhere else."

After he grabs his coat and hat, they depart, firmly in the midst of the lunchtime rush. The freight ride downward is packed with reporters, thick with bodies pressed panel to panel.

Cora tucks herself into the platform's far corner, Cal attempting to give her berth. As soon as the doors close, though, the freight lurches. She reaches out to prevent herself from falling, hands landing on Cal's impressively firm chest.

Cora's cheeks warm. "Apologies."

Cal clears his throat. "Quite all right."

They step out into the lobby and then the brisk late March air, Cal offering an arm as they fall in stride across the square.

He finally breaks the loaded silence. "Does, ah, my sister know you've come to see me?"

"No. And I'd like to keep it that way, especially as she is the reason for today's inquisition." Cora stops walking. "I'm . . . well. I am actually quite worried about her. Something happened last night and I . . . ." Cora trails off, searching for the right words. "I'm concerned that she is in over her head, only I can't be positive because she never tells me more than the barest essentials, and I was hoping . . . ." She huffs. "I was hoping you might trust me with the truth, Mr. Archer."

"Come on, it's Cal by now."

Her cheeks turn hot again.

Focus, Cora.

"The *full* story, as it were, Cal. I know she prefers to hold people at arm's length—me, it seems, especially—but that isn't how I want to live my life. Call me a fool, but I care about your sister very much. I desire to help, however I can, and . . . I cannot do that if she insists on shutting me out."

Cal stays quiet for a long while. So long that their stroll has returned them to where they started.

"I understand," he finally says. "And lord knows I can relate. I can provide context, I suppose, take you back. Maybe too far back, I don't know." He sighs. "Once upon a time, our family was old money, if you can believe it. Dad came from Puritan stock and Mama was Dutch New York, that kind of old. It was all inheritance, investments, that type of thing. We lived in a brownstone not far from where Alice is living now, although there was always talk about moving uptown, keeping up with the fashionable crowd. Never happened, obviously."

While he offers his hand, assisting her around a particularly ghastly looking smear of coal-colored snow, his eyes look distant, fixed on the past.

"Dad had this aversion to the men he'd grown up with," he goes on. "Something about being bullied at boarding school; he never went into details. Didn't stop him from hauling me off to good old Maidenhead Academy, same as him, but it did make him seek out friends among the newer crowd. The industrial rich. Businesspeople. Men who were, if I'm completely honest, much wilier than him. Men like—"

"Ogden and Ames," Cora supplies. "Vandemeer. Witt and Peyton, too, I suppose?"

Cal smiles ruefully. "Not Peyton. No, not him. The others,

though . . . yes. They were Dad's nearest and dearest. Or so he thought."

Cora shivers as they take another turn about the square.

"They were all in some way involved in the railroads. They all sat on various boards, held motley investments, hedging their bets, and Dad . . . well, he grew intrigued. Felt like an outsider. Until the day they brought him in."

Cal blinks, looking away. It takes him a second to shake his head and continue the story.

"I wasn't home." He says it bitterly. "I was off at school. But Alice tells me that was the happiest she'd ever seen our father, the day he breezed in from a meeting he'd had down on Wall Street. Popped a bottle of expensive champagne he'd been saving for a special occasion and whirled our mother around the parlor in a mad dance. Said he was a 'railroad man' now. Principal investor in Midwest Railroads, and yes, he'd put every bit of the family's holdings into the company's bonds, but it wasn't a risk. Far from it! Because his dear friends, his closest companions, they'd told him this railway was due to be bought by Manifest Rails the very next day for far, far more than what he'd put in. A key acquisition to fill a gap in their transatlantic line."

"Manifest?" Cora frowns, realizing. "That's Harold Peyton's company."

Cal points at her wryly. "Well, dear old Dad waited for the arrival of the papers the next morning, or a telegram, or a courier announcing the grand news. Nothing. Days passed. Still nothing. Not only that, but no invitations out to dine. Nobody home when they went out to visit, which was especially strange, as the wives of these men were some of Mama's closest friends since childhood. Something was wrong. They just didn't know what."

Cal scratches his face, sadness sweeping clean his story-teller's expression.

"It all became clear on Monday, May 1, 1871, when the papers ran their morning headlines, announcing the completion of the Manifest transatlantic line—and the collapse and bankruptcy of Midwest Railroads."

Cora shakes her head. "I don't understand—"

"Neither did he. Neither did Alice, not until years later. You see, our friends Ames, Vandemeer, Witt, and Ogden weren't just deep investors in Midwest Railroads; they were in the pocket of an even wealthier man—Harold Peyton himself. After negotiations to sell their line to Peyton failed, they scrambled to invest in Manifest instead. One problem: They knew damn well their bonds in Midwest would be worthless in a few weeks' time . . . unless they could sell it all off to some dupe. Some old-money Knickerbocker pal without a lick of business sense."

"They conned your father," Cora breathes, understanding hitting her in a cold wave.

She and Alice really are more alike than she ever realized.

"Took it all." Cal nods. "Never looked back."

He clears his throat, gaze turning toward the horizon, the magnificent bridge standing sentinel beyond. Cora has the gutting suspicion he won't get through the next part without looking away from her. "Alice was the one who found his body. Came home from her finishing school and found Mama in the parlor, sobbing in a ball on the ground, too distraught to go find out the source of the sudden thud she'd heard, the whining, persistent creaks in the rafters. So Alice did. She found Dad hanging in the study. She was all of fourteen years old. She was the one to cut him down, try to shake breath back into him, when he was . . . who knows, hours past help."

"My God." Cora's eyes well up with tears. "I cannot imagine—"

"Neither can I, not really," Cal says. "It all felt rather removed for me. I got the telegram the next day, came home to help settle what accounts we had remaining to us—not a whole lot—and to help Mama arrange the funeral. She insisted on Grace Church, despite the expense. Still thought she had standards back then, and you know what? Next to nobody came to that funeral. We hung those black silk drapes on the door and windows in mourning, but the only people who came to call were potential buyers, knowing we were ruined and would have to sell."

"So you moved to Poughkeepsie," Cora fills in, stitching Cal's story to the threads of what Alice had previously shared with her.

"To that lovely claptrap house we shared with six other families," Cal says dryly. "No more boarding school for me, one small consolation. I was thirteen, and this world of ours, it's different for boys. At that age, I could start to work, get my foot into an industry, and so that foot of mine was out the door almost as soon as we moved in. I reckon Alice has never really forgiven me for it. As a girl, she was both too young to leave and too old not to bear the weight of responsibility for what remained of our family after I took off to work as a runner in a newsroom. Like these lads you see hanging around here."

He tips his hat to a boisterous gaggle of newsies in flat caps gathered now outside *The Herald* distribution window. They salute him back in familiar greeting.

Cora's struck by something in his wording. "What *did* remain of your family? Alice, your mother . . ."

"And Rose," Cal says quietly. "The baby. We didn't realize Mama was expecting. I don't think Dad knew either, or maybe he wouldn't have . . . Anyway, Rose only made it two months. Caught scarlet fever from another family in the house and was gone within days. Mama never really came back from that. Slept all the time. Alice went out as a sort of cut-rate governess when she was about sixteen, I believe, teaching merchants' daughters penmanship and French and comportment and whatever else."

Cora can imagine that "whatever else," as she has been a beneficiary of those lessons herself.

"She came home night after night with whatever money she could scrape together for lodging and food, and she cared for Mama. Six years of that, until Mama finally gave up. Stopped eating. Died in her sleep."

Cal looks at Cora, eyes redlined and haunted in the midday light.

"I came for the funeral, but Alice . . . she was dry-eyed. I didn't understand why at the time, but now I know she was already starting to come up with her revenge. Didn't know she'd moved until several letters I'd sent her were returned to me in a bundle. Landlady in Poughkeepsie had no idea where she'd gotten off to. I dug around here and there, using newsroom resources, seeing if I could find anybody matching her description. No luck. A total vanishing act. Then, last spring, she turned up in Manhattan. Right here, as a matter of fact, up in the office, just like you did. I'd recently been promoted to the international beat, chasing my colleagues to the telegram, first to the story, first to the paycheck, that kind of thing. Not exactly rolling in dough, but I had enough to offer to help her financially. She wouldn't have it. Too proud, too angry at me for leaving."

He lets out a bitter laugh. "I'll admit, she looked like she was doing a far sight better than I was. Nicely dressed. This air of hauteur about her. You've seen it. You know exactly what I mean. She wouldn't let me apologize, as I'd already tried to do in those returned letters. She did let me take her to lunch and told me she had a plan and a part for me to play in it. These false stories about Württemberg. I wanted to help her any way I could, so I said yes, of course I did. But I'd be lying, Cora, if I didn't tell you that some nights I *still* stay awake wondering if I made the wrong call. If I shouldn't have taken her by the shoulders and said, 'No. I'll get you a job as a secretary, an apartment somewhere livable,' instead of all this madness."

Cora shakes her head. "I don't suppose she'd have listened."

Cal smiles sadly. "No. I don't suppose she would have. As you know, she's forged of steel, my sister. And now you know that it's life that's made her that way."

Cora nods absently as Cal's story washes over her in full, her mind drifting now to another corner of the world, her own farm, her own father. Another family with fragile, foolish hopes crushed by the tide of greed and deception.

She's struck again by how similar she and Alice are . . . though while Alice made it her life's mission to avenge her father, Cora has blamed hers, at least in part, for being an easy target, assuring herself she'd never be as foolish as he was. Cora has made it her own mission to be on the winning side of the con game, first with the troupe, then her petty thievery, and then with Alice herself. Now Cora wonders, though, if all this time she was really longing for something else. And if this game she's been playing is all far more complicated than she has allowed herself to believe.

Where is the point, she wonders, where shrewd scheming crosses into cruelty? Or when bald, desperate hope tips into foolhardiness, for that matter? She's suddenly struck by how unmoored, alone, she has felt these past eighteen months, ever since her home was taken from her. She assured herself that getting the farm back would fix everything . . . but the meaning of home, she realizes, might run deeper than just a place.

"She is lucky to have you, all the same," Cora whispers.

"She is also lucky to have you," Cal says, glancing at her. "Alice values you, Cora. Your earnestness. Quick thinking. Quick fingers. She was mighty impressed by the stunt you pulled at the opera. When I met up with her at the new embassy, she couldn't stop talking about it—"

"And yet she's said not a word of any of this to me." Cora blushes.

"Doesn't surprise me." Cal laughs. "Best not let anyone think they can affect the Unflappable Alice Archer."

"You managed to affect her, though, didn't you? At least a bit," Cora amends. "You convinced her to move up her plans, to expedite our timeline."

"Well. Even at arm's length, she has been known to acknowledge my insights from time to time. Especially when I refuse to leave until she does. And I can be convincing when I want to be."

Of all things, Alice's lesson from many moons ago floats to mind: *Pay as much mind to what people don't say as what they do.*

She'll never forgive herself if she doesn't try to press Cal further.

"And why did you? Want to be?" Cora swallows, heart thudding now. "I don't see any real advantage that convincing her to move up the plan gave you, or any of us, if I'm honest. It puts more pressure on us, affords us no slack of time to correct potential mistakes. I see no benefit at all, really, other than . . . well, altruism. Saving me from a fraught marriage and a lifetime of . . . regret . . ." She trails off.

Cal has stopped walking, staring at her now with those deep blue eyes.

"And why isn't that reason enough?" he whispers. "Though I'm not sure I'd call it altruism. Not when my own interests are involved."

"Your own interests?" Cora's voice comes out as barely a breath.

Cal reaches for the edge of her sleeve, pinching it between two fingers, the rest of his hand barely grazing hers. "I can think of few things more interesting than you, Coraline O'Malley."

A heat burns through Cora's abdomen, spreading like wildfire up her spine, down her limbs. Her real name. On *his* lips.

Of course she has feelings for him. She has since the first moment she saw him.

He's been honest with her. Now it's time for her to finally be honest with herself.

She inches closer. "What are we to do about this?"

"What do we want to do," he murmurs, "or what should we do?"

Cora lets out a shaky breath. My, how she longs to lace her fingers around his neck, pull his lips down to hers, here, in public, for all the world to see. No more lies or games or illusions, her heart laid bare. Despite everything at stake—or perhaps more truthfully, *because* of everything at stake.

"Cora," he whispers, searching her face. He nearly, *nearly* reaches for her.

A face catches her eye beyond Cal's left shoulder. She startles with a flinch.

Is it him? What on earth is he doing here?

Cora steps back sharply, heart hammering. Harry Peyton hasn't seen her, though, not yet. Beneath his tall top hat, his guileless face is angled up at the bridge, his brow stitched in deep thought, as if he's calculating the geometrics of the arch. He's headed in their general direction, his hands in the pockets of his fur-lined overcoat.

"I'm so sorry," Cora mumbles. "You'll understand in a moment."

She takes two more steps from Cal, spinning directly into Harry's line of sight.

"Harry?" she gushes. "Oh my goodness, a lovely surprise! What are you doing here?"

She winces at her own accent, perhaps a bit overdone.

Cora looks at Cal in earnest, hoping he'll play the game, but no need—he's already scrubbed his face clean of emotion, approaching Harry with a dapper stride.

"Harold Peyton the younger, is it not?" Cal extends his hand. "We met in the park. Good to see you, old chap."

Harry's expression of extreme distaste broadcasts that the feeling is far from mutual. "Are you well, Cora? Is this reporter harassing you again? Surely you've gathered enough quotes for your paper, sir."

"Goodness, no, how chivalrous you are." She laughs dotingly, wreathing her arm around Harry's. "I stopped by Mr.

Archer's office to see if he had received any news from home. We haven't heard from my cousin in quite some time, and I . . . well, I must admit . . ."

Cora wipes her eyes, her face crumpling.

Harry's expression softens. He takes her hand in his. "Oh, dear Cora."

"Believe this is my cue," Cal says ruefully. He nods, a sad twist to his smile. "I shall keep you abreast of any developments, Miss Ritter, if I hear anything from my sources."

He tips his hat and goes.

Cora tries hard not to obviously watch him as he passes the newsies, sharing a joke with them, before disappearing back inside.

Harry squeezes her hand as they begin to stroll.

"I know how much your homeland means to you," he says. "It pains me to see you so bereft."

"Thank you." She sniffs. "I must say, it's such a tonic to run into you. What, pray tell, are you doing downtown?"

Harry gestures across the square.

"Our family broker has offices here," he explains. "My father wanted to speak to him about potential investments."

"Your father!" Cora exclaims. "He . . . left the house?"

"I'm as surprised as you are," Harry says bemusedly. "He's upstairs now at the brokerage, discussing the details of his current portfolio. I was keen to listen in, I must say, but he made me take a walk. I figured I might get a closer look at the bridge while I was at it."

"Well, what delightful serendipity for us to run into one another."

He edges closer. "Cora, I know I can't solve this conflict in Württemberg, but I am certain I can help us. Er . . . *you*."

"You've helped me so much already," she protests faintly, edging subtly away so that he drops his hand.

"I can hardly convince my father of anything, but I believe the dynamic between us may finally be shifting. I explained the emerald mines opportunity to him, and he's now just as eager to invest as I am." Harry smiles, standing an inch taller. "The fact that half of my father's old associates are desperate to carve out pieces of the business for themselves didn't hurt matters."

Cora shakes her head, the very model of innocence. "I'm not sure I understand."

Harry cups her shoulders. "Cora, he plans to be the primary investor in your mines. The *primary* investor."

"That's . . . that's wonderful! I shall speak to my cousin about it, but I'm sure, given our engagement . . ." Cora lets out a tempered laugh as she embraces him. "Oh, Harry, for once, the future feels bright and grand and—"

"Free," Harry finishes, whirling her around in a sudden dance. "So very, very free!"

"Harry!" Cora laughs.

She closes her eyes as they spin, trying to pinch away the memory of Cal's somber face, the hitch in his breath as he shared his story, his father's ill-fated boast. *A railroad man now.*

And now the train she has helped put into motion, one built to correct the wrongs of the past, is garnering its final momentum. Hurtling forward, unstoppable now, just as Alice intended.

Perhaps that's why Cora feels as if she's stepped onto a runaway car, mere moments from careening off the rails.

CHAPTER 25

The Scorpion and the Frog

I do declare." Ward removes his hat as if in church, strolling about the soon-to-be Württembergian embassy, taking in the reception room's curtains, sofas, tables, and other furnishings—all included, thankfully, in the rental fee. "It is all falling into place."

"Béatrice is working on finding a flag," Alice says. Her footsteps echo across the hardwood floor as she walks toward the "consulate's" office and motions upward. "I thought to hang it here. And we'll have to find a way to install a double-sided wall safe. Directly beside the door of the ambassador's office."

"Perfection!" Ward cries, striding over to rap the edge of the marble fireplace. "Perhaps the mantelpiece for the market ticker, as the embassy has only brought it in for this rare occasion. I suppose you've got someone in mind to read it off to the assemblage?"

"Our ambassador himself," Alice answers.

"Quite right," Ward says with a smirk. "I'll look forward to meeting the esteemed gentleman. I thought I'd take on the task of marking down bids, unless you have any objections. One thing my unfortunate state of relative penury has afforded me is a gift for numbers."

"I'd be very glad for you to do that," Alice says. "I've a fair head for numbers myself, but I don't suppose anyone will trust the accounting of a woman on the day."

"I, for one, would trust nobody so much as I trust you, my dear," Ward says.

Alice looks away to hide her smile. After all the annoyances and setbacks she's faced of late, she must admit to a certain growing warmth in her chest tonight. Hope, exhilaration— but more than that, pride. No small feat, all this, and rather invigorating to stand here, on the invented ambassadorial grounds of a nation she has never set foot in.

And to have Ward McAllister by her side to witness it feels appropriate. Cora, Dagmar, Béa: They may live in her home, but the stakes are different for someone like Ward, who has no criminal record, no wolves snapping at his heels. He jumped aboard this little endeavor purely because he believed in the brilliance of it. And he's proven at every turn a stalwart and upstanding partner.

She's forming the right sort of words to express those thoughts without undue sentimentality when Ward turns to face her again. And Alice sees a glint in his eye that over the past year has become a familiar warning signal.

Though never before has it been pointed in her direction.

"Well, my dear duchess," Ward says. His grin widens like the Cheshire cat's. "Seems as good a time as any to revisit our arrangement."

Alice remains cool, her own porcelain smile fixed on her face. "In what sense?"

Instead of answering directly, Ward begins to prowl the edge of the room, trailing his pointer finger around the top of the wainscoting as if marking it all as his own.

"Yes, it is indeed all in place," he says. "Might not have been if I hadn't warned little Cora not to broadcast her nefarious intentions to the entire Metropolitan Opera House." He glances smugly at Alice. "And if I hadn't faked a faltering wheel on my carriage to prevent a catastrophic escalation of your flirtations with Brett Ogden, he might have lost his interest then and there once he'd gotten what he wanted."

Alice feels a chill from the calculation in his words. No concern for her welfare, no. Only for the plan.

"No, all of that was fixed," he croons. "But when I look ahead, puttin' myself in your shoes, as it were, I can identify a weak spot. Only the one, really, which makes it all the more remarkable."

"Care to illuminate me?"

"Why, none other than my dearest friend," he says. "Mrs. Caroline Astor."

Ward turns before Alice can hide her alarm. He smiles, eyes crinkling, at the unconscious confirmation in her pinched expression.

"The one woman everyone in New York society is desperate to claim as an intimate, and you, Duchess, avoid her like Valjean avoids Javert, if you'll allow me the literary reference. And why is that? Why *not* include her on your little list of marks? Or at least pay her a visit, enlist her help in deepening your ties to high society? Yes, yes, you've told me. You worry she'll recognize you from when you were a little whelp of a thing in white lace dresses. But I wonder if it's something else, something . . . more recent." Ward taps his head, playful. "I've often wondered, dear Alice, if you've already hit this particular mark. Perhaps before we had the happy occasion to meet?"

Alice lets out an impatient sigh. "In what direction are you pointed with this, Ward? It would be a relief if we could arrive there before daybreak."

"I propose to increase my take," he answers, leaning jauntily on the wall, "from fifty percent to . . . let's call it eighty-five and shake on it?"

Alice is too proud to laugh in incredulity. Her expression doesn't change one bit.

Ward blinks, squirms a little in his too-tight jacket.

"Our team has increased in number," she counters. "At your urging."

"All to the benefit, you must admit. The more the merrier."

"They'll each need to be paid their agreed-upon share. Even in our wildest calculations, we wouldn't be able to arrive at figures that would make a divided fifteen percent add up to what I've offered them."

"I'm afraid that's your concern, not mine, dear Alice. You see, I'm in a particularly strong position here. The closest personal friend of Lina Astor there is, ready and willing—nay, duty bound!—to tell her just who you are and what you're planning to do."

"I see."

Now Alice does laugh. Bitterly. "So my actual options, as you have just outlined, are to allow you to tell Mrs. Astor that I'm planning to defraud several members of elite Manhattan society, thus risking imprisonment, or to call the whole thing off due to an untenable financial situation of your making."

"Oh, Alice, tsk-tsk! I'd have given you credit for more creative flexibility than that. We've got weeks to go. Plenty of time to rope in another mark. Or two. Or three. As I said, I'm not even averse to taking my Mystic Rose for all she's worth, if that idea appeals."

"The more the merrier indeed," Alice says.

"Now you see the point!" Ward crows. "You've been too limited in your ambitions, my dear, hobbled by this petty revenge plot. It's beneath you. Now, I don't like turning brutish like this, not *entirely*, anyway—I have grown rather fond of you over this past year—but at the end of the day, one has to look out for the bottom line. I'm doin' you a favor, *Your Grace.* Widening your horizons."

"We'll call it a widened horizon of *three* choices, then." Alice counts them on her fingers. "One: Cancel it all and walk away. Two: Bring in more dupes in order to pay you what you demand. Three: Refuse and risk you telling Mrs. Astor, whatever the consequences."

"I'll give you a moment to mull it over," Ward says with a bow, as if the soul of graciousness.

What Alice mulls as she turns away, her fingers digging into her pocket for the reassuring solidity of her derringer pistol, is why exactly she feels so stung by this entirely predictable turn of events. She certainly wasn't under any illusion that Ward was a truthful person. But perhaps she did believe he was on the right side of dishonesty and for the right reasons.

For all his talk of infiltrating high society, of setting himself apart from them, condemning them . . . he is every bit the self-serving mountebank that they are.

So now she can take a risk, out of righteous anger. Call his bluff. Burn it all down if necessary.

Or she can continue to steer the course.

"Would you accept seventy-five percent?" she offers.

"Eighty," Ward counters.

"Done."

Ward brightens. He extends a hand.

They shake. Ward's palm is surprisingly sweaty. For all his bravado, he wasn't sure how this would play out himself. Perhaps she should have held out for seventy-five.

Not that it will matter in the end.

"I've left my driver idling out there long enough, wouldn't you say?" Ward perks up. He juts out his elbow in offering for Alice to take it. "Allow me to see you home."

"I'll stay a bit longer," Alice says, turning away. "A few more things to see to."

"At eleven o'clock at night?"

Alice doesn't answer.

Behind her, Ward sniffs.

"Very well, then, Your Grace, I shall see you at our next social occasion." He slips from the door and escapes onto the darkened street.

And Alice's knees grow too weak to hold her upright.

She sits on the reception room floor for a long while before finally picking herself up and seeing herself out, locking the door behind her. Her door. Her embassy.

The thought is a cold comfort, the thrill of achievement all but eviscerated now.

She's glad, at least, that she never entered her brother's name into her confidence with Ward McAllister. Still, the scoundrel knows far too much. She cannot risk him learning all of it.

A church bell rings as she passes the southern border of Central Park. Eleven o'clock, as Ward said. If there is ever a time when it would be acceptable for a lady of high station to walk alone on a city sidewalk, it certainly isn't now.

That's why I have this gun, she recalls, patting her pocket again in reassurance. In her early days in the city, she'd lived in places where women frequently walked alone and were subject to potential muggings, harassment, or worse. The gun was an investment against those possibilities, one she thankfully never had to use. Funny how it's here among the wealthiest that she's been forced to draw it.

But not to fire it.

She breathes slowly, walking against the blustery wind, and reminds herself that she is a person of free will, not to be battered about by the fates. No, not her. She is in control.

As she reaches the corner of Third Avenue and Forty-First Street, at this late hour entirely devoid of pedestrians, carts, and carriages, there comes a sound above her that sends the hairs rising on the back of her neck.

A crackling.

She looks up with a wild gasp. An electrical wire, the kind they use for the trolleys, has broken loose. One end is sparking madly, all of it shaking like a trapped serpent. Another barreling wind cuts through the narrow street, strong as a train itself.

Impulse reaches into Alice's gut and propels her backward, sprinting for the other side of the block. She turns in time to see the live wire touch down right where she was standing, sending a hiss of angry steam rising from the pavement.

Heart hammering, she doubles back to Lexington, coming at her house from a different angle. She's heard of the wires coming loose—they're assembled in such haphazard fashion, it's a wonder they stay up at all—but never has she come so close to being struck by one.

The lights are lit in her little apartment on Thirty-Eighth Street. Before she crosses to come inside, she watches the silhouettes in the window. Three women, all laughing. Singing issues from the windows—Cora's yodeling folk song. She's performing it for them at last. Dagmar is slapping her knee, doubled over with laughter. Béa's hands are pressed to her lovely face as if to stopper the giggles. And Cora is dancing between them with pure, joyful liveliness.

I could have died tonight, Alice thinks. *Forget Ward. Forget the embassy. No matter who I was or what I was doing, it all could have ended right there on Third Avenue, just the way it does for so many others. Abruptly. With no resolution, no justice, no revenge.*

I keep waiting to live. Why not do it now?

Feel something other than this endless . . . anger?

As she slips inside the house, she's careful to be quiet, to not interrupt their merriment.

Rather than joining in, she goes to her room and closes the door, shutting out good cheer, affection, all sentiment apart from that which is immediately useful.

Only ten days remain now.

This plan is a train, she reminds herself. And anger is its fuel.

Ye'r kordielly invited to a

Poverty Balle!

HoSTed bY
Missus Witt

Where yur fenciast clothin and
we'll be servin rotgut and vittles

~

Saterday, 29 of Merch 1884,
10 o'cluck

488 Madison Aveneu,
New Yerk

CHAPTER 26

A New Game

March 24, 1884

The oversize clock on the wall of the Lord & Taylor dressing room keeps *tick-tick-tick*ing. Is it growing louder, like Poe's tell-tale heart? Cora could swear it is. There is ever so much to do before Alice's grand scheme unveils its first and only performance—in precisely one week, the morning of April 1, Fifty-Seventh Street and Central Park, at the newly minted Württembergian Embassy—but still, here she is, whiling away an afternoon shopping for "commoner's attire" with Arabella on Ladies' Mile.

Arabella peeks her petite head out from behind a curtain. "Is a maid's petticoat meant to drag along the ground?"

Cora shifts, forcing herself to give the girl her entire attention, and grits her teeth into a smile. This ludicrous and wholly tasteless poverty ball of Mrs. Witt's has all the most fashionable families scrambling about town, clamoring to dress as shabbily as possible, gleefully spending far too much on bespoke, commissioned ball gowns that look, quite literally, like rags. "I'm not familiar with the customs of American maids."

Arabella blushes. "Right. Forgive me. I'm a bit preoccupied."

"Is the theme more beggar or servant, do you suppose?" Cora asks Arabella, wincing apologetically at the working-class seamstress who has hurried forward to help the girl with the necessary adjustments.

Arabella's brow scrunches in concentration, as if attempting difficult arithmetic, and murmurs ruefully, "Yet another confounding dilemma."

The seamstress barely disguises an eye roll as she kneels before the girl's skirt to fix the hem. A few swift adjustments, and then Arabella ducks again behind the curtain.

In moments, Cora swears she hears sniffles issuing from the dressing room, but when Arabella reemerges, cotton dress and matching bonnet in hand, she has adopted a stiff upper lip.

"Do you know what you will be wearing to the ball, Cora?" Arabella asks, once they've exited the crowded shop and taken to strolling Ladies' Mile southward, in the vague direction of Union Square. "Perhaps we can pop into Stern Brothers and have them craft you something."

Cora shakes her head, eager to part ways now that Arabella has secured her costume for the ball. Ever since Harry pledged his and his father's interest in Württemberg's mining company, she's loath to spend any more time than she has to around the marks. A late-game slipup would be devastating, after all.

The growing, gnawing guilt is quite bothersome too. It was kind of Arabella to issue this shopping invitation. Perhaps it was at her mother's insistence, an attempt to stitch closer ties to the royal family come hell or high water. But Cora's had the keen sense all day that Arabella is sincere in her offer of friendship to the woman who has stolen away her childhood love.

Which, of course, makes Cora feel all the worse.

"Thank you, Arabella, but I have already secured a garment from the McAllisters' scullery maid," she says quickly.

"How wonderfully authentic." Arabella smiles. "Aren't you clever?"

She would be if it weren't a lie, as well as another increasing worry—Cora has hardly seen Ward McAllister in the past week, and Alice has barely spoken his name. Nothing so blatant as bad-mouthing the man, just a conspicuous absence, a large hole where his boisterous presence once took up so much space.

"A cup of tea then, perhaps?" Arabella says hastily. A look of outright desperation is shining in her eyes. "Or perhaps a hot chocolate? My mother once took me to a charming place, a bit more uptown, near where we—"

"Arabella?" Cora asks gently. "Is something ailing you?"

"Is it that obvious?" Arabella slows her pace, swallowing hard. She looks, again, to be mere moments from bursting into tears. "I'm really trying very hard to hide it."

"And doing an admirable job." Cora fetches her a handkerchief, then leads the girl toward a wrought iron bench bordering the park, insisting she sit.

"Please don't worry," Arabella sobs. "I'm crying tears of . . . joy!"

"I see that," Cora hedges.

"I've received a formal proposal from your cousin, you see. Wilhelm. The prince."

"A proposal . . . via letter? A proposal as to what?"

Arabella looks up, her eyes as shiny as green glass. "Why, marriage, of course."

Cora's eyes threaten to evacuate her skull. "Goodness."

Arabella sniffs, pulling out a letter written on fine stock that appears to have been folded and unfolded many times. "He asked me to journey to Württemberg this very summer, spend some time there while planning a royal wedding. It's everything my mother hoped for me. Everything that *I* hoped for . . ."

Cora takes the offered letter. She knows Alice's writing as well as her own, after so many months. It's most certainly her handiwork, but why on earth would Alice require the girl to announce a proposal that will soon be revealed to be fake, given everything else at play? Just to take it away? To further crush and ruin her?

Thanks to Cal, Cora now fully understands just how completely and mercilessly these vicious families destroyed his sister. And yet, why enact such equally heartless vengeance upon their progeny? Will this awful cycle never end? What did Arabella do to deserve such manipulation and cruelty? It seems the one mote in Alice's eye. Cora wishes she could help her mentor see it.

She blinks away her own threatening tears, unsure of what to say to this girl who is going to, what? Travel across the Atlantic in search of a prince who has never heard of her?

Then Cora remembers that the con will have ended well before any travel ensues. Arabella will be penniless, same as Harry Peyton and the rest of them.

She supposes that's some consolation. That they'll be tossed out onto the streets together.

"Cora?" Arabella leans forward.

"Apologies." Cora sobers, passing the letter back to Arabella.

"Merely overwhelmed with joy myself, is all. My cousin is clearly very much in love. I will be honored to stand by both of your sides on your wedding day. And we shall be family!"

Not her finest nor most eloquent acting, and it's high time to flee, else she might say something she regrets.

Abruptly, she swipes at imaginary dampness on her forehead. "Do forgive me, dear friend, but I believe the oysters from lunch may not be agreeing with me."

Before Cora can fully take her leave, however, she swears she hears her name being called.

Not by Arabella. Down Fourteenth Street.

She turns and spies a dowdy woman dressed all in black, staring at her in disbelief outside of Tony Pastor's new theater.

Oh. God.

Cora glances at Arabella. But the girl is still lost in her own world, consumed in reading and rereading Alice's/Wilhelm's letter.

Cora looks back at Maeve with terrified eyes and mouths a simple, *Not now. Please.*

Her panicked message must register, because her former coworker nods, dipping her chin, and slips back inside the theater.

A hand wraps around hers. Cora nearly jumps.

"You do look quite pale, Cora," Arabella says, squeezing her hand, sniffling again. "You should get home, retire some, rest. Thank you for being such a good friend. I just . . . needed a trustworthy ear. And to know that I have your blessing."

Cora pastes on a smile that truly churns her stomach. "As we say in my homeland, 'the greenest of blessings.'"

And then, before she grows to fully hate herself, Cora bids her mark adieu.

She heads east on Fourteenth Street until she knows Arabella is well out of sight. Then she doubles back through the alley and into Pastor's.

※ ※ ※

"Still can't believe my eyes," Maeve says, looking Cora up and down after fully expressing her rightful shock and relief. "Not only alive, but doing quite well, it seems."

The two of them settled down for tea after all, just around the corner from the lobby of the theater. Hardly a soul is in here right now, which is why Cora agreed to a cup in the first place. Leora's is a modest tea shop, with a handful of white-cloth tables, a checkerboard tiled floor, and a frayed cushioned bench beside a smudged window overlooking Third Avenue. A world away from Mailliard's, and a place she is sure that neither Arabella Ames nor any of Alice's other targets would ever frequent.

"So good to see you, love." Maeve's tired eyes water. "Really have been worried sick, thinking the worst had befallen—"

"I've been well, Maeve, though truly regretful I didn't have the chance to say goodbye," Cora says sheepishly, eager to change the subject. "Though enough about me. Tell me about the troupe, all *your* latest adventures. How long is this latest run?"

"Two whole weeks. Prospero has been boasting about it since we left Boston. *Tony Pastor's new theater*," Maeve says, with mock stage gravity, "quite the coup." She slumps. "Up to Rochester after that, pitching a tent at the state fair. I get a chill just thinking about it. Anyways, no sense in worrying about that now. It'll be nice to stay in one place for a while. It's done near worn me out, this life, I've gotta admit."

"Indeed." Cora makes a mental note to avoid Union Square for the next couple weeks, before their ultimate play on the first of April. If Prospero himself were to spot her, no amount of silent entreaties would keep that showman from talking.

"Been really hard, you know," Maeve says softly, "since you disappeared."

Cora forces a laugh. "Oh, don't flatter me, Maeve. I was a backstage apprentice, nothing more. You certainly didn't need me then, and you don't need me now."

"It's different these days. Not getting any younger." Maeve gives her a rueful smile.

Buried memories of Prospero materialize, him snapping at the older woman, calling her a hag, ugly, washed up.

Why does she stay?

Only a few months ago, Cora might have instinctively blamed Maeve herself, dismissed her as a glutton for punishment.

But the truth, of course: Maeve has no other options.

Cora clears her throat, taking another sip from her teacup, trying in vain to put the memories back into their dark places, shut the doors and lock them tight—but she can't. It sounds as though Cora has only made things worse for the old woman. Did she even think about Maeve *once* when she took off that morning near Hell's Kitchen?

Despite all of Cora's supposed guilt—her sympathy for Arabella and Harry, her concerns about the ruthlessness of Alice's plan—is she really any more merciful than her mentor, not caring who gets hurt, not caring who gets left behind on her quest to right past wrongs?

"I never meant to vanish on you so abruptly," she finally says. "You have to understand, working with Prospero was a dead end for me. I made peanuts every week and Dinah was threatening to have me fired. I want to buy back my home, Maeve. I want to—I need to make what happened right." Cora steals a breath. "So when an opportunity came along that I couldn't pass up, to learn from someone, someone—"

"Is all this a job?" Maeve says quietly, vaguely gesturing to Cora's velvet dress and petticoat, her delicately made-up face and carefully arranged chignon. She lowers her voice. "Like your . . ." The older woman's eyes flit around before she discreetly mimes picking her own pocket, then flashes Cora a single raised, questioning eyebrow.

"It's more complicated than that, I'm afraid." Cora sighs. "In more ways than one."

"Is there a fella involved?" Maeve asks, rather shrewdly.

Her breath catches, her eyes sharpening on her old friend. Maeve would never try to blackmail her, would she? Did Maeve get a good look at Arabella? Would she sell Cora down the river for a chance to make a quick score with the smart set herself?

As if she can read her mind, the older woman shakes her head.

"Don't worry, love," Maeve whispers. "Ain't gonna rat you out. I want the best for you. Always did."

Cora hastily finishes her tea, attempting to mask the tears that have begun stinging her eyes. She suddenly feels like the loneliest person in the world.

Maeve glances at the tea shop clock, wincing. She finishes the remains of her own cup in one gulp. "I'd best return next door. Rehearsal's starting, and you know the great magician doesn't like to be kept waiting."

She reaches across the table, laying her calloused hand atop Cora's.

"I'd say take care of yourself, eh?" Her smile is flat. "But it seems you always do."

The words continue to burn as Cora wanders uptown, taking the air instead of hailing a cab. Her thoughts kicking up, twisting and turning like a Great Plains dust devil—painful recollections, people, uncomfortable truths all swirling together.

Maeve. Dinah. Arabella. Harry.

Da.

Is it the very worst thing to be a fool? Or could it be worse to be so clouded by supposed justice, so consumed by "winning" and revenge, that you lose all sense of decency?

Forget Alice; Cora may be no better than those vulturous bankmen from Ross & Calhoun.

She sniffs, shaking her head as she turns onto Madison.

Conmen. Victims. Victors. Marks. If no one is brave enough to break the cycle, when will it ever end?

A tear spills loose as Cora crosses Third Avenue, thoughts still churning.

Well, this performance is far from over, and Cora may have another trick up her sleeve. Though whether the twist will lead to one heck of a finale or ruin the show entirely remains to be seen.

CHAPTER 27

A Matter of Fairness

March 29, 1884

W hat do you suppose will happen to the marks after they're ruined?" Cora sits in her pauper's gown—a sort of cobbled collection of frayed rags sewn onto an evening gown frame, complete with a bunched cotton bustle—her face tilted upward, eyes closed, so that Béatrice can apply charcoal to the area around her lashes.

It's no easy feat to make someone look all the prettier for being filthy, but Béa has managed it, Alice admits— although she did draw the line when Béa offered to do the same for her.

Bad enough to be mocking the poor in her burlap gown and stained gloves. Her face can be left alone, thank you.

"In what sense?" Alice eventually replies. "Emotionally? Practically?"

"Practically," Cora says. "How long do you think it will be before they're forced to leave their homes?"

Alice can answer that from experience, but she refrains,

choosing instead to peer askance at her young protégée. "Why should you care?"

Cora averts her gaze.

Alice's own gaze narrows. "I'd think you'd be more pre-occupied with what happens to us."

"Okay then." Cora's eyes dart back to Alice's, brash now. "So what does happen? To us? Immediately following the successful completion of the fraud?"

Béa steps back from Cora, her work complete, and turns to Alice, expectant. Alice swears she can sense Dagmar listening from the kitchen too.

"Once we're out, we go to a secure location to divide our shares of the takings." Alice speaks slowly, as if to a simpleton.

"And then?" Cora asks.

Alice laughs in frustration. "And then I told you, that's up to *you*. You can hardly expect me to sketch out the rest of your life for you, not after planning everything leading up to that moment. Once your share is in your hands, it is yours to do with as you see fit."

"I suppose I just thought that plan might have changed a bit, given that you two are so . . ." Cora glances worriedly at Béa. "Are you suggesting we *all* go our separate ways, or just me?"

"I'm not suggesting anything," Alice says. "Merely stating a fact. When the job is done, we scatter. Nothing has changed, Cora. Why would it? This was never meant to be forever."

The room falls into a leaden silence, punctuated by the ticking of the mantel clock.

"And where will you be going, Alice?" Béa cuts in quietly, her eyes pained, unblinking.

Alice can't answer. Not for the sake of secrecy but because

she truly doesn't know. Something in her mind has not allowed her to think that far.

There's also the fact that, for all her bluster, the prospect of going her separate way from Béatrice is the most unthinkable thought of all. She wonders if Béa had assumed the plan would change too, after all these months of growing ever closer. Béa, dear Béa, who has been battered by life at every turn, is probably even more disappointed than sentimental Cora.

A rap sounds on the door. Béatrice turns away to answer it.

Cora glares at Alice accusingly.

"None of that now." Alice stands, reflexively brushing off her deliberately filthy gown. "If you're really that helpless, I can secure you a coach ticket under a false name for that afternoon. We'll need to be well out of the city by nightfall. I know you're going out west to buy back your farm—"

"So you did listen," Cora mutters.

"Just tell me, whereabouts is it?" Alice smiles, the very picture of patient amiability.

"Near Topeka. Kansas."

Alice winces in sympathy. "And you're quite sure you want to go home to . . . Kansas?"

Cora's cheeks redden with indignation. "Why shouldn't I? It's beautiful there. Not to mention peaceful, especially compared to the city. You can hear the birds sing in the morning and the evening, and you can look out on an actual horizon, not a man-made one. You ask me, it's the perfect place to go unnoticed for the rest of one's days and not mind one little bit." She gives a flat laugh. "I'll tell you one thing I'm looking forward to; it's taking off this damned French corset and setting fire to it out in the field. Never having to worry about which fork is which or how to make polite conversation with the likes of—"

"Mr. McAllister," Béatrice announces from the entryway.

Alice blinks. She'd rather been enjoying that rant of Cora's. "What?"

Béa glances behind her. "He's arrived to collect you for the ball?"

Shaking her head, Alice hurries to fetch their invitations from her study, then follows Cora down the front stoop, past Béa, who has trained her eyes firmly upon her own feet to avoid looking at Alice.

Alice's heart pinches. She swallows away the sensation and lifts her chin.

On the street below, McAllister is waiting for them from inside the open door of his carriage.

Ward, dressed in a head-to-toe hobo costume, is waving some sort of large frond about.

"An olive branch!" he crows.

Alice laughs in sheer incredulity. The man went down to the flower markets to buy an actual olive branch to hold. Why do anything subtly?

"Which I offer"—he bows deeply, branch extended—"to you."

Cora glances between them. "Are we going or . . . ?"

"Yes, yes, come inside!" Ward shakes himself out of his seat, lending them each a hand into the carriage. "We hadn't spoken of it specifically, but as I tend to escort you two to these events . . ."

"Of course," Alice says coolly. "Very gracious of you."

When the door shuts, Ward raises an eyebrow, the branch

still in his hand. Alice grudgingly takes it from him, sensing he's not going to relent otherwise.

"I realize," Ward starts, squinting regretfully, "that I came on unnecessarily strong with my demands. There was no need for all that . . . unpleasantness."

"It's fine," Alice says, peering out the window. "We came to an arrangement."

Cora's big eyes flash between them with interest Alice has no time or energy to entertain. To the girl's credit, she refrains from inquiring.

"Yes, but I realized belatedly, I could've approached it with a bit more gentility. After all, we are old friends by now, my dear, and if I'd only explained to you the *why* of it, I reckon you'd have offered to up my take without the need for bombast and bullyin'."

Cora draws in a sharp breath, but a glare from Alice sends her looking in the other direction again.

"I don't need to hear the why," Alice says, knowing damn well he's about to tell her anyway.

"For one thing, it's a matter of fairness," Ward plows on. "Who's done what and so forth. You're the brains of all this, no doubt about it, but there would simply be no opportunity without a person such as myself by your side. Cora, did Alice ever happen to tell you about the first time she and I met?"

Alice could slap the man for dragging Cora into this. She smiles vaguely instead and keeps looking out at the city scenes filtering past her isinglass window.

"No, she hasn't," Cora says, a hint of rebellion in her voice. "Do tell, Mr. McAllister."

"Why, it was a little more than a year ago, can you believe

that, Alice?" Ward continues to use her real name, she notes. Like a weapon. A bomb he could drop at any moment, should he choose to. "I was down at the Union Square flower market, pickin' out American Beauties for Mrs. Astor. She likes for me to select her flowers personally, you see. When along comes a woman in a lovely day dress—now, that was the first tell, right there. Ladies of that apparent station would send their maids, don't you know, not traipse down among the hoi polloi themselves. But I smiled politely, didn't I, Alice? Tipped my hat. Now, here's where the fun began. She was holding a vase, blue and white, in a Chinese style. As I took a step forward to point to a rose, she positioned herself *just so*, allowing me to knock straight into her, at which point the vase fell from her hands and shattered on the flagstones. Tears swirled in her eyes. The lady had brought it here to pair flowers with it, she told me. It was her mother's, Ming dynasty, priceless!"

Alice sighs. She knows the rest of this tale only too well.

"Now, at this point, any kindhearted gentleman of means would offer to pay for the damages," Ward says, leaning back to rest his hands on his "pauper's" waistcoat, the buttons threatening to spring loose from their seams. "In fact, that's exactly what I *did* do several months prior, when another, far less genteel woman had pulled the exact same trick on me down at the Canal Street flower market. Some luck you had, Alice, playin' the same tired, old con—but in the end, I'd say it was good luck, not bad."

He turns to Cora.

"Right then and there, I offered her my arm, and I said, 'I'm not gonna give you money for that piece of junk. I'm gonna offer you something much more valuable.' Took her out to tea and imparted my wisdom to her. 'You are clearly an elegant woman of fine breeding,' I said, didn't I, Alice? 'You can do better than two-bit street tricks.' And that was when she told me she spoke French. And German. That she knew all about European current events. And that she had a wild plan in that lovely head of hers. The rest, as the man says, is history."

"And I am truly grateful," Alice says placidly.

"Now that there is our history," Ward says, adjusting himself on the bench. "A fine story, but my future is looking even finer."

"Let me guess." Cora cocks her head. "You'll build the biggest mansion in New York, secure the best box seat at the Met, and throw the first and best ball every season."

"As enchanting as all of that sounds . . . no." Ward waggles his bushy eyebrows. "I'm taking myself off to Paris. I shall bid adieu to all of these pathetic, desperate, two-bit wannabe aristocrats and make friends with real ones. Oh yes, I'm going to live out my days as a wealthy expatriate, fill my salon with the handsomest men and most entertaining women I can find, and I will not spare a single thought for those I've left behind."

The implication is clear: including Alice.

"What of your wife?" she asks. "I can't quite picture her carousing in Parisian society."

The carriage stops.

Ward widens his eyes. "Funny. I can't picture that either."

He grins.

A chill sends goose bumps rising all over Alice's arms.

"Which brings me to my burning question," Ward says, his tone featherlight as he raises a hand to keep them from exiting. "Which additional marks shall we be adding into the mix tonight?"

Cora outright stares at Alice now but again has the good sense to stay quiet.

Alice shrugs one elegant shoulder. "None. But don't you fret, Ward. I've figured out a way to manage the funds in a manner that will suit us all to a T."

"Me?" Ward points to himself, mouth agape. "Fret? Never!"

He raps Alice lightly on the knee with his cane. "I always knew you'd work it out." He rises, waving for them to step down from the carriage.

"One last celebration before the biggest one of all," he announces grandly. "Now let's go slum!"

CHAPTER 28

Rotgut and Vittles

I f the Night of Illusions ball had been the overture to
Cora's New York social season, it is perhaps fitting that
Mrs. Witt's latest private banquet will be her final act.

The Witt estate has gone through its own extraordinary
transformation in the interim, Cora notes as they arrive on
Madison and Fifty-First Street, although one might more ac-
curately call it a *debasement*. Mrs. Witt's careful landscaping
of ivy, rosebushes, and potted topiaries is now covered in ratty,
tattered blankets. Her dozens of stained glass windows be-
smirched with dirt. A collection of buckets and dusters has
been arranged into a sculpture at the soot-stained, Baroque-
style entrance, with a handwritten beggar's sign atop the pile,
gleefully misspelled in accordance with the invitation posted
weeks ago:

Welckom to the Poverty Balle!
488 Madison Aveneu, New Yerk

Ward offers Cora a hand down from the cab, looking
around with a smirk as he adjusts his pageboy cap. "My, my,

better than I could've expected. Iris Witt may be many things, but understated ain't one of them."

They open the door themselves, in keeping with the theme, Cora supposes, not a butler in sight, other than the costumed guests themselves.

Inside Mrs. Witt's grand hall, the party is already in full swing, hundreds of partygoers in custom rag gowns and footman uniforms mingling about under the Witts' crystal three-tiered chandeliers, which are bespeckled at present by dirty mopheads. The parlor on the right—the one that was repurposed as the troupe's backstage space during the Night of Illusions, if Cora remembers the house correctly—has been arranged like a clapboard tenement, complete with cots on the floor and laundry lines ribboned like a spiderweb across the ceiling. On the left, the dining room chairs have been replaced by wooden boxes, and folded newspaper-napkins decorate the table.

The lump in Cora's throat grows into a ball as she follows Alice deeper into the manse, the overwhelming tastelessness of tonight very nearly derailing her intended mission. How on earth did she ever envy these wretched people, ever see them as the shiny American victors?

"I spy the Vandemeers," Ward murmurs, gesturing ahead to a refreshments table, which has been arranged like a food line in a lodging house. "Shall we make the rounds? Start handing out our coveted invitations?"

Alice nods, threading her arm through Ward's.

Cora shakes her head, following them. She's not sure she'll ever understand their relationship, which seems all the murkier after Ward's little walk down memory lane. Currently, he and Alice seem as tight as ever, though Cora can't help but worry that whatever "arrangement" they've come to likely doesn't bode well for the rest of them.

"Duchess," Mrs. Vandemeer says vacantly, lifting her glass as they approach, her silver bodice cascading into tiered bustles of rags. "Perhaps it's premature to celebrate our *company* . . . but ha, let us drink all the same."

Mrs. Vandemeer must have dipped into her snuff quite early tonight, Cora notes—the woman nearly knocks down the pyramid of bowls displayed on the table with her intended toast.

The rest of said company ignores her faux pas, Ward merely smiling coyly. "Perhaps not so premature."

He glances at Alice, then pulls a thick cream envelope from his hobo vest with enough dramatic flourish to rival Prospero.

Mr. Vandemeer takes the invitation as one would accept a Communion wafer, hands outstretched, face twisted with rapture. "Is this . . . what I think it is?"

Mr. McAllister winks. "You'll have to wait and see when you open it."

"Yours has been delivered first, naturally," Alice adds demurely.

"How many?" Vandemeer presses. "How many have you—"

"Only five," Alice says. "Including yours."

"You ask me, competition is the spice of life," Ward crows, helping himself to a glass of rotgut punch. "I myself keep urgin' our dear duchess to open trading on the exchange down on Wall Street, but her little heart is set on the embassy and the company of friends only . . ."

Cora drifts down the table, watching her mentors work with resigned remorse. *This* she will miss. Not Mr. McAllister, obviously, nor her mounting crises of conscience, but the team. The notion of being part of something bigger than the sum of its parts.

Alice's crew has become . . . well, her sanctuary, she supposes, a family she has made for herself. A family that will disband mere days from now, Cora realizes soberly, given Alice's unwavering vision. Despite what Alice had insisted upon, time and again throughout the season, Cora honestly believed her mentor's mind would change somewhere along the way. She feels like such a dupe even thinking it, but the emerald con seems far less valuable a score when Cora imagines herself alone at its end.

She laughs bitterly into her glass. Oh, the irony. To finally get Long Creek Farm, have the last laugh, only to realize that who she's with matters a far sight more than where she's going.

"Did you make a last-minute change?" The question startles her.

Cora turns to see Arabella standing before her, a faint blush across her cheeks. She gestures down toward Cora's dress. "I recall you were planning to come as a scullery maid."

Ah yes, the little white lie in Lord & Taylor. Cora glances over at Ward, who still stands gossiping, now a ways down the drawing room.

"He fired her," she says simply. "I had to pivot."

"Well," Arabella says brightly, "you are the loveliest pauper I ever saw." The girl winces, cringing at herself. Perhaps realizing she sounds like her obsequious mother? "I'm a bit out of sorts. Again, sorry. And this party is overwhelming. Hardly helping the matter."

Cora smiles, looking around pointedly, venturing, "Mrs. Witt has really outdone herself."

"It is all . . . a bit off-putting, is it not?"

"Ghastly."

"In terrible taste!"

Both girls burst into relieved laughter. For a moment, Cora conjures another reality, one where she and Arabella are actual debutantes, true friends.

"I want to apologize for the other day, Cora," Arabella says. "I really am very eager to marry your cousin—"

"You do not have to explain yourself to me."

"I just . . . I struggle to picture my future life abroad. When I try to imagine my home in Württemberg, with Prince Wilhelm, or the wedding, or even the gardens the duchess speaks so fondly of, I . . . well, I find I cannot conjure anything. It is as if my future is merely . . . blank."

Perhaps Arabella is more intuitive than Cora ever gave her credit for.

If ever there was an opening for her planned conversation . . .

"Something has been weighing on my mind too," Cora confesses. "I was hoping we might have a private word?"

Arabella's thin brows pinch, but still, she nods gamely. "Of course, dear friend. Lead the way."

The pair navigate through the crowd, Arabella trailing, with Cora bound for the one space she knows intimately in the Witts' grand home. On their way to the private theater, they pass a sprawling dice game spilling out of the adjacent parlor.

"Cora! Bella!" Harry leaps up, looking goggle-eyed between them. "Are you enjoying the party?"

He begins swaying. Is he tippled? Cora leans closer, catching a gag-inducing whiff of whiskey. Oh, most certainly.

"The game of craps is ever so much fun." Harry guffaws. "There seems a surprising inverse correlation between frivolity and affluence—"

"Do win one for Württemberg, won't you, darling?" Cora says kindly. "We'll join you shortly."

As soon as they reach the theater, Cora ushers Arabella inside and closes the wide double doors behind them. The large space is mercifully free of partygoers, as she anticipated, empty but for the long rows of wooden chairs, the majestic walls spangled in woodwork, and the wide, red-curtained stage. A room primed for her own performance.

"So grand," Arabella marvels.

Cora nods. "I thought it a fitting place to talk."

"Have you been here before?" Arabella says curiously.

Cora's breath catches.

"You were still in Württemberg, were you not, for Mrs. Witt's Night of Illusions? Though perhaps you came for lunch or tea?"

"I asked one of Mrs. Witt's servants for a quiet place, is all," Cora says breezily. *Focus, Cora. No need for any contradictions, not when we are so close.* "Please. Come sit."

Arabella slides beside Cora onto one of the nearby chairs.

"I know you are anxious about your future, Arabella," Cora starts. "But I assure you, Württemberg is a truly breathtaking place. Green pastures as far as the eye can see. Rolling mountain ranges. The Black Forest, with its shining lakes. Around every corner, there are treasures to rival even the mines themselves."

Arabella nods absently, studying her lap. "So I've heard."

"And yet I know all these things can feel so very . . . abstract," Cora continues. "Only painted in your mind's eye through Wilhem's letters, which can be unnerving." She steals a breath. "Which is why I think you should join us at the embassy next week."

Arabella looks up. "The embassy?"

"Mr. McAllister will be handing your parents an invitation at some point tonight," Cora explains. She takes Arabella's hand. "Despite to whom the card is specifically addressed, as your friend, I beseech you to be there as well. Württemberg is your future home, after all, and you should be fully informed about the mines and *your* company. How the new investment structure impacts your future."

Arabella lets out a soft laugh. "I'm not sure my parents would agree. One of our housekeepers was once dismissed just for allowing me a glimpse of a grocery bill. They prefer me to keep my mind . . . unpolluted."

"I don't believe a solid grounding in finance to be anything but useful," Cora retorts. "Do you think so, truly?"

"I would always prefer to know more rather than less," Arabella admits, rather shyly—though the girl's answer comes as no real surprise, given Arabella and budding scientist Harry have always gotten on so swimmingly. "But my parents can be quite forceful in sheltering me."

"I see." Cora sighs. "Then . . . tell them that you must be there for, I don't know, emotional support. For me. On such a momentous occasion. We will be cousins by marriage, after all. I should think our close kinship means a lot to your mother."

"Well. That is unarguable." Arabella smiles hesitantly, looking more resolute by the moment. "All right, Cora. Yes. I will try my best to be there."

"Wonderful. And one more thing . . ."

Cora hesitates. *How very important it is to walk the proverbial tightrope here.* "I should like to know that I can truly count on you for emotional support. If I ask you for something come

Tuesday, I would very much appreciate it if you would comply, with no questions asked."

Again, Arabella's brow wrinkles, but this time she smiles. "You can *always* count on me, Cora."

"Good." Cora squeezes the girl's hand before letting go. "Now that that is settled, shall we return to the madness?"

The girls exit, laughing. As soon as the doors are open, Arabella peeling off to greet others, Cora nearly wilts with relief.

"Everything all right?" Alice asks archly.

Cora startles, turning to find her mentor looming over her.

Goodness, was Alice following her? Did she know Cora was in the theater? Does she have any suspicions as to why?

"Right as rain, dear cousin." Cora offers a bland smile, steering her away from the theater doors. "Why wouldn't it be?"

The rest of the party is a sickly blur. A late dinner of mush and cabbage, another round of rotgut punch, and then, once the remainder of invitations have been delivered to their targets, she, Alice, and Ward take their leave—a quiet ride via Mr. McAllister's carriage to the apartment on Thirty-Eighth Street.

"Get some beauty rest, my dear duchess, my little heiress." Mr. McAllister winks at each of them. "Big day come Tuesday."

Alice retires to her chambers without another word. For once, Cora is relieved to have that door firmly shut between them.

Even so, she's too pained to sleep. Tossing. Turning. This will be one of her final nights, she realizes afresh, in this snug little bedroom she's come to regard as home.

She hears a whistle of a kettle from the kitchen.

Perhaps she's not the only one having trouble sleeping.

Cora ventures out to find Alice sitting at the table, one lone lantern by her side, brow stitched, poring over that damned ledger, as always.

She looks up curiously as Cora approaches.

We are all going our separate ways, Cora reminds herself. *If I do not say this now, I'll never have the chance.*

"I have something to tell you," she says evenly.

Alice leans back in her chair, placing down her pencil. "What a dramatic opening for a girl in a nightgown at four in the morning."

"And I need you to listen. For once." Cora is surprised to find her tone remains level, despite her nerves. Steely, like Alice's own. "Because I really must thank you, Alice. You've changed my life, taught me everything. I know I can't re-pay you. Nevertheless, I'm going to try right now." Tears, shockingly, sting her eyes, this little impromptu speech of hers suddenly feeling momentous. She blinks them back. "I know you think you are infallible. Unflappable. Brilliant and sharp as an emerald yourself, and well, you are, but . . ."

She takes a fortifying breath, ignoring the defensive skepticism playing over Alice's face.

"You have built something here. Something worthwhile. And I'm not just talking about the con. I know you think it's easier to burn it all down, every last bit of it, and walk away, but you would be making a huge mistake. An irrevocable one."

She dares a step closer.

"I've spent much of the past couple years convincing myself that vulnerability is stupidity, and in the process of trying not to play the fool, I've made countless foolish mistakes. If you want to pretend I'm just a pawn, just a cog in the wheel of your game, that's fine; cast me aside if you must. You've only known me for a matter of months, after all. If I had my druthers, I'd prefer to continue to know you, but that's your decision to make."

Cora presses her hands into the table, eyes sliding to the maid's chambers across the hall.

"But I'll tell you this as a parting gift. For all your grand plans and brilliant schemes, you are the most idiotic person I know if you walk away from Béa. You deserve true happiness, Alice, same as anyone else. Showing love and showing weakness are *not* one and the same. And of all the things I may have thought of you in private, I never took you for a coward. But here we are."

"Is that all?" Alice says, though there's an uncharacteristic hitch to her tone. A now-familiar wrinkle forming in her forehead.

"Yes," Cora says. "That's everything. Good night, Alice."

She closes her bedroom door without another glance. Buries her head under her blanket, her bittersweet satisfaction finally eclipsed by exhaustion.

An Exclusive Invitation

You are cordially invited

TO AN INTIMATE GATHERING
IN CELEBRATION OF
THE COMMENCEMENT OF TRADE
BETWEEN THE KINGDOM OF WÜRTTEMBERG
AND THE UNITED STATES OF AMERICA

TUESDAY, THE FIRST OF APRIL, 1884
UPON THE OPENING OF THE MARKETS
NINE O'CLOCK IN THE MORNING

AT THE EMBASSY OF
THE KINGDOM OF WÜRTTEMBERG
50 CENTRAL PARK SOUTH

REFRESHMENTS WILL BE SERVED
WITH LUNCHEON TO FOLLOW AT SHERRY'S

CHAPTER 29

The Sting

Arabella's father stares at the embossed embassy card with an unimpressed squint that makes his mustache twitch.

Arabella finds herself holding her breath. Could it be he's considering snubbing the invitation?

Not if her already red-faced mother has anything to do with it.

"Nothing here about financial dealings," he grunts. "Anyone would think this was a social call."

"Well, precisely!" Her mother flings herself beside him. "Her Grace can't very well write down the true purpose of the meeting, or any Tom, Dick, or Harry could lay eyes on this bit of paper and word would spread like wildfire, absolutely *everyone* wanting to worm their way in."

"Nothing here about Arabella either," he mutters with a droopy frown, his eyes lifting briefly to meet Arabella's. "Doesn't seem appropriate for the wife-folk to attend a business meeting, let alone our impressionable young daughter."

"It's only because Miss Cora has to be there," Arabella puts in. "She requires a friend close at hand or she'll be terribly bored. And if the bidding grows too heated, we'll excuse ourselves."

"Miss Ritter, eh? Maybe I'll write a note to the duchess, suggesting she keep her ward at home as well."

"You'll do no such thing!" her mother snaps. "This is no mere business meeting, my darling; it is a matter of family. Think of Arabella's future. Our *grandchildren*—"

Arabella's heart thuds wildly, as it always does when the two of them bicker. She retreats to the safety of her own bedroom, her thoughts in a muddle. Perhaps it would be easier to stay home and avoid the argument. The idea of capitulating comes as an instant relief.

It was odd, wasn't it? The intensity with which Cora implored her to come.

Something seems amiss. She can't quite put her finger on it.

But good heavens, if she cannot even brave a trip to the Württemberg embassy, how on earth will she manage to move to Württemberg itself?

She buries her face in her pillow to soak up her tears.

※ ※ ※

"This is a first," Iris Witt declares, racing through B. Altman with two shopgirls and a floor merchant tailing her. "What does one wear to an embassy luncheon?"

"Perhaps something in the style of the country in question?" the merchant suggests.

Iris sneers at him. "I think emeralds would be a bit obvious, don't you?"

"Or perhaps"—he frowns thoughtfully—"obvious is exactly what the occasion calls for?"

The shopgirls murmur between themselves.

Iris flings herself onto the closest settee. "Very well. Bring me everything you have in green. Quickly! Might as well collar a seamstress; the event is tomorrow."

As they curtsy, bow, and turn, she calls again, "While you're at it, show me some bags. Crocodile skin, large enough to hold two hundred and fifty thousand dollars in cash."

The color drains from the merchant's face.

Iris fans herself. "And if you breathe a word about anything I've said today, I'll tell all my friends that B. Altman and Company is infested with bedbugs. Now shoo!"

"Very good, madam," the merchant says, and just as they round the corner, out of earshot, he tells the shopgirls, "Raise the price of everything twenty percent."

🦂 🦂 🦂

"Are you sure I oughtn't accompany you tomorrow, my darling?" Priscilla reaches her vein-riddled hand across the table to grasp her husband's.

Revulsion ripples through Ogden, even as he smiles adoringly. "We've talked about this, Priscilla. It's a business meeting. You'd be bored to tears as we men talk of bonds and market share."

Dinner is the only time she doesn't wear her gloves. It's a wonder he can eat at all.

"But it won't just be men, will it?" Her hooded eyes narrow farther. "*She'll* be there."

"I'm not sure to whom you're referring," he says lightly, sipping his wine.

"Cora Ritter," she hisses. "That girl couldn't stop looking at you during their last visit. And that vulgar song she sang. She has aims on you, I know it."

"Now, darling, you know she's engaged to—"

"Which makes it all the more disgusting, how she flirts with you." Mrs. Ogden cuts into her steak with renewed vigor.

Does she? Ogden wonders. A secret smile plays over his lips. Perhaps he'll have the duchess as a main and the girl for dessert. Preferably before she's been sullied by the marriage bed.

"You've nothing to worry about, dearest," he breathes. "I am yours alone, body and soul. And the riches I bring home tomorrow morning will be mere icing on the cake of our felicity."

Priscilla lets out her broken-glass laugh. He guzzles his wine to dull the grate of it.

🦋 🦋 🦋

"Where is it?" James Vandemeer shouts, his cheeks reddening above his freshly trimmed beard. "I insisted it be ready by eight this morning!"

"It is eight now, sir," the valet says, handing him the heavy-laden folio case he requested.

"*By* eight," Vandemeer repeats disdainfully. "Do they not speak English where you come from?"

"They speak French, sir."

Far down the corridor, Olivia Vandemeer drifts like a ghost between rooms.

"Goodbye, my darling!" James shouts, hoisting the bag. "I'll be the first outside the embassy door. Position in the room is everything, you know. Let's get going. Time is money, and I mean to gain an obscene amount of it today!"

"Get me my cane!" Harold Peyton Sr. shouts.

Harry cringes. "I don't suggest rising from your chair, Father. Not without first performing a few calisthenics to strengthen the muscles—"

"It's not for walking, it's for beating people! Like my idiot son! Thinks he can tell me anything. Medical or otherwise." Harold Senior's voice falls into an incoherent grumble. Harry feels his own spine beginning to weaken once again under his father's glare. "You think you're a big boy now, don't you, Harry, with your fiancée and her emeralds, but I'll tell you something. They're going to be *my* emeralds soon. You are coming with me in order to roll my chair. Nothing more! You got it? I don't want to hear a damn peep out of you while the men are talking."

Harry sniffs, picturing the long Bow Bridge in Central Park. A stroll with his dear old dad. A feigned misstep, a hoist of the chair, his father tumbling straight into the lake . . .

"What was that?" Harold shouts.

"Nothing, sir," Harry says. "Didn't make a peep."

✿ ✿ ✿

"Test it once more," Alice says.

Béatrice sits before the telegraph machine and begins to type.

"And can you hear me through the wall?"

Silence. Then, on the ticker tape, the typed word: "Yes."

Alice laughs as she opens the door to the "ambassador's" office.

"Good," she breathes, leaning against the desk, close to Béa. She nods up to the wall, where a large clock is displayed. "If for whatever reason you can't hear the announcement through the door, you'll stick to the timings regardless."

"Announcement of lunch by ten fifteen, out the window before half past." Béa reaches for her hand. "It will all be splendid, Alice. No more arranging, no more planning. We are ready."

Alice lets her fingers curl into Béa's for a few blessed seconds before letting go and striding to the door.

"It's a quarter to nine," Béa says softly. "I suppose you should go out into the salon now. I'll . . . well, I suppose I'll see you at the meeting place."

Alice's hand lingers on the doorknob.

"For all your grand plans and brilliant schemes, you are the most idiotic person I know if you walk away from Béa."

Alice swallows around a vise-tight throat, then turns around. "As a matter of fact, there is one more matter to be arranged."

"Oh?" Béa frowns.

Alice glances over her shoulder, at the closed door leading to the reception room, and then joins Béa once again.

"I . . . well, you see, I've bought a set of coach tickets, heading west. First to Albany." Her feet fidget upon the floor. Lord's sake, she's more nervous about this conversation than she's been about any aspect of this plan thus far. "I thought we might lodge for the night there before we board a train to . . . perhaps somewhere in the Midwest?"

Good grief, where did that idea come from? Another influence of Cora's, no doubt.

Although, my goodness, she's surprisingly grateful for that influence now.

"We could go farther," she blurts. "All the way to the Pacific coast. Or even abroad, if you'd prefer?"

Béa slowly smiles. "I'm still puzzling over that 'we.'"

"I'm rather hoping you'll come with me," Alice says. "Stay with me. In fact . . . I'm desperate for it."

Béa stays very still. She closes her eyes, as if pained.

I'm too late, Alice thinks. *She's written me off as a poor investment.*

"I've been closed off," Alice says. "I know it. It was a struggle, often, and I fought to maintain that . . . distance. Which hasn't been fair to you. Not to Cora either—Dagmar I don't suppose cares either way."

Béa lets out a breathy laugh of acknowledgment. Her eyes still don't rise to Alice's.

"I pretended it was about the plan, keeping a steady heart and a cool head." Alice's voice comes out a little broken. She draws a heavy breath and forges ahead regardless. "But it was more than that. You have to understand, Béatrice, everyone . . ."

A sob chokes at Alice's throat. She whispers around it.

"Everyone has left me." Tears flood her eyes. She draws a stinging gasp. "My father. My baby sister. Cal, off to seek his own fortune. My mother, the way she hid inside herself and gave up and didn't spare a thought for . . ."

She can't say it. Her hands are shaking, her eyes streaming. This is the worst possible time to confess all of this, the most unstrategic display of raw emotion, and yet, what other time will there be?

"If you left too, Béa—"

And then Béa is there, rising from the desk in a blur, pressing her hands to Alice's cheeks, wiping the tears away with the tips of her fingers. "I will stay by your side, Alice. If you will have me, *mon Dieu, je resterai, pour toujours et toujours.*"

What could I possibly want apart from this? Alice thinks as she takes in humble, kind, brilliant Béa.

When she steps back and straightens her gown, it's with a rush of renewed purpose. Her eyes dry up in a blink.

Revenge has felt bitter all this time. Now, she suspects, it will only be sweet.

Béa returns to her station at the desk before the telegram machine, shooting her a grin from across the room as Alice opens the door. After clicking it closed behind her, she strides into the Württembergian embassy with her head held imperiously high.

Alice nods to Dagmar and manages not to laugh at her cook's getup—Alpine maiden garb purchased from a theatrical costumer, the look complete with two long, plaited pigtails. Dagmar picks up a tray of drinks and nods back, grave.

Alice glances reassuringly at Cora, who is pacing the room in her pretty pink dress. Cora answers the look with a nod of her own.

To Ward, seated at a table in the corner, his ledger at the ready, she grants a rather cooler smile.

Last, she inspects their ambassador, standing proudly beneath the mounted Württembergian flag.

Dagmar's bartender sweetheart, Konrad Weber, fits the bill even better than Alice could have hoped. In his tailored diplomat uniform decorated with dangling war medals, his bristled mustache trimmed and oiled, he looks every bit the Bavarian grandee.

"Zay are already waiting to enter," he notes, nodding to the front door. Even his accent is perfect, Alice marvels. "Care to do zee honors?"

Konrad steps gallantly aside.

And the Duchess Marie Charlotte Gabriella of Württemberg opens the parlor-level door to the entrance hall.

🦋 🦋 🦋

Cora has never felt so nervous and exhilarated for a performance in her life. Her heart takes off, galloping like a wild pony, as the embassy door flings open.

Mr. Vandemeer stands waiting in the vestibule, the first to arrive, naturally, looking as puffed and barrel-chested as a rooster in his trim business suit.

"Velcome, velcome!" Alice's newly minted ambassador cries, clicking the heels of his gilded and medaled green uniform. A bit on the nose, Cora had thought of the costume as a first impression, but Alice had insisted that subtlety is lost on these people, and now Cora can certainly see her point.

Konrad extends his hand to Mr. Vandemeer. "I am Gustav Roderick, zee Württemberg ambazeedor, yes?" He pumps Vandemeer's hand vigorously. "Zee well has run dry, eh? Now it ez time for a new type of green!"

Cora risks a glance in Alice's direction. Was that an ad-libbed riff on their Württembergian folk saying? And is it her imagination, or is Konrad's accent growing more pronounced?

Alice, though, remains placid, immovable as marble beside the man.

"Err, James Vandemeer. A pleasure, Ambassador Roderick."

"We make you at home." The ambassador waves them in. "Come, come, take ze seats."

As soon as Mr. Vandemeer makes himself comfortable in the embassy's sitting room, Dagmar moves from her position next to the wall, braids flopping as she hurries over to the serving trolley. She begins adding a thick brown mixture into a sherry glass, topping it off with a healthy pour of red wine from the nearby decanter.

Alice sits down prettily in an empty chair.

"An Esslingen cordial," Alice boasts as Dagmar hands James Vandemeer the glass, the contents of which are disturbingly murky.

"At nine in the morning?" Vandemeer raises his eyebrows.

"Our country's signature breakfast drink," Alice explains. "It is meant to bring good fortune."

Vandemeer takes a sip, sputtering, "Thick as molasses."

"It is mainly Württembergian berry wine," Alice adds. "Plus honey, spices, and a splash of fig liqueur. *Prost!*"

"*Prost*," Vandemeer mutters.

"And for zee young lady." The cook-turned-secretary hands Cora an identical glass of plain old juice.

How Cora wishes her own drink was spiked. She could use something right now to calm her nerves.

Entering soon after is Mrs. Witt, by herself. She struts inside, dressed to the hilt, a garish feathered hat, head to toe in blinding green. She's also clutching the largest crocodile skin handbag Cora has ever seen.

A minute later, Mr. Ogden arrives, alone as well. Cora imagines he must have suffered quite the argument leaving his clinging wife to venture out for a meeting with Alice.

Next come the Peytons. Harry, suit pressed, hair combed, wearing a cautious smile, pushes inside a golden wheelchair bearing a livered scowl of a man.

Alice and the ambassador hurry to greet them at the door, while Cora trails behind.

"Mr. Peyton," Alice says crisply. "What a pleasure to meet you at last."

"Are you the gal my blockhead son plans to marry?" Peyton Senior sneers up at Alice in appraising silence.

She stares back at the ancient man, every bit as coldly. To any unsuspecting onlooker, this would be the natural response of any upstanding woman to a man as boorish as this. But Cora can see a deeper satisfaction in the set of Alice's smile.

She's locked eyes on him at last. Drawn him out, into her web. The worst of them.

"Ah, no," Cora says quickly, stepping forward, lest the bald hatred playing over Alice's face becomes evident to everyone. "That would be me." Cora gives a deferential curtsy. "I'm so pleased to meet you, Mr. Peyton."

"Humph." Peyton Senior's eyes narrow as he studies her like a piece of meat. Cora resists the urge to squirm. She must have passed his examination, at least in some fashion, because the old man nods faintly, then shouts behind him, "Move it, Harry!"

Harry does as commanded, flashing Cora a manic smile.

"It's all very exciting," he murmurs, wheeling the chair forward. "My father hardly likes anyone, but I dare say—"

"Quit jabbering and let's get on with it!" Peyton Senior snarls. "What did I tell you, boy?"

"Simply waiting for one more," Alice says. "Please. Make yourself comfortable."

The marks attempt to mingle, a general air of expectation, discomfort, as the morning ticks toward the inevitable opening bell. Eventually, though, they all take their seats, accepting Dagmar's aggressive urging to try the Esslingen cordial, sipping on the oversweet beverage with barely disguised reluctance. The room now reeks of impatience.

Alice glances conspicuously at the clock.

"Nearly opening time for the markets," she says, feigning nonchalance. "Does everyone have their initial buy-in amounts at the ready? Am I saying that right, Mr. McAllister?"

She laughs helplessly.

"You are indeed, Your Grace," Ward calls out from his seat in the corner, a wide ledger on his lap, pen at the ready.

The ambassador adds with gravity, "I do hope you all understood zee need for an initial deposeet of zee cash."

This time Alice barely suppresses a glare. Yes, Konrad is most certainly overplaying his role—that was meant to be Alice's line, wasn't it? And she would have pronounced the words far more convincingly.

"Izz everybody here?" he adds curiously.

"What the hell is the holdup?" Peyton Senior snaps.

"We're expecting two more." Alice stands swiftly but keeps herself anchored to her silk-upholstered chair, knuckles turning white against its back. "Perhaps they've gotten lost."

The Ameses, Cora realizes, her thoughts beginning to freefall. *The Ameses are the ones missing.*

In a panic, she replays her conversation with Arabella during the poverty ball. Her request for the girl to not only join them but follow Cora's lead. Did Cora's appeal tip her off in some fashion? Could Arabella have sensed something amiss? Did she warn her parents, implore them not to come?

"Nearly nine thirty, Your Grace." Mr. Ogden leans across the arm of his chair to stroke Alice's hand.

She flinches so minutely Cora's sure the cretin hasn't noticed it.

Mr. Vandemeer puts down his glass. "Yes, let's get this show on the road."

Alice's gaze remains tenaciously fixed upon the door.

Cora ignores the muted pangs of guilt and shame coiling inside her. *No.* She made the right decision about Arabella, she's certain of it. *Someone* needs to break this vicious cycle.

Cora just hopes she didn't blow the whole sting in the process.

A minute later, the door slaps open once again.

Cora lets out a low whistle. *Abracadabra, there they are.*

Robert Ames skitters in first while Arabella trails behind him, looking guileless as ever, her hair prettily curled, her tiny figure flattered by a simple violet tea dress. If Alice is surprised by the girl's uninvited attendance, she doesn't let on, greeting her with a kiss to the cheek. Mrs. Ames brings up the rear and appears to have dressed for Arabella's royal wedding, puffed up in a huge lace hat and overly frilly ensemble complete with train.

The three of them sit down together on one settee, huddled, like three blind mice.

"I do hope you don't mind that Arabella has decided to attend as well," Mrs. Ames says, squirming to get comfortable. "It only seemed appropriate to Robert and me, given how this occasion will impact her future among the royal ranks—"

"Of course, the more the merrier."

Alice once more glances at the clock, her eyes now sparkling with resolve.

The game is on.

🪄 🪄 🪄

"Mr. McAllister," Alice demurs, turning to Ward in the corner. "Would you mind terribly outlining the financial proceedings, as you suggested them to me? You know I have a distaste of talking about money."

"It's one of the things we love most about you, our dearest duchess," Ogden says in a sultry tone. "The particular delicacy with which you wear your sex."

Alice becomes freshly attuned to the comforting weight of the pistol she wears in her pocket as she gazes up at the devil through demurely lowered lashes.

"I'd be more than happy to oblige," Ward drawls, setting down his oversize ledger. He steps to the middle of the room, assuming center stage. "For the purposes of our American partnership, we've created an entity we're callin' Württember-gian Gem Exports Incorporated, which will be the beneficiary of fifty percent of the profits of all Württemberg emeralds sold in North and South American markets."

"Not Europe?" Vandemeer cuts in.

McAllister looks to Alice. She shakes her head very slightly— enough to be seen, firm enough to preclude any argument.

"Not at this time," Ward goes on. "As we discussed, this is for American markets only, but if you'd like to walk away at this point, we certainly understand—"

"Zee markets have opened, ladies and gentlemen!" the am-bassador shouts from next to the mantel, where their "market ticker" has now clacked abruptly to life, threads beginning to unspool. Béa typing it all from the next room, unheard.

"Anyone?" Ward offers, motioning to the door.

"Enough," Peyton growls. "Let's get on with it."

"Very good." Ward bows, hands pressed together. *Lord, much as he disdains it, the man was made for the lackey role,* Alice thinks. "The corporation will now be issuing an initial

set of twelve hundred shares. We will look to the markets to
see where to start our bidding."

They turn to the ambassador, who is squinting through a
monocle at the tiny type on the ticker tape. "We have not yet
reached zee emerald value. Gold is steady at $1,894 per troy
ounce. Silver has dropped to $108. Emeralds . . . $64.78 per
one carat average."

"Shall we begin the bidding at one dollar a share, just for
simplicity's sake?" Vandemeer affects an affable smile.

"You and your goddamned suggestions," Peyton growls.

Vandemeer's face goes white, just in time for Ward to
chuckle and say, "I was thinking more like five. Do I have five?"

Five sets of hands rise in the air at once.

"How exciting this is," Cora murmurs. Alice turns to smile
at her over her shoulder.

"I, for one, feel thoroughly invigorated," Ogden breathes in
Alice's ear.

The ambassador makes a sputtering noise that draws everyone's eye. "I say! There has been a jump. Emeralds now at
$110.29 per—"

"Let me see that." Ward bustles over, peering through the
monocle at the tape. "Well, buff my buckles, quite a jump!"

Alice rises from her chair, partly to get away from Ogden's
attentions. "It is the abdication. It must be. My king has
capitulated and the news has broken—"

"Prince Wilhelm is going to be *king*!" Mrs. Ames squeals,
clutching a stunned-looking Arabella's hand.

"And the price of emeralds is leaping in joy," Ward puts
in, eyebrows high. "Everyone open those bags. Let's get your
cash deposits in at five a share, even split."

The cash is produced in haste. Harry Peyton, cowering

silently in the corner, at a threatening wave of his father's cane, hastens to draw stacks of cash from the leather bag hanging from the back of the golden wheelchair.

Arabella cranes her head over her dainty shoulder to watch him as he does so, a look of plaintive concern playing over her face.

The ambassador circulates the room, collecting each bundle with a grave nod of thanks, then places it into the double-sided safe set into the far wall—adjoining, conveniently enough, the ambassador's office. Alice had wondered whether the outward face of the safe was too ostentatious, with its large handle wheel and iron door, but if anyone here thinks it looks theatrical, it hasn't deterred them from filling it with bills.

"Now the fun begins," Ward says. "You'll all benefit from here on out, but the majority stakeholder will control the market. Anybody game?"

And again, Alice watches with rich satisfaction as five hands fly into the air.

$ $ $

Mr. Vandemeer slides a very large wad of cash across the parlor room table. "I'll raise to ten a share, for my part—*if* it means I can take the company majority. Six hundred and one shares."

"I think not." Mr. Peyton's tone is pure venom. "Harry, place the bag on my lap. My *lap!*"

Harry jumps to, rounding his father's wheelchair with the large, leather-bound case.

The senior Peyton grabs at it hastily and waves his son away. He fishes into the case, soon dislodging a wad of bills three times the heft of Vandemeer's pile.

Mrs. Witt lets out a shocked hiccup. "Now *that's* a lot of money . . ."

The ambassador looks up from his ticker. "Emerald price now at $120—"

"You are all . . . wasting . . . my . . . time!" Peyton tosses the heap onto the table as if kindling for a fire. "One *thousand* a share. For majority ownership. Just to get the rest of you to shut the hell up."

Cora manages to keep her face stone.

Good God, momentum is a beautiful, magical thing.

Mr. Ogden stands from his chair, his handsome face uncharacteristically thrown. "I must say, Duchess, Ambassador Roderick . . . I wasn't expecting the price to climb so high so soon. I do hope my lack of cash on hand won't preclude me from further bidding."

"I'm out as well," Mrs. Witt admits, slumping back onto the settee.

"Perhaps we can put a cap on the price, you know?" Mrs. Ames pipes up in apparent panic, clasping at her husband's arm. "Considering we're all friends."

Cora watches as Alice frowns, positing a discreet but nonetheless orchestrated glance at the running commodities ticker.

The ambassador nods gravely. He reaches for the ornate handle of the telephone. "Are you thinking, Your Grace, zat we open the bidding . . . ?"

Alice sighs. "I merely wish to consider what is best for Württemberg—"

"Hang on one gosh darn minute," Mr. Vandemeer interrupts hastily, scrambling to his feet. "No, don't offer to the larger market. Surely there's something we can do."

"Well." The ambassador frowns. "There *is* zee word as bond, as our people say."

"'The word as bond,'" Mr. Vandermeer echoes. "What the devil does that mean?"

Alice explains, "In Württemberg, there is always the ability to enter into a contract without money in hand. A note of . . . promise, is how it roughly translates."

"Why, we have promissory notes here in the US of A, Your Grace," Ward drawls. "If these fine investors would be willing to sign pledges to that effect."

He looks around the group, gauging their responses.

The marks give eager nods.

"Well zen!" The ambassador claps his hands. "Then let us resume ze bidding. Did ze man on wheels zay one thousand a share?"

"Two thousand," Vandemeer says.

"Three," Witt trills, petting her empty crocodile clutch. "I'm good for it."

"Five," counters Vandemeer. "Thousand."

"You think you've got me with five? Do you? Imbecile." Peyton Senior growls. "Ten!"

Mr. Ames stands, squeaking, "Put me down for the majority of shares at twelve thousand!"

Mr. Vandemeer scoffs. "I call humbug, Robert; you know damn well you can't afford that."

Arabella blushes, recoiling, as her father reels toward Vandemeer. "How dare you claim to know my business!"

"And yet I *do* know your business," Vandemeer goes on. "I thumbed through your financials during the Manifest merger, and unless you've received an unexpected inheritance . . . Oh, wait. You don't *come* from family money."

Ames clenches his fists, but he's easily held back by his much larger wife.

Arabella covers her face with both gloved hands.

Peyton's attempt at sardonic laughter rolls him straight into a coughing fit.

Cora looks to Harry, expecting him to lend a hand to his father, but he's walked away, gazing worriedly (longingly?) in the direction of Arabella.

Which makes Cora even more settled about her little amendment to the plan.

"*Fifteen* thousand." Ogden cuts through her thoughts, though he's looking a bit queasier, Mr. Vandemeer beside him a bit more deflated too.

"Sixteen," Mrs. Witt says, her voice a far sight less braying than Cora's ever heard it.

"Sixteen-five," Ogden croaks.

"*Twenty-five thousand a share!*" Mr. Peyton roars.

Harry flinches. The rest of the room falls silent.

"That's . . ." Ward looks taken aback as he scribbles down the calculations. "At 601 shares—"

"Fifteen million twenty-five thousand dollars, and none of you nitwits can outbid that, can you?" Peyton snarls. He stamps his cane beside his chair so hard, Cora suspects it'll leave a dent in the embassy floor. "Living your frivolous lifestyles, building your monuments to poor taste all over Fifth Avenue, your ugly castles in the clouds. I *will* own this company, same as I once owned all of you! I *made* you all . . . and I command you to stand down before you idiots ruin yourselves along with this opportunity."

His head swivels toward Alice like a reared rattlesnake's.

"But I don't want 601 shares. I want 700 shares at twenty-five thousand a share, and the rest of these peons can peck at each other for the scraps."

Alice stays silent, ostensibly waiting for someone to jump in, correct him, outbid.

No one does. Mr. Peyton has swallowed the room and spit out the bones. More vicious than all the rest of them put together. Alice and Cal were right.

How he produced a naive, harmless fellow like Harry, Cora will never understand.

"I can match that price." Mr. Vandemeer clears his throat. "For, let's say, a quarter of the shares that are left? Even split."

Mr. Ames, Mr. Ogden, and Mrs. Witt nod reluctantly, agreeing.

"Seven hundred to Peyton, with the rest split equally between Ogden, Ames, Vandemeer, and Witt," Ward announces.

The ambassador nods toward Dagmar.

From the nearby cabinet, Dagmar retrieves a pile of official-looking documents—the promissory notes, all teed up with fields for the investors' names, respective banks, accounts, places for an official seal—and hurries over with them.

The marks lean together over the table, reading, completing, signing.

Cora lets out a silent, exultant breath. Word as bond indeed.

The ambassador claps his hands again, and from the adjacent vestibule emerges a handful of young lads, dressed in modest suits and sharp hats. Cora needs to look twice before recognizing them.

Of course. Cal's young newsies.

"My couriers vill bring zeez to zee banks," the ambassador explains.

From her station near the windows, Cora watches as the

newsies scurry out of the embassy's parlor level, through the vestibule, and down the front steps, the notes safely tucked into their satchels. The lads disappear into the growing morning crowd.

Alice's eyes shine with thinly veiled glee.

"Thank you, dear friends," she cries, clasping her hands before her heart. "You have all made this a momentous day in Württemberg's history. Perhaps another cordial to celebrate?"

Mr. Vandemeer grimaces. "Might you have anything more palat—er, a bit less sweet?"

The ambassador laughs, both hands slapping his impressive belly. "Perhaps this calls for a toast of Württemberg rye."

"Quite like the sound of that," Mr. Ogden says.

Vandemeer nods smartly. "Hear, hear!"

Dagmar has a new pep in her step as she pours contents of a second decanter into seven crystal-cut glasses.

Alice's eyes flit to Cora's but do not linger. Still, the message is clear: *It is done.*

Now all they need to do is to get out the door.

"And to celebrate in true Württembergian fashion, I have taken the liberty of reserving a private room at Sherry's for our inaugural lunch." Alice downs the whiskey in her glass, eyes still bright with victory. "Shall we be off?"

🪷 🪷 🪷

The procession out to Sherry's begins with Mr. Vandemeer, naturally, resulting in an irate outburst from Peyton Senior, who apparently believes his superior stake in the mines should grant him the right of first departure.

Senior is further outraged when his son refrains from assuming his position behind the handles of the wheelchair, instead escorting Arabella Ames out the door. Not Cora, who trails behind them, Alice notes. Not that it matters one whit now.

She turns away to smile, catching Dagmar's eye, as well as that of her ambassadorial sweetheart.

Konrad leaves his place beside the still-unspooling ticker tape. "Vee vill just make sure everything eez in order."

"Very good, Ambassador," Alice answers with a satisfied nod, and allows herself the luxury of one little playful wink in Dagmar's direction.

In answer, Dagmar scans the departing crowd and, apparently assured no one is looking, hoists her skirts for a brief little tap dance before following her beau into the ambassador's office and locking the door behind them.

Now only Alice remains in the quiet, stately space . . . apart from one other, lingering by the doorway.

Alice stifles a sigh. She should have predicted Ogden would want to escort her out.

"How kind of you to wait," she says, approaching the exit.

"It is my pleasure, dearest," Ogden breathes.

But instead of holding the door open for her, he shuts it. Blocks it with his body.

"How else could I engineer a moment of celebration for just the two of us?"

Blood rushes cold through Alice's body. He can't mean to try again. Midmorning, in an embassy . . . with the door shut and, as all others have already departed in their carriages, no witnesses. *No one to hear me scream.* No defenses.

Except one.

As he draws closer, like a leopard stalking prey, her hand fumbles for the gun in her pocket. It cannot come to that, surely. This has all been so clean, and nearly completed. How could she not have guarded against this?

She'd been thinking mainly of Peyton, she realizes. That putrefying old man, as bad as she remembers. But she got it wrong, didn't she?

Peyton is the greediest of them. But he isn't the worst.

Ogden lurches for her. She reels back and slaps him, hard, across the face.

There's a moment of astonishment as Ogden processes the rejection. Alice uses it to dart backward, behind the table, as Ogden recalibrates, snarling, "Drop the pretense, Marietta. I know you want this as much as I do. And European aristocrats are not exactly known for their virtue."

He snatches for her across the table, coming up empty as she flies to the side. His arm, desperately grabbing, sideswipes the ticker on the mantle, which falls to the floor.

They both stare. Alice swears her heart stops beating completely for a good three seconds as she takes in what Ogden is seeing.

That ever-unspooling line of ticker tape, showcasing not what should be the current values of emeralds on the commodities market downtown but blank paper instead.

Because no one is typing false values. Because Béa is gone.

"You're right," Alice says quickly. "I want you desperately, but not here. Perhaps a hotel . . ."

His eyes rise to hers, hot with understanding—not of what she's just said, but rather, of what she's just pulled off.

She extends her arms in entreaty, but he rushes heedless past her to the door of the ambassador's office. One arm joggles with the false safe built into the wall, the other with the knob.

"Brett, please!" Alice cries. "I don't know what's gotten into you!"

With a roar of frustration, he steps backward, then charges at the door to the office with a fierce kick that splinters the edges of the doorknob. And then another, until the door is flung wide, revealing . . . very little.

An empty room. A telegraph machine. And an open window through which Alice's co-conspirators have already escaped.

"You *bitch*," Ogden growls. "You sharper, you swindling trollop!"

He whirls around, ready to attack.

But Alice has already crossed the room toward the window . . . and pulled out her gun. "I'd take care how you speak to me, Mr. Ogden."

🍐 🍐 🍐

Eyes trained ahead on Arabella, Cora follows the elated, boisterous crowd into the vestibule and then finally, blessedly, out into the shocking bright white of Tuesday morning. Her team's intended ride to this supposed luncheon, Ward's carriage, is parked down the road, near the corner of Fifty-Seventh and Fifth, and also houses a patiently waiting Cal Archer. Béa, Dagmar, and the short-lived ambassador Konrad have no doubt already climbed inside their own hansom cab, having left via the back room's window to the street. The marks' carriages, meanwhile, are still parked in the style of a front-and-center parade directly outside the embassy.

Vandemeer's coach pulls away from the curb, already off for Sherry's, Mrs. Witt's cab on his heels. Ahead, Harry and his driver attempt to lift the blustering Peyton Senior into theirs.

Now it's time for one more magic trick.

"Arabella," Cora calls as the girl climbs the carriage stairs to join her parents.

Arabella turns, looking curious, and doubles backward.

"Oh, Cora, I really must thank you," the girl says, eyes shining as she approaches. "You were right. I am so very glad I was here today—"

"As was I." *Not much time, Cora, best be quick.*

She gently leads Arabella away from the curb and out of earshot. "We are friends, are we not, Arabella?"

Arabella laughs, confused. "Of course, why—"

"Then before we lose ourselves to today's festivities, allow me the honor of presenting you with an engagement gift."

Arabella shakes her head. "Please, Cora, you've already given me so much."

"Well, this is a secret gift, to be revealed in due course, and meant only for *you*. Do you understand, dear friend?"

"Meant only for . . ." Arabella's hand drifts to her chest.

"Come now, Arabella!" Mrs. Ames barks, her bulbous frame leaning halfway out of the carriage. "You do know how your father hates to wait!" Her eyes brighten when they fall on Cora. "Miss Ritter, it is high time to royally celebrate, don't you think?"

"High time, indeed!" As soon as Mrs. Ames slides back inside, Cora presses hastily, "Promise me, Arabella, just for you?"

Clearly perplexed, Arabella says slowly, "I do not know what I am promising, but yes, I give my word that— *Oof!*"

Arabella startles, though soon relaxes into Cora's embrace, squeezing back.

When they pull away, Arabella's eyes are welling. "Goodness

me, always getting so emotional. Mother tells me it is most unbecoming."

Cora says kindly, "And I might tell her that she does not know everything."

Arabella flashes her a conspiratorial smile. "May I sit beside you, when we get to Sherry's?"

A strange sort of sadness overtakes Cora. A vague, regretful ache for what might have been, in another life. "It would be an honor, my friend."

Arabella climbs into her family's carriage . . . unknowingly carrying along with her the team's showstopper Colombian emerald, as well as Cora's engagement ring, both now tucked safely inside Arabella's purse, thanks to Cora's quick fingers.

Cora can only hope her friend will discover the bounty at an opportune time. Based on Alice's prior comments about the team's budget and the emerald's cost—plus Cora's new knowledge about the price of gemstones—Cora estimates there may be close to $25,000 now on Arabella's person. Nothing close to the *thirty million* they've just swindled, but certainly enough to provide the Ames girl a fresh start.

In a moment, the Ameses are off, following the carriage train of the rest of the defrauded investors, all but one car gone from the curb.

Cora frowns. She's certain she saw Vandemeer leave, as well as Mrs. Witt, the Peytons too, the Ameses. Which means . . .

Cora looks toward the doors, studies the flat windowed facade of the embassy, the sense that something is amiss only mounting.

She hurries toward Ward's carriage, where he loiters outside, smoking a cigar.

"Is Alice with you?" Cora asks.

Ward lazily turns around with a puff. "I'd assumed she was with you."

Cora pokes her head inside the carriage, finding only Calvin waiting there. No Alice.

"What's wrong?" Cal asks. "Where's my sister? Cora!" he calls after her, but she's already off and running, back around the block to the embassy, outside of which Ogden's carriage remains. And still no Alice or Ogden in sight.

Cal hustles to catch Cora, drawing up beside her.

She peers up at the embassy building, a sickening feeling growing in her stomach, just as a flash of blue silk slides by the elevated, parlor-level window. She can make out a hand pressed against the glass, scrabbling desperately inside the folds of fabric.

And emerging with a gun.

"No." Cora's voice quivers. "Cal, she's still up there with Ogden!"

Cal's jaw tightens. "I'll kill him."

"No, wait, just—" Cora huffs, grabbing at his arm to stop him, mind whirring like a magic lantern. "It would be far better to get out of this without adding murder to the tally."

She glances worriedly at the window. Alice—and her gun—are no longer in view.

"Listen," she says, drawing Cal closer. "I've got an idea."

🐟 🐟 🐟

Alice trains the gun, along with her gaze, on Ogden's face.

This is her mistake. The look in his eyes strikes her like a thunderbolt—the rage, the disdain, the primitive drive to rage and attack and claim—just like it had in the carriage that day.

That day she nearly shot him. And he very nearly . . .

Her thumb trembles against the heavy hammer, unable to cock it quickly enough. As the gun slides against her damp palm, her breath coming fast with terror, Ogden crosses the room in two feline strides and snatches the weapon from her hand.

"I'll talk to you however you like, you whore," he sneers. "I'm going to hand you over to the police, and they'll have their fun with you too, no doubt, you and your little criminal friends, but before I do that, I'm going to take from you what you have dangled in front of me for months. What I *deserve*."

He trains the gun on her lazily. Taking his time.

She raises her hands. Inches toward the exit.

"I don't think so. Get back where you were." He sniffs, his eyes cold. Utterly empty. "Take off your dress."

She makes no movement at all.

His face reddens in rage. "Or would you rather I rip it off you?"

He lurches forward when—

"You faithless little strumpet!" A new voice resounds from the vestibule.

The door is flung wide.

It's Cal, holding roughly on to . . . *Cora?*

Alice's heart leaps, but only for a moment. What is the damned fool doing, barging in here, putting more lives at risk?

Cal shoves Cora forward onto the floor. Cora sniffles and whimpers, trying pathetically to rise in her voluminous skirts.

Ogden, momentarily stunned, backs away from Alice.

"I don't know what these women have told you," Cal shouts, his face bright red with anger that Alice can sense is very, very real. "But they're nothing but two-bit frauds. This one had me out of thousands with some cockamamie story about a pearl farm. I managed to trail her here, but I'll need some help restraining her until the police arrive. This one too, I suppose."

Cal nods disdainfully in Alice's direction. "Is there anything in here we can use to tie them up?"

Alice steps toward Cal. Cal turns and spits on the embassy rug, inches from her slipper.

Nice, if revolting, touch, Alice concedes, her breath still coming fast and short.

Alice glances at the Württemberg flag upon the wall, with its many yards of gilded fringe pooled decoratively beneath it. Then she stares back at Ogden, expression drawn, as if caught.

His eyes narrow in triumph. "Over there. Use the flag."

As Cal goes to the wall to rip loose the flag, Ogden pockets the gun, content for the moment to have an ally on hand.

And now what? Alice wonders. Cal's managed to pause Ogden's attack momentarily, but he still has the weapon, and he's still eyeing the length of her body as if mentally preparing ever worse punishments for her. Her brother can't hope to wrestle the gun out from Ogden's pocket without a shot being fired—

And then she sees Cora, still on the ground—on her knees now, crawling closer and closer to Ogden. Her face is upturned, flushing seductively.

She always told Cora to keep her distance from Ogden. Her protégée has chosen the perfect moment to ignore that advice.

"Please, Mr. Ogden, don't turn me in," Cora coos breathily. "I'll do anything. I'll help you get your money back, I swear it. I'll do . . . anything you ask."

Now she has Ogden's full attention. Her hand creeps upward, lightly grazing the waistband of his trousers, her eyes wide and unblinking, lips parted.

"I know you will," Ogden whispers, leering down at her. "Because I'm the one with the—"

He reaches for his pocket. His eyes widen.

Cora rocks back onto her heels.

"With the *what*?" She smirks. "Don't suppose you're looking for *this*?"

She rises from the ground and points the derringer pistol she's just pilfered right at him.

"I . . . How?" Ogden sputters.

Cora shrugs. "A bit of misdirection. The simplest of all magic tricks. Must say, you're extremely easily distracted."

Alice's pulse lurches back to life.

"Down on your knees," she orders. Ogden ignores her.

Cora cocks the gun.

Ogden obliges, hands raised.

He turns to Cal in appeal. "St-stop them! Do something, man!"

"I am doing something." Cal smiles coldly. "Apprehending a loathsome criminal. Hands behind your back now."

It only takes a matter of minutes for Cal to bind Ogden's arms and legs and tie him to a sturdy plumbing pole in the corner of the embassy toilet.

"You vermin! You low-class swine," Ogden seethes. "You'll hang for what you've done unless I get to you first. I will rip—"

They use the rest of the flag as a gag, tied fast round his head.

"Don't worry, we're not complete monsters," Alice calls back from the doorway, using her own flat American accent at long last. "We'll send a message to your wife on our way out of town. We'll let dear Priscilla know exactly where you are and every little detail of what's happened to you. And to your money. It'll be up to her to decide whether to come collect you or not. Seems just, no?"

They leave him moaning mutedly in the water closet as they hurry at last out the embassy door.

Before they step into the carriage, Cora murmurs, "Alice? Are you—"

Without a moment of hesitation, Alice turns to her friend and embraces her tightly, gratefully. Cora laughs, surprised.

"I'm absolutely golden, thanks to you. You were brilliant, Cora. *Are* brilliant."

"How do you know it wasn't my plan?" Cal puts in.

Alice and Cora look at each other and burst out laughing.

"It's not *that* ludicrous a suggestion," he protests, holding the carriage door open for them.

"You truly are a fool," Cora teases as she accepts his hand up.

"Only for you, darling," he answers.

She swats him at that—and then, so fleetingly Alice almost misses it, leans in to press her lips to his cheek.

Not much of a kiss, but it's enough for Cal to look positively gobsmacked.

Alice has to clear her throat to get him to help her up.

She takes a seat opposite Ward McAllister, who has a sheen of sweat beading on his forehead and a smattering of cigar ash dusting his cravat.

"What took you so long?" Ward asks. "I'd started to think you'd skipped out on me."

"No." Alice smiles, peering out the isinglass window. "Not yet."

As the carriage pulls away from the embassy, Alice feels stress beginning to melt from her entire frame like snow in a spring thaw. She's not clear yet. Not entirely. But she's on her way out, rather than in, and she feels it.

"I must say," McAllister drawls, "I'm dyin' to see what little hidey-hole you're takin' us to for the divvying up of our winnings. Don't think I didn't notice you talkin' to my driver in whispers, not lettin' me hear the address you gave those newsboys. I don't blame you for bein' cagey, dear Alice. Did you think I might turn up to—what is it? A tenement house? An old shanty by the river?—and take all the money for myself?"

"Something like that," Alice says, still staring placidly away.

"No, eighty percent is what we agreed, and that's fine and dandy with me," Ward says.

Alice feels Cora stiffen beside her and feels a small pang of regret.

She should have told Cora about this last bit of the plan. Spared her the worry over her own stake that no doubt is racing through her mind right now.

But it's too late to correct that error. All she can do is slide her foot onto Cora's and give it a reassuring, surreptitious tap.

Her eyes meet Cora's, conveying a message she hopes her young student can now decipher: *Do not worry. You can trust me.*

Cora stares back for a moment, pondering. Then, with a quirk of the corner of her mouth, she taps her foot against Alice's in reply. *Message received.*

The carriage stops. The driver jumps down to open the door. Alice steps out. Then Cora. Then Cal.

They have arrived, not at a seedy warehouse but at a stately four-bay townhome on 350 Fifth Avenue. The very epicenter of New York high society.

As Ward emerges, his jocular grin sinks steadily into slack confusion. "Why, this is . . ."

"Mrs. Astor's house." Alice smiles from the front stoop. "Won't you come inside?"

CHAPTER 30

Salve Regina

I t's been fifteen years since Alice last set foot in this vestibule, but she still knows the path to the sitting room, even without Mrs. Astor's butler showing them the way.

"It's good to see you again, Thomas," she says.

"And you, Miss Archer," the butler replies, just as formal as she remembered him. "If you'll allow me a moment of sentiment, it is lovely to see you all grown up."

"Grown tall but too skinny," comes a retort from the sitting room. "Now that all this nonsense is over, perhaps Alice will finally take my advice and allow her figure to fill out a little more."

Mrs. Caroline Schermerhorn Astor, queen of New York society, strides across her Louis XV salon toward them, eyebrows raised, brown eyes sparkling.

"Exertion does not become you, my dear," she says, offering her cheek up for a kiss.

Alice obliges with a peck. "So you've told me many times, Aunt Lina."

"*Aunt?*" Ward sputters a cough, his hands clasping at the cravat at his throat.

"For heaven's sake, Ward," Mrs. Astor snaps. "Cease your conniption and sit down."

She points to the settee. Like a well-trained puppy, Ward obeys.

"Now, Calvin. Let me look at you." She squints as Cal presents himself for inspection, her discerning eye catching on his cheeky grin, making her own face break into a grudging smile upon seeing it. "Hopeless as ever."

Alice sits in a high-backed chair, her vision almost blurring with relief. Thomas wheels the tea service into the room, leaving it for Mrs. Astor to serve.

As Mrs. Astor sets out saucers and cups, she addresses Cora. "Do you know, my dear, that this young man used to terrorize my daughter Carrie with tales of goblins and wicked ghosts roaming the city streets? I always knew he had a gift for fiction, but I never dreamed he would use it in quite *this* capacity."

"You haven't been formally introduced," Alice realizes. "Lina, this is my good friend Coraline O'Malley."

"The belle of the season." Mrs. Astor sniffs, taking Cora in, head to foot. "And already engaged."

"Oh. Well." Cora's throat bobs as she swallows. "That's obviously not happening. Given current events."

"I meant *this* one," Mrs. Astor snaps, nodding to Cal. She turns to Alice with a frown. "Has he not proposed yet?"

To this, Alice can only shake her head in honest befuddlement.

"I might have stopped by Aunt Lina's for a few visits." Cal winces, caught. "She wanted to know how things were going!"

"Not that he indulged my curiosity," Mrs. Astor comments dryly. "I could scarcely glean a single insight as to your little confidence game, because all this young man could talk about was Miss Cora O'Malley, the clever, beautiful, and kind."

The outrage that floods Alice's veins at hearing of the absolutely reckless, unnecessary, and frankly typical risks her brother has taken fades surprisingly quickly. Yes, he was a fool. But that no longer matters. Much has taken place unseen, without Alice there to pull the strings, and when all is said and done, the realization comes as a rather immense . . . relief?

She's done controlling every possible angle now. She can let it all go.

"So?" Mrs. Astor demands. "Are you or are you not engaged?"

"Give me a minute to catch my breath, Aunt Lina." Cal laughs, loosening his collar. "Anyway, I'll be able to offer Cora a much finer ring after we divide up our takings than anything I could've afforded on a reporter's salary."

Cora looks like she might cry from happiness.

Cal gazes back at her in open adoration. "Maybe even diamonds and emeralds?"

Cora's expression morphs from rapture to a laughing wince. "Anything but emeralds."

"If you'll beg my pardon," Ward cuts in, apparently recovering from the first wave of his surprise, not yet predicting the greater shock soon to follow. "I hadn't realized you were all relations."

"Not by blood," Mrs. Astor says, pouring Alice's tea. "They call me aunt as an endearment, much simpler and more affecting than anything you've concocted, Ward. 'Mystic Rose' indeed."

Ward's face goes mottled with embarrassment.

"Mrs. Astor was my mother's dearest friend," Alice says. "And my own godmother."

"She was the only one to attend our father's funeral," Cal recalls, his eyes distant.

"I offered financial assistance after the disaster, but Mary wouldn't have it." Mrs. Astor sets her own tea aside with a leaden sigh. "Alice and I kept up our correspondence over the years, but I found that in adulthood she'd inherited her mother's stubbornness."

Alice shakes her head. "I only wished to keep you clear of all this, dear Lina. It was not your vendetta."

"Oh, but there I disagree," Mrs. Astor says, a vicious smile spreading across her face. "I always hated them. The lot of them. Ogden's predations and his wife's hatred of her own sex. The Vandemeers with their unseemly competitiveness. Those new-money Ameses, desperate for legitimacy. I have half a mind that Iris Witt killed her husband for the fun of it—it's a wonder she hasn't offed those dreadful children. And Peyton. Well, he's the very symbol of everything rotten in society today. Honor means nothing to this breed. Only cold hard cash, earned by any base means. I'm glad to see them as thoroughly ruined as poor Mary, who deserved it not a whit."

Ward nibbles a cookie, trying valiantly to puff himself up again. "What divine felicity that I happened upon your own goddaughter that day at the flower market!"

"Divine poppycock!" Mrs. Astor turns to stare at Ward in sheer incredulity. "It was my own handiwork, you fool."

Ward drops the cookie. Scrambles to pick it up from the silk settee.

"I sent you to the market that day to fetch me roses. I directed Alice to run the same con you'd fallen victim to months prior, knowing you wouldn't be able to resist assuming the role of wise mentor. You do enjoy the sensation of feeling far more clever than you actually are."

Cora lets out a snort, then stares into her teacup. "Excuse me. Bit of dust in the air."

"I'd have done far more myself," Mrs. Astor says. "But Alice thought it might be more prudent to drop you into it instead."

Ward glances between them, his eyes at last flashing panic. "I thank you for that decision, my dear Alice. It's proven to be a rather lucrative one for both of—"

Mrs. Astor rolls her eyes. "Oh. That."

She rises with a sigh, motioning for everyone to join her.

"We may as well get the vulgar bit over with. Come on."

Alice, the least bewildered among her crew, follows behind her godmother, treading a track from her childhood, down the back corridor of the house, into the servants' stairway and down to the kitchens, where she and Cal used to hide with the Astor children to steal any treats left cooling from the oven.

The treats in question today are spread about the wide servants' dining table. Stacks upon stacks of money. Béa stands counting the last of it, clutching Alice's old ledger, a charcoal pencil pressed between her lips. Absolutely adorable.

Surrounding Béa, Dagmar and Konrad—both swilling beer from pewter mugs—are the half dozen newsies they employed, all happily tucking into jam tarts and milk, just as Cal and Alice used to when they were about that age.

Béa's eyes spark with happiness as she looks up and sees Alice. "Thirty-two million one hundred and sixty thousand dollars. All here, cash in hand."

Dagmar lets out a long, low whistle.

"The emerald itself has gone amiss, I'm afraid," Béa continues, "but with this amount of takings, I should hardly think it matters."

Alice's eyes dart to Cora, who stands staring at the ground, a small smile playing over her face. Perhaps she kept the stone for herself as an unsanctioned bonus?

She'd look the other way, if so. But she suspects Cora has used that stone to help defray the cost of all this to her own stung conscience.

Ward steps forward, irate. "Like hell it doesn't matter. I want every bit of our winnings accounted for."

"Oh, shut up, Ward," Mrs. Astor says. "Surely by now you can see that you've won nothing."

"I'd have happily given you half," Alice says calmly. "If you'd only refrained from threatening me, I'd have honored our agreement and bid you farewell as a friend. But now?"

She shakes her head.

His face goes white with indignation. "I say—"

"*I* say," Mrs. Astor cuts in, "that if you stay quiet, like the sycophantic little worm you always were and always now will be, I will stay quiet as well. I shall not tell the truth about your role in all of this to my friends in society. I shall not turn you away or shun you, much as I now long to. All will remain exactly as it is. Picnics in Newport, Patriarch's Ball in January, evenings at home with your lovely wife. How is dear Sarah, anyway? You hardly mention her lately. It's almost as if you've *designed* it so that she's sick all the time."

Her glare says it all. Alice knows that with Mrs. Astor's own husband forever "off on his yacht," the older woman holds a strong opinion or two about marital neglect.

Ward swallows. "She . . . she sends her regards."

Mrs. Astor rolls her eyes. "Come now. Leave them to conduct their business now that you're out of it. I have some curtain patterns I want you to look at for the east guest room. I simply cannot decide on my own."

Ward glances over his shoulder in desperate, ineffectual entreaty as Mrs. Astor drags him out of the kitchen and back upstairs.

"Leave him two hundred dollars," Alice says. "For the use of his carriage."

"Maybe he can finally buy himself a suit that fits," Cora suggests.

And Alice lets out a laugh so big, it startles even herself.

※ ※ ※

They bid goodbye to Dagmar and Konrad downtown. Other than the German woman's insistence that she "earned her place in thees city and will not be geeving it up for anybody," none of the rest of them are any the wiser about what she plans to do with her winnings.

"Perhaps she'll open a theater," Alice muses as Mrs. Astor's carriage drives away from the bar down on the Bowery. At Cora's incredulous expression, she grins. "She's quite the dancer, and she didn't break character for a second at the embassy. I could see a future."

"Nothing compared to Cora's groveling act, though," Cal says fondly. "Right here's the true actress."

"Never again," Cora groans.

She motions down at the outfit she's now wearing—simple gingham and a straw hat, to all appearances a Midwestern

LEE KELLY & JENNIFER THORNE

tourist heading home from her idyll in the big city, just like the rest of them.

"From now on, I am plain old Coraline O'Malley. I never want to see a fine gown again for as long as I live."

"How are you going to spend all that money, then?" Cal cocks an eyebrow.

Cora scowls thoughtfully. "Well, maybe not as *long* as I live. That pink chiffon was rather nice."

"And what about you?" Béa cocks her head to gaze at Alice.

"You mean 'us'?" Alice peeks out the window. "I'm tired of deciding everything. I thought I might let you pick."

They are dropped off just outside the Brooklyn Bridge. The driver tips his hat and steers the carriage away, no doubt realizing what a wash the fine vehicle will need after braving these mucky downtown streets. After the tip they just gave him, he can afford to buy several new ones instead.

Alice breathes in the salty air of the river. She takes in the incredible feat of engineering with a wave of wonder, of aliveness, that she hasn't allowed herself to feel for as long as she can remember. It's almost humbling, this marvel of a bridge.

Almost.

Alice smiles, thinking of the tangle of confusion they left behind. Even if, as she expects, their ruined victims have made their way to a police constabulary to demand the identification and arrest of a group of flagrant frauds, it will take untold hours to sort through their muddled story to reach the heart of it. A Württembergian duchess, you say? Here because of a resistance, and emerald mines and a called-off engagement to which far-flung prince . . . ?

By the time anyone even believes them, Alice and her funny

little family will have disappeared into the middle of this sprawling continent like so many anonymous others, only the stories of the great confidence game they pulled remaining in this shining sham of a city.

Now *that* is a feat of engineering.

Béa comes to stand beside her. Alice slides close, so their wrists and pinkies touch.

"A school," Béa says quietly.

Alice looks at her.

Béa smiles out over the shining river. "For girls of all stations. Not to teach them how to quiet their voices and select the right fork at dinner, but real things."

"Such as?"

Béa thinks. "Financial management, for one."

"World history, current events?" Alice suggests, only half sardonically.

"Why not? We'll make independent young ladies out of them. Nobody's victim. Nobody's fool."

At that, Alice glances at Cora, standing beside her brother, the two of them the picture of innocent courtship, their fingers idly playing in each other's as if no one else can see—just as her own fingers play against Béa's.

"Where are you headed then, Cal?" Alice calls.

He lifts his hat. "Why, wherever Miss O'Malley goes."

Cora's cheeks turn pink.

"Then I suppose you're headed to Topeka, Kansas," Alice replies.

"Topeka, you say?" Cal smiles. "I like the ring of that. Sounds far away, for one thing."

"I've heard it's known for its beautiful countryside, birdsong galore, endless horizons," Alice muses. "The perfect place to go unnoticed for the rest of one's days and not mind one little bit."

Cora's eyes spark warm as they meet Alice's. "Not to mention a very long and shining creek running through it all. Enough room for several houses. And . . . Béa, did I hear you mention a school for girls? Well, as a matter of fact, you might have just helped me solve the biggest problem I've got with my plan to buy back the family farm, one I simply couldn't come up with a solution to until now."

Cora links arms with a smiling Béa as Alice cocks an eyebrow.

"Oh really? What's that?"

Cora grins, cheeky as the day Alice met her. "I *hate* farming."

Encore

Happiness is a work of art. Handle with care.

—EDITH WHARTON

CHAPTER 31

All In

October 31, 1885

The morning sun winks beyond the pastures, the hardened soil track that leads to the school cutting like a muted pink ribbon through a swath of golden silk. From her vantage at the window, Cora can just spot where the wheat fields crest into rolling green pastures in the distance, and just beyond, the sparkling, serpentine creek where she learned to swim, fish, and scheme. This very image, serving as her motivation and beacon for years—although now, Long Creek Farm is far more than a birthright or a conquest. It's just home.

She fixes her hair, pressing her school mistress dress just so as she admires herself in the mirror. Gone are the days of rented ball gowns, costumes, tailor-made ensembles for private dinners and affairs. Today's dress suits her far better.

She takes the stairs down to the open first floor, where she's surprised to find Cal still sitting, hunched over his notebook.

She raises a quizzical eyebrow at her husband.

He drops his pen, leaning back with a tired sigh.

Cora clasps her hands behind her back, dancing over to him. "I believe I left you in this very same position last night."

"I'm on a roll." Despite his heavy-lidded eyes, Cal rallies a smirk, rubbing his hands together like a schoolboy. "I've crossed the midpoint of the novel and can't seem to stop. Words are just pouring out of these puppies."

He waggles his fingers like a two-bit magician.

She laughs, closing the remaining space between them, delighting as Cal puts his arms around her.

"If I didn't know better, I'd think you were having an affair with this story."

"Funny you should mention. I just introduced the heroine, a strawberry-blonde, beguiling, mischievous creature that I can't stop writing about. Or thinking about. Even when she's right upstairs."

"Are you ever going to tell me what the devil this book is about?" Cora asks, hands on her hips in mock outrage.

"I'd have thought you'd have guessed it," Cal says, leaning back, boasting in his very serious literary voice. "A story uniquely of our time. A tale of two brilliant women beating the cheats at their own game, and me, but a humble narrator bearing witness to the spectacle."

Cora arches an eyebrow. "Sounds familiar."

He winks. "Don't worry. It's a hugely fictionalized account. No one could possibly trace it back, with all the details I've altered. Trust me."

"I trust you entirely," she says, and means it.

He kisses her then, his scent a delicious and decidedly odd mix of coffee and pencil shavings, and whispers, "I'll make it up to you tonight. I promise you'll have me in time for dinner."

"And you can have me for deezzzert," she says, with perfect

flirtatious Württembergian inflection. She rustles his hair as she goes. "Make one of the ladies a secret pickpocket and I'm yours forever."

She takes the path toward the school, passing the second of the three new farmhouses they had built on the lot after buying the farm back from Ross & Calhoun. Alice and Béatrice's little slice of heaven only about twenty paces away.

And dear Béa is sitting on her own porch now, reading a book. Lord, it's nice to see her finally sitting idle.

She looks up, waving to Cora as she passes.

"Is Alice already at school?" Cora asks.

Béa smiles. "Can't keep her away."

"These Archer siblings." She winks. "They do tend toward obsessiveness, do they not?"

She follows the path to the largest new structure, which stands where Da's old barn used to sit, the newly minted Archer School for Girls. Their pride, joy, labor of love.

The school is the first of its kind in the area, a finishing and grammar school for young ladies of Shawnee County and surrounds—Alice as headmistress, Cora as instructor of mathematics and fine arts, Béa handling afternoon French and cooking instruction. Even Cal pitches in from time to time, especially last summer, when it took all hands on deck to get the school off the ground.

And then there's the den matron, who takes gentle care of their lodgers.

Cora waves to Maeve, who's sitting on a bench with a homesick younger student, playing cat's cradle to distract her. Maeve responds with a nod and a smile before returning her attentions to the child. It's a perfect job for her—nurturing, fulfilling. And absolutely no heavy lifting. Cora had sent a letter to Maeve via the Rochester fairgrounds on their way out of state, with a job offer and an address: Long Creek Farm, Topeka, Kansas.

Maeve arrived a mere week after the rest of them. She completed their little makeshift family. For now, anyway.

Da would be happy with what they did with the place, she thinks.

And she, Coraline O'Malley Archer, is happy indeed.

The only member of their tight-knit crew not living in community is their beloved cook Dagmar . . . but she has much to do in New York, Cora knows. She and her sweetheart bartender, Konrad Weber, have both entered the theater world as budding actors, although Dagmar is clearly the natural talent and has also turned into a bit of a Bowery Robin Hood. Alice gave Dagmar a double share of their score from the emerald sting, it turned out, with specific orders to spread the wealth around to the many in need in the city.

Cora still has Dagmar's letters to look forward to—as well as fairly frequent posts from Mrs. Caroline Astor herself, keeping Alice and the rest of them abreast of all the latest gossip and scandal from New York society.

As it happened, their great sting did not remain long in the forefront of drawing room whispers; only a month later, two fraudulent brokerage firms went under, sending the entire economy slipping under the waves in their wake. The so-called Panic of 1884 was welcome news to Alice, who saw the ensuing financial chaos as not only further assurance of their scot-free getaway but an unbelievably close shave. Upon reading the newspaper, Alice granted Cora a fervent hug, in thanks for, as she put it, "Setting us all on the right timeline. If we'd stuck with my original plan, we might have been sunk!" The banking scandal also managed to move the glare of opprobrium away from Ward McAllister, Mrs. Astor reported, allowing him to step back into his timeworn role as Manhattan's social arbiter with renewed, if chastened, enthusiasm.

Mrs. Astor's latest register was particularly interesting to Cora, as it included news of the recent nuptials and decidedly modest wedding between spoiled Mimi Vandemeer and seventy-eight-year-old lifelong bachelor and leather manufacturer Matthias Turner (Cora couldn't suppress a triumphant guffaw at reading that, having recalled Mimi's very lofty suitor standards—and fellow debutante sabotage—at last year's Patriarch's Ball).

The post also included in welcome detail the latest goings of Mr. and Mrs. Harold Peyton Jr., the new couple last reported to be rounding out their delightful, yearlong honeymoon somewhere along the southern coast of France, at least if Mrs. Ames's crowing is to be believed. As society's grand dame, Pearl Ames has grown wincingly desperate in her boasting around town, ever since circumstances have forced her to rely on an allowance provided by her generous daughter—who came into a surprise inheritance from a mysterious godmother in Chicago soon after Cora and Alice skipped town, fancy that! Apparently, when the young couple returns, Harry will be formally enrolling in medical school—although a facility will be providing care for his father now, one better equipped for the old man's very particular needs and extremely limited budget.

Cora steps onto the front stoop now with a shiver. The school year is flying by, the brick building already decorated with pumpkins, a class-made scarecrow, papier-mâché ghosts hanging from the apple trees.

Upon entering, Cora is immediately warmed by the sound of chatting and giggles—the halls full of eager students, despite class not starting for more than twenty minutes. She spies Alice in her front office, brow stitched, hovered over a new ledger.

"Care to dance?" Alice asks her flatly.

Cora blinks. "I believe we're both spoken for."

"With the girls." Alice sighs, leaning back in her chair. "Frivolous as it may be, they keep asking for instruction, so I was thinking about a new studio. Ballroom dancing, ballet. Even—dare I say—Irish jig?"

"I think it a fine idea." Cora smiles. "Count me in."

Alice beams in return—the expression no longer a rarity. In fact, her new headmistress position has unlocked something within Alice, Cora has noted, like a key to a secret heart chamber. She's a lot kinder and gentler with these little ladies than she ever was with Cora.

Cora tries not to take that personally.

She climbs the stairs to her second-floor classroom, where some of the students are already sketching on their easels, gossiping and laughing in the corners, their typical blouses and skirts exchanged today for costumes, given the All Hallows' Eve festivities. For today, they're not the daughters of shopkeepers, farmers, and factory workers, but fancy princesses, goblins, ghouls, whoever they want to be.

"Mrs. Archer!" One of her favorite students practically leaps out of her seat, auburn pigtails flying wild. "Mrs. Archer, what are you supposed to be today?"

"The grandest costume of all," Cora says, bowing dramatically. "Myself!"

Truth be told, she forgot this morning . . . but no matter, Alice has thought of everything, per usual. She spies a black witch hat waiting on her desk and puts it on.

"By which I mean . . . the most terrifying witch in all the land!"

All the girls giggle and shriek, feigning fright. Cora begins stomping down the aisle between desks, sending her wards into laughing fits. A different sort of costume ball, she supposes, the most rewarding one she can imagine.

And, at last, a home—*her* home—full of people she would follow anywhere.

※ ※ ※

After lunch, as the girls of the Archer School spill giddily outside, Alice takes a little stroll along the dusty cart path, gazing out upon that horizon—all natural, just as Cora had described it. She was right about the farm. It is restorative. The sun glitters on the creek that stretches through the farmland, and the handful of low-maintenance animals they keep on hand for eggs and milk punctuate the birdsong with charming calls of their own.

In the far distance, Alice can hear the long insistent whistle of a train passing by, a reminder that beyond this honest oasis they've carved out for themselves, the great wheel of the nation keeps spinning, the railroads expanding, the wide lands east and west filling up with dreamers and schemers, all driven forward by "manifest destiny," to no real end but bigger and greater and more.

Alice leans against a fence post and takes her braid down from its pinned bun for a moment, letting it hang loose while the students play. She feels the breeze sweeping by to say hello, the sun enlivening fresh freckles on her skin.

It's life, this feeling, she realizes. *One hundred percent genuine, actual real life.*

She's still wily enough to know that this land, however beautiful, is far from immune to deception. Look at Cora's father, after all, defrauded by those bankers—Ross & Calhoun— who, at the end of the day, were paid off for this land and went away perfectly satisfied with the outcome of their swindle. Alice read in the paper just this morning of a local mayoral candidate who campaigns by standing on a wooden crate, promising free ponies and electric lights for every house in town. He's projected to win, of course. She saw another story about a preacher touring the area with his little daughter, whom he swears has been blessed with the power of healing. Folks are lining up to donate any amount just so she'll lay hands on them.

But for the first time since she was a child in pretty dresses, Alice Archer feels some relenting of her cynicism, a small measure of trust in the future. It doesn't seem *entirely* impossible that truth and fairness will win out over glitter and grift in the end. Maybe not in her own lifetime, no. But she has the next generation to consider.

She looks at them now, these twenty girls, running and chasing and laughing in the sunlight, freer than she ever got to be. But it's up to her and Cora to make sure they're no less savvy for it.

Alice pins her hair briskly back into its bun, brushes the prairie dust from her cotton skirts, and heads homeward again.

Back to work.

A NOTE FROM THE AUTHORS

I f it isn't obvious by now, we love pairing up to write big stories: novels with high stakes, cinema-worthy plots, and immersive worlds. After tackling a globetrotting archaeological adventure in *The Antiquity Affair* and a 1950s Hollywood caper in *The Starlets*, we knew we wanted to write something equally sweeping and challenging—but fresh. Different.

We've always loved the long-game feel of movies like *The Sting*, as well as the timeless impact of Dumas's *Count of Monte Cristo*, and soon came around to the idea of centering our story around a revenge-driven confidence game. We arrived at the setting quickly from there. What better time and place for a con than Gilded Age New York, when social, political, and economic deception was practiced rampantly and as a matter of course?

It was important to us to keep the Gilded Age setting as accurate as possible and for the story to feel authentic within this era of contradictions. We decided that our two main protagonists would come from very different corners of this world: Alice Archer, we decided, would be the daughter of a hapless "old money" investor swept under the tide of a rapidly changing world, destroyed alongside his family by the bad faith of his robber baron "friends." Coraline O'Malley, by contrast, would come from a poverty-stricken farming family in the Midwest, one that fell victim to the pressures of industrialization and local banks' all-too-common avaricious lending practices.

But we also wanted to faithfully depict the glitz and glamour of the age, and thus, we set the book's action over the course of the very real New York social season of 1884. While some parties were fabricated (Mrs. Witt's Night of Illusions and Mrs. Ames's Midwinter Night Costume Ball, for example), all the little details were ripped from history. High-society parties of this era would indeed often feature such extravagances as theater showings in private ballrooms, gowns commissioned for a single night, ten-course dinner parties—even, yes, carousels of live animals. The Witts's poverty ball, too, was based on cringingly real "servants' balls," which were thrown in jest by various wealthy families over the course of the Gilded Age, complete with purposefully misspelled invitations, custom rag dresses worn by guests, and mush served for dinner. The night of the Patriarch's Ball at Delmonico's was a real-life event, meticulously recreated here, as was the *Carmen* performance at the Met in March 1884.

As for our central scheme—the Württemberg con—this took several iterations to get right. We wanted to concoct a scheme bold enough to be fun and daring but not *so* bold as to be unbelievable . . . Our five families were astute, well-connected members of society, after all. Our story's first draft actually featured a fictional homeland for our fake socialites (RIP our made-up homeland of "Linsbourg"), but we soon came around to the idea of using a real place and real nobility. The sovereignty of Württemberg, its tumultuous relationship with the rest of the German Empire, the Battle of Tauberbischofsheim, King Charles I, and Prince Wilhelm II are all real, just as Alice explains to Cora when she first takes her protégée under her wing. The only things we made up are the considerable fabrications that Alice herself added to the story.

Like in our prior novels, *My Fair Frauds* features several real and infamous characters from the era, most notably Ward McAllister and Mrs. Caroline Astor. We've obviously taken ample liberties with these larger-than-life figures, creating a wild (though, who knows, perhaps possible?) backstory for this unlikely duo of Gilded Age tastemakers. Many other real-world figures make cameos inside these pages as well, including William Vanderbilt and Sarah Newbold. And our main con artists and side characters, while all fictional, were heavily inspired by legendary swindlers of the era: Ellen Peck, Cassie "Carnegie" Chadwick, and Marion LaTouche.

In any event, we do hope that all our gambles were worth it . . . and that you felt fully taken in by our schemes.

ACKNOWLEDGMENTS

In a way, a novel is like a confidence game itself—a grand, 80,000-word swindle where a writer attempts to immerse her marks so fully that fiction feels like truth. Historical adventures are especially difficult cons, with plotting, pacing, and sweeping period detail all needing to come together *just so* to hoodwink the reader. Naturally, this takes an expert team. A big one.

Our insightful and supportive editor, Kimberly Carlton, believed in our vision from the start, championing us every step of the way and pushing us to add depth and heart to our heroines, as well as nuance and further twists and turns to every scene. We are in true debt to you, Kim. You take each of our stories and up the ante. We are extremely grateful for your insight, guidance, and advocacy.

Our thanks, too, to our whip-smart line editor, Julie Breihan, who never misses a trick and brought her genius and commitment to making *My Fair Frauds* shine. And as always, many thanks to the rest of the Harper Muse crew: Amanda Bostic, Savannah Breedlove, Caitlin Halstead, Margaret Kercher, Colleen Lacey, Nekasha Pratt, Kerri Potts, Taylor Ward, and so many others. We're also so thankful to the art and design teams, with special thanks to Lila Selle for her commitment to creating such a playfully elegant cover for this novel.

Endless gratitude to our dynamite agent, Katelyn Detweiler, our tireless advocate for this and every story. We feel so incredibly lucky to be on this journey with you! Many thanks as well to Sam Farkas, Denise Page, and the rest of the wonderful team at JGLM. We're thrilled to call you our agency family.

And as always, a special thanks to our fellow con artists, our writing community. We can't imagine surviving this topsy-turvy game of publishing without you all. Thank you for your ongoing friendship, support, and camaraderie over these many years.

From Jenn: My most fervent thanks go to my co-conspirator, Lee Kelly. I have rarely had more fun than when I'm scheming with you. I'm thrilled to be your writing partner, but even more grateful to be your friend! Speaking of friends, shouts to my Minchinhampton and La Mattina Vocal Ensemble crews. Thank you all for the laughs, the music, the sage advice and encouragement. So much love to my parents and my wonderful brother, Ryan, the current bearer of the Biggest Jenn Cheerleader crown. Well, actually, he might have to share that crown with my husband, Rob, who has steadfastly supported my ambitions in words and deeds for the past sixteen years. None of this is possible without you holding down the (substantial) fort. I am forever grateful. Lastly, to my two sons, Oliver and Henry—you're right. You are much funnier and smarter than me, but hey, I don't mind. Being your mother is an absolute blast.

From Lee: This past year has been one of the most challenging of my life, and somehow through it all, I still was able to team up with Jenn, my storytelling partner in crime, and spin

Alice and Cora's caper to life. All credit to my unbelievable support team: my loving parents, Linda and Joe Appicello, my best friends and sisters Jill and Bridge, Jon, Mike, my Kelly family, Alice and PK, Susan, Peter, Alicia, Kevin, Laura, and Will. The Cookies and Gtown reunion crews, my Oak Knoll gals. Lindsey, Jenni, V. And of course, to Jenn: I treasure our jam sessions—working and shirking with you is the absolute best (here's to the Saloon). I love you all and thank you for being there, always. And finally, all my love and gratitude to my rocks, Jeff, Penn, and Summer. After this past year, I honestly believe we can weather anything. Accomplish anything. Even high society cons (a joke, P&S, don't get any ideas).

Finally . . . to our readers. This book is one of the most complicated plots we've ever attempted, with one teeny change, tweak, or addition sometimes rippling into tidal-wave proportions. And yet it was all worth it because we can imagine you holding this book in your hands. Hopefully you're smiling. In any case, we're beyond grateful you picked it up.

1. Although primarily a fast-paced caper, *My Fair Frauds* is also an examination of a complicated, polarizing time, a period in United States history when the "haves" and "have-nots" of the country were separated by an extremely wide chasm. As you were reading, did you notice instances of history repeating itself—any similarities between the Gilded Age and our current times?

2. Both the story's protagonists—Alice and Cora—are skilled con women, each shaped in different ways by family circumstances and tragedy. How do Alice's and Cora's grifting talents and approaches differ? How do these talents and approaches evolve, individually and collaboratively, over the course of the novel?

3. All the players in Alice's Württemberg con (Alice, Cora, Ward, Béa, Dagmar, and Cal) are in the game for different reasons, with "success" carrying a distinct meaning for each of them. How would you describe each character's motivations at the beginning of the

novel? How do those motivations change throughout the story?

4.   According to Alice, each of the five families she is targeting is guilty of duping her father and destroying her family, as well as guilty of a particular vice that she plans to use to destroy them in turn. Did you find that all five families are as villainous as Alice thinks they are? Were you satisfied with who was ruined and who was "saved" at the end of the story?

5.   *My Fair Frauds* is a story about greed as much as it is a tale of revenge. At one point in the story, Alice notes that all she can imagine once her vengeance is enacted is a "massive void." In what ways are greed and revenge similar preoccupations, and how are they different? Do you believe it is possible to "right" a personal wrong? If you were part of the con, what might you have done differently for moral reasons?

6.   The motif of deception is prevalent throughout the story—Cora's background in magic, the storytelling required for the Württemberg sting, even the lies some of the characters tell themselves to survive and thrive. At one point, Cora notes that deception may be more of a sliding scale than a black-and-white matter of right and wrong. Do you agree? Where should the line be drawn, in your opinion?

7.   As Kelly and Thorne discuss in their authors' note, the Kingdom of Württemberg was a real place within the

German Empire, as were the nobility that Alice "borrowed" as her relations. Do you believe that real-world members of Gilded Age high society of a similar station as the Vandemeers and Ogdens could ever be taken by such a ruse? Do you think a scheme on this scale could be attempted today?

8. Kelly and Thorne also explain in their authors' note that they took serious artistic liberties in reimagining high society "arbiter of taste" Ward McAllister. What did you think of McAllister's role in the con? What did his inclusion add to the story? Do you think the real McAllister would agree with fictional McAllister's declarations that high society is its own swindle?

9. Did you find the ending of the story satisfying? Do you think that Alice and Cora are truly done with the grifting life? Is this a happy ending, in your opinion, or merely a happy-for-now?

From the Publisher

GREAT BOOKS

ARE EVEN BETTER WHEN THEY'RE SHARED!

Help other readers find this one:

- Post a review at your favorite online bookseller

- Post a picture on a social media account and share why you enjoyed it

- Send a note to a friend who would also love it—or better yet, give them a copy

Thanks for reading!

ABOUT THE AUTHORS

LEE KELLY is the author of *City of Savages*, *A Criminal Magic*, *With Regrets*, and *The Antiquity Affair*, *The Starlets*, and *My Fair Frauds* (co-written with Jennifer Thorne). Her short fiction and essays have appeared in various publications, and she holds an MFA from the Vermont College of Fine Arts. An entertainment lawyer by trade, Lee has practiced law in Los Angeles and New York. She currently lives with her husband and two children outside Philadelphia, where you'll find them engaged in one adventure or another.

JENNIFER THORNE lives in a cottage in Gloucestershire, England, with her husband, two sons, and various animals. She is the author of horror novels *Lute* and *Diavola*, picture book *Construction Zoo*, and, as Jenn Marie Thorne, YA novels *The Wrong Side of Right*, *The Inside of Out*, and *Night Music*. Jennifer is also the author of three historical novels, *The Antiquity Affair*, *The Starlets*, and *My Fair Frauds*, co-authored with Lee Kelly.